THE EVOL

COMI

Life is full of complications

Vanessa
xx

ISBN 13: 978-1480136557
ISBN 10: 1480136557

Discover other titles by Vanessa Wester

The Evolution Trilogy
HYBRID

Seasonal short stories by a range of authors
OUT OF DARKNESS

THE EVOLUTION TRILOGY

COMPLICATIONS

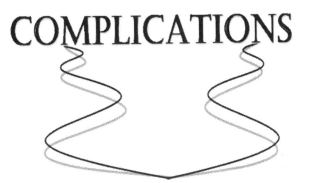

Vanessa Wester

Acknowledgements

Since I published my first novel, HYBRID, I have been on the sharpest learning curve of my life. The highs and lows of self publishing are immense, but the influence and use of social networking outweighs this.

I am now on Twitter, update several blogs, liaise with authors and readers of Goodreads and the Amazon Forums, and am more active on Facebook (with mainly family and friends). My life has changed overnight, so much to do, so little time. I can honestly say that I have learnt more from being on Twitter than any other site. Authors write insightful informative pieces, or highlight noteworthy articles, you learn a lot. You receive up to date information on news, sports results, everything really…it's a minefield.

The Twitter and Goodreads communities are incredibly supportive.

I have also been encouraged by a range of friends, family and readers. All of the reviews left for me on Smashwords and Amazon for HYBRID and OUT OF DARKNESS have certainly made me smile. I thank you readers for taking the time, it means a lot.

I do have a few special mentions. To Katy, Sarah, Chalis, Lynn and Adam – thank you for reading COMPLICATIONS prior to publication. Your feedback was fantastic.

Also to my sister in law, Minka, thank you for letting me use the amazing cover picture.

Finally, to you the reader, I hope COMPLICATIONS meets your expectations. I look forward to completing the final book in the Trilogy.

Best regards,
Vanessa Wester

For my parents, Marie-Carmen and Malcolm

PROLOGUE

Southampton, England, 1991

Emily fidgeted with her bracelet and kept her eyes to the floor. 'I've been hiding something from you. I don't know how to tell you the truth.'

'There's nothing you can't tell me. You know I love you no matter what,' Paul replied. The warm, irresistible smile he gave her nearly melted her resolve.

Her hands started to shake, the charms rattled. 'Do you want to know where I go at night? I don't want to tell you, but…'

'What's going on?' Paul took a seat placed his hands on hers. His grip tightened, as though he was trying to help them keep still.

She kept her head low. She could not meet his gaze. The words were hard to say, harder than she imagined. She could not tell him the truth. He would never understand. 'I can't stay here anymore.'

'I don't understand.' Paul froze. His hands automatically let hers go.

Emily got off the bed and made her way over to the window. It was dark outside, the time drew near. 'I can't live here anymore. I don't belong here.'

'Of course you belong here, what are you saying?' Anger seeped into his tone.

She swallowed hard and continued. 'I don't love you and I can't look after Steven. Motherhood is not what I thought it would be.' She turned around to face him, but his eyes were far away. His frame had gone rigid.

He looked away from her as he spoke. 'Are you serious? Please don't say things to break us.'

Emily fought hard to keep her emotions in check and made her way out of the room. It was best if he mulled it over alone. She needed to see her baby again. She did not have a lot of time. Once in her son's room, she edged over to the side of his cot. Steven gave a deep sigh and turned on his side, deep in sleep. She was biased, but as far as she was concerned he was gorgeous, a perfect baby boy. There was nothing she wouldn't do to protect him.

She kissed her fingertips and placed them on her little boy's head, then eased out quietly and made her way back to Paul. He was still sat on the bed, head in his hands.

Without a hint of emotion, she said, 'I'm leaving now. I have a taxi waiting. Please look after him for me and tell him I was just protecting him.'

Paul flinched and looked up. His eyes glazed, distant. He opened his mouth and then closed it shut. He didn't or couldn't say anything. His head slumped back into his hands. She had broken him.

'I'm so sorry,' Emily whispered.

It was only when she had closed the door that her chest heaved and she broke down. Somehow she got to the taxi. Somehow she did not turn back. Somehow she thought she had done the right thing.

CHAPTER 1

Back To Civilisation

A mixture of excited, concerned, and confused faces waited. Judith held her head high. None of them understood. The young ones, in particular, could not grasp the decision to leave. In times like these, she was glad she only had four children. Saying goodbye to three was hard enough. She blinked consecutively and took a deep breath. She had made a vow to remain calm; she would not lose control of her emotions here. Not now. The tears that threatened were kept at bay.

A thought crossed her mind. There was a distinct possibility they might never return. It was strange; a part of her was convinced *she* would never return. It was the reason why her chest ached. It was a silly notion. They would be back in no time. She had no idea why she thought this would be the last time she would ever set foot on her beloved Amazon Jungle, her home and sanctuary. Regardless, she could not help the feeling of unease.

It was hard to acknowledge the facts. She had not left the community they had built within the Amazon in over sixty years. It was a long time – too long, probably. Now, she was about to return to normal civilisation, a place she feared. Not for what it would do to her, but for what she could do to it. Again, even though there was no real reason for *her* to be scared, she was. It was a fear of the worst kind, a fear of the unknown. Her uppermost concern was whether she would be able to resist the *normal* humans, or more to the point human blood.

A vague recollection of the taste remained. It was the burning desire to have it which she remembered the most. Up close, it would be hard to say no. In the Amazon, it was easier to abstain. In a few days time, humans would be all around her, enticing her. For Steven's sake, she hoped she would be strong. She owed her grandson that much. She gave a deep sigh and turned. Her eldest daughter, Catherine, came up alongside.

Catherine threw her arms around her and the sobs began. Judith felt the lump on her throat expand.

A minute later, Catherine eased back and wiped her face with the back of her hand. 'Don't do anything reckless.'

Judith smiled at her beautiful, fiery haired daughter, the hair a constant reminder of her grandfather's Scottish roots. 'Catherine, why do you worry so much? We'll be fine.' She knew her daughter was right to be afraid. Catherine found it impossible to control herself around humans. That was why Catherine never left anymore. The guilt was too much to bear.

Catherine gave a half smile. 'Just try to keep away from them.'

Judith nodded as Steven's mother, Emily, came into view. Her now short, black hair glistened as the early rays of sunshine beat down on her head. It was hard to distinguish her from her twin sister Anna now. They looked identical. Judith recalled how as a child Emily was always the carefree, happy little girl. After the accident, she became so serious, so lost. It was sad. Judith never realised how bad things got for Emily.

It wasn't until they had found out about Steven that she realised the extent of her inner torment. What mother would not grieve the loss of a child and partner? Judith could not imagine what it must have been like for Emily. It must have been hard to let go of her only son and the love of her life, even if he was just a normal human. It was typical of Emily to fall for a normal human, she was always a rebel. Yet, to sacrifice everything and return to the community to lead a life she hated. Judith could only now begin to understand what she must have been going through. In hindsight, it explained a lot.

Through the corner of her eye she saw Steven arrive. Emily watched him, a look of despair etched on her face. A second later, Emily adopted her usual aloof expression. She was such a brave girl. She would have made an excellent actress if she had ever been allowed to follow that dream. With the aid of two wooden crutches Steven made slow progress. He had the same, almost angry, expression his mother carried. She could not blame him; an attack of the kind he had endured would have shaken any of them.

Steven reminded Judith of Emily in so many ways. His dark, raven colour hair and piercing amber eyes were certainly like her daughters. Yet, there were other qualities that were alien. His height and build for a start. She would have liked to have met the man who stole her daughter's heart.

Of course people would assume Emily and Steven were siblings. It was useful Emily would always look aged twenty, and now so would Steven. None of them ever looked old. Yet, because she changed when she was older she would always look old, she would always be taken for their mother. No-one would ever suspect Emily was Steven's mother. It was the only thing that alienated her from the community. The more the community grew, the older she felt. There were times when she grew tired, tired of the existence. She wondered what the point of it all was. But, then she had her husband. Jeff was the reason to live, the reason to exist. And now they had a new adventure to look forward to, an adventure on the outside.

'So, there's nothing we can say?' her youngest son, Ian, asked, as he eased up alongside. 'You're ready to brave civilisation?'

Judith shrugged her shoulders. She would miss him. 'Absolutely, what will be, will be.'

At that, Jeff came up beside her. He slipped his hand in hers. 'Neither your mother nor I intend to become killers. Hiding isn't always the best course of action. We can't go back in time and change what we are. If Steven feels he doesn't want to become a killer then we must try to follow the same route. To be honest most of us have been too scared to try.'

'But what if you can't stop and you *do* kill? Doesn't that go against everything?' Ian threw his hands up in the air.

Judith gave a curt reply. 'No, we always said that to kill to save someone's life was acceptable – this is no different.'

She recognised the problem. It was probably their fault Ian

was institutionalised. Blind to any view other than what he had been taught. After all, he was only ten when they had arrived. This life was all he knew.

'Steven isn't dying, he's *injured*.' Ian rolled his eyes.

'He is severely impaired from leading a normal life. Of course there is nothing wrong with having a deformed foot.' Judith sighed as she felt the strain. She did not want to argue before she left.

As if sensing her unease, Jeff took over. She was grateful for the interruption.

'Ian you have to agree. If his foot does not heal, he will be unable to do a lot of the things we take for granted. He has a long life ahead of him. It's not a good idea to let him stay like that if we can fix it.'

'So there's nothing I can do to change your minds? I'm not allowed to come with you?'

Judith and Jeff shook their heads in unison. Even if they thought it was a good idea, Judith knew Emily would not stand for it. Emily never saw eye to eye with her younger brother.

***

Steven glanced at Jensen, who he now considered to be his best friend, and nodded. He then turned to face the rest of the people he had met in his last few months at the community. He saw in their faces a mixture of hope and fear mangled together. Without a doubt, some were glad he was leaving. He had confused many of the young ones, who now demanded the right to leave. His uncle, Ian, was fuming about the decision. Ian wanted to take Steven back. Ian did not seem to understand why Jeff and Judith had decided to take responsibility. Steven suspected deep down Ian understood all too well. He suspected Ian did not think his sister Emily deserved to leave. She always broke the rules. Steven had yet to see why she was considered to be such a threat. Either way, Steven was sure Ian would be glad to resume normality, even if it meant losing Jeff, Judith, Emily and himself.

As the time to go approached they made their way to the exit. Ian and his wife, Carmen, got into the lift last. All ready, Jeff inserted the key to enable access to the exit. The doors closed and Steven mentally said goodbye. He might never see any of them ever again. Not if he could help it. With a jolt, the motley crew made their way up. Once outside, Steven reflected on the last time he had walked this route. He had known nothing back then. He had no idea of the life they led. Now, he knew different. It was amazing what a few months could change. It was not a life he would choose, but it was still a good life, a decent life.

The community looked out for each other. They maintained valuable principles and taught lifelong lessons. Most of them were happy. The life they had chosen to create was self imposed. They acknowledged they were dangerous to humans, and so opted to keep away most of the time. Steven recognised the fact each of them had to kill a human to change – he'd had to. Yet, as far as he could tell, death was restricted to necessity. Greed was not allowed to flourish. A lot of their principles were commendable.

In mid thought, he crumpled in pain and winced as his ankle gave way again.

'Let me help,' Jeff said, as he placed his arm around Steven's waist.

With no choice, Steven accepted the assistance and ignored the throb. Progress was slow.

'There's no hurry, you go ahead and get the ship ready,' Jeff barked at the others. It was not a request. 'Tell me if the strain gets too much. I can carry you.' The voice was more subdued, compassionate.

The vessel looked smaller than Steven remembered. It had lost its mystery and charm. Now it was a means of escape.

The Amazon River bustled with activity. A pair of macaws flashed their impressive blue and yellow colours overhead. Monkeys chattered and played in the trees to the sound of snapping branches, and river dolphins swam alongside the boat. They were all oblivious to the danger within the boat. Finally, they arrived at the junction where the Rio Negro and the Solimões River clearly distinguished themselves. For a second time, the sight took Steven's breath away. The dark waters of the Rio Negro contrasted against the lighter shade of the Solimões River. Steven watched as they refused to mix, stubborn in their quest for independence. He half-smiled as he contemplated the view. The water was a metaphor for his life – two sides that might never be compatible.

Even though they would be keeping him under close surveillance, he could taste freedom for the first time since he had boarded the plane at London all those months earlier.

He was getting out at last.

CHAPTER 2

FINDING A BASE

After about half an hour, they arrived at the busy entrance to the City of Manaus. Disembarkation was smooth. Before Steven had a chance to think about it, he found himself back in the car with Ian at the wheel again. There was something déjà vu about the trip. Only difference being, this time there were more people in the car. He glanced at Judith as she waved at her daughter-in-law, Carmen, who remained on the boat. It had to be strange for Judith. He could see a trace of emotion on her face. He had not seen her cry yet. He had obviously inherited her tenacity. He did not do tears.

As Ian drove, Judith talked. She had perked up since she waved at Carmen and was now animated and chatty, as though in awe of everything around her. Civilisation – someone found it exciting. Jeff, on the other hand, nodded off and made very loud snoring sounds. He resembled a wounded animal.

Judith laughed aloud. 'That explains why I never get a good night's sleep.'

After that, silence ensued as everyone took cover within their own thoughts. The only sound that remained was the car engine purring along. As they started to approach the centre of the city the surroundings changed immediately. It was the middle of the day and people sold a variety of goods on the roadside. Some even braved running alongside the car, touting for business.

Ian veered away and parked the car in a quiet side street. It prompted Judith to wake Jeff by giving his shoulder a nudge. Jeff huffed aloud and stretched. His lazy eyes took in his surroundings and he nodded in apprehension. He opened the car door and got out as Judith passed him a small black rucksack. Then he made his way into a small building. The cash points at the entrance marked it out as a bank.

Steven glanced at Judith. 'Do you have money then?' The question was innocent enough.

'Yes,' Judith beamed. 'We have money. The bank account has changed names many times of course, to keep up appearances. It was opened in Manaus in 1943. We have done very well over the years with investments. Your grandfather, Jeff, is a very prudent man. It's time *we* got to spend some. I might even go shopping,' Judith giggled.

'I'll come,' Emily said, with what looked a like a smile.

'Done,' Judith said. She turned, held Emily's hand and gave it a squeeze.

Ian rolled his eyes. 'You come back out and the first thing you think of is shopping – typical.'

Judith guffawed. 'Now, you see my cunning plan. I just missed real shops.'

Steven was amused by the exchange. For the first time, he started to see them more as people, not potential vampires. Vampires seemed like such a stupid description now. He certainly wasn't one.

After twenty minutes Jeff sauntered back and returned to his seat, a cocky smile on his face.

'Done?' Ian asked.

Jeff patted the bag on his lap. 'No problem.'

Ian started the engine. Ten minutes later they stopped again at a run down garage. A selection of cars with hand drawn for sale signs waited on the forecourt. None of them had any appeal for Steven so he opted to wait in the car as the others looked around. It was unfortunate Emily decided to stay in the car too, but he was not going to leave because of her. His ankle alone was a good enough reason not to move.

Emily turned to face him and said, 'they're going to buy a car.'

'Right,' Steven replied. It was obvious. Did she think he was stupid?

Emily turned away and stared in the distance. She spoke again without facing him. 'Are you comfortable?'

Steven shrugged, but did not answer straight away. He wondered if it was a serious question. 'Sure, I'm just fine.' There was a hint of sarcasm in his reply, he couldn't help it.

Emily nodded and did not say anything else. They sat in silence, an awkward silence.

After what must have been a painstaking half an hour Ian came over to the passenger side and leant on the door frame. He glared at Emily, then Steven. 'Don't do anything stupid now. I'll be going. I guess…good luck seems apt.' There was a hint of menace in his tone.

Emily kept her eyes on the dashboard and remained tight lipped as she replied, 'we'll be fine.'

Ian huffed, unconvinced.

Steven figured there was nothing he could do about it. When Ian gave his parents a giant hug, Steven figured Ian might actually be capable of some emotion. The moment did not last as he narrowed his eyes in their direction, got back into the other car and drove off.

It was time to go it alone. Well, with his grandparents and mother. Happy days.

When the cheap hotel, with its tacky fluorescent sign, came into view Steven's shoulders slumped. Inside, Jeff spoke the local dialect of Portuguese and secured the rooms. A man with a missing tooth and greasy shoulder length hair handed over a set of keys and winked at Emily. Steven glared at him and the man's face paled, before he turned and practically ran into the back office. Was he intimidating now? Perhaps, there was something positive about his change. It was interesting. Steven had no idea what the man saw.

A sweet smell, mixed with cheap aftershave and pungent body odour, tempted. Was the sweet smell of blood? Could he smell it? Steven was not sure. Even so, the bad smell overpowered the good. The man was not on the menu. He could not believe he had even contemplated it.

Once in his room Steven collapsed on the bed. In the doorway, Emily stopped for a second before coming in and taking a seat on the twin bed opposite his. Jeff and Judith followed.

'This is hard.' Judith leaned into Jeff, her hand fused into his. 'I am hungry, or thirsty. I don't know – I could barely smile. The last thing I wanted was for my extended fangs to come into view. We are monsters.'

'We're not monsters. We just have different needs.' Jeff enveloped her in his arms and kissed her head.

The show of affection was nauseating. It was great they were still in love, but it was the last thing Steven wanted to see.

'Monsters that drink blood.' Emily stared out of the window. Did she ever smile?

'I could smell it,' Steven admitted. His head low.

Jeff paced slowly in the small space. 'Scientifically speaking we could lead symbiotic relationships with normal humans.' He always spoke like Steven's old school professors. Anything he said always sounded plausible.

'So what do they gain from us?' Emily looked over her left shoulder as she rolled her eyes.

'Nothing much necessarily, I grant you that. They help *us* stay alive.' A broad smile set across Jeff's face.

'Look, we are not here to become something we are not, but we can't feel bad about what we instinctively want to do,' Judith added. Her tone serious now, this was no joking matter.

'Well I'm glad that you're all happy. So what happens now?' Steven asked.

'You have to feed and so do we. We just have to maintain self control. That is the *little* problem.' Jeff grimaced.

'I won't have a problem with that,' Steven stated, his head held high, defiant.

'You can say that now, but you can't be certain,' Emily snapped.

Steven had noticed the way she clenched and unclenched her fists. Was she already finding it hard?

'Look, we have to stay focused,' Judith said. It seemed like some of her earlier enthusiasm was starting to wane. 'We are here to help Steven get better, not to argue.'

Jeff started to laugh and sat down on the wonky chair in the corner of the room. 'Now we're acting like a family.'

Judith was entranced as she walked down the street. It was such a simple thing; walking, holding hands. Yet, it was a new experience. It had been a long time since she had been out in the open. She felt exposed, overwhelmed and yet, liberated. Unfortunately, the moment was short lived. All around her temptation beckoned. She would not remain relaxed for long. The taste and smell of human blood hung thick in the air.

'Shall we have a drink?' Jeff motioned towards the café.

'Why not, we'll sit outside.' She did not feel brave enough to go inside. Not yet.

At a small table for two she watched the array of cars zooming past. She could not understand why everyone seemed to be in such a hurry. Had the world sped up whilst they were away?

A petite waitress came up to the table and took their order. Judith diverted her gaze.

When the waitress had gone Jeff placed his hand on hers. 'We have to look for a place to stay. There are many abandoned buildings that are reasonably habitable around. We just have to find the right one.'

'Why don't we drive around and find somewhere?'

'That's a good idea.'

A few minutes later the waitress arrived with two coffees and two huge helpings of bolo de macaxeira, the local speciality. Judith was momentarily distracted from the temptation to feed by the cake. It looked and smelled delicious. With the small fork she took a piece and savoured it. It tasted just as she remembered.

Jeff followed suit and washed it down with some coffee.

Once she had eaten half the cake Judith had to tell Jeff what was on her mind. 'This is very nice but you know it doesn't really help. We will have to go and hunt soon, otherwise I might do something I'll regret.' She glanced at the table nearby where two men sat deep in conversation. By the cut of their suits she could tell they were businessmen, foreign by the sound of it. Would anyone notice their absence? They spoke Spanish, probably Mexicans. It would take only two seconds to snap both of their necks. Judith shook her head in an attempt to erase the thought.

Jeff followed her eyes and frowned. 'I'm tired of ignoring what we are.'

She nearly freaked. It was as though he had read her mind.

'We should do the right thing,' Jeff said. It was an afterthought.

Judith finished her drink and stretched out her hand to touch Jeff's face. 'We made our choice many years ago. We can't change now. Let's go and find somewhere to stay and then decide on a strategy to make our grandson better.'

'You know, for the first time the word grandson makes me feel old.'

'We've always been old in the community, at least, compared to everyone else.' She picked at the placemat.

'In my eyes you've always been the prettiest.'

Judith ran her hand through her hair. 'Always the charmer.'

She could not help a quick glance at the men. It was hard to ignore the smell, the lure. It was driving her crazy.

For the first time, in a long time, she had found a new sense of freedom but she was torn. Life in the community revolved around chores and roles, routine was a good thing. It did not put her in the path of temptation. Yet, it felt so good to just spend some time with her husband without responsibility. It was tiring for Jeff to be in charge. He played the role well, but it was demanding. They were carefree again, with no burden or responsibility. They were just another couple in love.

CHAPTER 3

RECOVERY

Emily had not left Steven's side. She suspected he would be glad to get rid of her. His face had said it all when he was told he would have to share a room with her. In the stifled silence that followed Steven fell asleep. She would wait even though she had never been the patient type; it gave her too much time to think. The last thing she needed to do was to over think her plan. She had to take her time. When her parents returned they would finalise a plan, then she would know what she would do. It was too early to leave. She needed to know if Steven needed her. There was a near enough certain chance he didn't.

They needed to find somewhere inconspicuous. Time stopped for no-one. Steven's recovery had to get into motion. She heard a huge yawn, and realised Steven was finally coming back to earth. Her baby had become a man. As he rubbed his eyes, stretched his arms up into the air and sat up she found it hard to believe he was her son. Unshaved with wake up hair, he did not resemble the cute baby she had left. He did remind her of Paul. She wondered what Paul looked like now. She hoped to find out soon.

A barely audible grunt followed. 'I'm starving, when can we get some food?'

'We have to wait for Jeff and Judith to return.' She did not know if he would ever call them grandfather and grandmother so she decided to use their Christian names. 'Here, you can have a chocolate bar in the meantime.'

Steven un-wrapped the bar and wolfed it down in three bites. 'Now that hits a tiny spot.'

'I'm glad. How's your foot?'

'I try to ignore it, when I move it's in agony.'

21

'Did the plaster cast they put on it help?'

'I guess. More pain relief would be good.'

'We'll get you some.' Emily stood up and looked out of the window. The pane was dirty. The place was disgusting. A group of children played in the basketball court across the room. She wondered what it was like, to be so free. She turned her thoughts to the present. 'Look I know that you don't want to feed from a human, but you do understand it's the only way right?'

'If I am due to live a long life, yes I get the point.'

'Good, so are you up to going out tonight?'

'Tonight?' Steven's eyebrows narrowed.

She could not afford to sound apprehensive. In a confident voice, she replied, 'the sooner the better. We need to know what difference it'll make.'

Steven stared at the floor. 'Fine, I'll do whatever you need me to do. Tonight it is.'

Emily suppressed her concern. She hated what he was going to have to do. It would change everything. There was a strong chance it would bring out the hunger. He could become just like her.

***

Jeff and Judith made their way back into the hotel, and knocked on the door.

Emily opened it, a look of exasperation set across her face. 'Finally!'

The honeymoon period was over. Peace never lasted. Emily stepped aside and Judith noticed Steven raise his head.

'We have found a house where we can stay. It's safe and habitable and not out in the open,' Jeff said.

'Oh, great.' Emily's features relaxed.

Judith was glad Jeff got straight to the point – they *had* actually been doing something useful. She hoped Emily would loosen up soon, she seemed so tense.

Judith looked in Steven's direction. He did not look good. 'We got you some more pain relief.'

Steven nodded.

'The city is huge and there are plenty of opportunities

available. The fact that Steven looks frail will also be an advantage,' Jeff said. 'Steven, we are not asking you to kill. You just need to take enough to survive and more importantly to heal.'

'We can go to one of the areas where the homeless hang out if you would prefer?' Judith asked. She did not know if that would ease the blow.

'Whatever. It's too late for me to have a huge amount of input. If it relieves the pain I'll do it. I won't kill, I know I won't.' Steven voiced his thoughts but his eyes betrayed his true feelings. You could tell his heart was not in it.

'Right, let's go then,' Jeff said.

No messing around, as usual. That was her husband.

**

'Do you know much about Manaus?' Jeff kept his head forward, his hands firmly on the steering wheel.

'No.' Steven replied. Why would he? Steven was loathed to admit the place intrigued him. One moment the buildings were grand, almost regal, the next they looked like they would blow down if someone sneezed. It was weird.

Jeff started to talk; he obviously did not need a show of enthusiasm. 'The city was extremely affluent at the beginning of the twentieth century. The rubber industry made it a lot of money, as you can see by the grand cathedrals and impressive buildings. However, when the monopoly was broken by seeds being taken out of the city to other countries, the decline began. Some areas of the city are now ghost towns, with dilapidated and unwanted buildings left to crumble. It leaves us with an excellent place to hide. No-one there would ever be taken seriously if they started rambling about a supposed vampire attack.'

The car jumped suddenly as Jeff inadvertently drove over a huge pot hole. They all made disgruntled noises.

'Sorry,' Jeff said. 'It's like driving through Swiss cheese.'

Finally, he parked the car in front of a large house. The weeds and climbers covered most of the exterior of the house.

'This is it,' Judith pronounced. 'Doesn't it look great?'

Emily wedged her arm under his shoulder to help him get

out of the car. He considered trying to get out alone and telling her to leave him alone, then he realised it was fruitless. He had no choice. She passed him his wooden crutches and he got a grip. Slowly, he made his way towards the house. Jeff and Judith unloaded the car of their meagre items. From what Steven could see it was a bare shell. It would take some time to clear it up and make it habitable.

'We suggest that we clear up the back room, we don't want to alert any passers by to our presence,' Jeff said. 'Steven, don't strain yourself, you should get back into the car. This is a perfect time of day to remain inconspicuous.'

Steven grunted. He had made all the effort to get to the door for nothing. He turned round and started to make his way back, it was easy to simulate a snail. It was all he could do to delay the inevitable.

Jeff drove for about fifteen minutes until he came across a populated area housing a bar, off license and several small shops that were still open. A few people could be seen casually drinking with friends outside. The park opposite looked like a natural breeding ground for vagabonds.

Jeff parked the car and sighed. 'This is it.'

'What now?' Steven asked.

'We hunt,' Emily replied.

The glint in Emily's eyes and slight curl of her lips gave her away. There was no ignoring the *we* – she was also a player. He had no idea what she was capable of or what he was capable of. He clenched his teeth and tried to stay focused. There was a lot at stake. He would not kill. Even if it was to spite her, he would find a way to stop.

The decision was made to go in pairs. Judith decided to go with Steven. Something told her she could not trust Emily to act rational. Steven was supposed to be the only one who got close to humans. She watched Jeff drive off with Emily and gave a wary smile. She was glad they were going to the other side of the park. The smell of humanity drew them both in. After twenty minutes they were deep within the wooded area. Judith knew humans were around, she could smell them. She stayed alongside Steven and waited for him to speak. Would he know where they were? She had no idea if his sense of smell and sight was as good as hers.

As if reading her mind, Steven stopped. He stared at a small bridge. 'I think there are people sleeping under there.'

Bingo. He had found them. There was nothing wrong with his senses. 'Then that's where we go.' Judith took another step.

Steven froze. 'I'm not sure I can do this.'

'I will help you.' She was sure that once he was close enough he would know what to do.

'No, I want go on my own. I can't run anyway so you don't have to worry about me escaping.'

Judith gave a slight nod. 'Do what you think is best. I'll wait here.'

It was just as well. If she got any closer she would do something she would regret.

***

Steven hobbled off, his crutches firmly ensconced under his armpits. He hated being so weak and helpless. Was his recovery worth it? Was it selfish to want to heal? Closer now, the smell intensified. Out here, other smells did not overpower. He loathed what he was about to do. A shuffling noise could be heard under the bridge and the faint sound of snoring. He could also detect the smell of alcohol. He moved on. Barely a metre away, a twig snapped under his foot and a female voice called out. The other person remained fast asleep, probably drunk.

The female did not sound scared or threatened, just curious. Even though he knew Spanish it did not help him with Portuguese. He carried on and got closer to the dim light, it had to be a fire. The voice belonged to a girl who now walked towards him. She looked young. She stared at him with huge brown eyes, transfixed. She glanced at his crutches, then smiled and repeated the question. He stared in silence unable to reply.

She took a step closer and he realised she was not as young as he had at first thought. Her features were more womanly, and she had long brown hair that hung loosely around her face.

He was drawn to her – he could not deny it. Instinctively, he smiled, keeping his mouth closed to hide his now extended canines. His tongue explored them. It was loathsome, but still amazing.

The woman remained calm. She was now inches away, asking the same Portuguese question. Steven got within touching distance. She was silent now, just watching. Her eyes glazed over, as though in an awed trance. He remembered Ingrid and her piercing stare and momentarily faltered. Could he really do this? Could he not? He leaned in. As he did, she tilted her head to the side and exposed her neck. He closed his eyes and lowered his head; instinct told him where to go.

The blood coursed down his throat and initiated an unexpected rush. It urged him on. He began to forget his promise to stop. In mid frenzy, a face appeared – Caitlin. He was doing it for her. He was getting better for her. He would not kill the woman. He could not kill. What would Caitlin say? He could stop. He groaned as he wrenched himself off the woman and gasped. The woman stood still with her eyes closed.

Steven backed away as the woman waivered and collapsed on the floor. He had not killed her, he was sure of it. He whispered 'thank you' and left, carefully retracing his steps. As he got up the bank, he threw one of the crutches on the floor. He did not need two anymore. His injury was better, much better.

CHAPTER 4

JOANA

Emily narrowed her eyes and watched Steven make his way towards the car. He only had one of the crutches now. He must have done it. A jealous pang made her clench her teeth. The thought alone of fresh human blood made her canines extend and she savoured the night air. It reeked of human scent. She reminded herself to stay calm and controlled. She could do that. Once Steven and Judith got back into the car, she snapped. She needed to leave before it got too late. 'Let's go,' she urged, her lips taut.

Jeff nodded. The stiff way he moved made her wonder if it was possible he was also finding this hard?

Once they got moving, Jeff broke the silence. 'It went okay then.'

Steven wore a smug look. 'I left her alive of that I'm sure.'

Jeff laughed, 'Good for you. So, tell us your secret? How did you manage to stop?'

'Willpower, I guess. If I want to get back home I have to earn the trip.'

The casual way he said it stung.

'You really think you can live amongst humans?' Judith asked, her face pensive.

'Of course I can. I *will* do whatever it takes to get back to those I love.'

Now Emily was angry. She wanted to hold back the words, but they burst out. 'Love? I had plenty of love to give. It didn't help me. I can't control it.'

'Well, I can.' Steven folded his arms over his chest.

There was nothing more she could say. He really thought she did not love him enough. She was sure Steven thought she had not tried hard enough. She looked out of the window again and closed her eyes, overwhelmed by anger. She could not believe he thought it was so easy. He had no idea of the hardship she had endured, the pain. She had tried everything to control the thirst – nothing ever worked. Her chest burned and she swallowed. Was there anything she could do to make her son forgive her? Would he ever consider her as his mother? Somehow, she doubted it.

'Half of your genetic make up is human, so perhaps that is the reason you can do what we find so hard,' Jeff mused, a light huff followed.

***

Steven unfolded his arms, and leaned closer to the driver's seat to chat to Jeff. 'If I can control it, then I'm not a threat to human life am I?'

The question hung in the air.

'If you can, then I guess you're not,' Jeff declared, ruffling his hair with one hand.

Steven was not completely sure. This close, it appeared as though Jeff had aged. Was his hair whiter or was it Steven's imagination?

'So when I am fully recovered there is no reason for me to return with you, is there?' Steven pushed the point. A light glimmered at the end of the tunnel.

Jeff looked at Judith next to him, who raised her eyebrows.

Emily continued to look out of the window. She obviously did not think love was the answer. He had hit a raw nerve – he was glad it hurt her.

'It would certainly leave the floodgates open for others who want to integrate. For years we have thought the younger ones seemed to be more in control,' Judith sighed, getting closer to Jeff.

Emily sharply moved her head to face Steven. In a voice laced in venom, she spoke, 'we can't allow that yet, not until we know for sure. Some of the members of the community can never be allowed to leave. We know they can't control themselves. It would lead to revolt, jealousy and uncertainty.'

'Just because *you* can't control yourself.' There was a bitter edge to his tone. She flinched, but he ignored her. 'You could

28

say I died.'

'You would prefer that to living with us?' Jeff asked, in a bewildered tone.

Steven paused to consider this. 'No offence to you all, but yes.'

'You don't know what you're saying,' Judith added. 'You've barely lived this life, neither have we to be honest. There are risks.'

'Life is a risk,' Steven replied, hands held out in protest.

Emily lowered her shoulders. She felt defeated. 'Okay, tell you what – you prove to us that you are fully recovered and that this was not just a one off.' She paused to sigh, and then continued in a mellow voice. 'It would give me a great satisfaction, one you can not even comprehend, to know you could lead the life that I can't.'

'No offence to you Steven, but we find it very hard to smell humans and repress our needs. Emily you sound on edge.' Judith leaned her head over the headboard, to face Emily. Then she gave her a reassuring smile.

Emily remained straight faced.

'You put us to shame Steven. I will try to follow your example and not kill a person – no promises though,' Jeff smiled, as he stopped the car. 'You wait here whilst we go to feed.'

Steven barely looked up as they all left him alone. He was amazed his foot had made such an amazing recovery. He played back the conversation he had just had in his head and could not believe they were going to help him. For the first time, he truly believed they did have his best interests at heart. If his ability to control himself was true, then he could return to England and resume his previous life.

He wondered whether he would be able to obtain his old identity back. He groaned as he realised Eilif would be unable to help him if he thought he was dead. He would have to think of a way in which he would obtain, at least, his nationality back. At a price, he was sure anything was possible. Regardless, the issue was how far his family would go to help him.

A sound made him turn around to see if they had come back. In the distance, he saw a silhouette against the moonlight glow. Whoever it was stopped moving when he turned. Then the body started to gain momentum and walked faster and faster to stand a metre away from him. Steven realised who it was and remained glued to the spot, stunned. Still on the border of the park, she had found him. It beggared belief.

***

Joana looked at the man standing before her. He couldn't have been much younger than her and he took her breath away. It was so strange. She dreamt he had visited her. She could not remember what had happened, just that the experience was heavenly. She knew now he was not a dream – he did exist. He was standing right there. His mesmerising eyes, they were like jewels. She needed to touch him – to check. She took a step forward, knocked on the window pane and smiled.

Then she faltered, her body felt weak. She had hardly had any food and was hungry, but this was different. She was dizzy. Stretching out her hand she leant against the glass. He blinked. It was not a dream – he was real.

'Olá! Como vai você?' She called out, knocking on the window again. Her voice rasped, so weak.

No reply.

'Como vai você?'

His eyes narrowed and he bit his lip. Then she heard the click of the door as it opened. She stood back and let him get out. He watched her, and then held his hands up in the air. 'No speak Portuguese.'

He was an Englishman. She knew a little from school. 'H-hello. H-how are you?' She could not understand why he continued to watch her as though scared, with a pained expression on his face. She could wait; they did not have to talk. She could not understand the need to throw herself at him.

***

Steven was shocked to hear her speaking English.

'I'm okay,' he answered. He shuffled around knowing it was a stupid answer.

30

'Wh-why are you here?' The woman persevered and cocked her head to the side, as though confused.

What on earth was she doing here? Why was she talking to him?

'Just visiting.' He did not know what else he was supposed to say.

The woman laughed before she stumbled as her eyes rolled back towards her head. She looked like she was about to faint. He had done that to her.

She managed to raise her head. 'Sorry, n-not well today.'

'I have to go.' Steven turned; he didn't want to see the effect he'd had on her.

'Take me,' the woman pleaded, as she reached out for him. Her hand gripped his arm.

He grabbed her small hand and eased it off. 'Why?'

She hugged herself and looked at him with huge eyes. She gave a huge gasp and then broke down into tears. Through the stifled sobs she pleaded. 'I-I don't know. I have to go with you.'

It was clear to Steven he had done something. She seemed obsessed. It was crazy. He'd had admirers before, but this went onto a whole new level. Either way, there was no way she could go with him. He cursed under his breath, and he saw her flinch. The tears escalated again.

'Sorry, you have to stay.' He could not look at her. He took hold of the door and made his way in. If he had to, he'd drive away.

The woman stared through the glass, her face distraught. 'Please, take me,' she screamed, desperate.

'Sorry,' Steven mouthed, as he put the key in the ignition. Even with a slightly dodgy ankle he would find a way to drive the car. As the car came to life, he saw her stand back and turn around.

It was only then, as his foot was about to hit the accelerator, that he saw them. Jeff, Judith and Emily had returned.

***

Joana heard another voice and turned around. There were even more strangers at this time of night. Something told her to run, but she couldn't – she was finding it hard to stay awake now. All that crying had exhausted her. Unable to stand any longer, she collapsed on the floor and just looked at them. The man had a round face, bushy eyebrows and kind eyes. He reminded her of her grandfather. The older woman looked afraid. That was weird. The younger woman looked like her angel. She had to be his sister. Something made her uneasy, she was not sure she could trust the young one. Was it the way she looked at her?

Perhaps, if she fell asleep they would all just go away. She was so tired.

***

Steven could not believe the woman had fainted. What exactly were they going to do with her? He was responsible, it was his fault.

'Who is this?' Judith leaned down and pushed the woman's hair away from her neck. 'Is this your victim?' She frowned. A set of pin prick marks gave him away.

'Yes,' Steven said, through gritted teeth.

Judith stared at the floor. 'This is not good. We have to take her to safety.'

Jeff glanced from Steven to the woman, then back again. 'Did she *follow* you?'

Steven nodded. 'It looks like it.'

'She can't keep away from you, can she?' Emily huffed, as she circled the woman.

'I don't know.' He did not want to admit the obvious.

'We'll take her back to where you found her. She won't be able to track you over distance,' Judith said, as she took a tube out of her pocket, opened it and applied a lotion onto the woman's' neck. The moment she did, the marks vanished.

Jeff leaned down and picked up the woman. He turned towards the park. The woman gave a little whimper, and then snuggled into his arms. 'I'll be back soon. We'll talk later.'

Steven could hardly wait for their little *chat*.

'What shall we do?' Emily asked, her eyes to Judith. 'It's inhumane to leave her like that.'

'What do you suggest Steven?' Judith asked.

Steven stared at floor, speechless for a moment. Everything had changed. 'Leave her to it; I will not end her life. You can go and check on her tomorrow if you like. I doubt she was following me anyway.' He knew he sounded defensive. He was not prepared to let this hiccup spoil his chance of going back home.

Judith pursed her lips. 'Steven, she was desperate to be with you. Face up to the truth.'

Emily gave another patronising shake of the head. Would she ever be a supportive mother? Would she ever be on his side?

He had no idea how to get out of the situation. He was not exactly an expert on cause and effect. 'I don't know what to tell you. We'll talk to Jeff when he gets back.'

The way Emily's eyes fixed on the direction Jeff had gone made Steven wonder what thoughts were running through her mind now.

He did not trust her.

CHAPTER 5

EMILY'S CHOICE

The floorboards creaked under his feet as Jeff made his way up the staircase. They would have to repair them if they intended to stay. He mulled over the fact that Steven's injury seemed to have healed significantly after one feed, it was incredible. He would not be surprised if he would be back to normal in no time. He had not expected the recovery to be so fast. If he had known, perhaps the trip could have been avoided. The thing was he was glad to be away from the community for once. He was not in a hurry to return. There was so much to discover.

Yet, he wondered whether they should take Steven back to the community. It was the right thing to do. He just did not want to go back. He wondered how Judith felt about it all.

The reason to go back to England with Steven was partly selfish. He longed to be on English shores again, his home soil. He longed to see how it had changed. He imagined seventy years would bring about a lot of change. He had followed the news and seen pictures, but it was not the same. He wanted to see it all for himself.

He just could not avoid the facts.

The woman.

Even though Steven had not killed her, she was obviously unstable, unpredictable. They had no way of knowing what the repercussions of his feeding would be. To add to it all, it was going to be impossible for any of them to hold back from killing for much longer. The need was becoming unbearable.

Jeff opened the door and took in the high ceilings and worn coving. Grandeur long lost. Judith had her back to him, as she looked out of the window. She was barely concealed behind a transparent, tattered curtain. He could not believe how beautiful she was. He admired the way her hair rustled as the wind played with it, it called to him. From behind, he cradled her in his arms and kissed her head. 'How are you coping? Be honest.'

'I'm fine...what was that tonight?' She was avoiding the question. 'Steven has healed faster than we expected. And what did he do to that woman? Have you seen that before?' She turned to face him, her eyes wild as they darted around.

Jeff placed his hands on her face and stroked her cheek. 'Calm down, don't panic, we've been through worse than this.'

She focused on his face and then pursed her lips, as though holding back tears.

Jeff lowered his head and kissed her lips. He could feel her body relax as he did. Physical contact could always perform miracles.

***

Steven stared at his ankle which looked significantly better. The last time he had seen it out of the cast it had been twisted. Now, it was swollen, but not deformed. He gave a low snort as he remembered the bloody tapir. He had no idea a tapir, of all animals, could be capable of such an act of aggression. He guessed all animals instinctively defend and protect. With a lick of his lips, he remembered the taste of the woman's blood. It was totally different to tapir blood. It was amazing blood could be so powerful.

A part of him equated human blood to Chateaubriand, whereas tapir blood would be more like stewing beef. He recalled the rush. When he started to feed on that woman a force surged through his body. The effect on his foot had been near enough instant. He never believed in magic, but he guessed there were a lot of things he could not understand. The events of the past year spoke for themselves.

Outside, the sky thundered. He made his way over to the window, leant against the swollen wooden frame, and watched the rain. It was torrential. He wondered about the woman in the park. Would she be okay? Would she survive? More importantly, was she looking for him?

He was proud of the fact he had been able to stop.

Somehow, he had heard her heartbeat and known. He would not kill, stubborn to the end. Over the past hour he had come to a decision. If they would not take him back to England, he would escape. He knew he was not completely healed, but at least he could now walk unaided.

It was confusing.

Deep down he knew his grandparents had his best interests at heart. He had no idea why Emily was there. She was not exactly doing anything to help.

The truth was he wanted to stay a little longer. He wanted to learn. He had so much to learn. His dream of returning to England and continuing with his old life had changed. He wanted to do it right. If Caitlin remembered him, or even allowed him back into her life, he would have to start from scratch. He resolved to find out as much as possible before he opted to brave the real world again. The last thing he wanted was to cause Caitlin any harm and now he knew that was exactly what he could do.

***

Emily could not understand the tangled web forming in her gut. She could not keep still. In a ball on the floor she rocked back and forth. Every now and again she paused and stared at the night sky. The dark called as her thoughts raced in confusion. She was out now. She was free. It was what she wanted, wasn't it? Steven had given her an excuse to leave. Even if she had planted the seed, they had trusted her to look out for Steven. Her parents trusted her. Could she betray them again? She had helped to build the community. Did it matter? Probably not, most of the people in the community would be glad to see her go. Wouldn't they?

Yet, she wanted to hold on to the idea that she could protect Steven, that *she* could help him return to his former life. She gritted her teeth, who was she kidding? He did not need her.

She longed to kill.

The fact she had managed to resist so far was incredible. Her lack of self control was embarrassing. Had she really tried as hard as she could in the past? Perhaps, if she'd had more faith in her self control she would have been able to lead a reasonably normal life with her husband and child. It would have taken a few years before they noticed she did not age.

The thoughts tormented her. Only one thing could interrupt them. The pull she was now unable to resist. She had tried, but she could not fight the hunger. The image of the defenceless woman swam in her mind.

No-one would notice if she slipped out. It was the most humane thing to do.

***

The sky was pale blue and completely clear, not a single wisp of a cloud in sight. The advent of daybreak brought life seething to the surface as the sun rose over the horizon. It had a direct hit on Steven's face. He put his hand to his forehead and squinted. He had been awake for a while, restless. Curtains would be a welcome addition to the room. In daylight, the room left much to be desired.

He could not believe he had slept on the floor. It was hard, cold and filthy. To top it all, his stomach growled. It needed food, proper food. Visions of an English breakfast swirled in his mind and he salivated at the thought. Sausages, bacon, eggs, hash browns, baked beans, toast covered in real butter – if only.

Resigned, he stretched his arms above his head. His body ached. The floorboard made a loud noise as he moved. He fidgeted as he made his way down the hall. Inside, the bathroom was filthy. To top it all, there was no running water – it was just what he needed. He had never been the self conscious type, but basic hygiene was something he had learnt to take for granted over the years. At least the community had a waterfall. Surely, they would not stay in this dump for too long?

Out in the hall, he cut his losses and made his way downstairs. The ground floor of the house looked totally different in the morning light. There was no furniture, but a faint discoloration of paintwork on the walls indicated the presence of large paintings at some point in the past. With a touch of fresh paint, furniture and basic appliances the house had potential.

In the kitchen, Judith and Jeff bustled over the table. Emily sat on the floor. On the worktop was fresh bread, butter, jam and a carton of orange juice. They all faced him.

'There he is,' Jeff exclaimed. 'Are you hungry?'

'As always,' Steven replied. It dawned on him that they must have been up very early. 'Can I help myself?'

'Of course,' Judith answered. She stepped back with a slice of bread smeared in jam and a glass filled with juice.

Steven wondered when they had gone shopping. 'Thanks, I needed this,' he said, as he picked up a slice of bread, hastily buttered it and devoured it in a couple of bites.

Emily was lost in thought. Even though he did not know her that well he was not stupid, something was up.

'Are we going to check on that woman today?' Steven asked, after he had washed a second slice down with some juice.

'No,' Emily snapped. She flicked her hair back, smiled and continued. 'There is no need to make her suffer further by going to see her.'

It sounded forced.

Steven frowned. Why did he have to have such a strange mother? 'She would not have to see us.'

'I'll go and check on her then.' She rose and started to walk to the entrance.

Jeff raised his hands in the air. 'You do that Emily and make sure you tell us what you see.'

Steven suspected Jeff was wary, it surprised him to see him let Emily go so easily.

'Great, I'll head off now.' Her juice remained in her cup, untouched.

Once she had left, Steven voiced his concern. 'What's up with her?' he asked, as he prepared another slice of bread.

'Nothing for you to worry about.' Judith's expression was kind. 'Emily is just Emily. Sometimes you just have to let her go.' It sounded like she was speaking to herself.

Jeff made his way over and sat on the floor next to Steven. 'Now that Emily has gone we can talk to you about your future. I have to be honest, as much as I love my daughter I know she has to return to the community. She cannot live out here. She did it once and could not cope. She can be of no help to you if she starts to lose control.'

'Go back then, I can take care of myself.' Steven pulled a poker face.

'Can you really?' Judith narrowed her eyes. 'You don't know much about what you can handle if you're honest.'

It was time to take the defensive. 'Maybe, but I have proved to you that I'm not a killer.'

'You might be able to control yourself now, but will you later on? You can't be sure of it.' Jeff paused, and then looked to Judith.

Steven continued, 'I know I have a lot to learn, but I can't go back. I just can't.'

What Jeff said next left him dumbfounded.

'We have decided to take you back to England ourselves. We would like to see our hometown again and we our prepared to keep an eye on you until we are sure that you're under control.'

Steven raised his eyebrows and could not withhold a smile. 'Really?'

'Really,' Judith repeated, a smile made its way across her face.

Steven narrowed his eyes. 'And how are you so sure that *you* will not be tempted?'

'We're not sure, in the same way you are, but we both managed to resist last night and are prepared to try. We also have other ways to help ourselves. The truth is if we'd helped Emily when she was younger she might have stood a chance. Now, I doubt she can resist. You did notice how erratically she was behaving?' Judith sighed.

Steven wondered what other ways Judith was referring to but he decided to let it drop. He was curious about Emily. 'She resisted last night, didn't she?'

'Unfortunately she didn't, I heard her go out in the night. And the signs this morning indicate that she fed. She looks different, couldn't you tell?' Judith asked.

'She seemed guilty about something that's for sure, but,'

Steven paused. He felt sick. 'The woman – did she kill the woman?'

'We don't know for definite, but it's likely,' Jeff admitted, his shoulders dropped.

'All because of me,' Steven said, his eyes fixed on the knife. 'Will she come back?'

'We don't know,' they both admitted simultaneously.

Jeff put his hand on Steven's shoulder. 'Don't worry, if she doesn't come back we will find her.'

CHAPTER 6

DECEPTION

Emily savoured the remnants of blood left in her mouth and licked her lips. It was official she was a monster, nothing but a ruthless killer. She had concealed the body in a familiar crypt she had used in the past. It was unlikely there would be a thorough search for a homeless woman but it was better to be safe, no-one would look there. The woman had been so easy to kill, they all were. She had found her soaked to the bone, lost and disorientated. As far as she was concerned, she had done the woman a favour by taking her out of her misery.

The woman had welcomed her as though she was seeing an angel. Emily was an angel, an angel of death. A series of faces flooded through her mind, strangers she had killed for her satisfaction. She had never been able to control herself. The only exception had been Steven's father, Paul. Her abstinence *had* come at a price. So many lives had been lost to enable her to live with Paul. It had been a selfish decision on her part. Either way she could not regret having experienced true love, even though short lived.

When she came up with the plan to take Steven out of the community her ultimate aim was to escape. The question was when and how? Her parents had no idea what she was capable of. No-one knew. Now, out in the open she was free to lead a new life, they could not stop her. She wondered if the time had finally come. Was she free to go? Would they follow? Steven had made it clear he was indifferent towards her. He did not love her and certainly did not look upon her as a mother. Would it be better if she left and let her parents look after him? The only thing stopping her was her irrational nature. She was a killer. She deserved to live a life of exile in the Amazon. She should curb her bloodlust.

Emily had never been very good at doing what she should.

The questions continued to play in her mind as she drank the cup of coffee in the tiny cafeteria. She could see the locals watching her, as though evaluating her presence. She certainly did not look like a backpacker. Yet, a female of her age, alone, in a place she did not belong, left her vulnerable. Her features marked her out as European, her skin would always be too pale no matter how much she caught the sun. The only reason they had left her so far was the fact that she spoke perfect Portuguese. As if reading her mind, the waiter came up to her again and asked if he could get her anything else. Emily looked up, smiled and declined a refill. She took out the correct change and got ready to wander the streets. She needed to think, to plan.

***

Steven mulled over the conversation with his grandparents. It was interesting. He accepted them as his grandparents, yet, he had trouble accepting Emily as his mother. She looked too much like a sister. It was hard to accept the truth. How could she be his mother? And was it true that she was a ruthless killer? How many had she killed already? His grandparents could only guess, only Emily could answer for her actions. He had a feeling she would never be that forthcoming.

He looked up at the clouded sky. The rain had started to fall and was beginning to intensify. It would probably turn into another deluge. The day had started out so positive, yet a few hours into the day the weather was unrecognisable. The climate here was so different to back home. It was hot, sticky and humid. He longed for a cool English breeze. He leant his head back and let the rain run over his face. Childishly, he stuck his tongue out and let a few droplets run down his throat. The taste was pure and natural.

'Are you planning to sit out here all day?' Judith asked, as she came up behind him. 'Meditating or can I join you?'

Steven gave a half smile. 'Not meditating, that's too much trouble. Take a pew.' He had heard her. Her footsteps were slower than Emily's and lighter than Jeff's. His hearing was so fine tuned. He could make out the subtle differences.

Judith sat next to him. It didn't look like she minded the rain. She must have been used to it by now. 'So how are you really doing?'

That was a loaded question. 'I'm fine.'

'You're just like you're grandfather you know and I've known him for years. You don't fool me for a second.' Judith paused and gave a low chuckle. 'What is different about you since the change? You need to tell us about anything that is confusing you. We can help.'

Steven studied the grass and ran his fingers through a few strands. He pulled a few off and played with them. Could he trust her? He didn't have a lot of choice in who to confide in. 'I can hear everything around me as clearly as if it were next to us.'

Judith ran her hands through her hair. 'How far can you hear? Do you have any idea?'

When she lowered her hands he noticed they were really bony, with long fingers. They were very different to his, almost fragile.

'Not really. In the jungle the sounds were more natural. Here the manmade sounds are magnified to a level I have never experienced before. When I fed off that woman every sound became crisper, clearer. I don't know how far I can hear.'

'It'll be interesting to see your gift develop. The first year is always when things tend to happen.'

Steven dropped the strands of grass, his curiosity sparked. 'Do you have anything special you can do?'

'Apart from the fact I don't age?' Judith had a hint of a smile on her lips.

Steven smiled. Ironic, was life a big enough gift?

'All of us have qualities that seem to have become more exaggerated. Some can solve incredible calculations, others have fun learning every language under the sun, and others know how to make the most of the land. I was naturally inquisitive before the attack. After, I guess I became the ultimate problem solver. I love the challenge of figuring out a puzzle. I was the mastermind of the new habitat in the jungle.

Jeff and the others were all scientists. There was nothing they could not figure out. We were a dream team. Together we created the security systems, access to the community, lighting, and amenities. Everything you saw for yourself. It was fun to create something out of nothing.'

Steven frowned. 'No offence intended, you seem nice enough, but don't you think you ended up making a large prison?'

Judith looked him straight in the eyes. 'It was necessary. We saw what was happening and how we seemed unable to resist. None of us wanted to become killers. Don't forget we witnessed the horrors of the Second World War. We had seen enough bloodshed and death. We did not want to add to the carnage.'

'So you ran away?'

'I guess we did,' Judith said. 'Do you think we should have stayed?'

Steven thought about the question, torn on the answer. He knew there was no way he would ever understand what they had gone through. Even so, he could not help feeling that human nature never exerted the same effect on different people. 'It seems a bit strange to make the decision to leave civilisation and create a new home without actually knowing more about what you had become. Would it not have made sense to have waited a while?'

'Maybe, I don't know, we were hasty I guess. But then all the children started to change too and what about the fact that we did not age? How could we remain inconspicuous? No, I don't believe that living away from humanity was a bad decision. The question now is can we ever realistically rejoin it?'

'I'm willing to try,' Steven added.

'I know you are,' Judith sighed. 'Perhaps we could try. Your mother has to go back to the community, you know that don't you.'

'It doesn't bother me.'

Judith scowled. 'She is your mother. I know she is an *interesting* individual.'

Steven suppressed his laughter – that was an understatement.

'But she is still your mother. You should come to terms with what she did. You would not exist were it not for her recklessness. I do believe she tried to protect you. Besides, you've opened up possibilities we had not dared to consider. It's going to take some time for people to adapt.'

Steven changed tack. 'Anyway, how are we going to get her to return if she refuses?'

The smile was back. 'We'll find a way.'

***

Emily walked around the streets admiring the stunning architecture. It appeared out of place when you considered the Amazon Jungle was just around the corner. Yet, this place had seen electric lighting before many places in Europe, it was prosperous and exclusive. Now, it struggled to compete in the World economy, the mighty fall eventually. Just look at the British Empire, in her lifetime it had gone from having a say over a fifth of the world's population to having not a lot of say at all.

She had no idea where she fit into the world puzzle.

Even though it was wrong of her to follow her instinct and kill, it was the most natural thing she ever did. She never consciously chose to commit murder, she just could not resist. All the years of seclusion in the community had been a complete waste of time. They had taught her nothing. They had changed nothing. She was what she was. And if she was destined to live as a twenty year old forever wasn't it time she started to enjoy herself? She had been twenty for over seventy years. Enough was enough.

The impressive building in front of her pulled her in. The church offered a sanctuary. When she had fallen in love with Paul she had walked into a church and asked for God's forgiveness. A peace so pure had descended upon her that she had been reassured to stay. Acoustics did strange things. The church beckoned her again. A few people knelt over the pews and some candles burned on the altar. It was the middle of the afternoon so it was not busy.

It always amazed her how many statues and saints the

Catholic Church had. Idolisation was certainly not frowned upon. The main stage belonged to the image of Christ on the Cross. Her family had never been overly religious, but she had heard enough from living with the Santos family to know not to talk lightly of faith.

Sat down, a peace descended on her again. It was bizarre.

She needed guidance. She wanted someone to tell her what to do. She knelt down and leant her head in her hands. All she could do was pray for a solution to her wretched existence.

She did not know how long she stayed there, but the sound of footsteps eventually disturbed her. When they stopped next to her, she looked up, unsurprised. 'Hello Carmen.'

'Emily.' Carmen sat down next to her.

Emily tensed. 'How did you know where I was?'

'We've been tracking you.'

'Why?' Emily snapped, her voice louder than intended. A few heads turned in their direction. Silence was sacrilegious in these kinds of churches.

'There is no need to draw attention to us,' Carmen whispered. 'We know what you did last night.'

'Great, so where's my brother? Was he spying on me as usual? Why have you been tracking me? You have not answered my question.' Emily could not help being bitter.

'You know why we're here. We have to take you back. You can't be allowed to run around jeopardising what we have spent years protecting. Did you think we were going to let you go without keeping an eye on you?' Her speech sounded rehearsed.

'I should have guessed…where is he?' Emily looked back, and grunted at the silhouette by the entrance.

Carmen glanced back momentarily.

'What if I don't want to come back?' Emily hissed.

'It's not an option. Your son is safe with your mum and dad. His path is different to yours.' Carmen nodded at Ian. 'We don't need to do this the hard way.'

Emily locked eyes with her brother as he winked in his usual cocky manner. She felt defeated. She looked at the image of Christ ahead and bowed her head. In the house of God she had no fight left. Carmen was right about one thing, Steven would be better off without her.

Carmen always did what Ian said, she was his bitch. They never put a foot wrong. All Emily had was left feet. From a young age, Ian had always shown leadership qualities that had gone on to mature and develop – he was *so sensible,* a natural leader who loved to be in charge. She had been indecisive where Steven was concerned, but Ian had gone behind her back to bring her son to the community. Steven was her son, *her* responsibility. She would have known what to do if Ian had given her the chance. At least she liked to think so.

Emily was fed up of being overpowered by her dominant siblings.

She narrowed her eyes and made a decision. Not today. Not ever again. An alternative scenario unravelled in her mind. It was time for her to take charge of her own destiny.

CHAPTER 7

A FRESH START

'Emily's not back yet?' Judith had waited long enough, it was time to talk.

Jeff frowned and whispered, 'I was thinking that.'

'You know ignoring it won't help. And I can hear you,' Steven said, from the top of the stairs.

Judith glanced at Jeff, shrugged her shoulders and called out, 'we can't keep things from you. You're right.'

The sound of Steven's broken footsteps stopped as he came into the room, he held his head up. He hobbled and yet maintained a confident air, he reminded her of Ian. 'I'm glad you're talking English now. If you spoke the other language I wouldn't have a clue. Shall we go and look for her?'

'Probably best,' Jeff said. There was an undertone to his voice, one of disappointment.

Once in the car, Judith leant her elbow on the window sill and studied the road. When they approached the city centre she closed her eyes and imagined it as it had been. Now, it was dated. Brick glass houses, there was nothing interesting about the buildings. The car eased into one of the concrete monsters, the multi-storey car park of a large shopping centre.

'We should really get mobile phones,' Steven suggested.

Jeff sounded excited as he replied. 'I have heard of those, but I've never used one. It is fascinating that you can walk and talk. Things have changed so much where technology is concerned and yet people remain the same.'

'Well, not necessarily the same,' Steven countered.

'Emotions and characteristics can't have changed at all – more habits I imagine,' Judith speculated. 'We use computers too. We are not behind the times. But I sense that our community must be totally different to how mainstream society works today. Money has always been a cause of conflict. As you know, we have no need for it.'

Jeff continued, 'it's interesting really, in modern society introverted people have the opportunity to live their lives uninhibited by protocol. They don't have to socialise or talk to anyone outside of the work environment. Frequently, people also live far from their families, don't they?' he asked Steven.

'I guess. I practically grew up in boarding school. I don't know much about living like a grown-up, I was not allowed to become one.' His reply came with a bitter edge.

Jeff laughed aloud. 'Still resentful are you?'

The pout was confirmation enough.

Jeff rubbed his moustache. 'You have a lot to learn about living. Sometimes sacrifices are needed for the greater good.'

Steven kept quiet on the point. Judith had noticed he had lost some of his fight recently.

'Anyway, it's a good idea. We'll get mobile phones if we come across the right store,' Jeff added. 'I'm always ready to explore new technology.'

***

At times Steven felt like he was being babysat, yet he had to admit that he liked his grandparents. It was hard to explain. He was almost in awe of them, of what they had achieved. They were visionaries. He had to respect them.

His view of his mother was clouded, very clouded.

At first he understood the dilemma she had faced and a part of him was sorry for her. Now, he wondered whether Emily had been hiding something else. She said she did not want to be a killer, but she never admitted enjoying the kill. It was obvious she never held back. She lusted after human blood in an uncontrollable manner. It was amazing she had managed to walk away from humans for him. It must have been hard if she was so weak. It made him wonder whether something else had made her leave. She did not give him the impression that she missed being his mum. Emily was not the kind of woman he classed as the maternal type.

'How much money do we have anyway?' Steven asked.

'Plenty,' Jeff answered. 'It's amazing how the value of

money has multiplied over the years. Our modest savings have grown a lot over the years.'

'And we have some pretty savvy minds that know how to play the markets.' Judith winked at Jeff.

'Not that it matters. We have ways to get money. People tend to do what we want.'

'You use mind control?' Steven asked.

'It works.' Jeff gave a slight shrug of his shoulders.

'So what do we do now? Are we likely to find Emily?' Steven asked.

'The truth is that we don't know for sure, but we know where to start,' Jeff added.

'She always had a weakness for chocolate. If I know Emily at all, she will have been to the best chocolatier in the city,' Judith smiled.

Once out of the car, Judith passed Steven one of the crutches. She offered to help, but he was determined to go it alone. His foot was much better, but it still ached if he stood for a long period of time. He would try to keep up. As they walked around the main street Steven took stock of their surroundings. The shopping centre was busy at this time of day and a lot of people barely glanced at them as they rushed passed. A few mothers grappled with their young demanding children that were either refusing to go in their pushchairs or refusing to get out. The people around them were mainly mestizo in features, a term affectionately used to describe the outcome of being born of a mixed cultural heritage.

It was obvious to anyone that observed that they were not locals. However, it appeared to Steven that in a city like Manaus, foreigners were no strangers to the local people. He guessed they brought lucrative business opportunities. The locals casually glanced, but did not stare. It was like they knew not to trouble newcomers. The shops bustled, a lot of glamorous displays on the shop windows sought to lure people in. It was very different to the basic setup they had back in the community. Large posters claimed discounts of extraordinary proportions. It was difficult to believe the shops made any profit.

Judith stopped at a clothes shop in front of them. 'It's not there anymore,' she sighed. 'I should have realised that the last time I came was a long time ago and things don't always stay the same.'

'We'll try the one over there,' Jeff said. He gave her hand a squeeze and they walked side by side.

A confectioner's with a large display of handmade chocolates on the shop front made a good effort to lure them in. Steven had never really been that bothered about chocolate. He liked it. He liked other stuff too. The display was impressive; he had to give them that.

Judith took the lead and went in to talk to the sales assistant.

After a few minutes, she came back out again looking pleased. 'Emily was here this morning.'

'Well at least we know that nothing has happened to her,' Jeff looked relieved.

A male voice interrupted them. 'Still lusting after chocolate, mother?'

They all turned around.

Ian.

'No need to look so surprised, you did not think I'd just leave without seeing whether you'd be okay did you?'

'Ian, we don't need you to keep an eye on us,' Jeff said. From the way he stood straight, Steven could tell he was not impressed.

Ian did not back down. 'Well, you certainly lost track of my sister, Emily, didn't you?'

'Do you know where she is?' Judith asked.

'Of course, Carmen is staying with her so that we can take her back. This is not the place for her, is it? She could easily give us away. I don't know why you brought her with you in the first place.'

Jeff and Judith glanced at each. Steven sensed trouble.

Ian folded his arms and studied Steven's foot. 'So, are you coming back with us? Steven looks much better now.'

'No, we are not son,' Jeff replied. 'Your mother and I would like to take Steven back where he belongs. He does not belong here.'

'You think so?' It was Ian's turn to get angry as his face turned on a shade of red.

'Definitely,' Steven spoke up. 'You should never have brought me here in the first place.'

'No need to be like that. You might have stopped yourself from killing that woman, but you're not exactly normal now are you?' Ian sneered, his hands in fists.

'So, you've been following us?' Steven added.

'Anyway,' Jeff interrupted. 'At least we know what's happening. You take Emily back, before she does something we'll all regret, and we will continue on our journey. I'm looking to you to keep the community strong Ian.'

'If that's what you want. I just wanted to let you know where Emily was. You were *trying* to find her?' Ian was so obnoxious.

Judith went up to him and gave him an embrace. 'Look after yourself. Try and trust us. We've been at this longer than you have.'

'Resisting after time is harder than you think. It does not get easier, it gets harder. I've been out in the open longer than you have. You look tired, Mum. You are, aren't you?'

Steven was impressed with the way Ian showed concern for Judith. Now he mentioned it her face had paled.

Judith glanced away as she spoke. 'I'm fine. We'll bear it in mind.'

Jeff shook Ian's hand. 'Look after the community for us whilst we're away. You make a fine leader. We are both proud of you son.'

Ian nodded and gave a half smile. Then he made his way into the crowd and disappeared.

'At least we know where Emily is,' Jeff said. 'Let's make preparations. We have a long trip ahead of us.'

'Are we really going back to England?' Steven asked, incredulous.

'We're going home,' Judith replied. Her arm went over his shoulder.

Home.

Steven couldn't believe it. It was hard to understand why

they had agreed to take him back. Ian did have a point. Steven had no way of knowing what would happen the next time. Whatever their reason he was not about to complain.

***

A piece of paper flitted through the air, bounced off the floor and flew back again playfully, teased by the wind. Emily looked at its free spirit as she sat alone inside the café and mulled over her plan. Through the corner of her eye she watched Carmen. Carmen could not read her mind, it was very lucky. She took the opportunity and got up. 'I'm going to the toilet.'

'Okay, but we have to go soon.' Carmen did not suspect a thing.

*

The large prominent building oozed importance. From its detailed carvings to the intricate archway welcoming people in, there was nothing inferior about it. There were fifteen minutes left until closing time, so Emily made her way in whilst pretending to brush her hair aside as she passed the security camera. A few people queued for the tills so she stood patiently behind and waited. There was only one cashier which would simplify things. She glanced at the clock again, ten minutes to go.

At last, it was her turn.

She smiled at the male bank clerk and gazed into his eyes. In perfect Portuguese, she said, 'you are going to help me. Ask someone to take over for a few minutes. We have to talk in a private room.'

The man called a lady over and was replaced. Moving over to the side door he opened it, walked in, and gracefully ushered her into a small room. Once inside the room he stared at her robotically whilst she gave him further instructions. Obediently, he left the room.

Emily looked around the bare room. She knew he would talk to no-one.

After five anxious minutes, he returned. 'Here is your deposit. You do not need to sign for this. Thank you for doing business with this bank. Come back soon.'

The artery pulsed on his throat and she became aware of his aroma. In this confined space it intoxicated her. It was tempting, so tempting. With a snarl, she pulled away. She had to resist, for now. It would not hurt *later*. 'You will meet me outside the back entrance in twenty minutes.'

The man nodded like a puppet and held the door open.

Emily walked out smiling, the black bag tucked under her armpit. Life was looking very good. Her future was rosy.

***

Ian's phone rang. He hit the receiver button. 'Carmen, how is my darling sister?'

'Bad news, she's gone!' Carmen screamed.

'What do you mean, she's gone? You were supposed to stay with her.'

'I can't watch her every second, she's made a run for it and I can't figure out where she went.'

'Great, that's just great.'

A pause followed, before Carmen asked. 'What shall we do?'

'We'll have to tell Mum and Dad.' Ian hung up and wedged the phone in his pocket. Now he was pissed off.

CHAPTER 8

AN ENLIGHTENING CONVERSATION

The day was eventful to say the least. Ian had been following them, Emily had gone astray but had at least been found, and his grandparents had stood up to Ian.

'So, when should we move on?' Steven was eager to begin.

'Well, we have to obtain false documentation first so that we can travel. Unfortunately, none of us exist anymore so we'll need birth certificates and passports. I have a contact we can use. I'll sort it out tomorrow,' Jeff said.

It all sounded so easy. 'Right, so can I keep my real name?'

'Why not,' Judith smiled. 'You're entitled to use the name you know.'

Jeff narrowed his eyes. 'Are you happy to return to Southampton with us?'

Steven was embarrassed by the question. He had not really shown any gratitude. Whatever their reasons, they were still taking a huge risk. 'I would really like it if you came back with me. It'll be a great help. I have no idea what'll happen and I think I'll need all the help I can get,' he paused and scratched his head. 'Do you think, well I can hope, there is a chance they'll remember me?' He knew he had talked too much.

Jeff replied. 'We can try. We are no experts in mind manipulation. You know as much as we do. There is one catch.'

It sounded ominous. 'What's that?'

Judith squirmed.

'We will all need to feed before we leave for England, and I do mean human blood. We can justify it. This is an exploratory trip for us as much as it is for you.''

'Right, okay. If you think it's a good idea.' What else was

Steven supposed to say? Was it selfish to do whatever it took to get back?

'You're okay with that?' Judith sounded surprised.

'I know what we have to do.'

'How's your foot?' Judith asked.

'Near enough back to normal,' he replied.

Jeff nodded. 'Tonight we should see another improvement.'

'I guess tonight then…?' Steven left the suggestion hanging.

'Tonight,' Jeff committed.

*

The next morning Steven was overcome by guilt. He had done it. He had played a part in another person's death. They had killed a man together, so much for his principles. It did not seem so twisted last night. It had all been very peaceful. No screaming, no gory death. The old man did not seem in any pain. It was over quickly. And it had worked, he could now walk normally again. The difference in Jeff and Judith was obvious, with their appearance alone. He had not realised how dull and lacklustre Judith's hair had gone until he saw the colour come back.

The deed was done, and in a way he was glad the man was dead. The woman had suffered, he could see that now.

His mind was now fixed on his future. He needed to do some research.

He relished the ease with which he walked down the stairs; he did not need any support now. He would not push it too much but he could tell the damage was now minimal, a minor sprain, nothing more.

'Good morning, do you mind if I grab some breakfast in town and check some things on the internet?'

Jeff smiled. He looked so much healthier. 'If you need to, we also have to book flights so maybe you can check availability for next week. The documents should be ready by then.'

'No problem.'

Trust had to be earned. Steven figured he had done enough. He sat on the broken leather seat and got ready to drive. A weight had lifted. Finally, he was on his own. They trusted him enough to leave him alone. It was a breakthrough.

The streets were near enough empty now, people had gone back home. There was something peaceful and serene about the environment. A band played a reasonable tune on the local radio station and for a moment he could have closed his eyes and been anywhere – like he used to when he was normal. For the first time in months, he did not feel like an alien.

After ten minutes he came across the internet café he'd spotted on the previous day, there was nothing wrong with his navigational skills. As he made his way in, he got a few glances from a couple of teenage girls in the corner. He avoided their gaze. He managed to order what he hoped was toast with scrambled eggs and a coffee and paid for an hour. He took a seat on the other side of the room and got ready to surf the net. Eager to see if anything had happened whilst he was away, he logged on to the BBC website and saw that nothing out of the ordinary had occurred. Then he checked out his local football club, and was dismayed with the volume of defeats. Everything was as he left it.

He was happy to see what he had ordered brought to him. There was something red on it, but he guessed it was herbs. He took a sip from his coffee and relished the taste. Then he cut a piece of toast and heaped some eggs on top. When he put it in his mouth he was convinced he was on fire. Chilli, the eggs had chilli in them. He took another glug of coffee and managed to burn his mouth further from the hot liquid. He got up to order some water and saw the girls laughing at him. He was glad he could provide some entertainment.

After he had swallowed a whole glass of water, he ate the toast. The eggs would have to be wasted. It was an acquired taste, one he had not acquired!

Back on the net, he made a note of the flights and then logged into his Facebook account. He had left it for last on purpose. There was a high chance no-one would have contacted him. His jaw dropped when he saw he had one message. He clicked on the shortcut to reveal her face. Caitlin had sent him a message. A little flutter of butterflies ran through his stomach as he clicked on it to see what she had written. As he read the message a huge smile spread across his face.

Steven got back into the car deep in thought. Since he had left England he had dreamed that she would remember him, he had hoped. Now, his prayers had been answered. She knew of him. He stood a slim chance. As he rounded the corner, he braked in surprise. Emily was walking straight towards him. She had a look of contentment on her face and there was something different. He was about to call out to her, but he stopped himself. She was alone. He knew she was supposed to be with Carmen and Ian. There was no reason why they would have left her after what they'd said.

Impulsive, he parked the car, got out quickly and followed.

He dodged in and out of shop fronts as he tried to blend into the background. He nearly lost her track. Something told him to head down the alleyway. He felt like an amateur sleuth as he edged into the dark narrow tunnel. There was no sound up ahead. All he could do was walk in and hope that it wouldn't result in a wild goose chase.

Once in the dark, his eyes refocused.

A sound ahead startled him and he stopped.

She sounded bitter and angry. 'Stop following me, Steven.'

'Emily?'

'I guess you'll never call me Mum,' she snapped.

'What are you doing here? Where are you?'

'I thought you had excellent echolocation skills, you should know where I am.'

Concentrating on the sound of her voice, he scrambled along the tunnel. Light broke ahead, so he eased out and looked up. She was perched on the roof, her legs dangling over the side.

Without thinking, he scrambled up the wall, and sat next to her. As he looked down, he realised they were quite high up and he had climbed up with practically no support. 'How did I do that?'

'There are a lot of things you can do now.'

Everything was calm and quiet up on the rooftop. The street lights twinkled below giving the streets a play set quality.

He repeated the question. 'What are you doing here?'

'Escaping,' she said in an amused tone. 'I'm breaking free.'

'Really?' he mused, unafraid but nervous. 'I can't say that I blame you for wanting to leave, but will you be able to live with yourself. How are you going to stay undercover?'

'I'll find a way.'

'So, is this goodbye?'

'Until another time, not goodbye – that's too final.' A smile spread across her face. Then she cocked her head, as she swung her legs alternately over the side. 'I really am sorry for everything, but I hope you get a chance at a good life. That's not something I can help you with. I'm not good for anyone.'

'Are you always going to be a killer?' He needed to know how bad things might get.

'I don't know. I'd like to think not. Sorry I'm not a mother you can look up to.'

'Don't apologise to me, you're only letting yourself down. You don't have to be driven by your needs. You can fight it. I did.'

'What if I like being driven by my needs, what if I can't stop?'

'Mind over matter,' he stated.

'Drug addicts never get over their obsession. I don't hold up much hope for beating this.'

'Just try,' he hesitated and bit his lip. 'You should really go back.'

'No, sorry, I'm not going back. I'd rather die, as would you. Do you think I can't tell that you've fed again? Your foot is back to normal. I bet my parents fed too. We all have to in the end.'

Before he could say anything else she got up. He noticed a black bag strapped over her shoulder.

'I do love you.' Emily threw herself back down into the dark alleyway. She seemed to float through the air. He did not hear her land. He distinctly made out her faint silhouette as she disappeared into the distance.

All this time, he had failed to think of her as a person.

Now, for the first time, he saw her for what she had become – a caged, dangerous animal that had obtained a set of keys.

Was he destined to be no better?

***

Ian could not believe it. First, his sister went missing and now there was no sign of Steven. He made his way to the back room to confront his parents. Carmen shuffled after him. He could not even look at her, he was so angry.

'Where is Steven?' he shouted, his hands in fists.

Judith replied casually without lifting her head, her eyes transfixed on a newspaper. 'He'll be back soon. He had some things to do.'

'You let him go out alone? Are you crazy?'

Judith looked up now and folded the newspaper away. 'No, we are not crazy. Anyway, why are you here? You were supposed to take Emily back.'

'Emily escaped.'

Jeff fumed, 'you let her go and you have the gall to tell *us* off.'

Ian leant against the wall and folded his arms over his chest. 'It's hopeless. I'm not ready to take charge of the community. I need you to come back Dad. I can't do this.'

Judith got off the floor and made her way towards him. 'You can and you will. Steven will come back and we will find Emily. As hard as this is to believe I really don't think she will do anything stupid.'

Jeff remained pensive. 'It's a test. Steven can not run like Emily. We know where he wants to go. We would find him easily. He will come back. By the way, don't shout at us again. If there is one thing I have learnt it is that anger is never the solution. You can take charge. Keep a clear head and don't lose your nerve. Things have a way of working out in the end.'

Ian felt like a child all over again. He could not understand how his father could spin any situation. Like a petulant child, he spat back. 'We'll see.' He turned round and wandered into another room. He couldn't bear to wait with them. He needed to pace.

***

Steven knew they had visitors. His senses became sharper

every day. It was just what he needed, another confrontation. As soon as he walked in the door he got accosted.

'Did you find what you were looking for?' Ian's dry and condescending tone was starting to get irritating.

'I did actually, thanks for asking. Did you find Emily? Oh, no wait, I can answer that. NO. I just bumped into her. It was most enlightening.' Steven could not help himself, he had to grin.

'You saw her?' Ian's jaw dropped a split second before he composed himself. 'Where is she? Where was she going?'

'Do you honestly think she would tell me?' Steven rolled his eyes. Ian did not look as stupid as he acted.

'So, you let her get away?'

'And how exactly was I meant to stop her?' Steven huffed, he was getting impatient now.

Judith saved the day. 'Leave him be Ian. Come in Steven, tell us what she said.'

Steven eased past Ian, who was still partly blocking the corridor, and made his way into the kitchen. He took a huge slug from the orange juice carton on the worktop.

Jeff, Judith, Ian and Carmen followed. Carmen stayed at the doorway. She did not look too happy. Steven assumed she had experienced the wrath of Ian.

'So, is she okay?' Judith asked, still the compassionate mother.

Steven shrugged his shoulders. 'You know what? I think she is. She wants to be alone, to be free. I didn't get the impression she would do anything stupid.'

Ian guffawed. 'As if!'

Emily was not his best friend, but Ian's reaction grated. He was a real asshole sometimes. 'What would you know about her? I don't think you ever even tried to get to know her.'

'And you did?'

Steven fumed, anger brewing. 'No, I didn't, as you well know.'

'Enough!' Jeff exclaimed. 'No-one really knows Emily. Anna is her twin. She is the only one with a direct link to her emotions. Ian, ask Anna how Emily is. She will know. As for the situation, it's done, it's over. Emily is gone. Deal with it Ian. Our plans remain unchanged. We leave for England as soon as possible.' He turned and faced Carmen. 'Carmen. Thank you for trying to help. It can't be easy. My daughter is a live wire, always has been, always will be. All we can do is hope she has some common sense.'

Just as Ian opened his mouth, Jeff gave him a look and said, '*we* will figure out what's best.'

Steven hoped Jeff knew what that was.

CHAPTER 9

SETTLING

From the tiny window of the plane it was difficult to see what the weather was like outside. The air hostess flashed Steven a set of pristine teeth. They were so white against her tanned complexion. There was no way she had been in England recently.

'Can I get you anything else sir?' she asked.

Somehow, he got the feeling she would have given him *anything*.

'I'm good.'

'If you think of anything just press that button over there.' She half smiled, as though disappointed, and wandered off.

First class was a great place to be. At least his grandparents had more sense than Ian and Eilif. If he had travelled in this style going out he might have been less bitter.

After a sleep in the comfy spacious chair, which was more like a sofa chair, he heard the instructions from the Captain. They were making their final approach. It was time to belt up, and get ready for landing.

Steven could barely contain his euphoria.

When the engine died down the plane came alive, it was a hive of activity. As soon as the seat belt sign went off the noise tripled. Overhead lockers opened, bags and coats materialised out of nowhere and the passengers started to talk simultaneously, as a few children shouted and a baby cried. Everyone wanted to leave. They were so loud. He would give anything for a pair of earplugs. They'd been stuck in there for long enough.

Steven was desperate to leave and by the look on his grandparents' face they were too. Long haul flights were not ideal for people like them.

He gave a half smile as he imagined Ian scouring obsessively through every news report around the world. He was determined to keep track of anything suspicious that would lead him to Emily. Apparently, Anna was also to tap into Emily's feelings, to try to keep tabs on her state of mind. It was the only thing they could do for now.

'Home at last,' Judith said, her hands clenched tight.

'If that is what it is, then yes, we are home again,' Jeff replied. Was he sceptical?

As they walked past the stewardess, she grinned in Steven's direction. 'Thank you for travelling with us.' He heard her heart skip a beat as she swallowed involuntarily.

Steven had to be careful. He barely managed the attention he used to receive. He did not even want to consider how he would cope with any more.

At passport control the queue was no better, it was tempting to use mind control to cheat.

Eventually, Jeff approached the passport desk. As he handed over the passport, he leaned in and said something to the inspector. The expression on the woman behind the desk went blank and she handed back the passport without scanning it. When Judith approached the same thing happened. Steven took a deep breath and stepped forward, his turn. He handed over the passport and remained silent. The woman glanced at the passport and robotically handed it back. He walked on in utter bemusement.

'What did you say to her?' Steven whispered, once out of earshot.

Jeff gave a small chuckle. 'That she was to let us through of course.'

'And it works, just like that?'

'Just like that.'

'Wow!' He held his mouth open a second too long.

Jeff nudged his shoulder. 'All of us can do it to some extent. Some are better than others. It's like any skill really. I'm pretty average, but I can do enough to get by without giving rise to any problems.' His cheeky smirk was familiar; Ian looked a lot like his dad.

'I'll have to practice that one. It could be handy.'

Judith gave an amused huff. 'Don't think you'll have any problems. The stewardess would have done anything for you just then and you barely said a word to her.'

'So, could I make people remember me?' Steven's eyes came alight. A new possibility dawned on him.

'No idea. I know what you're thinking though. Be careful with mind control, we don't know what the lasting effects are,' Jeff said, his brows furrowed.

With their luggage in tow they made their way out of arrivals and headed for the taxi stand.

'Where are you heading then?' A balding, overweight cabbie with a strong cockney accent asked.

'Southampton,' Jeff replied.

'Do you have a postcode?'

'Yes, this is the address. We will pay cash.'

'Right then, as you wish,' the man replied, as he entered the postcode into his satellite navigation system. As the distance and location came up he nearly coughed up a lung in shock. It was a fair distance. 'You realise that'll cost over 200 quid right?'

'Yes, that's fine,' Judith replied, her voice crisp.

'Thank you very much. Enjoy the trip,' the man spluttered. It was obviously his lucky day.

Jeff and Judith started talking in their unique dialect to prevent the man from listening. It also stopped Steven from listening. For once, it did not bother him. He stared out and watched as teardrops of rain traced their way down the window pane. The weather outside was dismal for the end of November. It was near freezing and the rain seemed incessant. A news update on the radio even mentioned the possibility of snow. It was unheard of at this time of year.

They still had a way to go so Steven leant his head back and closed his eyes. He dared to dream.

***

Judith noticed Steven was asleep, his face angelic, at peace at last. She nudged Jeff. 'Look at him, can you believe he's Emily's son.'

'He sure looks like her. It's weird isn't it? I think we get along just fine, don't you?'

'Yes, we get along better with him than we do with Emily that's for sure,' she sighed.

Jeff squeezed her hand. 'Nothing we can do about that just now. I have faith. Hopefully, Emily will find her path and in time it'll lead her back to us.'

'You always were the eternal optimist.' She loved the feel of his hand, it always reassured her.

Jeff looked out of the window as he spoke. 'We'll have to think of a cover. The locals will realise we're back if the lights are on. If we start living there they will ask questions. I might apply for a job in the New Forest, there's bound to be something. My background will not be hard to bluff.'

'I think I'll clear up the house. I dread to think how much work needs doing.' Judith had no intention of going to work in the modern world.

'Good idea. What about Steven?'

Judith knew the answer to the question, the how was what bothered her. 'I think he is keen to continue where he left off. He wants to go back to University.'

'Is that wise?' Jeff ruffled his hair with his hand. She took it as unease.

'If it's what he wants, then we have to help him. That's why we came back, to enable him to regain normality.'

Jeff leaned closer. 'Darling, I know why we are here, but let's face it we are not normal.'

She smiled. 'I know that, but, he still has to learn that for himself. We have to let him lead as normal a life as possible. In a few months, he might see things differently.' She was not trying to kid herself.

'You're right, you're always right. But, maybe we could convince him to try to get a job for now. He could always apply for next year,' Jeff replied, with a shrug of his shoulders. Reverting to English, he asked the cabbie. 'Excuse me, how much time will it take to get there?'

'It depends on the traffic. I wouldn't say it would be much longer than two hours.'

'Thank you.'

Judith looked out of the window and studied the cars and buildings they passed. So much had changed. Even though the weather did nothing to welcome them she was happy to be back. A lot of good memories ran through her mind of a time before war. It made her reminisce.

'Do you still remember the first time we met?' Judith asked.

'That was a long time ago.'

She knew he did remember. He was just playing hard to get as always. 'I remember it like it was yesterday. I fell in love with you the first time I saw you.'

Jeff hummed in agreement without repeating the sentiment. He never opened up to her when she wanted him to. Touchy feely was not how she would describe her husband.

'I stared at you through the corner of my eye the whole night. It was only at the very end when you were about to go that you acknowledged that I existed by nodding in my direction. You didn't dance with a single girl even though we were short of partners. It was shameful.'

'What can I say, I have two left feet,' he said, his face serious. Only his moustache tweaked.

'Poppycock, you couldn't be bothered to make the effort.'

'Well, that too.' His eyes came alight as the smile broke free.

'I couldn't believe it the next day when my parents told me they'd invited your parents round for tea. I almost died in shock. I didn't know what I'd say to you or if you'd come. I nervously waited and bit my nails in annoyance until four o'clock when you did finally make it.'

Jeff nodded. She could tell he was enjoying the story. It had been a long time since she'd talked about it.

'Finally, at four o'clock sharp – you were all very punctual – you arrived. I don't think I said a word for an hour, did I?'

'No, you looked very shy and beautiful. You certainly deceived me by appearing to be quiet that's for sure,' he huffed.

'You know you'd get bored if I didn't talk to you. Anyway, I couldn't believe it when I realised our parents had mutually set us up. But, it all worked out in the end and you became mine,' she beamed. He had always been hers.

'Well, I got you first,' he mused.

'Infuriating man, you'll always have me in the palm of your hand.'

'I sure hope so,' he replied. As he leant in to kiss her, Judith sighed. After the short kiss, she nuzzled into his chest. Home was where he was.

***

Steven had been awake for a while. He could not sleep. He could not understand what they were saying, but it was obvious they were still madly in love. It was strange to see true love. It existed. His dad and Clara had a real meaningful relationship, even if they just never seemed to have a lot in common. Love seemed to work in different ways for different people. It made him hopeful. Even someone like him should have a shot at love. The question was could it be with someone like Caitlin?

The message Caitlin had left on Facebook had initially given him hope. On further analysis he'd started to wonder if he'd misinterpreted it.

The message still rang clear in his head.

You were in a dream I had last night. It seemed real. Do I really know you? The dream was confusing. I would like to talk. Caitlin.

At first, he had been overjoyed by the fact that she had remembered him. All he could think about was whether she remembered that she used to be in love with him. But now he wondered about the dream. What did she mean by confusing? The more time went by, the more he was convinced that perhaps what she had dreamt was a very bad thing, not the kind of thing you would want to remember if you loved someone. All he could do now was to wait until he was back online. By then, he would hopefully have figured out what to do.

CHAPTER 10

LIFE IS CONFUSING

The drive lasted for three and a half hours. As they took the turnoff Jeff studied the surroundings, they were back. Steven was apprehensive, yet he looked forward to the adventure.

'Excuse me Gov' do you know the way from here? The sat nav doesn't give me an exact location,' the taxi driver asked.

'Sure,' Jeff replied. He knew the route had not changed. It was still deserted. They owned the land surrounding the house. He gave the taxi driver final instructions and sat back.

His mind drifted, as it reflected on the past. A childhood playing with tin toy soldiers in the back garden. Born in 1893 his childhood was idyllic and innocent, pampered really. The eldest of a family of five, he was used to being in charge and generally enjoyed bossing his siblings about. His youth was too innocent. It did not prepare him for life. He was naïve.

He imagined glory when he signed up for the Great War. He would have been proud to die for his country, just like all the other fools. It was a strange time. The unnecessary death still haunted him. For two years he witnessed the carnage, and by sheer luck he survived. Aged twenty five he returned a man, a troubled, traumatised man.

Judith was the reason he regained reason.

A sucker for punishment he felt duty bound twenty years later to join the team of scientists that would discover the nuclear bomb. The fight resumed. It was a battle to find the ultimate weapon, the decider. It was no surprise they found it. They were responsible for more death, more destruction. Jeff was convinced it was karma they were attacked. They never stopped to consider what the radiation would do to the bats, the *vampire* bats. It was their deadly bite that initiated their evolution.

Had they become vampires?

He did not like to think so, none of them wanted to think that. And yet, perhaps the mutation had happened before. Perhaps, they were not the first. He shuddered at the thought that the story of *Dracula* was true. At least they were outwardly normal, their deception was too good.

It was no surprise he took charge. A natural leader, he set in motion the chain of events that would lead to the establishment of their new community. The place he now knew as home deep within the Amazon.

Officially, he had died during the Second World War so his family house remained derelict for a few years, but they managed to make a successful claim in Ian's name and the property reverted to the Roberts family. None of his brothers and sisters had survived the war and any relatives had long since forgotten about the house.

So it stood alone, on the top of the hill amongst its pastures of land, deserted and lonely until some of *them* arrived.

'Are you sure you're at the right place?' the taxi driver asked. He looked around and studied the dark and secluded environment. It was practically black, the only light coming from the full moon and headlights.

'This is it,' Judith cheered. 'I'm *thirsty*,' she whispered.

'I know but you'll have to wait,' Jeff said, his tone wavered. 'Here is the money as promised, thank you.'

The taxi driver took the money greedily. As he counted Jeff saw Judith's face change, her canine's extending. He gripped her hand and held back the urge to react. 'No!' he stressed.

'Sorry mate, can I help?' The man looked back absentmindedly.

Jeff opened the door and practically pushed Judith out. 'Nothing, we're just glad to be back.'

The man shrugged and put the money down. He opened the car door to get the luggage.

'No, we'll do it,' Jeff hissed.

The man frowned, it was a worried look. 'If you're sure.'

'I've got them,' Steven said, hauling the bags off the taxi. Finally, he was awake.

'Sure, thanks then,' the man shut the door and turned on the engine. The tyres screeched as he turned the corner in a hurry.

As he drove out of the drive Judith broke down. 'I was really close. Was I the only one tempted?'

'To me he smelled of cigarettes,' Steven replied.

Jeff had smelt the cigarettes, along with the other tempting, sweet smell. 'We need to feed soon,' he said. 'Or we will not remain strong and might do something we will regret. We don't want to attack anyone inadvertently.'

'Fine, lets leave the bags and find a sheep or two that won't be missed,' Judith laughed, the tears gone.

Steven groaned.

Judith countered. 'You can always go for rabbit. I make a fantastic rabbit stew.'

'That's a pet, not food, ugh,' Steven winced.

Jeff watched the exchange in amusement. 'Let's drop off the bags and we'll see what we can find.'

The outside lighting transformed the building as the full grandeur was revealed. Jeff turned to Steven. 'The house was built in 1854 for my great grandfather. He worked the land and became a successful landowner. It's got a lot of original features. You can have a good look around it tomorrow. It's the only real link we have to the past.'

'It's lucky you found a way to keep it in the family. Who owns it now?' Steven asked.

'Ian, but since he is apparently approaching the age of seventy, we might have to consider faking his death to allow someone else to inherit. You could be a prime candidate you know. You could be his grandchild,' Jeff said, with a hand gesture.

'Can't you amend all the records? It's what you do, isn't it?'

Jeff was reminded of the way they had erased his existence. He was not surprised Steven brought it up. 'If you intend to stay here it would be easier to just add you as the owner.'

'I guess it would give me an identity,' Steven said, he shuffled from one foot to the other.

Jeff nodded. He had never been one to get into an argument. 'We can say you inherited it. I'll discuss it with Ian when the dust settles.'

Steven looked up, casual. 'Fine.'

'Time to go,' Judith said, robot style, her expression devoid of all emotion.

Jeff could tell she was struggling more than he was. It was interesting. In the community he had never stopped to think about their differences. He was starting to realise that Judith was weaker, it worried him. He slid his arm around her waist and gave her a squeeze. 'Yes dear, it's time to go.'

Outside, it was dark but Jeff's eyes adjusted quickly. 'Steven, are you alright to walk?'

'I can manage.'

It seemed as though Steven's foot was back to normal, but Jeff was wary. The recovery had gone too smoothly. 'Are you alright to hunt? Do you know what to do?'

'I got the idea back in the community. I doubt I'll get attacked by a bunny.'

Jeff scoffed, was that an attempt at humour? He was hopeful.

'No, there shouldn't be any killer rabbits out here,' Judith said, with a chuckle. When she recovered, she added, 'although we could try to find deer? I used to love venison sausages.'

'Deer are protected,' Steven said.

Jeff laughed, 'not from us.'

Steven pursed his lips. 'I'll just do what you say.'

Jeff was finding it hard to figure out what was wrong with Steven. He was a lot snappier now he was back. 'Are you okay?'

The question seemed to catch Steven by surprise as he stopped. 'I guess I just find it hard to be so close to Caitlin and yet still not be able to see how she is.'

'Caitlin, it's a nice name,' Judith said.

Jeff rolled his eyes. Love caused an awful lot of problems. 'You'll get to see her eventually. First, let's sort ourselves out and see how we go. The last thing you want is to put her in danger.'

'You're right,' Steven admitted. 'Sorry, for being such a

grump.'

Jeff relaxed. 'It's alright we'll come up with something. Now, less chatter, follow our lead.'

On a full stomach it would be easier to think clearly.

***

The next morning Judith woke up refreshed and energised. She stripped the skin from the deer as soon as she got downstairs. It was something she had known how to do for years from hunting in the Amazon. She made thin rashers in an attempt to imitate bacon. Jeff had already left. She had sent him on a mission to buy provisions.

As she worked, she thought about what they were doing. She could not understand why they had decided to be so impulsive. Were they reckless? Had they made a huge mistake by coming back to England before they knew what Steven was capable of?

She saw so much of Emily in Steven and yet he seemed so much calmer. In character, Steven reminded her of Jeff. Was that why she wanted to help him? Was she prepared to do what it took to enable Steven to be happy? Could she tell Steven the truth? She had not discussed the idea with Jeff, but she would not be surprised if he realised the possibility. Was it time to let everyone in on their secret or would it be like opening up Pandora's Box? Could they deal with the consequences, whatever those were?

Bag in hand, Jeff walked through the door and broke her trail of thought. 'It's amazing Judith, the service station…'

'Service station?'

'…yes, the service station stocked all sorts. It's so easy to shop here.' Jeff's cheeks were flushed.

'I guess now you can buy what you want when you want. It must be nice. Just think of all the time people must have on their hands. From what we know they don't have to do manual chores. What do people do?'

'I guess they replaced servants for convenience. With all the machines to do the work they found other things.' Jeff scratched his head. 'They have T.V., the internet, computer games, another thing called tablets or the iPad. And it goes on,

73

new gadgets for each generation.'

'And this makes people happy?' Judith spoke in a puzzled, but judgemental, voice.

Jeff shrugged his shoulders. 'I can understand the appeal. I would love to see how they all work.'

'Always the scientist,' she scolded. 'Don't you ever learn your lesson? New inventions are not always a good thing.'

'I know that, but man is a curious beast. We can't help ourselves.'

'Jeff Roberts, I hope you didn't want to come back to spend the entire time ogling at new technology.'

He eased up behind her and wrapped his arms around her stomach. 'I wouldn't ogle at technology, I only ogle at you.'

Judith giggled. He could still get to her.

'Now, where is my breakfast woman?'

'Yes, my master,' she sighed, sarcastic.

He spun her around and kissed her, she could not resist. After this entire time one thing never changed, she was still in love with her husband. She knew he would do anything for her, he always had.

The remains of Steven's breakfast sat alone on the table. Judith tried to relax. They had gone to find Steven, but his room was empty. She hoped he had not done anything foolish. She immersed herself in the text of an old favourite she had found in the bookcase. The paper was old and fragile. She remembered when it had been new.

Had so many years really gone by?

The sound of the front door alerted them to Steven's return. Trust was going to be important. She did not want to rush to any conclusions. Without raising her eyes from the book, she continued to read and waited.

Steven made his way in. 'Hey, just went out for a run.'

'Feel better?' Judith asked, she glanced up from the page.

'Yes, thanks. I think I'll go shower.'

'There's some food for you in the kitchen. Might be cold now but you can always put the plate in the oven again.'

'Sure, okay,' he awkwardly backed away.

After she heard the sound of water, Jeff turned to her and

74

said in their dialect. 'His hearing will be as good as ours so we have to make sure that we say nothing to upset him.'

'Mmm,' Judith answered, deep in thought.

'You trust him don't you?'

Judith stared into Jeff's eyes and said, 'completely.'

'I thought so. You always had a good judge of character.'

'Emily never thought so.' She had made so many errors where Emily was concerned.

'If it hadn't been for you, Emily would have gone off the rails many years earlier. If you had not insisted that she had to stay in the community in the early days just think of the damage she could have done?'

Judith wondered a lot about that recently. 'Perhaps…let's not talk about Emily, we are here for Steven.' She was just not sure if she could help Steven without letting him in on the secret. She wondered whether to discuss it with Jeff and then reconsidered. It was easier to read, it was an escape.

An hour later, Steven returned with wet sleek hair and a revived expression. 'Cosy.'

'You like the fire?' Judith asked.

Steven looked at the flames. 'Who doesn't like fire?'

Jeff stood up and made his way over to Steven. 'Breakfast?'

'Sure.'

Judith watched them go together. It was nice to see the way they seemed to bond. She just did not know why she was thinking strange thoughts. When she left the community she was so excited, now she was overwhelmed. She wanted to see the modern world. She wanted to come back to England. Now she was back in their house she felt at peace. This was where she belonged. Yet, she was so tired. She did not want to kill anymore, she wanted to rest. She could not explain why a part of her seemed to let go. A part of her wanted it all to end.

She didn't dare to tell Jeff. He would not understand.

CHAPTER 11

AN OLD ACQUAINTANCE

Steven appreciated the character of the old house. From the wooden beams, to the high ceilings, to the log fire, he liked it all. It was the kind of house he could see himself in. It was weird to think it could actually become his. He wouldn't say no.

'Do you like the house? It's been in my family for over one hundred years.'

Steven could not lie. 'It's in need of some modernisation, but other than that it's great.'

'Glad you like it. You are the new generation. Maybe we should go and get some things to bring it up to date,' Jeff said, as he took a seat in the kitchen chair.

Steven nodded. 'Shopping, hey why not, nothing else fazes me anymore.' He got the plate of food out of the oven with a cloth and sat down to eat. It looked good.

'Where did you go this morning?' Jeff asked.

Steven finished his mouthful and washed it down with some juice. 'Not far, I just needed some fresh air.'

'Try not to get noticed.'

'I know the drill.' He heaped some food onto his fork, and asked, 'so how do we travel?' He savoured the venison, Judith was a good cook.

'Now this might interest you. We own some classic cars. If we pump the tyres they should run like a dream.'

He swallowed and said, 'classics, now this is interesting.'

'When you finish I'll show you.'

As soon as the plate was empty Jeff leapt off his seat. 'Ready?'

There was never a dull moment. 'Sure.'

A separate outbuilding on the side of the house acted as a

76

garage. Jeff opened the doors and revealed three cars.

'So which one do you want to drive?'

Steven only had eyes for the Bentley, a car he had always dreamed of since he developed an infatuation with old cars at a young age. 'Are you kidding?'

'No, take your pick.'

He went straight for the Bentley and ran his fingers along the side of the car. Then he stopped to open the door and look inside. Even the smell was incredible. 'This is the car for me,' he said.

'Let's fix this baby up then,' Jeff said, getting the equipment ready.

'Absolutely.'

Half an hour later the car was ready for a test drive.

'We can only go for a short spin today. We still have to update the insurance and tax disc. Don't want to attract any unnecessary attention. I'll go and get Judith,' Jeff said.

Ten minutes later Steven sat at the wheel. He turned the key and the engine purred to life. He revved the engine, put her into gear and let go of the handbrake. The car cruised out of the garage, smooth.

***

The drive along the familiar sights seemed to be a revelation to Judith. Everywhere they went there was something old and new that made her ramble on about the changes. Jeff kept glancing back at her. It had been the right decision to come back with Steven. She was excited again, for quite some time she had seemed indifferent. He had hoped that by being outside of the community she would get a new lease of life.

As they rounded the corner a small platform came into view.

'Do you mind if we stop? We can get the train into town and leave the car here,' Steven suggested.

'No, not at all,' Jeff replied. 'Do you know? I think it might actually snow.'

'Not in November, silly,' Judith laughed.

'We'll see,' he smirked. Jeff looked up at the grey clouds and wondered if he could still tell a snow cloud from a rain cloud.

77

Steven rubbed his hands together as they waited for the train. 'What would have happened if you had not found me?'

'If we had not found you it's likely you would have killed someone without having any idea why.' Jeff put his hand on his shoulder.

Steven kicked a small stone. 'I guess I knew that.'

A few hours later, on the drive home Jeff gave a half smile. It had been fun. He never thought he would actually enjoy shopping but the range of stores, machines, opportunities and the sheer mix of people left him giddy. 'I hope you know how all of that works,' he said, his eyebrows raised.

'Definitely,' Steven replied.

'Once I know how to use this mobile phone, it should be useful,' Judith said, a worried expression on her face as she stared at the shiny box.

'I'll teach you. That's a promise,' Steven assured.

As they rounded a corner a small pub nestled within a range of deciduous trees came into view.

Jeff glanced over. 'Anyone fancy some food?'

'We'll go food shopping later then.' The way Judith said it worried Jeff. She sounded deflated, zapped. All her enthusiasm seemed to have vanished again.

***

Steven was not surprised when a few heads turned in their direction when they entered the pub. If they knew what they were, they would do more than give them casual glances. The furniture was wooden and aged; it was not one of those that had undergone modernisation. It was what Steven would class as homely, with a patterned carpet and dim lighting.

Jeff walked alongside. 'Is it strange to be back in Southampton?'

Steven did not know what to say. He knew he wanted to be back, he just did not know if it was the right thing to do. 'Yes and no, it was not that long ago I was here, not as long as you anyway.'

'No, it's strange for me to be back too,' Jeff replied.

Judith held Jeff's hand. 'It reminds me enough of what it was to still feel like home. Although, the shopping centre looked like it had come from another planet. The old city walls are the same. It's nice to be back.'

The pub was only half full. The weather might have put people off. Steven was sure he'd never been to this particular pub before. It was on the outskirts of Southampton, so it was not on the radar for first year students. He could not believe he would have been a second year student now.

They took a seat at one of the tables and perused the menus.

Judith peeked over the top of her menu. 'You're still thinking of the girl, aren't you?'

Steven faltered. He could not lie. Caitlin was the main reason he was worried. There was a possibility she would never remember him. 'Yes.'

Jeff glanced at Judith then went all serious. 'It's not a good idea to go back to university yet, you know that right?'

As much as Steven wanted to find Caitlin and probe the university files, he knew he had to wait. 'I understand.'

After they had all made their choice, Jeff went up to order. Steven took the chance and made a break for the toilet. On his way he nearly turned around and scarpered. It was Julia, one of Caitlin's old flatmates. He kept his composure and hoped for the best as they brushed past each other. She turned to face him and smiled. It was a blatant take me to bed look. He raised his eyebrows. He realised she had no idea who he was and had no reason to avoid him.

On his return, Julia caught his eye. She was only a few tables away. She leant towards her friend as though pointing him out, then giggled as the friend looked over. Steven smiled at them as he took a seat. He was up for stringing her along. Julia had not known Caitlin that long at university, but from what he recalled she hadn't exactly been that nice to her either.

'I've come up with a plan,' Jeff announced.

'I knew something was on your mind. So, what is it?' Judith became more animated.

Jeff began, his voice lowered. 'The fact is we need *extra* to survive, things are beginning to get difficult. We need to ensure we have a steady source of nutrition.'

'So how are we going to do this without making mistakes,'

Judith interrupted.

'I think we should reopen the farm, offer abattoir services. We've been doing it for years anyway. All we need to do is fill in the right paperwork and we kill two birds with one stone. We keep what we need, deliver what people want and at the same time give ourselves the perfect cover, unlimited animal blood. What do you think?'

Judith frowned as she mulled it over. 'It would give us a cover *if* animal blood was the only thing we needed.'

Steven averted his eyes. Judith had a point.

In a haughty tone Jeff added, 'we might have to supplement, but it will make things easier. Anyway, I've also thought of something for you to do Steven.'

Steven half smiled. His grandfather had been busy. 'I'm all ears.'

'You can apply for a job within the New Forest. If you still want to go back to university after that we'll find a way.'

'Sounds fair,' Steven said. 'When did you think this all up?'

'It's been on my mind since we decided to come back. Tomorrow, we'll start making preparations.'

It all sounded good. 'That's great for the short term, but I'd like to have my identity back. When will that happen?'

Jeff started to get flustered. 'I have to look into the records, see how camouflaged they are. It might not be hard to reinstate things back.'

Steven pressed the point. 'Will I get my qualifications back? I worked hard for those.'

Judith sounded tired again as she attempted to reassure him. 'Your grandfather will do the best he can, of that you can be sure.'

Jeff looked put out. His grand idea had not got the reception he hoped for. The food arrived to break the moment and they fell silent.

Steven relished the taste of his fish and chips, whilst drowning it down with a Coke. His stomach seemed to bulge under the weight of the food. He should have been full, but he still felt empty. As much as he was able to resist the lure of human blood, he knew he craved it. It was comforting to know that they'd have a steady supply of animal blood soon. He liked to think it would help.

'Can we head back now?' Judith asked.

'Sure, are you better?' Jeff sounded worried.

'Are you not well?' Steven studied her features. Her hair had lost its shine again and her face was gaunt.

Jeff replied. 'She's just tired. We've probably overdone it. We'll head back so she can rest.'

Steven decided not to question further. He knew *he* was not tired.

When he got up to follow, Julia stared right at him and gave a tantalising smile. She was asking for it, for sure. He stared for a moment, then looked to the door and smiled. If she wanted to talk to him she would follow.

Outside, a steady stream of snowflakes settled on the ground. It transformed everything in sight.

'Snow in November!' Judith exclaimed. 'I can't remember the last time I saw snow. It was a long time ago.'

Jeff gave her the answer. 'It was 1940 to be exact, the year before we left England for Los Alamos.'

'Was it really that long ago?' Judith said, as though struggling to recall the memory.

'Afraid so,' Jeff sighed.

Steven took his chance. 'Do you mind if I make my own way back?'

'Not at all,' Judith added. 'You remember the way?'

'Course, I've got an inbuilt sat nav.'

Now Judith looked puzzled. 'A what?'

'Don't worry about it, I'll find my way back.'

He watched the car drive away and noticed the snow fall was getting heavy. It dawned on him that before long he would look like a snowman if he did not move.

He heard Julia come out of the pub and turned to face her.

'Hello there. It's cold, I could warm you up.'

He could not believe Julia, of all people, was flirting with him. 'I'm fine.'

'I can't help feeling like I know you,' she continued, as she got closer.

'Maybe you do,' he said. He wanted to challenge her.

'Yes, maybe,' she mused. 'Can I give you a lift anywhere?'

'Sure,' he replied.

After they settled in the car, Julia commented on the cold several times as she rubbed her hands together. 'Where shall I take you? Do you want to come to mine for a coffee?'

'Coffee it is.'

Julia was not ugly, by any stretch of the imagination. *Coffee* sounded like a good idea.

CHAPTER 12

JULIA

After a slow drive through the slippery snow they made it back to a block of apartments. He had never been to this street before, but he knew where it was in Southampton. The university was a twenty minute drive away. He was so close now. Since Julia was in her second year she'd had to get new digs outside campus. He doubted she'd be living with Caitlin, they had never been close.

Julia struggled with the keys and opened the door with a shaky hand. For the first time she showed signs of nerves as she said in a high pitch, 'please come in.'

'Thanks.'

The corridor was narrow and it led to a small living room that was open plan with a tiny kitchenette.

'Do you want tea or coffee?' She asked.

'Coffee please.'

'Milk and sugar?'

'Lots of milk, one sugar.'

He took a seat on the double sofa, picked up the local newspaper and sifted through the pages.

Julia made casual conversation. 'So, what brings you here?'

'I just moved back, family reasons.'

'Oh, you used to live here?' He could hear the kettle start to boil as she prepared some mugs and spooned in some coffee granules.

'Yes.'

The spoon rattled in the mugs.

Julia made her way towards him and handed him a mug.

'Thanks.' He leaned in and took a sip, then rubbed his lips together. It was still too hot.

She took a seat next to him and placed the mug on the coffee table. He followed suit and put his mug down. When she turned to him and bridged the gap he was not surprised. The kiss was not unpleasant. He was surprised at his reaction as he kissed her back and slid his hand behind her. He enjoyed running his hands through the contours of her back. She grasped his neck and then slid her hands through his hair.

When they took a breath Julia was even more forthcoming. 'Do you want to go to the bedroom?'

His head was exploding. He could not believe that he was making out with Julia of all people and that she was trying to seduce him. 'Not yet.'

'Right,' she replied, her eyes to the floor.

He gave her a quick kiss on the lips and eased back. 'I'd like to talk for a while.'

She jerked her head back and stared at him in shock. 'Talk, now that's new. Where do you come from to get in touch with your feminine side?'

That was more like the Julia Caitlin had told him about.

He gave her a deep stare and saw her expression change to one of awe, her eyes wide, transfixed. Whatever he was doing it was working. Before he chickened out, he leant towards her and kissed her again. He kissed her chin, then made his way towards her neck and made his final move. His fully extended canines knew exactly where to go. Julia gave a low groan, putty in his hands.

After a minute, Julia started to go limp and he knew to stop. He withdrew and placed her carefully on the sofa. She would wake up again none the wiser, he hoped. He turned her head to the side and inspected the mark. It was small. At least it was winter, so she could hide it under a scarf. Hopefully, she'd think it was a love bite.

He let himself out of the apartment, his stride strong, head in a buzz, as adrenaline coursed through him. Using someone was not as difficult as he first imagined. He could return if he needed more, unless his grandparents considered it too risky. Time would tell. He put more pressure on his weak ankle as he walked, to test it. There was no pain anymore.

The snow continued its relentless descent. At least Steven's tracks would get hidden in no time. He was a fair distance from the house after his detour. If he walked it would take hours. Impulsive, he started to jog. Comfortable, he increased the pace. He moved even faster and turned into a wooded area. Once the trees enveloped him he let rip. A series of shrubs blocked his path so he jumped up to avoid it. He could not believe it when he soared high up into the air. His arms flew out as he tried to keep balance and he gave a shriek of exultation. When he landed safely he stopped and looked back at the distance he had covered. It was practically a football pitch. He had jumped *off* great heights, but he had not tried to jump *up* heights before.

They had kept that one quiet.

At the base of a huge oak tree, he wondered if he would be able to reach the top in one go. He took a few steps back, judged the distance and then ran as fast as he could before propelling himself up into the air. In his mind he visualised the top, he could touch it. And then, as if by magic, he was there. Perched on the top branch, his cast his eyes down below and feasted upon the magnificent view. It was a winter wonderland. He was the king of the world. Everything appeared so distant and far removed, tiny – like a model village with a sprinkling of lights.

In that moment of serenity he took stock of his situation.

Was he foolish to think he could waltz back into Caitlin's life and resume where they left off? It was extremely naïve of him to consider his life normal, especially when you took into account what he had just done. He could never be the same person he used to be. The need for blood grew, like an uncontrollable virus, and he was beginning to develop a taste for *human* blood. He liked how it made him feel.

The snow had started to settle on his shoulders so he brushed it off. He wondered if he could sweep aside his doubts and remain positive. He would not abandon Caitlin. They were meant for each other. He just knew. It was worth a shot. They were worth a shot. He could not live with the regret his mother had experienced. When he leapt off the tree he wondered what his grandparents would think of his decision to use someone as a donor. He doubted they would object. They wanted him to make a full recovery.

After dark, the house had a majestic presence. Its vantage point helped. It sat on top of the hill basked in the moonlight glow, surrounded by countryside. One of the lower windows shed some light on the shrubs at the side of the house. It could only mean one thing; Jeff and Judith were still awake. Steven made his way to the sash window and peeked in. As he did, the window slid open in front of him.

'Welcome back Steven. Is the front door not good enough for you?' Jeff asked, a grin on his face.

Steven shrugged, slid in through the window and straightened up to face them.

As they studied him, Judith frowned and Jeff scowled.

'Why Steven?' Judith shook her head.

'Why what?' he asked confused.

'We know you've had human blood, don't lie to us. Have you killed someone?' Jeff was blunt and straight to the point.

'No, no, of course I haven't killed anyone. But…'

'Oh no,' Judith sighed, easing her arm into Jeff's for support.

'But, what,' Jeff interrupted as he patted his wife's arm. 'What excuse could you possible have? We trusted you.'

'Look, I didn't kill anyone. I just …'

'Just what?' Jeff stressed, impatient. 'If you drank someone's blood you broke the rules. We should have been there. What happens if she behaves like that girl in Manaus?'

'I'm sorry okay. I know it was stupid.'

'Damn right it was stupid,' Jeff huffed.

After a few minutes of silence, Judith spoke. 'Jeff, it's done. Let's hear what he has to say. He does need it to recover after all, regardless of how risky it is.'

'Fine,' Jeff said, as his shoulders relaxed.

They simultaneously turned towards the fireplace, took a seat on the sofa and waited in silence. Steven paced the room. He could not understand why he had acted so impulsively. Finally, he sat down on the old fashioned armchair opposite them and placed his fingertips together as he leaned on his hands. 'Okay so I recognised the girl at the pub. Her name is

Julia, Caitlin used to know her. She couldn't remember me so I played along for fun. I don't know, I guess I liked seeing her in a different light. We were alone when it happened.'

'Too right,' Jeff guffawed.

'But I stopped before I'd done her any harm. She'll be fine right?'

'You are sure she was alive?' Jeff asked.

'Positive.'

'Okay, we'll have to check on her. We'll do it tomorrow. Let's get some sleep,' Jeff said, as he helped Judith up.

'Are you feeling okay?' Steven asked. He realised something was amiss, Judith did not look well.

'No, I'm not doing so well. But, we'll talk more tomorrow,' she replied, the smile on her face forced.

As he watched them leave the room guilt overwhelmed him. At the back of his mind a thought lingered. Was it his fault Judith was unwell?

The patterns on the ceiling formed irregular and interesting shapes as the curtain moved. The cool breeze wafted through the barely open window making goose pimples form on his arm. Steven lay on the bed and stared at the display. He could not sleep. He kept thinking of the blood, Julia's blood. It had a different taste from the girl in Manaus. It seemed blood was not just blood. He knew human blood satisfied in a different way to animal blood, and he had noticed a difference between the tastes of different animals. He never thought humans would taste different too. It was like trying out different flavour ice-creams – all good, just different.

His only regret was the lack of guilt. It was *only* Julia. She made him want to take the risk. If something had happened to her, honestly, he would not have been sorry. He knew it was wrong, but it was different to feeling remorse. For the first time in a long time, he was ashamed of his behaviour. He knew it had been wrong, he just wanted to do it again. The lure of the adrenaline kick was overwhelming.

He was beginning to understand why his mother had turned to the dark side. It reminded him of Anakin Skywalker in *Star Wars*, one of his favourite series. A good person can turn to evil in a quest for power. He laughed at the thought – he was such an anorak when it came to science fiction.

***

Julia woke up dreamily and remembered the eyes that had captivated her. She blushed as she realised she had fallen asleep. With a sigh, she covered her eyes with the back of her hands. She could not remember anything after they kissed. Groggy, she got up. Lightheaded and off balance she turned on the light to look around. There were no signs of a burglary so he couldn't have drugged her for money. And she was definite that nothing had happened so he did not use her for sex. But, something made her think that he had come to her apartment for a reason.

What that reason was she had no idea. She could not ask him, he had obviously left. She ran her hands under her thick wavy hair. As she did she brushed against her neck and felt a sharp stab of pain, just like pins and needles. She made her way over to the mirror and tried to angle her head to look, whilst holding her hair back, but she could not see clearly. It looked like some sort of love bite. Annoyed, she brushed her teeth, grabbed her pyjama's and put them on hastily before making her way towards her bedroom.

As she drifted off she groaned. There was nothing she hated more than to be marked by a man and yet, even though it was against her nature, she wanted him to do whatever he had done again. His eyes danced in her mind as she went to sleep and dreamt of going to find him.

CHAPTER 13

ATTRACTION

When Steven went into the bathroom to shower he paused to appreciate it for the first time. It was a bathroom suite worthy of being a museum piece. The bath was inset into the wall surrounded by a mosaic depicting a fish swimming in a pond. The sink was huge with a set of brass taps that had seen better days. The toilet was in a separate room between the sink and shower. Steven had not seen anyone cleaning; even so, it was obvious someone had. The fresh scent of vanilla and magnolia lingered.

Hidden within the alcove of the bath was a set of shower handles and a large round shower head. It was a shame the water pressure was so weak. He had been so hopeful the other day, before he turned it on. Maybe, he could convince his grandparents to upgrade the boiler. Then again it would mean they'd need someone to come to the house. He could wait.

Refreshed and revitalised he sauntered down the stairs and wondered what his grandparents had bought at the supermarket. In a way, he wished he'd gone with them. He wanted to stock up on his favourites. He missed Marmite.

'Good Morning.' Judith's voice was croaky. Steven wondered if he would find out what was going on.

'Morning,' he replied. 'I'm sorry about last night.'

'No you're not, I can tell. It felt natural to do what you where designed for. Just be careful, you don't know what your limits are yet. But, let's talk later okay.' She barely got the words out as a cough took hold.

Steven frowned. 'You're not feeling better? What's wrong?'

'Nothing for you to worry about now, it's just an adjustment, that's all.'

'Adjustment?'

'Don't trouble Judith with questions, you have enough to answer for already,' Jeff snapped, as he walked in from the dining room. 'Come and have something to eat.'

Steven felt like a child. His hand had just been well and truly slapped away from the cookie jar. Obediently, he made his way to the dining area. The table was laid out with toast and the usual condiments, boiled eggs, and a range of small cereal packets. He whistled in admiration. 'This is great.'

'We heard you taking a shower so we got it ready.' Judith beamed, as she slowly made her way in and sat down.

'She always loved mothering her children, you're lucky,' Jeff grumbled.

Steven resisted the urge to ask him what his exact problem was. Instead, he sat down and helped himself to an egg and toast. The egg was warm so he cut into the shell with his knife, removed the hat, and dipped the bread into the runny yolk. After devouring the remains he helped himself to a packet of corn flakes and poured on some milk.

'Hungry?' Judith asked, as a laugh coaxed its way out before the cough took hold again.

'Just a bit,' he admitted, a frown now set upon his face. 'Okay, so are you going to tell me what's going on?'

'We will tell you when you need to know!' Jeff snapped. Was he angry or upset?

'Calm down Jeff,' Judith interrupted. 'He needs to know. I think I have to feed soon, that's all,' she said, her voice subdued.

Jeff pursed his lips, but Steven continued and rephrased the question. 'Has anything like this happened to you before?'

'Well, no, I guess not,' she replied.

'Do you need human blood?'

'We don't know.' Jeff's shoulders drooped. 'Out of interest, how do you manage to stop yourself from killing? You've consciously done it twice now. It appears that you can control yourself.'

'Surely, others have done it?'

'Very few of us have been known to stop once we start. The

90

victim usually dies. But no-one we know could do it straight away. They had to teach themselves to stop by reading the signs. You just know when to stop. It's insightful.'

Steven thought about this and cocked his head to the side. 'I'm the first to know when to stop naturally. Do you think that's because I'm more human?'

'Who knows?' Jeff said, with a quick shrug. 'The point is can you teach Judith?'

'It's worth a try.'

'No, it's not!' Judith retorted. 'I won't do it anymore, I told you Jeff.'

Immediately, Jeff's hand was on her shoulder. 'No-one will force you to do anything, but,' he paused. 'Won't you please reconsider?'

'No,' she replied, determined.

Steven sensed there was more to this discussion. He thought it wise to change the conversation. 'Shall we go and check on the girl?

Jeff turned to face him and then paused, eyes narrowed. A moment later his expression relaxed. 'Good idea, I'll come with you. Judith, try and rest, please.' Jeff took hold of her hand and kissed her forehead.

'I'll take it easy,' Judith replied.

She did not look good. When they got back Steven intended to find out more. He didn't want to think about what could happen if Judith did not feed. It was obvious she needed human blood, the sooner the better.

***

Steven enjoyed the ride on the Bentley. They certainly didn't make them like this anymore. It was a shame they'd have to get a different car. This one was way too conspicuous for the locals.

'By the way, I had a look into your paperwork. I don't think it will be too difficult to make Steven Thorn reappear. It would be easier to use your middle name with people you meet, just in case.'

'Simon?'

'It's a good name.'

'Great. Can't say I ever liked it much. But hey, it's better than nothing. It would be nice to get my identity and qualifications back.'

'You don't need a piece of paper to tell you that you're smart.'

'No, but it helps if I want to get back into university.'

Jeff huffed, amused. 'I guess nowadays qualifications are important. Not that they weren't in my day just that the measure of a man was more by his brawn and tenacity than by his intellect, even though intellect helped my case.'

Steven had no idea what it must have been like in the roaring twenties. It was nearly one hundred years ago. He rose to the bait. 'It's not that those qualities are not important anymore, just that for certain career paths qualifications are important.'

'Oh, I see. You mean to study Law.'

'Exactly, Law, you remember then.' Steven was impressed. His grandfather paid attention. He only mentioned his interest when he first arrived within the community. He recalled the fact he had not made a great first impression. It felt surreal. Steven wanted to believe that his time in the Amazon Jungle had been a dream. It was wishful thinking.

Jeff drummed his fingers on the beige leather dashboard. 'Your great grandfather was also passionate about the law. He had a real sense of right and wrong. He died for his conviction, during the First World War. Right and wrong had nothing to do with it then, it was carnage.'

'I'm sorry.' Steven had not even stopped to consider his great grandparents.

Jeff carried on, obviously lost in his own thoughts. 'People always said I was like my mother. She was always interested in new developments whilst maintaining a passion for the rights of workers in industrial sites. She was particularly interested in the suffragette movement, to my father's horror. I searched for the impossible, I dreamed of the ultimate invention. That's what motivated me.'

'Is that why you created the new community?'

'Yes. In a way it was an experiment. A flawed one if I'm honest. Necessary though, without trials it is not possible to seek the best solution.'

'The community works to an extent, doesn't it? I mean the people I got to know, Jensen, Susanna. They seem happy enough.' The stilted pause made Steven uncomfortable. 'We don't have to talk about this.'

Jeff clenched his hands into fists. 'No, we don't. But, you should know that I'm not proud of certain things, your mother for one. I let her down. She was not happy, never was. Nothing we did could ever change things. Then she had you and she gave up on the only motherhood she has ever known. As a father I know how that must have hurt. You can't understand how much she loves you, if she was prepared to abandon you. I am sure she was trying to protect you.' He hesitated for a few seconds. 'What did I do to protect her? I coveted her, smothered her – I killed my little girl. The only thing left is what she has become.'

Steven felt sorry for Jeff. 'She can't be that bad. I have no idea what she plans to do. You never know, she might not kill.'

'It's nice to think so. Unfortunately, she is past that now. All we can hope is that she stays in the shadows,' Jeff paused. All serious, he continued, 'promise me something.'

'Sure.' What could Jeff want from him?

'If you see her, tell her I love her. Tell her I'm sorry for what happened.'

'You'll tell her yourself someday.' The last person Steven wanted to see was his mother. Whatever Jeff said, Emily meant nothing to him. He tried to sound positive for Jeff's sake, not for Emily. He didn't hold on to a lot of hope for her.

Jeff fell silent again and looked out the window.

'Shall we park here and walk the rest of the way?' Steven suggested.

'Sure.'

Of one thing they were in agreement, they needed to blend in.

The street where Julia lived was different without a layer of white snow. The temperature had not held and most of it had melted away. A cafeteria opposite the block of flats provided a good vantage point.

Steven took a seat as Jeff ordered the drinks. The table gave a perfect view of the entrance to the accommodation block.

'Now we wait. It's still early,' Jeff said, as he placed the tea in front of Steven.

'Or not,' Steven retorted.

The wait was not going to be long at all. Julia was walking out of the main door. She paused on the pavement and then stared right at Steven, eyes locked in some form of recognition.

'Stay sitting down,' Jeff snapped.

As the pedestrian lights turned green she practically jogged across the road. She was coming over.

Jeff had a change of heart. 'No, don't stay sitting down – go. Go, now!'

Steven got up and looked around. 'Where?'

'Toilet, be quick.'

As Steven scampered off, he caught sight of Jeff grabbing a newspaper from the adjacent table. He had no idea what Julia wanted, but whatever it was he was not planning to find out.

***

Jeff heard Julia enter the cafeteria. It could be a coincidence. Somehow, he doubted it. With a casual glance he flicked a page of the newspaper to see what she was doing. She was by the counter, eyes fixed on his table.

'Can I help you?' the waitress asked. 'Latte, as usual?'

He could hear the hesitation in her voice as she replied. 'Y-Yes, my usual.'

'Take a seat, I'll bring it over.'

'A seat,' Julia muttered. She walked over to Jeff and stood next to the chair Steven had just been in. She turned to head for the toilets.

'Can I help you?' Jeff asked, as he put the paper aside. Now was as good a time as any.

She stopped and stared, confused. 'No, I mean, yes. No, no, of course you can't help me,' she said, a nervous laugh followed.

'I might. Are you not well? I'm a doctor.'

94

'Really?' Her eyes alighted.

'Please, take a seat.'

Julia looked nervously from side to side. 'Thanks.'

He could see a smile surface as she sat down. She could smell Steven – he knew she could. He had seen this before. Not in a victim, in animals. When they are close to a familiar scent animals relax.

It was most interesting.

CHAPTER 14

A FEW LOSSES

'Do I know you?' Julia scrunched her eyes.

'No, you don't. My name is Jeff, nice to meet you.' He held out his hand.

She held out her hand and gave a firm handshake. Confident, even though momentarily weakened.

'I'm Julia. You know I never sit with strangers. My parents would not approve. I don't know what's up with me. I'm not myself.'

'So, did you have a rough night? Why were you confused as to whether I would be able to help you or not?'

'Well,' she squirmed in the seat. 'I was just watching television. Then I felt the sudden urge to come down and stand right here next to you. Although right now I'm drawn to the toilet. It's bizarre. I don't even know you. Yet, there is something about you. Am I making any sense at all?' She gave a nervous laugh.

'Absolutely. My diagnosis is that you needed some company. Not mine of course. Maybe you're lonely.'

'Lonely,' she paused. 'I'm never lonely.' She looked affronted.

'Hmmm... tricky then.'

Her next question caught him off guard. It was true after all.

'Was someone else with you? I was sure I saw someone with you a minute ago.'

'He left.'

She knew.

'Who was he?'

This was worse than he thought. 'My grandson actually.'

'I met someone last night. I don't know why I'm telling you this, but I-I.' She stopped talking and started to get up. 'I think I should go and see a real doctor.'

'I am a real doctor.' His turn to look annoyed.

'You seem nice and all, I'm sure you're a doctor, but I think I should see *my* doctor. If you know what I mean.'

He smiled. 'No offence taken. Good idea. I think your drink is waiting at the till.'

'My drink, I forgot all about it. See you around then and thanks for the chat. I'm not usually this erm…scatty. Honest.'

'I believe you.' He really did.

Jeff turned back to his newspaper. After a few minutes, he peeked out and saw she had gone. The coast was clear. He sipped the last of his coffee and got up to alert Steven. Once in the male toilet, he knocked on the door. 'Time to go.'

Steven shuffled out. 'So?'

'Not good. She's hooked, but doesn't know why. But all the same she's disorientated.'

Steven studied the floor.

'What's done is done. Let's go,' Jeff said, as he put his hand on Steven's shoulder.

When they rounded the corner Julia came into view. Not good. She was still there.

With narrowed eyes and a scowl, she hurtled into a barrage of questions. 'I knew he was with you. I don't know why I knew. I just did. Who are you both? Why are you here? What do you want?'

'Young lady, you are confused. You said so yourself. Take a seat and I'll introduce you to my grandson, Steven.'

'We already met,' she snapped.

'Please sit down.' It was not a request.

Julia's face became calm. In a robotic voice, she replied. 'Okay. I will sit down.'

***

Steven glanced at Jeff. He could tell Jeff was controlling her. 'Is it necessary?'

'You bet it is,' Jeff replied.

Julia stared into space.

'Have your drink Julia.' It came out as a command and it worked like a charm. Julia raised the polystyrene cup to her mouth and took a sip. Then she looked at Jeff and waited.

'You will forget Steven and me. We have never met. You will not talk to anyone about us. You will never see us again. You understand.'

'Yes.'

It was sweet and simple.

'It's time for you to go now. Goodbye.'

Julia smiled, got up and started to walk out. It felt so cold, so calculated. Even for someone like Julia, it was harsh. She was not a bad person. Confidence was not the worst quality anyone could possess.

'Sorry,' Steven whispered.

Julia seemed to freeze at his words, but she shook her head and continued to the door.

The next minute seemed to go by in slow motion. Steven suppressed his horror as he watched Julia walk across the road without looking. There was nothing he could do as the large supermarket truck rammed into her.

Absolutely nothing.

***

The highlight of the following week had to be when Steven held a valid birth certificate in his hands, he finally had an identity. His name was officially Steven Simon Thorn and both his father and mother were unknown. Supposedly, he was an orphan. He hated that. He did have a father he loved. His biological mother did not deserve to be on his certificate, but his father had earned the right. Either way, it was not in his hands. It was under the control of his grandfather or evil controller, as he now thought of him.

As much as he had grown to like him Julia's death had changed things. He could not accept what Jeff called a reasonable loss. Was everyone he was with destined to die even if he did not actually commit the murder? He could not accept that. With his foot completely recovered he wondered if he actually *needed* human blood.

A knock on the door interrupted his thoughts.

'Steven, can I come in?'

Jeff.

'Sure.'

Jeff opened the door. He stood at the entrance for a few seconds and rubbed his hand, his eyes fixed on the sash windows. Steven carried on downloading apps for his iPad. He had been dying to get an iPad since it was released. It made him feel like he was back in the land of the living. His grandparents never questioned the purchase. He would never have got away with it with his parents; his dad never bought him a gadget on a whim.

Finally, Jeff spoke up. 'I'm sorry the girl had to die. I really am. It just happened. Mind control is a powerful tool. I-I have not used it very often. It was my mistake and I apologise. Please, can we put it behind us?'

Steven shrugged his shoulders and continued, still focused on the amount of free stuff he could get his hands on. 'It's done.'

'I came to talk to you about something else. Can I sit down?'

'Sure.' Steven shuffled up the bed and reluctantly switched off the machine.

Jeff walked slowly towards him and sat down. 'Judith is very ill. I'm sure you've noticed.'

Steven glanced at the small, ornate fireplace. 'I have.'

'I am also getting weak. The truth is we don't really know why. Animal blood does not seem to satisfy us anymore. We think we need human blood. I want to look after Judith but sh-she is refusing to drink human blood. I-I...'

Steven noticed Jeff's hands were shaking. He swallowed his pride and stretched out his hand. Jeff's hand was frail and thin against his. He was sure if he tried he would be able to crush it.

Steven had to ask. 'Are you planning to kill again?'

'No, I-I think I will steal it. Mind control has its uses. I'm sure someone at our local hospital can help. I'll bring some back for Judith, just in case.' He gave a weary smile.

There was no point in holding a grudge. 'I'll stay with her, you go. By the way, I know you didn't intend to kill her. Apology accepted.'

Jeff gave a half smile. 'That means a lot. Thank you.' He turned to go but then paused, his hands now on Steven's shoulder. 'Whatever happens I am already proud of you. You have inner strength; a quality no-one can ever take away. Hold on to your convictions. In time, every wrong will right itself.'

Steven was winded by the words. After a few seconds, he managed to splutter. 'Thanks.'

Jeff had already gone.

Steven knew he had to keep his promise and keep an eye on Judith. First, he had a more pressing matter. Caitlin. It was time to track her down. He flicked the iPad back on and turned to the Facebook page. The page dared him to write back. He already knew what to say. He had written the same speech out many times but he found it hard to follow through. He couldn't contact her via the internet. There was no point in replying.

For what felt like the millionth time, he logged off and took a swig from his water bottle. The internet was a blessing and a curse rolled into one. It seemed like an easy way to find things out. Yet, nothing could substitute human contact. He needed to see Caitlin, not her words.

He flung the iPad on the bed and got up to see Judith. He knocked on the door and waited. A faint voice replied. He turned the door handle and made his way in.

The sight of her made him wince. She looked worse, a lot worse.

'Can I get you something?'

'Did Jeff go out?' she whispered.

'Yes, he did. I know it's probably not my place to say this but death is not necessary. He will find a way to get blood. You don't have to kill.'

Judith gave a low chuckle. 'Come here.'

Steven moved closer and sat on a chair opposite the bed. The room had a rancid smell.

'You don't need to control yourself, I know I smell.'

She must have noticed the fact he scrunched his nose.

Judith coughed. 'I've been around for a very long time. Do you know that I'm 116 years old? My body is just starting to show its age. Thing is, it's not impossible to live this long. The longest living human being was a French woman – she got to the age of 122. And did you know that there's a woman still alive in the United States born in the same year as me? Water, please?'

Steven reached for the glass on her bedside table and passed it over.

She took a sip. 'Thank you. I was born in 1896, a couple of years before the turn of the century. Edwardian Britain, a Britain with no real knowledge of war, an invincible empire.'

Steven could not help wondering if she should be talking so much. 'Don't strain yourself.'

'No, you have to listen. It's important you understand. The Great War changed the world. Did you know that? Millions of people died. I was your age when friends, relatives and acquaintances died to preserve our freedom. Your grandfather was one of the lucky ones, although he did not feel so lucky to survive at the time. It was the worst thing we thought we'd ever see.' She coughed again and took another sip.

Steven waited. He did not want to interrupt.

'We were wrong. It was not the worst thing. It was the beginning of the end for many. The roaring twenties brought many good things. Automobiles. Moving pictures or *talkies* as they then became known as. Walt Disney produced Mickey Mouse. And of course Jazz and the infamous Charleston,' she giggled. 'I was quite good you know.'

'I imagine you were.'

'You are such a charmer, just like your grandfather. Anyway, I got to dress as I pleased, was wild for a while and even got to vote like a man. What a privilege! You should have seen us girls lining up the street. Imagine. Well, I guess you can't – you take that for granted now.'

'Sorry.'

'Don't apologise. Each generation is faced with a different set of problems. The thing is it couldn't last. As you must know, or they surely teach you nothing at school, the bubble burst in 1929. The Great depression brought hard times.'

'Not that different to now. The latest recession has brought a lot of problems.'

'Yes, life has a way of repeating itself. Or, humans have a way of making the same mistakes,' she chuckled.

Steven was mesmerised, he had no idea Judith was so fascinating.

He could not wait to hear the rest. The past was a scary and yet very insightful place sometimes. If only people paid more attention, the world would be a lot simpler.

CHAPTER 15

JUDITH'S STORY

Steven eased back. 'When did you meet grandfather?'

Judith smiled. 'I met him in 1920. I was twenty four – quite old to still be a spinster in those days. I had rebelled and become a member of the suffragette movement. I refused all of my parents' suitors.' She gave a cough that got mixed in with a laugh. 'They got me in the end. I was bowled over by your grandfather. I didn't stand a chance. We got married and I had Catherine the following year. The twins followed barely a year later. For some reason I found it hard to have more children until Ian came along ten years later. After that the Second World War consumed us. We had to go to America. Your grandfather could not miss the opportunity to be a member of the most exclusive scientific team ever created. And he would not leave us behind, he always put family first.'

'That was where the attack happened?' Steven could not help being sucked in completely.

'Yes, we were attacked. My children and Jeff, they were worse off. I-I just got involved.'

Steven found it a strange thing to say. He dismissed it for now.

'You have to understand that after everything we had been through. After the death we had seen. We could not be a part of it. We could not become killers. We accepted some death to survive, but we did not want to kill. You get that, right?'

Steven did not want to argue, he just couldn't help it. 'I never had a problem understanding it. But, your experience and mine are two very separate things.'

Judith coughed, took another sip of water and held out her hand. 'Steven, people do strange things for love. I understand that. Just make sure you don't end up hurting those around you. Love does not give you the right to end someone else's life. Death is death. And it comes to all of us, even me.'

She was definitely rambling. 'Unnecessary death is still confusing. You don't have to *die*.'

'I do have to die!' The effort made her erupt into a violent cough. 'Have you not been listening to a word I've said?'

'Calm down, don't overexert yourself.'

'You don't understand. No-one does. I should be dead. I was not meant to live so long. I was not like them. I was not *one* of them. Emily guessed. She was the only one that guessed the truth.'

He had no idea what she was talking about now. 'Judith, you need to calm down. I'll go make some tea.'

'Tea? Good idea, go make tea. You are such an Englishman.' She nuzzled into her pillow as a glazed look came over her face.

Steven found her chatter interesting. She just made no sense. The bats bit her like everyone else. She had told him so. At least, Emily had. Or maybe it was Jeff. She was definitely bitten by the bats. Someone had told him.

When he returned, Judith was fast asleep, her breathing forced. He left the tea next to the table and sat down. She looked so old all of a sudden, ancient – fragile. The hum of her breathing had a soothing effect. He eased into the chair and closed his eyes, he could not leave her. He did not know how much time had passed when the sound of footsteps roused him.

'How is she?' Jeff's hair had regained its vibrancy and it was definitely darker, as though he had lost some of the grey. His face had been stretched, the wrinkles now barely visible, and his posture was now firm. Youth was on his side again.

'I guess you were successful.'

Jeff made his way over to Judith and sat at her side. 'I was. I brought some back for her. Did she talk to you? Did she say anything?'

Steven was not sure what she hadn't talked about. 'Quite a lot. She talked of the war, the Charleston…'

'Charleston?' Jeff interrupted, eyes raised.

'Yep, apparently she was quite good.'

Jeff nodded, his moustache twitched. 'She was, I mean, is.'

'She said some strange things. She said she was not *meant* to live so long. She said she was not like you and that Emily knew. Does that make any sense to you?'

'She's losing it. I'm afraid she doesn't know what she is saying.'

The way he said it did not leave Steven convinced, Jeff was holding something back.

Jeff stared at Judith; it was a look of despair. 'Anyway, you can go off now. I'll stay with her. Thank you for staying with her.'

'Anytime.'

Steven glanced back when he reached the door. Jeff was stroking her hair. The difference was striking. Judith looked like Jeff's mother, not his wife.

***

The sight of her pale and practically lifeless complexion made Jeff sick. Her refusal to drink human blood was having dramatic consequences. The blood of animals did nothing to improve her state of health. Jeff could not understand why was she giving up on life, why was she giving up on him? They had always vowed to stay together. What had changed? He saw her stir and he leaned in closer. Her eyelids fluttered, her pale amber eyes in view for a split second, and then closed. They refused to cooperate. Her eyes were always the same, just as beautiful as the first day they met.

'Something's happening to me. I can feel it,' she whispered.

'You need human blood? Here have some,' he said. Desperate, he brought the cup he had prepared closer.

She kept her eyes closed, but he could tell she was tempted by the smell. In a pained voice, she said, 'I don't want to drink blood anymore. I'm ready Jeff, I want to go now. I'm tired. We never expected to live forever. The extra time I had was a bonus. You know I was never meant to live this long.'

A lump caught in his throat. 'Why now? You seemed so excited to come back. We've barely enjoyed it. I don't want to lose you.'

She gave a throaty chuckle. 'Don't be silly. You'll never lose me. This is just the way things are meant to be. I wanted to come home and end it here. I guess it happened sooner than I imagined. It's time. It's time for me to rest.'

'Are you sure I can't convince you to live?'

She shook her head, raised her hand up to his face and caressed it gently. 'Not this time. I love you, my darling.' She lay back on the pillow as a barely audible sigh escaped her lips and she exhaled.

Jeff was torn with indecision. Should he respect Judith's wishes? He could make her drink. There was nothing he would not do to try and save her life. Was it possible she was actually dying? A lifetime with Judith had taught him that once she had made her mind up only a fool would try to go against her. Head bowed in defeat he wept for the first time in years. As he cried his chest heaved. After a huge intake of air he held out his now shaky hand. With her hand in his he held on to a faint shred of hope. There was still some time left? She had not left him yet.

A knock on the door startled him. 'Can I help you Steven?'

Steven opened the door and eased in. 'Are you okay? Can I do anything to help?'

Jeff could not take his eyes away from his wife. 'No. Not really. She's given up on life.'

Steven took a step back. 'Is she in any pain? I could get some extra blankets.'

'No, thank you.' Jeff squeezed down harder on her hand. 'We just have to wait and see.'

'I guess she said no to the blood.' Steven stepped closer, but kept a fair distance. It was obvious he was not comfortable.

Jeff wished he could give a different answer, but there was nothing to be done. 'It's her choice. She doesn't want to live. None of us have ever died after the change.'

'Is there nothing else *we* could do?'

Jeff shook his head from side to side. 'I know what you're thinking, but she doesn't want us to interfere. She's happy to go. She's home.'

Steven took a seat next to him on the edge of the bed. He

stared at his grandmother. They sat in silence for a while. Finally, Steven stood up. 'I think I'll give you some time alone.'

When Steven left, Judith's weak voice called out. 'Jeff.' She made an effort to open her eyes.

He held her hand tighter. 'Yes, my darling, I'm here.' Her eyes could just about be seen through thin slits. He controlled the emotions that threatened to overwhelm him.

She spoke in their disguised tongue. It was clear she did not want Steven to hear what she said.

'Th-thank you, I know this is hard,' she paused for a breath. 'I don't have much time.'

'You don't know that.'

'I know.' She paused. 'You have to promise me something.'

'Anything.' He hoped she would ask for her life, he doubted it would happen.

She spoke slowly. 'You must help Steven to lead a normal life. He might stand a chance. We were too scared to try.'

'You know I will do that.'

'Promise me.' Her hand squeezed his faintly, before a violent cough took hold.

'I promise,' he added, desperate to appease her. He picked up the glass of water and held up her head. 'Drink, my love, drink.'

When he removed his hand from behind her head a clump of hair came with it. He shook it off and tried to act as if it did not matter. It did.

She swallowed and carried on. 'You must find a way to help Emily. We failed her. We caged her up and made her what she is. It's our fault, *you* have to fix it.'

What she was asking was impossible. Emily was a lost cause. He hated thinking it but he could not deny the truth. 'I'll try.'

'That's all I can ask,' she sighed. 'These past weeks have been liberating for me. I remembered our life before things got complicated. I can't think of a better way to say goodbye to this world. Do you think there is another place for us to go from here?'

'Of course there is.'

'In that case I'll meet you in paradise,' her voice croaked.

Jeff leaned in to kiss her on the lips. She barely kissed him back before she closed her eyes. He panicked and checked her pulse – a faint, weak heartbeat remained. Confused and tormented, he curled up next to her and put his arm around her now thin and frail body.

The tears flowed freely.

***

The sound of a car door slamming in the middle of the night woke Steven up. Dazed, he sauntered down the steps and peered out the window to see who it was. To his astonishment, his Uncle Ian and Aunt Catherine stood on the doorstep surrounded by a few bags. After fiddling with the door latch, he opened the door and stared in silence.

'Aren't you going to welcome us in?' Ian sneered.

'I don't have time for your nonsense,' Catherine blurted, as she gave Ian an annoyed glance. 'I need to see my mother, excuse me.' Confidently, she made her way up the steps and disappeared.

'Why does trouble know where to find you Steven? If my mother dies, I'll hold you personally responsible,' Ian snapped, as he threw the bags into the hallway and followed in his sisters footsteps.

Mentally, Steven groaned. It was nice to know that he was a problem.

He needed some space away from the visitors. Back in his room he shut the door and went back to sleep. Now, *he* was the guest. For the first time since he'd come back with his grandparents, he did not feel welcome.

CHAPTER 16

FAMILY REUNION

The morning frost bathed the streets and cars in a sheet of white ice. The sky, dotted with a few stretched clouds, glowed in amber and russet colours. Daybreak, a breathtaking sight usually missed by many. Steven imagined most people missed the morning twilight, unobservant and subdued as they dealt with day to day routines. Perched on the ledge of the rooftop things were different for him, he had everything to play for. Judith passed away shortly after seeing Ian and Catherine. It seemed they had brought her a final closure.

It was weird. He had only started to get to know her. Now, she was gone.

Her death changed everything.

He was also going to die. Obvious to most, but he supposedly to had eternal youth. It appeared death was now an option and his life revolved around one thing, blood. He could take it and stay young. Or refuse, age naturally, and die. He wondered if he would die if he did not drink any blood at all. Was he willing to test the theory? A question nagged. Why didn't they age in the Amazon? What was it about the Amazon that kept them young? It was a puzzle he intended to get to grips with.

For all his principals and self imposed values, he now understood how easy it was to take what you needed. Blood was addictive, it was a drug. After the girl in Manaus and Julia he had felt a surge of energy and power, the adrenaline hit of a thrill seeker. It was easy to talk about giving up blood, the question was could he do what Judith did. Could he kill himself? Would it be so wrong to take occasionally? Just to survive.

An image of Caitlin flooded his mind. Recently, the picture

had started to fade. It would be easier to let her go. It would be safer for her. But, if there was a chance that he could lead a reasonably normal life and have her as well, should he not at least try?

He scrunched some of the leaves that had accumulated on the ledge in his hands and got up. Slowly, he opened his hand and watched the shattered pieces fly away.

He suspected he was acting like a fool. He had no way of knowing if Caitlin would even give him a chance in the first place. He just did not want to let her go without a fight. She meant too much. He did wonder if his obsession was real. Had he imagined a Caitlin that was perfect for him? Why did she have such a hold on him? Was she *the one*? Or did he just want her to be the one? Did his reluctance to accept his new life have a wider role to play?

All of this was immaterial. The arrival of Ian and Catherine changed things. Would they try to convince Jeff to go back? There was one thing he knew, he was not going back. Not without a fight. As the final pieces of leaves fluttered to the ground he threw himself off the rooftop, somersaulted in the air and landed perfectly on his feet, completely unharmed.

He glanced at the house silhouetted by the morning light and frowned as he considered his options. Did he want to talk to Ian right now? He knew the answer to that.

Without any further thought he raced down the hill and lunged into the trees for cover. Then he started to run like he never had before. He wanted to make it into Southampton before the students woke up. He needed time to do research. It was time to track her down.

*

Steven made his way on to the University Campus. It was still quiet, too early for most students. A sprinkling of lights adorned some buildings. Steven could not believe it was nearly Christmas. The previous Christmas he had only just got together with Caitlin. He remembered the night he took the plunge and went to see her. She had only just got assigned her new room, after she'd left when Georgina died. He did not know why he'd gone to check on her. He wanted to, he guessed.

It had been a good decision at the time.

Now, he wondered. If he hadn't gone, she would be better off. She would not have a hybrid after her.

He knew what he was about to do was stalking. He was about to hack into the computer files. He was about to track her down without her consent. He was about to find out where she lived. And he was planning to follow her. Love made a man go to great lengths. Not lengths he was particularly proud of, but still lengths he had to take. He just had to know if he stood a chance, if there was any hope.

Could he hope to achieve a different future?

Was he being foolish?

He did not care. He was going to do it anyway for one simple fact…because he could.

***

The sight of his familiar heirlooms caused Jeff to pause in the hallway. He was visibly shaking and had to lean on the wall to not collapse on the spot. Judith had been his life. He could not go on without her, his life had no meaning. He pushed off the wall gradually and carried on walking. It was such an effort. He had made her a promise. A promise, he had to fulfil. He could not give up on life yet.

When he reached the kitchen he made his way over to a seat and sat down. He put his head in his hands and stared at the wooden grain of the table. His eyes followed the lines, anything for distraction.

He heard Catherine come in. 'Dad, are you okay?'

Catherine and Ian deserved to see their mother. Judith had made so many sacrifices for her children. Anna and Emily should have been here. He had no idea how to even contact Emily.

'No, of course I'm not.' He could not help being short with Catherine, even though he appreciated the concern. He lifted his head and dropped his hands on the table. In an apologetic tone, he added, 'don't worry. There is nothing you can do.'

Catherine flicked her curly red hair out of her face as she bit her lip. After fiddling with her hands for a second, she moved towards the worktop and the kettle. 'Maybe I can make you some tea or coffee? I know you like it black.'

'Tea,' he pondered. Tea had been Judith's favourite drink. 'No, not tea, coffee, you better make it strong.'

'Sure, Dad.' She picked up the kettle and filled it up with water. Every sound seemed magnified.

Jeff could tell Catherine was holding back the tears. She was always the strong one, yet nothing could have prepared her for this.

His wife was dead. It should have been impossible.

He heard Ian's heavy boots coming down the stairs, his son always stomped. Is that the kettle I hear? Make me one sis?'

His casual manner helped. Ian could never be serious for long.

'Sure Ian,' Catherine said. 'Coffee right?'

'Nah, I'll have tea. When in England,' he smiled, all jokey as usual. Was it an act?

Catherine frowned at him.

'No need to look at me like that. Mum wouldn't have wanted me to change. I don't know why she did what she did, but I'm sure she had her reasons.

The sound of the spoon rattling in the mug echoed in the large kitchen. Catherine handed the mug to Jeff.

'I'll take it upstairs.' Jeff needed to get back to Judith.

When he was in the hall he heard Catherine whisper, disgruntled. 'Now look what you did.'

'What?' Ian pleaded innocence.

Jeff could not help a small smile. Ian was impossible.

Once in the room he put his mug on the bedside table and stared at the aged and still body of the woman he had shared most of his life with.

He could not believe his love was dead. They had sworn to stay together, no matter what. Now, she had decided to go against their promise. His head understood why, his heart could not accept it.

***

Shortly after Jeff had gone Ian watched in horror as Catherine broke down. He made his way over to her, let her cry on his shoulder and gave her a hug. He was not completely insensitive. After a few seconds he felt her shudder as the tears rescinded. When her breathing calmed down, he eased back and looked at her. 'Feeling better?'

'Marginally, thanks little brother. You're very annoying, but you have your uses.'

He smirked. 'Any time sis, I'm not so good at wearing my emotions on my sleeve. But I know enough from being married to Carmen that women need to release. Even if I don't show it, I'm just as shattered as you are. I just figure dad doesn't need to see me upset.'

'Well,' she sniffed. 'I guess someone has to keep a level head.'

Ian picked up his mug and took a sip. He licked his lips, got a spoon and helped himself to another sugar. 'Talking of that, I think Steven is up on the roof. He went up there after he found out mum died.'

'Should we check on him?' Catherine asked. She rubbed her eyes.

Ian took a sip before he shrugged. 'Nah, he'll have to come down eventually.'

Catherine stood very still. 'Are you sure he's still there? I don't feel his presence close by.'

'I hadn't thought of that. I don't feel things like you do.' Ian frowned. 'Are you sure he's not here?'

'Pretty certain,' she answered after a moment. 'But, he could be around. He might have gone for a walk or something.'

'We'll worry about Steven when he returns. I think dad needs us more. I knew something would happen when they left. I should have stayed with them,' he grumbled. Some days he felt like the fate of the world rested on his shoulders, today was one of those days.

'We couldn't babysit our own parents. Besides, they would not listen.' The tears welled in Catherine's eyes again. 'Sh-she promised me she'd come back.'

'She only said she'd *try*,' Jeff said, from the doorway. 'Look, as much as it hurts me to have lost your mother, she made the choice and we have to respect that. She wanted to die here, where she thought she belonged. She lived a full and happy life.'

'I'm sorry, Dad. Did you hear us talking?' Catherine put her hand to her mouth.

Jeff nodded. 'She was happy to return just to reminisce. This is a lot for you to take in. I-I have to tell you though. Now that she's gone, I don't think I...'

'Dad, no, not you too?' Catherine interrupted, her voice pleading.

Ian could not believe it. Was his dad going to give up on life too?

Jeff ran his hand through his hair and then rubbed his overgrown moustache. 'Not yet, I made a promise to your mum. But, after I have fulfilled her request I will also make my choice. It is clear to me now that we always had a choice. We should never have forced everyone to stay secluded. But, what's done is done. We have to look to the future now, to all of our futures. You have a heavy weight on your shoulders. The community needs to know the truth. That is what you have to do for your mum. You have to go back and talk to the others and explain that things have changed. We are not immortal.'

'Hang on a minute. If Mum had fed from a human she would have healed wouldn't she?' Ian protested.

Jeff narrowed his eyes. 'We don't know. She was convinced her body had had enough. She said it was her time to go. I guess that's the point. We can all choose the right time. The question is; do you want to live indefinitely knowing that you will have to feed off humans or do you choose to end you life when your body starts to fail? Mum chose, and so must we.'

'What about Steven? What promise did you make?' Ian asked, wary.

Jeff stepped forward and took a seat. Only now did Ian notice how frail he appeared. 'We will help him to lead a normal life. We will not force him to return. It was your mother's dying wish.'

Ian bit his tongue. He would have something to say about that when the dust settled.

'Talking of Steven. Where is he?' Catherine asked. 'I know he's not here anymore.'

'Really, has he gone?' Jeff seemed distracted. 'Probably for the best then, let him go. He has to find his own path now.'

Catherine stamped on Ian's foot, just as he was about to protest. She could always anticipate him.

'I'm going to sit with your mother again. Could you go and get some supplies? We are short of food. I did not have time to shop with...well, you know,' Jeff said.

'No problem Dad, we'll get on it,' Ian sounded assertive. He had to. 'Let's go Catherine.'

'Are you sure you want to be alone?' Catherine asked.

'Yes, I'd like to be alone with your mum. Don't worry I won't do anything stupid. I have a promise to keep.'

'Okay Dad,' Catherine smiled. She made her way over to Jeff, and gave him a hug.

Ian was nowhere near as sentimental as his sister. Sure, he was gutted – his mum had died. He was also angry. His mum did not need to die. He felt responsible; he should have stayed with them. Either way, it was Steven he blamed. If his mum thought he was going to let Steven gallivant around town unsupervised, she was sorely mistaken. He was going to do whatever it took to keep his kind safe, even if that meant defying his dying mum's last request.

CHAPTER 17

DÉJÀ VU

Catherine could tell Ian was angry. The way his eyebrows narrowed and his hands tensed was always a dead giveaway. Hell, she was also upset. She just couldn't be angry with her mum. She wanted to try to understand what she had done. Eternal life was not something any of them should have taken for granted. Judith was now at peace. What it meant for the rest of them was anyone's guess.

'You know death is not such a bad thing. It's natural. Mum knew that.'

Ian hummed.

'Perhaps, we're not the monsters we always thought we were. Maybe there is another way.'

A grunt.

'Talk to me. I know you're seething. Don't go thinking of doing anything stupid. You know Mum wouldn't want that.'

Ian banged the steering wheel with his hand. 'So, she would want more people to die? Really?' There was true venom in Ian's tone.

'You don't know if more people will die. This is another step in our evolution. Maybe we got it wrong. Maybe we should have thought of a way to fit in, rather than a way to get out,' Catherine said. She was worried. Ian had a tendency to go crazy if he lost his temper, she did not want to incite him.

'Easier said than done, anyway Steven doesn't know anything. He is an *infant* for goodness sakes. Is he to be our first guinea pig?' He was gritting his teeth now.

Catherine took a deep breath and waited before she replied. 'He is the first to be born half human.'

'And that changes things, does it?' Ian was drumming his fingers on the steering wheel – he'd leave dents soon.

She tried not to sound condescending. 'Yes, you know it does. If Mum wanted Dad to help Steven, we must not interfere. It is not our place to interfere. Dad knows what he's doing.'

Ian turned to face her, his cheeks aflame. 'A husband following his wife's dying wish does not know what he is doing. It's like the blind leading the blind.'

Catherine closed her eyes. After a minute had passed and she could hear a change in Ian's breathing, she slowly said, 'Ian. Stop. Let it go. We must not follow Steven. We'll talk to Dad in a few days. For now, let Steven go.'

'I guess I have to.' Ian sounded deflated now. 'Just like I had to let go of Emily...you know, everyone's going to want the same freedom back home. You know this is the worst thing that could happen for our community.'

'You don't know that. No-one does. Fate is allowed to have a hand in our destiny. Fate brought the bats to us. Fate allowed Emily to conceive Steven. Fate allowed Mum to die. We have no right to interfere. We are not God.'

That shut him up.

***

The sound of the bleeping clock got louder and louder as it drilled its way steadily into Caitlin's head.

'Ahhh, shut up,' she shouted, as she hurled a pillow in its direction. But, the noise was relentless – it would not give up. In submission, Caitlin rubbed her eyes and looked at the radio alarm clock. 'Oh no, I'm so dead. I am sooo late.'

In a split second the covers were hurled off as she run towards the bathroom, sat on the toilet seat and willed her pee to hurry up. Then she turned on the taps to run a shower. As she placed her fingers along the trickle she flinched, the water was freezing. After a painstaking few minutes, it became lukewarm. She cursed again as she washed quickly.

Once out of the bathroom, still dripping with suds, she browsed quickly through her cupboard and picked out an outfit. She caught a glimpse of her face in the mirror and scowled. Make up was a luxury item she had no time for. In a last attempt to remain decent, she grabbed the makeup bag, stuffed it in her rucksack and then made her way down to raid the larder.

A cereal bar would have to do.

She opened the fridge and took a quick swig of orange juice direct from the carton. If her flatmate found out there would be trouble.

Only fifteen minutes had passed. She might just get there on time.

A light drizzle welcomed her when she slammed the door shut. Before she could think of getting an umbrella she saw the bus cruising into the stop so she made a sprint for it, whilst yelling, 'hold it, please.'

As luck would have it there was a queue so she managed to get on before it started to move. With a sigh of relief, she took a deep breath and stared out of the window. The sky was grey and overcast. It was a miserable day.

'Having a bad start already?' a voice asked from behind.

'Every morning is bad where I'm concerned,' she blurted out, as she turned to face the voice.

'Things can't be that bad?' he asked, a quizzical expression plastered on his perfect features.

Dark hair, thick eyelashes, amber irises. She knew him from somewhere. Perplexed, she stared. The face reminded her of Steven, the one from her dreams. Yet, she couldn't be sure? 'No, I guess not,' she replied. She lacked conviction.

As the bus stopped, she was pushed forward so she turned to face the front again. Those pesky butterflies were swirling in her stomach in a state of frenzy. She turned around to face him to check whether it was *him*, but he was gone. She blinked, looked around, went on tiptoes to look over some shoulders and then did a three sixty degree turn.

Nothing.

Her imagination was running wild again.

***

As the bus pulled away Steven paused. He had made the first move, he had established contact. He was sure from the look on her face she remembered him. That was good news. Now all he had to do was come up with the next course of action. In fairness, he had acted impulsively. He just wanted to do this alone. It had to be feasible. His grandfather could not help him in his current state and he did not want Catherine or Ian poking their noses in his business.

The question was how?

It was all well and good to drop everything and get here. It was another to live on his own in the full knowledge of what he was capable of. Unless he was prepared to go back to the house he would have to use the art of persuasion to survive. For now, until he got a job. If he tried to use his *vampire* powers once no-one could blame him. Could they? He rationalised the argument in his head and ploughed ahead.

He knew the bank opened in half an hour's time so he went for a walk around campus first. He would just pretend he belonged.

An hour later, he made his way towards the main street in Porchwood. He had no problem imitating students with an old pair of jeans and moth-eaten sweater. Not a trendy one at that. Under this guise he was invisible, just another body. It surprised him. When he was smartly dressed a lot more heads turned in his direction. He had always considered his features to be the main attraction, now he reconsidered.

The imposing stone entrance to the bank made him gulp. He took a deep breath and walked in, it was now or never. The queue was not too long so he waited and tried to keep calm. Nerves were starting to get the better of him. At last it was his turn. A middle aged woman with a short frumpy haircut sat behind the glass panel.

He gave his best gleaming smile. 'I'd like to open a student account please.'

'Certainly,' the lady responded. 'If you wait there someone will come to help you.'

'Thank you,' he replied, and stepped back.

After a few minutes, a slightly flustered lady appeared. She was in her twenties – the perfect age range. She was wearing a smart standard bank uniform and a pair of trendy glasses. She gave a fake smile in his direction and held out her hand, more as an afterthought. He doubted she was impressed by what she saw.

When his hand made contact, she blurted out in a slightly edgy voice. 'Nice to meet you.'

'The pleasure is all mine.'

She gazed into his eyes, stopped and then gave a coquettish laugh. Her cheeks blushed. 'Right, Mr., erm,' she paused.

His looks still factored after all.

'Mr. Thorn.'

'Mr. Thorn, these are the forms you have to fill in,' she said, as she handed them over.

'Can we talk in a private room?' He asked. He hoped the piercing stare was enough. Her eyes seemed in awe.

'I-I was just about to suggest it, of course,' she stuttered. She signalled for him to follow and led the way down the corridor to a small room at the back.

Once the door was closed she made her way around the table and sat down. He sat down on the chair opposite, fixed his eyes on hers and calmly stated. 'You will give me two thousand pound in cash.'

Transfixed by his voice, she repeated in a robotic manner, 'of course.' She fiddled with the screen in front of her for a few minutes. 'How do you want the money?'

'Mixed notes, no fifties please.'

He could not help being polite.

'You will forget me, this transaction and how it came about. Thank you for helping me,' he added.

'Of course, please wait here.'

As she walked out his internal alarm bells rang as he panicked that his powers of persuasion would fail. That was way too easy. It couldn't be that easy. Could it?

After ten painstaking minutes she walked back in smiling.

In her hand she held a huge brown envelope. 'Two thousand pounds as requested. We look forward to doing business with you in the future.'

'You will wait here until I am gone.' His eyes instructed.

'Of course.' She stood still, just like a robot. He was not proud of himself.

He tucked the envelope under his waistband and covered it

with his sweater. He strolled out, at ease. The truth was he wanted to run. He nearly laughed out loud.

It was so easy.

***

The phone rang a couple of times before Jeff managed to pick it up. 'Catherine, did you find him?'

'Yes, I did. It's just like Ian suspected he's tracking Caitlin down.'

Jeff did not really want to act as a vigilante, but he knew he had to make sure Steven did not fail. 'Well, we'll have to help him. Can you keep an eye on him until we get down there?'

'Of course, but, he's already figured out how to use his hypnotic powers. He just walked out of a bank with a grin that would challenge a Cheshire cat.'

'Really,' he laughed. 'He's a natural, just like his mother. Okay, well in that case just follow him and see what he does. I'd like to stay here to prepare your mother's grave. She must have a proper burial. You know that's what she always wanted.'

'I know,' Catherine paused. 'I'll be back tonight. Don't worry. I know what I have to do.'

'Thank you.'

Jeff put the phone down and removed the lone tear running down his cheek. It still felt like a dream.

CHAPTER 18

RECONNAISSANCE

After Caitlin's usual nightmare start of the day the brief encounter, or whatever it was, with that guy had doubled the impact. Unfortunately, things had gone from bad to worse. When she had got off the bus and started to make her way towards the faculty building a car swung closer and cruised on top of a huge puddle. She had been drenched from head to toe, the youths in the back of the car had cheered and laughed. She still couldn't believe that anyone would be that mean.

She leaned against the radiator for a moment.

Everything had become harder this year, both academically and socially. She had to admit that the thought of going home was actually a good one for once. Her little sister had grown up a lot recently so she didn't dread holidays anymore. It was fun to take her out shopping and to the movies. A year earlier it would have been likened to the prospect of hell.

A lot of eyes stared and smirked at her ruffled and chaotic appearance.

A few girls walked past and laughed. She could have sworn she heard one of them say, 'if only I'd feel comfortable looking like that.'

Annoyed, she stormed down the hall to the lecture theatre and took a place at the back. With great care, she laid out her coat to dry and shook out her hair. At least her bag was dry; it had been shielded by her body.

Whilst in the process of removing her pen and notepad she saw her best friend making her way towards her. Gemma made her laugh, she was such a flirt. It was accentuated by what she wore. Her latest outfit was a blue, elbow length tight top, black fishnet tights, an electric blue rara skirt and high heeled black leather boots. Her spiky jet black hair, heavily black outlined eye make up and nose piercing completed the look. She was a big softie really. Caitlin did not know how she would have coped at the end of the last year without her. Gemma had become her rock.

'You look terrible!' Gemma exclaimed. Her Welsh accent always made anything she said sound good.

'Thanks.'

Gemma plonked her stuff next to her and sat down. 'Seriously, what happened? I nearly knocked on your door this morning but I wanted to get an early start so I left you to it. Should I have woken you?'

'Nah, I made it in the end, as you can see.' Caitlin took out her makeup bag and quickly and expertly applied some mascara and lipstick. 'Better?'

'Yeah, you look more human. Oh, well, here we go again,' she sighed.

The lecturer was making his grand entrance. If only.

'Can't wait.' Caitlin's voice dripped with sarcasm.

The lecture started so Gemma took her cue and whispered. 'I saw Mark again last night. I am soooo in love. His friend might be interesting for you. Shall I set up a double date?'

Caitlin harrumphed. 'No thanks, I'm not in the mood to make idle chit chat with someone who only wants to manhandle me.'

'Hey, you might actually enjoy it,' Gemma giggled. 'Mark can manhandle me anytime he wants.'

'Spare me the details. Honestly, all students want is to do *it*. Sorry, if I want more,' Caitlin said, as she tapped her pen on her folder.

Gemma rolled her eyes. 'Trust me, if you *wanted* someone you wouldn't say that. Hormones woman, where are yours?'

Caitlin scrunched her nose and whispered, 'buried, deep down. My libido is lost in the abyss. Now let me listen.'

'You got to dust those cobwebs or you'll become an old woman prematurely. Saying that they probably get more action than you,' Gemma scoffed, her laugh twisted. A few students gawped at her.

Caitlin glared. 'Keep your voice down. Jeez, how is it

possible for anyone to be such a pervert? And more to the point, why do I put up with it?'

Gemma leant back. 'It's a gift. Anyway, I'm trying to listen here.'

'Whatever,' Caitlin sighed, she focused on the notes on the interactive whiteboard. 'You do your thing, I'll do mine, okay.'

'Okay,' Gemma said.

Caitlin scribbled furiously. 'Let's take notes or we're going to fail.'

'Fine.'

After ninety minutes the lecture hall had a subdued, stuffy atmosphere. A proportion of the students seemed to have reached a comatose state, others looked totally lost, and only a few seemed to have understood what they had actually been taught. Caitlin had diligently taken notes, but it did not help. She was very confused. It was a huge relief when the lecture was finally over.

'Remind me again why we chose to take maths as a degree option?' Gemma asked, sullen and depressed.

'We are sadists, naturally, but we can make mumbo jumbo make sense, right?' Caitlin attempted eternal optimism.

Gemma finished packing away her things. 'Whatever. Thank God for tutorials, that's all I say.'

'Definitely, talking of which, have you done the assignment yet? It's due in tomorrow.' Caitlin stood up, ready to go.

'Really, tomorrow? I thought it wasn't due until the end of the week. Will you help me? Pretty please?' Gemma pleaded, her puppy dog face on full display.

'You know I will, but are you sure you can keep away from Mark for one night?'

'I have the night. We'll get it sorted before then,' she replied, all coy.

'How silly of me,' Caitlin replied. Gemma was exasperating. In a motherly tone, she added. 'I hope you use protection.'

'Duh, I'm on the pill.'

'Fine, just remember, until you know Mark better I suggest

you use something else. Haven't you heard of S.T.D.'s?'

Gemma's jaw dropped. 'Caitlin! You are worse than my mother. I promise I'll be careful. So will you help me even though I'm a disgrace to the female race?'

'You are so melodramatic; just get back quickly today okay, I don't want to be working late. I have training tomorrow morning.'

Gemma had a dig as they started to make their way out of the lecture hall. 'It's true. I forget that the swimming pool is the love of your life.'

Caitlin nudged her in the ribs. 'You are so funny. I guess you keep fit your way, I'll do it in mine.'

'It's no substitute for sex, I can *guarantee* that,' Gemma replied, with a pout. 'Apparently, you can lose a lot of calories after a night's *workout*.'

'I wouldn't know,' Caitlin sighed.

'Seriously…' Gemma lowered her voice further. 'If you've never been with anyone you have not lived. I need to get you some action. Sure I can't convince you about the double date, he's really hunky.'

'Thanks, but I don't think I'm missing out,' Caitlin replied. Now she was seriously unimpressed. Her nymphomaniac flatmate was not going to give her lessons on sex education.

'Right, well, you can keep on deluding yourself, but someday you'll know what I'm talking about. Anyway, I'll see you later. I've got some financial accounting to look forward to. Enjoy your Spanish.' Gemma picked up her things and hurried off.'

Caitlin watched her go amazed she could talk about that stuff with her. It was annoying Gemma had found another boyfriend. She was fun to hang out with when she wasn't loved up. In fairness, it was not very often they actually got to hang out.

At the exit, her mood darkened. It was raining really hard outside and she was about to get wet *again*. Bracing herself for the onslaught, she raced out the door and grimaced as she splashed across the open ground.

***

The manager of the Bed and Breakfast looked Steven over as he walked in the door. With his dishevelled and soaking attire he was not exactly selling himself as a good tenant.

'Are you planning to stay long?' the woman asked.

'I'm not sure yet,' he answered.

After filling in the paperwork he handed over the cash payment. It seemed to make her happier. Real cash always compensated for any doubts.

'Right, if you need anything just let me know.' She led him up a set of stairs and stopped in front of a locked door. After unlocking it she handed him the key. 'This is the room. Hope you enjoy your stay. Breakfast is served between seven and nine in the morning.'

'Thank you.' Steven replied. He walked in and heard her quiet shuffle fading in the distance. Once in the room, he noticed the kettle. A cup of coffee could do wonders. He took it to the sink and filled it up to boil. A few biscuits wrapped in some coloured cellophane looked tempting, so he hastily unwrapped one and ate it in one bite. The remnants of a chocolate chip lingered in his tooth so he licked it off with his tongue. He missed home baking.

The kettle whistled and the switch flicked off. He picked up one of the mugs, popped a sachet of coffee and sugar inside and poured in the water followed by the cream. Whilst he let it cool, he picked up the bags he'd brought with him and started to unpack the new clothes and toiletries. A few minutes later he picked up the mug, took a sip and let the hot soothing liquid take effect. He seized the remaining biscuit, dunked it in the coffee and ate it whole for a second time.

A small television sat in the corner of the room so he turned it on, picked up the remote control and flicked through channels. It was weird to be doing something so normal again. In the time he had been away nothing had happened to improve the quality of day time television. He settled on a music channel and decided to have a shower. A shower and change could perform miracles. He had missed his designer gear.

It was time to get the old Steven Thorn back.

He took the neatly folded towel and made his way into the ensuite facilities. Inside the bathroom, he was pleasantly surprised to see a power shower over the side of the bath. Eager, he slipped off his clothes and made his way into the bath and turned the nozzle. At first the water was freezing but gradually it got burning hot. In no hurry, he put the plug on the bath and let the water collect so that he could lie in the water to think.

***

Catherine sat in a café across the road from the bed and breakfast and sipped her hot chocolate as she pretended to read the newspaper. She quite liked the role of vigilante. She was only supposed to only keep an eye on Steven, but they had not said she couldn't talk to him. It crossed her mind that it would be simpler to ask him what he was planning to do. In a way, she might be able to help him better.

It was strange to sit out in the open with normal people.

It was no different being around them than it was to be around ordinary animals. She did not attack the livestock in the community at will so she was not going to attack out in the open either. The smell was different, she had to admit to that, but only in that it made her crave it more. It was like comparing chocolate to bread, both different yet delicious. So far, she had not been overpowered by an urge to have human blood.

Her need for blood would arise eventually. That would be the next challenge.

After exhausting all the newspapers articles and rereading some several times she finally saw Steven walk out of the exit. She noted his change of clothes and wet hair and wished she'd also had the chance to freshen up. This cloak and dagger routine was not going to work for her in the long run. She'd never followed anyone in her life, she had never been known for her tracking skills.

She sighed inwardly, got up and got ready to make chase.

CHAPTER 19

CATHERINE

The wind, rain and chill took Catherine by surprise. She was not used to this weather. She knew all about rain from the Amazon, but she had forgotten how cold and drab it could be in Southampton. It was just as well she was wearing a coat. She did not want to draw attention to herself. To fit in you had to look miserable. To be honest, it was not hard. The climate in England left as lot to be desired. She was depressed already and she had only been in the country for a week. She would not trade the tropical climate of the Amazon for anything. It was where she belonged.

It was ironic. She obtained no sense of freedom here. In contrast, she knew the confines of the community had stifled Steven. It was sad for her to think that he had not given himself time to appreciate the true nature of living in harmony with nature. The life they had carved out in the Amazon was so much simpler than life here.

Lost in thought, she nearly missed the fact that Steven had jumped on the bus. Unsurprisingly, it was the one leading to the university. Seeing an empty taxi in the nearby taxi stand, she jumped in and asked to be taken in the same direction.

The bus stopped opposite the huge Hartley library and she asked the taxi driver to stop. She paid quickly and followed him into the entrance of the library building. When she got to the entrance, she paused and looked around casually.

'Lost?' a male voice asked from behind.

Startled, she turned around and came face to face with Steven.

'I knew someone would figure out where I was eventually and you're not that stealthy. How are you doing, Catherine?'

Catherine chuckled. 'I'm as well as could be expected. I

didn't really like following you around so I'm glad you figured it out. How did you see me?'

'I didn't, I sensed someone was around. When I looked out of the bus window I saw you getting into the taxi. Like I said, you're not very stealthy,' he grinned.

Catherine was amused. As much as she wanted to be annoyed with him she couldn't be. She had always liked him. He was different to Emily. 'Fair enough. Well, in that case I can cut to the chase. Can we talk?'

'I thought we already were.'

'No need to be like that,' she frowned, suppressing a smile. 'You know what I mean. Look I'll get to the point. My mother wanted us to help you. So what do you need?'

Steven shrugged his shoulders. 'I don't need your help. I'll manage on my own.'

She could not help being impressed by his attire. His smart casual look oozed confidence. With his dark jeans, shirt and dark brown leather jacket he was dangerous for any human girl, for sure.

'Really?' she scoffed aloud. 'You can't confuse everyone you meet. I figured what you got up to at the bank. Trust me, mind games only work for a while. Eventually, you'll get found out.'

'I don't see how.' He shrugged his shoulders in a childish manner.

'Someone will notice eventually. They have a pretty good audit trail in the banking system.'

'A what?'

'You know, when people check that all the money's accounted for. Eventually someone would notice that money was missing. You need to be cleverer than they are. We have been doing it for years, I can help you.'

Reluctantly, he gave a huge sigh. 'Okay, I have been trying to figure this out in the dark. If you are serious about helping then I accept, but I don't intend to go back. I hope that's clear.'

Catherine smiled. 'Crystal, we don't intend to take you back, unless *you* change your mind.'

'Not going to happen.'

'We'll see,' she mused. 'Anyway, Mum didn't want us to take you back and I would never go against her wishes. Look, Dad will help you, when he's more stable. When he does I intend to return to my family. So I'll do what I can until I leave.'

'Okay.' He surveyed the library entrance and challenged, 'how do I get back into university life? It's nearly Christmas.'

Catherine started to walk away from the library, Steven followed. 'It seems to me that you should think of where you want to be. Then we'll arrange it. So, *where* do you want to be?'

Steven's shoulders slumped. 'I want to be near Caitlin but I'm rubbish at mathematics, so I don't know how to get close to her. Studying Law I'd never be in any of her lectures.'

Catherine grinned. 'Did you say mathematics?'

Steven shrugged, still in the dark.

'Don't you remember what I teach?'

'Mental agility… oh,' the penny dropped. 'But, you know how rubbish I was.'

'What you used to be before the change has no bearing on what you can do now. Trust me. Let's get to work.'

At last, there was something she could teach him that he would appreciate.

***

Catherine turned out to be a huge help. Not only had she managed to get them into the library using her means of persuasion, she was now on a mission to help him. Steven was not convinced the help she had in mind was something he welcomed. She was trying to convince him to become a maths geek. Not that he saw Caitlin in that light – he just didn't see himself in that light.

A series of thick and heavy books with all sorts of strange mathematical symbols emboldened on the covers laid wide open on the table, a range of topics and calculations on display. Weird thing was they made sense. That was the underlying problem. Maths had never, ever made sense to him. Yet, strangely now it did. He had never figured bats could be mathematical in nature.

'Have you had enough yet?' Catherine asked, a playful smile on her lips.

'Yes, I have. But, seeing as this is what I *have* to do, we'll carry on with it.'

Catherine frowned. 'Aren't you enjoying this at all?

'For the first time in my life, I can learn mathematical things immediately. Trust me it is impressive. But I still would not call maths fun, sorry.'

'Well, you'd better change your tone if you are going to pretend to be a maths student. Don't you see from everything you've read how important maths is?' She leant her chin on her tightly clasped hands.

'I do get it, really. I never appreciated how much the world relies on calculations. It's just that numbers were never designed to be my play toy.'

'Fair enough, but you do understand it all now, at least. So, if we get you on to the system to start as a new student after Christmas you can fit in with the others. We'll think of a way. All you have to do is pass the exams for the term and you'll be like everyone else. Trust me if you can master the stuff we've just covered the rest will be child's play in comparison.'

'I'll take your word for it.' He still preferred Law.

'And you are sure this is what you want? You want to go back to your old life, with that girl. Caitlin, isn't it?' Her eyebrows were raised.

He was tired of justifying himself. He had enough doubts of his own. 'Yes, that's her name. I fell in love with her and I am pretty sure she loved me. I have to know if she'll love me again. I know it's pathetic, but I need to know.'

'Okay, if that's what you want. Just try not to be too disappointed if things don't go to plan. She might not be that happy to find out what you are.'

'Why do I have to tell her?' He didn't want to scare her off immediately.

'Great place to start in a relationship, with one lie after another,' Catherine added.

Did she have to sound so judgemental? 'I can't tell her

straight away, can I?'

'No I guess not. Steven, can I just remind you of something important. You still need human blood. Feeding off humans, as you have discovered, has its risks even if you don't commit the crime.'

'Jeff told you about the girl.'

'Yes, he did.' Catherine leaned back on the chair and folded her arms over her chest.

'So, what do I do? Rob a hospital?'

'It doesn't do any harm. I'll help,' she replied. 'Just don't feed off any more humans. It's too risky.'

'Point taken, don't worry there are plenty of animals I can feed on without raising suspicions. If you help me get human blood via a safer source it'll be better. You will want some too I imagine.'

'Yes, so we kill two birds with one stone.'

'So, we're agreed. We won't kill anyone?'

'Right.'

Not on his watch.

'So, did you need help finding her? I guess you still don't even know where she lives?'

Catherine was obviously one step behind for a change. 'I already tracked her down.'

'Impressive.'

She flicked back her hair behind her ears and clasped her hands together, all business like. 'It would help if you knew as much as possible. Shall I do a thorough check?'

'See if you can find out something I didn't?'

'Exactly.'

An hour later, they knew everything about Caitlin Chance. Her address, grades, report on the suicide – the lot.

'She's a smart girl,' Catherine said, as she flicked through the papers.

'I know. Not that she'd admit to it,' he laughed. Caitlin was one of the most insecure people Steven had ever met, she never acknowledged her ability.

Catherine's next question threw him off guard. 'So, now you know where she is, what are you planning to do?'

He shook his head and looked away. 'I had not got that far. Start lectures and see?'

'Maybe. I don't suggest you follow her around. If she catches you you'll only make her suspicious.'

'I was not planning to become a stalker.' If he was honest he would have admitted the thought had crossed his mind.

'Good. Keep your distance for now, be patient. Time is your friend.'

The way she said it like it was true was silly. He did not know if she could see that he was not impressed.

'Anyway, we have to bury my mum. Are you coming?'

Steven took a deep breath and sighed. 'I owe her that much.'

'You do.'

***

Jeff decided to lay Judith to rest in the sheltered section of the garden. A beautiful spot surrounded by a range of evergreen shrubs and majestic oak trees. A wreath of fresh flowers leant against the paved grave. It brought colour and beauty to the sombre scene.

'Freesias were her favourite flower,' Jeff reflected.

'They do smell nice,' Ian added. 'Do you think she's at rest now? I mean, do you really think there is an afterlife, heaven and hell and all that?'

Jeff knew he could always trust Ian to bring in a moment breaker. 'Of course there is, without a doubt. Do you think we'd exist at all if it wasn't for the greater good? Nothing happens in isolation. God does work in mysterious ways. It's not up to us to question what the motives are behind every event.'

Ian tensed. 'Sorry Dad, but I can't accept that Mum died for the greater good. She had so much more to give. I know that death is a natural part of life but, I never thought *we'd* die.'

'What? Did you think we'd be *immortal*?' Jeff tried hard not to sound condescending. 'No-one knows what happened to us. In the past few years, your mother and I started to notice that we were not the same.'

'What do you mean?'

Jeff had not wanted to burden his son, he wished he had. It

would have made it easier now. 'We needed more animal blood. It seemed no matter how much we had we never felt satisfied. When we got here and your mother started to get ill it was purely a coincidence. She just knew she was home, I guess she was ready. There is no way of knowing whether by having human blood she would have healed. Personally, I think it might have extended her life by a few more years but that's all. The truth is that none of us will live forever. If we tried to I'm pretty sure it would not be much of an existence. I believe our need for human blood would become insatiable. Then we would truly resemble vampires. I don't want that, do you?'

'Vampires, sounds so macabre. Millions of predators in the world, including humans, and yet you say vampires and everybody runs for the hills. It's ludicrous really. We are human beings with different needs. That's all. Doesn't every species do what it can to survive?'

Jeff faced Ian, resolute. 'Yes, to a point. The thing is not all predators have a conscience. We do. I don't think you'd ever see a shark stopping mid bite, would you? They don't think about the animal they've killed for food? They just take what they need. Do you think any of *us* can kill and not be burdened with guilt indefinitely?'

Ian pursed his lips. After a moment, he added, 'no, I guess not.'

That had given him some food for thought.

CHAPTER 20

FIRST CONTACT

Jeff turned to face the house as he heard a car arrive in the distance. Two sets of doors opened and slammed, he gave a half smile. Catherine was back with Steven. She reminded him so much of Judith. She could convince water to turn into wine.

He was glad Steven was back. At least they would get a chance to talk. He had to be strong for Judith. He had promised to help him.

'Catherine's back,' Ian said, his tone hostile.

'Not now Ian, not now.' Jeff did not feel like putting up a fight.

'Fine, I'll go off for a walk. I'll be back later.'

'Good idea.' Jeff watched Ian saunter off and sighed. Ian was just like him, he wanted to protect everyone. This was not his fight.

Jeff stared at the gravestone. He wanted more than anything to fully understand why Judith had left him, it was just hard. They had decided years earlier to stay together. They had made a pact. Why had it ended? He could not believe another lone tear had run down his cheek. He ignored it. He did not want to move. He knew he was vulnerable. Even when he heard the gravel crunching as Catherine got closer, he stayed still.

'You don't need to be brave with me,' Catherine said, as she placed her arm over his shoulder.

He wiped the tear away from his face and rubbed his eye in a vain attempt to pretend he had grit in his eye. 'I know.' Catherine would know the truth anyway.

'Mum loved you so much. We all knew it. She would do anything for you. Remember that.'

Jeff thought about this and swallowed as he tried to get the words out. 'She did everything for me. What did I do for her?'

'What do you mean? You did everything you could to keep us safe. What else could you have done?' Catherine stared at him with huge eyes.

'Nothing, I guess.' Jeff knew he could not tell Catherine what was on his mind. He would have to tell someone eventually, but he just could not tell her. If Catherine found out, he was sure she'd feel deceived. They had deceived them all. Now was not the time. He just could not figure out when? He knew that was what Judith wanted. He knew she wanted him to tell Steven, to explain, to give him hope. He would find the right moment. Now was not it. 'So, how's Steven?'

'Fine, he's waiting inside. He wanted to give us some time alone. Shall I go and get him? Is Ian around? I don't want Ian to start a fight.' Catherine was worried. He did not know what he could say to put her at ease.

Catherine was always the thoughtful one. 'Ian's gone for a walk. Let Steven come, let him say goodbye. Judith would have appreciated it. She loved him a lot.'

Catherine looked to the house and whistled a slow melodic note.

A minute later, Steven started to make his way up to where they were standing.

Steven gave Jeff a hug which surprised him. He had never seen Steven show any affection. It was a nice gesture. Then Steven turned to the gravestone, bowed his head and closed his eyes in prayer. Again, Jeff was taken aback. He never realised Steven was religious. After a couple of minutes in relative silence, other than the odd sound of nature, Steven opened his eyes and nodded at Jeff. 'She's at rest now.'

'She is,' Catherine added.

Jeff pursed his lips and took a deep breath. He needed to get what he was thinking off his chest – at least partly. 'I need a favour. When I die, and that will happen soon, of that I'm sure.'

Catherine protested. 'Dad, no, not you too…'

'Let me finish Catherine. Steven, I need you to make sure I am laid to rest next to my wife.'

Steven seemed shocked by the request, but he managed to stutter back an answer. 'Th-that's a promise.'

'I will do it Dad, I will be here,' Catherine said, her eyes glazed.

Jeff did everything he could to keep it together. 'No, you have done more than what any of us expected. Your family needs you, the community needs you. You have to go back with Ian. You have to take care of the community. You have to explain...about your mother.'

Catherine bit her lip. 'You're sure you want us to go back? Steven needs me.'

Jeff adopted a stern tone, he had to. He did not want them here when he told Steven the truth. 'No, I will keep my promise. I will be here for Steven until he does not need me anymore. You are needed back home.'

He fixed his eyes on the gravestone and willed Judith's face to reappear. She could not be lying amidst the rubble. She could not be dead.

'You can trust me. I won't let you down,' Steven said, subdued.

You could have cut the air with a knife.

Finally, Catherine asked, now composed. 'Are you ready to go?'

'Not really. I miss her so much already.'

'I know Dad. We'll come back later. Let's go back in. It's getting late.'

The walk away from the gravestone felt long and slow, like he was being dragged away from a burning fire, out of breath, near the end. Back at the house he had to confess, face crestfallen. 'I need some blood.'

'I'll take Steven back,' Catherine suggested. 'You should probably meet up with Ian.'

'I'll find him.' Jeff did not know how he was going to convince Ian to go back, but he would find a way.

**

Caitlin loved the sound of Christmas music. It gave the busy shopping centre an extra touch. All around busy shoppers rushed around looking for the ideal gift. Shop fronts were decorated in a range of festive pictures and Christmas scenes. It was a shopper's paradise. At the entrance of one of her favourite shops, Caitlin stopped.

'Do you like this one?' she asked, holding up a red top with sparkly sequins.

'It's alright. How old is your sister again?' Gemma perused the rail.

'Twelve.'

'That's perfect then,' Gemma replied. She rolled her eyes. It was obvious it was not her idea of a cool top.

Caitlin pressed the point. It was fun to see Gemma squirm. 'You think, or do you prefer the blue one?'

'I have no idea what your sister is like, but I'm sure she'll be happy with either. They are both perfect for a twelve year old. Not that I would know what they're into now.'

'Come on, you were twelve not that long ago,' Caitlin said, amused.

Gemma scowled. 'I never went for the glitzy, Barbie type clothes. But I'm sure she'll love anything you get her, doesn't she worship the ground you walk on?'

Caitlin laughed. 'You know, you're right. She'll be amazed I got her a present in the first place.'

'Exactly,' Gemma smirked. 'Anyway, enough family shopping…shall we go and grab a cookie, all this decision making has made me hungry?'

'Good idea, I'll just pay for the blue one first. It'll match her eyes.'

'Can I meet you upstairs? I need the toilet and from the sight of that queue you're going to be a while.'

Caitlin stared at the long queue trawling down the aisle. Saturday's were always so busy. Christmas was always the same. 'Sure, I'll meet you up there.'

After waiting in the queue for ten minutes Caitlin finally paid and made her way out of the shop. It was bizarre. She couldn't recall that much about the previous Christmas. She remembered feeling irritated and annoyed at her sister but there was something important that eluded her. Either way, she was actually looking forward to going home for a change. She was fed up of having to cook and clean. The laundry in particular drove her insane. And none of them had any motivation to clean the bathroom. It was a case of clean it if it's dirty rather than because it's time.

Some things were definitely easier in self catered halls.

Living in a house with other students was nice, more homely than halls of residence. There was just a lot more to consider. Sometimes she was not sure going on to adulthood was as much fun as she thought it was going to be.

As the escalator started its accent her eye glanced around. A figure caught the corner of her eye. She turned and was stunned to see a guy staring at her. Reflexively, she turned away but in her mind she was sure it was the same one she had spoken to in the bus – the one that reminded her of Steven. But, the truth was that she'd only briefly met him so there was no way for her to know if it really was Steven.

She mustered up some courage and turned back to look. For the second time he had vanished amongst the crowd. It was so annoying. She'd never even heard back from Steven. Maybe her subconscious was telling her something.

'There you are,' Gemma exclaimed, waving frantically from a small table at the side. The area was crowded and there were practically no seating spaces left.

'Busy, isn't it?'

Gemma laughed. 'It always is at Christmas. Do you want me to go get the food whilst you wait? Or we'll lose the table.'

'Thanks, can I have a tuna mayo baguette and a bottle of water? Here's some money,' Caitlin asked. She took out her purse and handed over a ten pound note.

'Coming up, hope I don't take too long,' she sighed.

Caitlin watched Gemma join the queue by the food counter. Then she stared into the distance and focused on the huge glass windows on the periphery of the eating area. The sky looked grey and angry.

'Weather's awful, isn't it?' a male voice said next to her. He sounded so posh, what she called *polished*. The sound was familiar. She couldn't think why.

Coming out of her daydream, she turned to see who was speaking and gawped. It was the same guy. He smiled at her and waited, patient.

'Do I know you from somewhere?' she asked. She could not help it.

'I don't think so. My name is Simon Thorn,' he said, as he politely introduced himself and held out his hand.

The feel of his strong, yet soft, hand in hers made her stomach tingle.

'I'm going to start at the University of Southampton in January. Are you a student there? I can see the university waterpolo emblem on your top.'

Distracted, she glanced at her breast pocket and saw the logo for the swim team. That had to explain why he was talking to her. Wary, she answered back in a confident voice. 'Yes, I go there. So, I might see you around after Christmas?'

'Yes, you might, it was nice to meet you, Caitlin.' Then he walked away giving her a fleeting and friendly smile. It was *too* friendly for her liking.

A few minutes later Gemma arrived with a tray full of food.

'Finally...who was that guy talking to you? He looked yummy.'

Caitlin picked up the bottle of water, unscrewed the lid and took a swig. She nearly choked as her eyes came alight and she exclaimed, 'I never told him my name!'

'You really are a dim wit sometimes,' Gemma blurted out. 'A handsome guy speaks to you and you don't even tell him your...'

Caitlin grabbed her hand and pressed hard. 'Listen,' he *knew* my name, but *I didn't* tell him.'

'Ouch,' Gemma said, as she shook her hand and rubbed it. 'A handsome stalker, like wow.' She picked up her baguette and took a bite.

'No, trust me, he's *not* a stalker. I'm sure I've met him before. He just didn't admit that he knew me, but then, it's like, I don't know, like he said my name to give himself away.

Like some sort of test.'

'You're rambling now,' Gemma scoffed. 'You really need to get away for Christmas. You're losing the plot.'

Caitlin frowned, picked up the baguette and got ready to take a big bite. She paused, waved her finger in the air and added. 'I'm telling you Gemma, I know him.'

'Fine, so marry him then. It'll be nice to see you with someone for a change. Even if this guy is a weirdo, do it. Tell you what, let's make it interesting. If you see him again, I dare you to go up to him and kiss him. If you know him like you think you do, you'll have nothing to lose. But hey, if you're not up to it, I'll kiss him for you,' she added, her Cheshire cat grin on full display.

'You're on,' Caitlin swallowed her mouthful. 'If, and that's unlikely anyway, if I see him again I'll kiss him.'

Gemma squealed aloud like a little girl.

Caitlin couldn't help it, she had to join in.

CHAPTER 21

HUNGER

The body of the old man, lifeless on the floor surrounded by crumpled old newspapers and a few empty alcohol bottles, reeked of death.

'Should we leave him?' Ian asked.

'Yes.' Jeff found it hard to look at it. The alcohol in the blood made him disorientated. 'No-one will care how he died. This society doesn't care about all its inhabitants.'

Ian shrugged his shoulders. 'If you're sure.'

'I'm sorry old man.' Jeff gave the corpse a final glance. It was a waste of a life, even when the man was alive.

'I feel great.' Ian had a renewed bounce in his step. 'I feel the need for speed. Fancy a run back?'

'Let's not draw any attention to ourselves.'

'What? Not up it anymore, old timer?' Ian teased.

'Don't make fun of your elders.'

Ian smiled. 'You are *old*.'

'Let's get back then joker. I don't know why everyone back home seems to think that you are too serious,' Jeff sighed. He could not believe the cheek of the boy.

'It's an image,' Ian scoffed. 'What I am in public is not who I am in private. Some cards have to be played close to the chest.'

'Funny, I never took you for the gambling type.'

'Strategy, that's what life's about. Keeping ahead of the game by making the right moves,' Ian declared, confident.

'Maybe, do you think life is a game?'

Ian paused, as though taken aback by the question. 'Honestly, no, it's the worst hand I've ever had. I guess sometimes you have to bluff your way out of a situation. I'm here to help you, but when I'm not needed any longer I'm going back home – where I belong.'

Ian had just made it easy.

'In that case it's time for you to go home.'

Jeff could see the confidence evaporate.

'Now?' Ian stopped and frowned, 'I didn't mean…'

'I talked to Catherine,' Jeff said. 'She has a few more things to do and then you can both go back. I will take over from here. You're needed back in the community. You know as well as I do that it's for the best.'

Ian stopped walking and placed his hand on Jeff's shoulder. 'You will call us if you get sick? You will ask us to come back?'

Jeff patted Ian's hand. 'My life doesn't matter. I'm staying here to help Steven. Then I'll live out my days until I can rest with your mother.'

Jeff could tell Ian was holding back his anger. His reply didn't surprise him.

'If that's what you want.'

After a minute of walking, Jeff had to break the ice. 'Thank you son, I am very proud of you. I should say that to you more often.'

In a half grumble, Ian replied. 'I appreciate it. Let's get back.' Without a second glance Ian started to run. He went too fast. Jeff doubted Ian cared if anyone saw.

***

Catherine was smug, everything was in place. As agreed, she waited to fill Steven in on her success.

A few minutes later, Steven cruised in to the café and took a seat opposite. 'Any luck?'

Catherine smiled. 'Did you doubt me? You start university in January under your new name. You've transferred from the University of Leeds, the paper trail is flawless. We will receive your examination certificates shortly. You'll be pleased to know that you got A*'s in A Level Maths, and Further Maths.'

'Genius that I am,' he smiled.

'Steven, come back to the house. Caitlin is going back home, she won't be here either.'

'I guess.'

'I'll ring Dad and Ian. By the way, I got you an apartment close to the university after Christmas. I didn't think you'd fair well in halls anymore.'

'You've thought of everything.'

'Nearly, after we get your identification papers we'll open a student account and set you up with some money. Then it's up to you how you get more. Remember stealing is a crime. Try and follow the rules.' Catherine got the impression he was more inclined to follow *some* rules more than others.

'Yes, yes, I'll get a job.'

'Are you ready to leave?' Catherine added.

'Yes, I believe so.'

Catherine could not help thinking he was up to something.

*

The diner at the side of the road surprised Catherine. She had never been in a diner before and the prospect of unhealthy food seemed strangely appealing. The sound of fifties music played in the background, the walls plastered with fifties memorabilia. The menu revealed a plethora of steaks, burgers, fries, and hotdogs with a range of sauces and condiments. Her mouth watered at the thought of a chilli hotdog and fries.

'What are you having?' she asked, as she reconsidered again and continued to peruse the menu.

Steven studied the menu and flicked the corner of the laminated sheet. If he continued to do that she would get irritated.

'Don't know, but I'm starving so I'll have the biggest thing on the menu.' Steven sounded like such a teenager. He was young after all.

The waitress came up and smiled sweetly, 'hello there, what can I get you?'

Catherine looked up and made her decision. 'Chilli dog and fries.'

The waitress scribbled on the notepad, then asked, 'would you like a drink?'

'I'll have an orange juice please.'

'No problem, what can I get you?' The waitress took a deep

breath and stared at Steven.

'I'll have the diner special with a large lemonade, thanks,' Steven added.

'Coming right up,' she smiled, batted her eyelids seductively and left. She fanned herself with the notepad as she walked.

'Don't get too used to that,' Catherine warned.

Steven followed the waitress with his eyes. 'I don't intend to.'

'Saying something and doing it are different things. Why do you think it's easy for us to lure victims? No girl can resist you now; make sure you don't confuse love with infatuation.'

'I'll bear it in mind,' he said, disinterested.

'Do it,' she snarled. 'I mean it Steven. If you expose us your life with Caitlin will be over. You can dream all you like but don't live in a bubble. You are what you are and if you can't control yourself you'd better be upfront about it now. You don't want to end up like your mother.'

Composed, he replied. 'I will not expose you; don't worry about your precious community. Soon you'll be able to forget I ever existed.'

'I hope so, for the sake of my family and friends, I hope so.'

The food arrived. The smell was a welcome distraction.

'Can I get you anything else?' the waitress asked, eyes leering at Steven.

'No thank you,' he replied, he avoided eye contact.

Her shoulders slumped and she scuttled off.

'Don't you get tempted?' Steven asked.

'Of course I'm tempted. It's all about control. I need blood. I'm resisting human blood to the best of my ability. I can't change what I am. We'll have to stop in the New Forest before we go back to the house. There's no way either of us will hold out much longer.'

Before Steven devoured another mouthful, he asked, 'remind me again. Why is it okay to kill an animal and not a human?'

'We can take the body and use it for food, I don't think either of us would want to eat a human,' she noted, sarcastic.

'Fair point, but I thought none of you could resist if humans were around.'

145

'I don't intend to resist, I will feed before I go back home. I'll choose someone that won't be missed.'

'I get the feeling that you like everything in its proper place.' It was Steven's turn to be sarcastic.

'That's the best way, it's a shame your mother didn't see it that way.'

'Most people I know don't stick to rules,' he added.

'We are not most people,' she concluded. There was a definite finality to her tone.

***

Jeff draped his arm over Catherine's shoulder and gave her a squeeze. He could see Judith's smile on her face. As much as he tried to ignore it he could not ignore the heartache. Ever since Judith passed away a part of him had died.

'What's up with Ian now?'

'For once, he's right to be worried,' Jeff replied. 'Let's get inside. Can I make you a drink?'

'Sure, I'll have a cup of tea.'

Steven seemed to linger in the hallway for a moment. 'No, thank you. I'm going up to my room.'

Catherine nodded. 'Did you go shopping, Dad? I've only been away a few days and you look gaunt.'

'We have. They stock everything. It's lucky for us incompetent males.' He winked at her. Catherine was so motherly, just like Judith.

Catherine smiled. 'Yes, it's lucky.'

'How is Steven holding up?' Jeff added, as he looked behind her.

'Okay, I think.' Tentatively, she added. 'I lost my patience with him earlier.'

'Nothing serious I hope,' he added.

'I just miss home, I don't like the fact that he thinks we're freaks,' she stressed.

'He doesn't know any better, give him time.'

'I don't think I want to,' she paused. 'I'm sorry, Dad. I like Steven and all but I've made up my mind. I'd like to go home now. You said you didn't need us so I don't want to delay any longer.'

'I never expected you to stay any longer. Don't apologise. Thank you for coming in the first place. I'm sure you've helped him,' he paused, distracted. 'What's that noise?'

'Two male bulls in full charge,' Catherine said, as she rolled her eyes.

They followed the noise to the lounge.

'Who do you think you are? Do you really think you know more than us? I was right to take you to the Amazon and if I have to force you to come back with us again – I will. You are a liability, you're dangerous, you're the reason we chose the life we did. I can't allow such an unpredictable force to stay out in the open. Frankly, I don't care about Caitlin. We should have killed her when we had the chance,' Ian added, his voice filled with malice.

'If you had killed her, I swear I would kill you,' Steven spat, as the distance between them became an arms length.

'Just try it,' Ian laughed. 'You're a child, I would rip you apart.'

Steven lunged at Ian and knocked him to the ground. Ian threw him off easily and sprang back up on his feet.

'Stop it,' Jeff shouted, as he stood between them. 'Ian, let me talk to Steven.'

'I am NOT leaving here,' Ian shouted.

'Yes, you ARE,' he ordered. 'Ian, you are not responsible for Steven – I am. I made a promise to your mother. I intend to keep it. If you don't want to help Steven I suggest you return with Catherine to the community. I appreciate everything you've done but you don't have all the answers. You're needed back home.'

Ian huffed and shouted, 'I don't have any answers at the moment.' He threw his arms in the air and pounded out of the room at a brisk pace.

Catherine raised her eyebrows, shrugged her shoulders and then gave a smile of encouragement to her father before she followed.

A few minutes of silence ensued as neither Steven nor Jeff spoke. Steven sat on the sofa, head in hands.

Finally, Jeff broke the silence. 'You have to make a choice,' he paused. He hoped Steven would look up. When he didn't, he carried on. 'Two girls have died after you fed. The first under the hand of your mother, the second under mind control. You made it clear that the only reason you would come to live here was if you did not kill anyone. You now know when you do feed it has an effect. So, we have to come up with a solution or you return with Ian and Catherine tomorrow and forget about this life.'

'What if I don't want to return regardless?'

Jeff feared that answer. He tried to sound nonplussed as he replied. 'Then I will have to help you, but you might have to face up to the fact you have some hard choices to make. Hospital blood is not a long term solution. Your needs will develop. You have not fully matured yet. The need for blood gets stronger in the first year. After that it grows like a virus. You *might* be different but if you're not, you have to be prepared to do the right thing.'

'Fine, I will make the choice if it comes to it. I just can't return *now*.'

Jeff bowed his head. 'If that's your final answer, I will help you.'

CHAPTER 22

UNIVERSITY

The studio apartment Catherine found Steven was basic but convenient since it was only a ten minute walk from campus. In two rooms, one of which was the bathroom, he had everything he needed. The best part was that she had paid the rent and council tax for six months in advance. He had a student bank account and his card was due to arrive in the following days. Financially, his situation had never been healthier. There was no way he would ever resort to travelling by bus again. Jeff had offered to lend him a car, but he had decided against it. Those cars would definitely draw unwanted attention.

Catherine and Ian made the journey back to the Amazon before Christmas. Steven had spent Christmas at the house with his grandfather. It worked to an extent. He had watched a lot of television and accrued an impressive collection of fiction novels. Time vanished.

It was time for a new term to begin.

Steven sat on the double bed alone. He hoped to rectify that problem soon.

It was lucky Jeff trusted him. The last thing he wanted was to let him down. With his ankle healed he had no need for human blood. He would only feed from animals. That was the plan anyway. It was a shame Jeff could not follow the same rules.

Steven got off the bed and walked to the small window. He was right in the centre of Porchfield, with a view of the main road. It was busy outside. People just went about their business. Work, school run, shopping. Life seemed normal again.

It was as good a time as any to take stock of what he was

about to do. He was going back to be a student, a student of mathematics no less. Catherine had reassured him that his knowledge was more than adequate. He still found it hard to imagine he was actually good at maths. Anyone that knew him from school would have laughed – he had always loathed the subject.

The past had no bearing anymore.

Since he had changed it made sense. It was beautiful in a way. It was unbelievable that *he* should call a subject like maths beautiful, but that's how he saw it now. The way numbers entwined to give answers to a lot of life's challenges was mind boggling. It did make him think of Caitlin. She always talked about the beauty of maths. Either way, he still considered himself to be a fraud. He braced himself for the performance of a lifetime. He had to make an effort to fit in, drawing attention; was the last thing he should be considering.

***

Caitlin collected her bits and pieces and made her way down to the kitchen.

When Gemma saw her she pulled back in horror. 'Are my eyes deceiving me? Who are you and where is Caitlin?'

Caitlin half smiled, half scowled. 'No need for that.'

'Seriously, you're never on time. You must have had a nice Christmas break.'

'I did, and I'm going to make an effort. Today is the first day of the new me; positive, alert, and punctual.'

'Seriously, who are you?' Gemma joked, as she held her hand to her forehead.

Caitlin laughed as she helped herself to some cereal. She smothered it in milk. 'Make yourself useful and make me a cup of tea, will you.'

'Now, that's back to your usual self. Coming right up,' she replied. As the kettle boiled, Gemma took her first shot. 'So, did you hook up with anyone over Christmas?'

With a mouthful of cereal in her mouth Caitlin replied, 'did you?'

'Obviously, but don't make me change the subject. Did *you* have any luck?' she stressed, as she passed her the mug.

'With what?' Caitlin raised her eyebrows, played innocent and swallowed her cereal.

Gemma's eyes enlarged. In a split second she was in the seat next to Caitlin. 'So, there *is* someone. Who, when, how? Tell me everything.'

'Hmmm, maybe,' she teased. It was fun to keep Gemma in suspense. 'I'll tell you on the way in.'

'You're going to make me wait until we go. Come on. Spill the beans!'

Caitlin shook her head and placed a massive helping in her mouth.

'Caitlin!' Gemma leapt off the seat and made for the corridor. 'It's time to go,' she said. A minute later she was back in the kitchen. She held both of their coats.

'You are such a curious thing you know,' Caitlin laughed. 'It might not be that exciting.'

'Humph, let's go,' Gemma protested, as she plonked Caitlin's coat on the table.

'Alright, alright, I'll burn my mouth with the tea.'

'Forget the tea, we'll get one when we get there.'

'No thanks, the vending machine one tastes foul.'

Gemma sat down again, opposite this time. She twiddled her fingers as she watched Caitlin scrape the bowl and drink the tea. She blew out several impatient breaths and raised her eyes to the ceiling. This was fun. Caitlin wondered whether to string it along by drinking the tea really slowly.

'Isn't that cup empty yet?' Gemma asked, as though reading her mind.

'Not yet.'

A few minutes later Caitlin got up and picked up the coat. It was nice to have a new one for a change. The only downside being it was a bright red colour. It was warm and comfy, she couldn't complain. Christmas was always a good time to pick up useful and useless gifts.

Gemma eased up next to her and locked her arm in Caitlin's. 'Now start from the beginning, I want to hear it all.'

Caitlin filled her in on the mundane gossip first.

When they arrived at the forked junction leading to

university road, Gemma's lips twitched at an angle, her eyes narrowed. 'I didn't want to know what your granny got you. The *real* gossip, *please.*'

Caitlin shook her head dismissively and raised her eyebrows. 'Well, I did hook up with my brother's best friend, if that's what you mean.'

'Really? What's he like then?'

'Tall, dark, handsome, great sense of humour. He pays for everything.' Caitlin was enjoying herself.

Gemma scowled. 'Are you having me on?'

'No, for real, he's a great guy.' Caitlin suspected she would not believe her.

'Really?' Gemma beamed. 'Amazing! You'll have to tell me the rest later, I really have to go.' Gemma gave her a huge hug. 'You're so lucky, about bloody time!'

Caitlin watched Gemma jog off as she heard the familiar beep in her pocket. She got out her phone and smiled.

It was a text.

It read 'Good luck today, missing you already, Daniel.' A warm feeling ran through her and she smiled involuntarily as she reminisced on their last date. She had never expected to fall in love over Christmas, especially not with one of her older brother's friends, his best friend in fact. It was awkward, but not awkward enough to make her have second thoughts. Her brother, Mark, was not happy. She didn't care what he thought. She couldn't believe Daniel had been there all along and she'd never noticed him. Fate was stupid.

She put the phone back in her pocket and made her way to the lecture hall. Once inside, she sat down in her usual space and noticed that the lecture amphitheatre was only was half full. It was unusual for her to be there so early. With time to spare she glanced around discretely until she stopped and stared in utter amazement.

It was him. That guy, Steven or did he say Simon? She could not remember. What was he doing in her lecture? As she gawped his eyes met hers and he smiled. Annoyed, she focused on her folder. The last time she'd seen him she had vowed Gemma to kiss him when she saw him again. She was not going to keep her promise, she had a boyfriend. It was very lucky Gemma was in a different lecture today. There was no way Gemma would have let her get away with it.

***

When Steven saw Caitlin walk in he felt a wave of relief wash over him. She was here at last. Now he could put all of his efforts into winning her back. To his astonishment she walked past him, lost in her thoughts. It was infuriating. He was tempted to get up and sit next to her, just to see whether she would follow through with her bet. He resisted. He had heard Gemma dare her to kiss him and he could not wait for Caitlin to deliver.

As she went to take a seat she looked around and her eyes locked on his. He was unprepared for her reaction. It was not a look of admiration, it was one of shock. Something had happened since he last saw her, something had changed. He just knew.

The lecture seemed to go on forever. Everything the lecturer said made perfect sense, he learnt nothing new. His Aunt had already gone through the topic with him. He glanced back to make sure Caitlin had not left. As the lesson came to a close, he got his things together and casually made his way in her direction. Luckily, a few students had cluttered at the entrance as they chattered and blocked her exit.

He eased up alongside. 'Fancy seeing you again, I never asked what course you followed. What a coincidence.' He was sure his attempt at being friendly was not working.

Caitlin pursed her lips. 'What a coincidence.'

Her manner made him feel unwelcome. Neither spoke as they finally found the path clear to leave. He opened his mouth to say something but then his nerves got the better of him. He didn't know what he had expected, but a cold shoulder was not something he had considered. Without turning around she briskly walked away. She did not look back.

His muscles tensed. It was like being rejected all over again. 'Are you new?'

He turned to face the female voice and had to look down at

153

the petite brunette, with a set of small angular glasses, smiling in his direction. 'Yes, I just started today.' He could not help glancing in the direction Caitlin had gone.

'Well, I hope you settle in alright. I'm the student representative for the faculty. I'm Louise. I was told you'd be starting. If you need any help let me know. It is Simon Thorn, isn't it?' She cocked her head to the side.

He knew he was being rude by looking in another direction. He did not mean to be. 'Sorry, yes, my name is Simon Thorn. Thanks a lot, Louise. If I need anything I'll let you know.'

'Great, see you. She ambled off quickly as he just stood on the spot, transfixed. At least someone welcomed him.

***

Caitlin resisted the urge to look back. Something about him unnerved her. It was strange. She could not explain why she thought she knew him. He reminded her of the guy in her dream, the student called Steven. Yet, it had been so long ago. She did not even know if he really did look like that. Frustrated, she made her way into the room for her tutorial and sat down.

She dumped her rucksack on the floor and removed the things she needed. She had tried really hard to do the work they had been set over the holidays, but she had been unable to complete it all. She didn't have anyone that could help her with the complex calculations at home.

She did not notice Louise take the seat next to her, but her shrill voice could not be mistaken for anyone else's. 'Did you manage it all?'

First dagger plunge.

Caitlin had made a fundamental error. She had left a space next to her. Louise was always so smug, perfect and responsible. People like her always made Caitlin feel intellectually inadequate.

As if to dig it in, Louise continued twisting the knife. 'I found some areas challenging, but my daddy helped me with the things I could not do.'

'Lucky for some, I managed fine.' Caitlin squirmed. Louise was like a walking computer.

Louise stuck her nose in the air.

Caitlin looked away and doodled on her notepad. More students walked in and sat down, before the tutor made his entrance. She could not help checking the tutor out. He was only a few years older than her, was incredibly cute, and was Spanish so had the most amazing accent. As he was about to speak, the guy she now preferred to refer to as the stalker guy, walked into the room and took the last seat, which happened to be opposite her.

'You must be Simon, welcome. I've heard great things about you. Please join our soiree.' The tutor adopted an easy-going and welcoming manner.

'Thank you,' Steven replied.

Caitlin scowled. He could not be the person in her dreams. It was ridiculous. There was nothing she liked. He sounded and acted like a *know it all* snob.

CHAPTER 23

ANGST

The tutor nodded. 'Excellent work Simon. I'm sure they must have been sad to see you go at your last university.'

Steven knew his last answer was short of spectacular. If he was honest, he had no idea where it came from.

His name bugged him, Simon. It sounded all wrong. It would take some time to get used to. What made him swallow involuntarily was the look of disdain Caitlin gave. If looks could kill, she had just pulled off a corker. He could not understand what he had done wrong. As a means of self preservation he decided to avert his eyes for the rest of the session. It was obvious he had more work to do than he thought – it just wasn't of the academic sort.

Twenty minutes later, he had managed to solve every problem with ease. Louise was in awe of him, he could tell. She was practically drooling.

The tutor tried to act as though it was normal. 'Very impressive, Simon, have you covered this work already?'

'Yes,' he answered. It was as good an answer as he was prepared to give.

'Well, hopefully, we'll find some other things to challenge you further soon. That's all for today, see you all next week. Caitlin, can I have a word please?'

Caitlin looked up and nodded, as everyone packed up and made their way out.

Steven pretended to do his laces and waited outside. He could hear every word in the conversation.

'Feliz Navidad. Did you get to grips with the extra material I gave you?' the tutor asked. Nice, he wished her a Merry Christmas in Spanish, he had to like her.

Caitlin replied. 'Kind of, but I still found some of it

difficult.'

'Have you thought of getting some extra help? Or joining a study group? This year is important. You need to keep your grades up.'

He could hear the hesitation in Caitlin's tone as she replied, 'I know, I'll think about it.'

'I don't like to see good students struggling.'

Steven heard her sigh. She was not good at handling failure. Of course, her problems could give him a window of opportunity, a breakthrough. He casually went back in, looked around and pretended to have forgotten something. Then he shrugged his shoulders and turned to leave.

'Simon?' the tutor called.

'Yes?' Steven feigned ignorance.

The tutor motioned for him to come closer. 'You seem quite ahead of the game and I'm sure you'd like to get to grips with this place. Perhaps, you could give Caitlin a hand with the latest assignment in exchange for some introductions?'

Caitlin pulled a face of utter disgust, her eyes virtually popped out of their sockets.

The tutor looked at Caitlin then back at Simon. 'Erm, I'll just let you discuss it. It was just an idea.' He grabbed his things and skittered out. He seemed only too aware he might have put his foot in it.

Steven paused for a moment, unsure on best practice. He had no idea what he could have done to upset her. 'Caitlin right, I thought I'd introduce myself properly. Like I said in our brief introduction before Christmas, I'm Simon.'

'I heard.' It was a curt reply.

'Do you need some help? From what the tutor said, it sounded like a good idea. I don't mind giving you a hand, you don't *have* to help me settle in.' He was rambling, he could not help it.

With a blank expression, she stared. 'With what?' She frowned as she placed her hand on her hip and gripped her rucksack with the other hand. 'Are you now listening in on my conversations? It was weird enough that you already knew my name.'

'I know your name is Caitlin. The tutor just said it aloud.' He knew he sounded defensive.

'No, actually you called me by my name *before* Christmas.' She was pouting now. It was hard to resist the urge to kiss her.

Finally, the reason for her anger was revealed. He could not keep the corners of his lips from twitching. He knew she would pass his test, nothing ever got past her. 'No, I didn't.'

Nostrils flared, Caitlin raised her voice. 'Yes, you did!'

'Anyway, I overheard you talking as I approached the room. If you need help, I'm your man, if not, don't worry about it.'

'You must have really good hearing.' The frown was severe. Not a great start.

'I just want to offer my help with your maths. If you want to make me feel welcome then that's your choice.' He knew the only card he had to play was to appeal to her usual good nature.

Flabbergasted, she remained silent, eyes to the floor. After a painstaking minute, she looked at him. 'I'll think about it.' The answer was noncommittal. She did not break eye contact for a few moments, as though transfixed. Then she blurted out. 'Do I know you? I mean, from before. The last time we met I could not help feeling like I knew you already.'

He blinked and broke the impasse. Should he tell her the truth? 'I don't think so.'

'Silly, I know,' she smiled. 'You know, I'd be a fool to not take you up on some help. I've been struggling for a while. It's just that...'

At last. 'Good, it's settled then. Do you want to have lunch together and we'll tackle today's work first?'

'Erm, the thing is that...,' she faltered, nervous.

He waited and relaxed his shoulders. He could not help wondering what he had done now.

'I have a boyfriend,' she blurted out.

His shoulders hunched in response. Desperate to relax, he gave an awkward laugh, as he added. 'I'm happy for you, but I was not asking you out on a date. I never assumed you wouldn't have a boyfriend already, in fact, I knew you probably did.' He noticed her blush, so he carried on.

'Whatever your relationship status is, I'd just like to help you, and in return you can show me the ropes. Deal?' He held out his hand to make the arrangement binding. It was physical contact of some sort. He would have to comfort himself with that for now.

She shook his hand quickly. He felt the shock all the same, an electric spark.

He could not believe she had a boyfriend. That was not supposed to happen. It explained a hell of a lot.

***

Caitlin held out her hand to shake. As her hand came into contact with his the nerve endings on the back of her neck rose in response, electrified. Reflexive, she let go, even though it was likely to come across as rude. 'Can we start tomorrow? I have a few things to do today.'

'No problem, I'll meet you tomorrow in the students' union café, at say, one o'clock.'

'Fine, I'll see you then. I've got to go, see you around,' she replied. She rushed towards the ladies' toilet. Once inside she slid into a cubicle and leant her head against the door. It was incomprehensible. Something about him drove her crazy, but she was not going to let his looks or whatever it was overcome her feelings for Daniel.

For the strangest of reasons she had decided to let him help her.

It was weird. She still thought he was lying.

She was sure he called her by name before Christmas. She just could not shake the feeling she knew him from somewhere. Her memory was not that bad and she certainly was not stupid, or was she?

***

Steven walked out of the building and breathed in the cold air. It was so stuffy in old buildings, the smell musty. He had become so much more aware of the scents around him. His only comfort was the fact that they had a date, a work date, but still a date. It was obvious she was resisting him, but, at least now he knew why. She got a boyfriend. That was why she had not followed through with the bet. There was no way she

159

would two-time. A wry smile eased across his face.

He could do friendship, for now.

A few drops of water fell upon Steven's face. Since he had an hour to kill he decided to take cover and head for the cafeteria. As he walked the drizzle became a torrential downpour. By the time he got in the building he was wet through. Once inside, he shook some of the water off and ran his fingers through his hair smoothing it down.

The entrance was quite full. There were stands selling cheap CD's and DVD's, T-shirts and a range of jewellery by various merchants.

In the mood for a short browse he made his way around the stalls, stopped at one that caught his attention and started flicking through the CD's. After a few minutes he found a few that he wanted to buy so he handed them over to the attendant.

'That'll be eight pounds. Can I get you anything else?' The woman winked from behind the stall.

'No, that's all, thanks.'

'Come back if you change your mind. I can make time for a cuppa.'

Taking the CD's he walked away and reminded himself to be careful. It was incredibly easy for him to lure women. Before the change he had always drawn attention, but now it felt like he was irresistible. It would be so easy for him to take advantage of his magnetic pull. For some reason, Caitlin seemed to be the only girl who was not overcome by his charms. It was disappointing.

A long queue snaked away from the food counter so he took his place at the end and studied the CD's in an attempt to look inconspicuous.

'Excuse me, do I know you?'

He glanced at the student briefly, before replying. 'I don't think so.'

'No, I'm sure I've seen you before,' the student pondered, twirling a strand of hair in her fingers, before exclaiming flamboyantly. 'That's it; you were talking to my friend Caitlin before Christmas. I'm sure it was you. I'm not just trying to chat you up with a sad line, I promise.'

'Oh, maybe you have seen me then. Sorry, I don't remember you,' he apologised. He looked at her properly for the first time. Her spiky black hair and nose piercing gave her an edge. Other than that she looked normal, if a bit Goth.

'That's alright, I'm not memorable. Not like Caitlin, red heads always stand out right?' she said, as though checking his reaction.

'I guess so,' he shrugged, in a bid to keep his feelings hidden.

'I'm Gemma by the way.'

'Oh, nice to meet you Gemma, I'm St-Simon.'

'St-Simon, nice to meet you.' Gemma laughed, amused at his near error. 'I'm seeing her in a minute. Do you want to join us for lunch?'

'No that's alright. Thanks for asking.' He breathed a small sigh of relief as he reached the front of the queue and got busy filling the tray with a slice of pizza, chips and a drink of lemonade.' He paid, smiled and rushed away.

From the sanctuary of the far side corner he observed Gemma as she embraced Caitlin and they made their way to a seat. The last thing he needed was to fan the flames of friendly gossip.

CHAPTER 24

St-Simon

'I just saw your sweetheart. I nearly convinced him to join us for lunch. So, did you kiss him yet? I was looking forward to the snog you promised,' Gemma teased, twirling her fingers through her hair.

'My, who?' Caitlin asked, in a vain attempt to act confused.

'You know who I mean. Mr. tall, dark and handsome, St-Simon…the one you met before Christmas, the one who *knew your name*.'

Caitlin allowed herself to smile. She knew she had not imagined it. He *had* called her by name, Gemma had just confirmed it. Even though Gemma had not heard it, Caitlin knew she was not mistaken. The truth always outs. She smirked. 'If you are referring to the dare, the bet's off. I've got a boyfriend now, remember?'

'You took up the challenge fair and square. You can't back down now. I don't care that you said it before you met your lover boy. Besides, Daniel's not here now anyway, is he? How would he find out?'

Caitlin scrunched her nose. There had to be a way out. 'What's the forfeit?'

'Oh, I don't know, a box of *quality* chocolates, maybe. Not the cheap sort mind.'

'Deal, I'll get you some chocolates.'

'So, does this mean I can snog him instead?' Gemma asked, practically jumping off the seat.

'If you like, I barely know him.' She took a bite from her sandwich, and then casually added, 'although, you'll never guess what?'

'What?' Gemma asked, drawn in.

'He's a genius mathematician.' Caitlin shrugged her

shoulders.

Gemma gasped. 'No way, he's a maths geek.' Her face was scrunched up, appalled.

'Hey, are you calling us geeks?' Caitlin nudged her elbow.

'Technically, we are both not studying maths, it's just an add on. You have Spanish, I have Accounting. If he's *only* doing maths, he is a maths geek,' she rationalised, with a giggle. Gemma grabbed Caitlin's arm. 'So, you've *talked* to him already?'

'As a matter of fact, I did. And he's offered to help me – he's very smart,' she added.

Gemma took a huge bite out of her sandwich and scoffed. After taking a few chews and gulping down some drink she protested. 'So unfair, you have a boyfriend now. And you get the hunk of the moment offering to help you. Am I the only one missing the injustice? Hey, maybe I could also join your tuition sessions? Bet they're not exclusive.'

'I'll ask him if he minds. Sounds like a good idea.' It would mean she would have company during their sessions, which would be a bonus. 'So, come on, tell me about your conquests this Christmas,' Caitlin added. A change in conversation was necessary.

'No big deal, just a few snogs here and there. No-one *special*,' she emphasised.

'Come on, who knows what's going to happen. I only just started seeing Daniel.'

'And you're loved up already, which is great by the way. About time!'

Caitlin shrugged her shoulders. 'I'll be a spinster again soon, you'll see. Then we can wallow together.'

'Good.' Gemma smiled. Semi-serious, she added, 'I'll look forward to that. I know being single is *much* more fun than being used and abused.'

Caitlin rolled her eyes. 'If you say so.'

Gemma sipped her drink, and then winked at Caitlin. 'So, you have not told me anything yet. Have you, I mean, has anything *of interest* happened with Daniel?'

'Not what you're suggesting,' she sighed. Why was Gemma

so predictable?

'Boring. When it does, promise me that I'll be the first to know if the earth moved.'

'Okay, I'll tell you when the earth moves.' Caitlin frowned, bit into the remains of her sandwich and played for time. Once finished, she made to leave. 'Anyway, I'll speak to you later. I've got work to do.'

Gemma was scanning the area, now looking for someone. If Caitlin knew her at all she'd bet she was keeping an eye out for Simon.

'I have stuff to do too, I'll have you know. We'll talk later.'

As Caitlin walked off, she could not help wondering why Gemma had called him St-Simon. She'd have to ask her later.

***

Steven watched Caitlin go. He had not missed a thing. The conversation had been amusing. It was only now as she walked away that he became aware of his hunger. If he did not know any better, he would have thought he was coming down with something.

The food on his plate had done nothing to abate the thirst. The crowded, stuffy environment of the cafeteria only made things worse. He had to get out, now. Otherwise, he would be tempted to lure someone else just like he had with Julia, it had been so easy.

Outside, the fresh air cleared his head for an instant. He knew he would face the same problem during the next lecture. It was tempting to skip it, yet the only way he would master his thirst would be to maximise his exposure. There would be plenty of time to hunt under the cover of night. Or, he could just raid a blood bank. Either option, he loathed. It was a choice he wished he didn't have to make.

With long strides, he made his way along the route leading to the maths block. As he turned the corner, a group of girls blocked his path. He slowed down and said, 'excuse me.'

'Don't honey, why don't you stay and chat to us?' A long legged brunette with an American accent gave him a cheesy smile. She was confident and cocky, the worst combination for his current mood.

'Sorry, not today,' he mumbled.

'Awww, he doesn't want to play girls. The English are so polite. I don't bite you know, but you can bite me any day.'

The four girls alongside all burst into giggles as they eyed him up. He felt like a piece of meat.

'Let me through,' he glared, in a loud timbre. The American had no idea what she was up against.

The reaction was instant. The girl's faces transformed and they drew back.

In a less confident tone, the American girl whispered, 'let's get out of the way girls. He's too serious for us.'

It was just like with the man in the hotel. Something about him had scared them. He just did not know what they saw. Whatever it was, it worked. He doubted they'd follow him. Back on route he mulled over his predicament. He drew too much female attention. He had no idea how to change that. As the maths block came into view he took a deep breath. He had no way of knowing if this was going to be difficult.

Once inside, the smell hit him again and he faltered. With complete concentration he continued and eased into a seat at the back of the lecture hall. He did not need any stationery, courtesy of his photographic memory.

The scent was driving him crazy all over again. He leant into his hands and attempted to cover his nose. As he did, he brushed against his canines and realised they had started to extend. The situation was more precarious than he imagined. His eyes focused on the carpeted floor and he did everything he could to calm down. His canines started to retract, and then he noticed Louise.

She sounded genuinely concerned. 'Are you alright? You look ill.'

'I'm fine,' he replied. 'Must have been something I ate.' He could not believe his canines were staring to extend again. The temptation to grab Louise overwhelmed him. With a grunt, he snapped, 'can you leave me alone?'

'Charming.' Her lips curled back. She gripped her rucksack and continued down to the front, he could hear her tut as she went.

In the split second that followed he became aware of several things at once.

First, Caitlin was a few rows away.

Second, he wanted to attack someone – anyone in fact.

Third, his canines were fully extended again.

And fourth, if he did not leave *right now* he would do something he would regret.

***

The sound of the monotonous dial tone echoed down the hall. The phone went unanswered. After going through a collection of old family photographs, Jeff came across one of Judith and him a few months after they first met. It was such a happy picture. A memory of the past, a fragment of life before everything changed. He was sure he was suffering from depression. He did not care. He no longer had the strength to fight. He lay on the couch, closed his eyes and let his memories take him back in time.

The end of the Great War was marked with jubilant celebrations. Aged twenty five, Jeff had returned to a hero's welcome. Every girl in town admired him. He was one of the lucky ones to return. He did not consider himself lucky. He had seen too much bloodshed; a part of him would never be the same. He remembered being overwhelmed, so much admiration and attention. He was tempted to make the most of the situation, but a part of him had died during the war.

A spark of life resurfaced when he met Judith, he only had eyes for her – no-one else stood a chance. From that first glance, he wanted to settle down and have a family with her. She was the woman he wanted to marry. It had happened at a dance. He had so much choice, so many single ladies for so few men. That was the war. Men were few and far between. When he saw Judith he knew.

He did not approach her that night. He did not dare. His parents arranged it instead.

The next day the match was made. Her reaction had amused him. Her cheeks bright crimson as she maintained eye contact. Her amber eyes dotted with gold were almost magical. They only sought to capture his heart further. They had talked under the watchful eye of their families and the pact was made. Everyone realised the inevitable.

They were married six months later.

The phones incessant ring tone continued so Jeff cursed and got up. He could not ignore it anymore. Reluctant, he returned to the present with an aching heart and picked up the receiver.

'Jeff, I need your help.' It was Steven. 'I'm very close to breaking point. What do I do?'

'Calm down. What do you mean, close to breaking point?'

'I nearly attacked someone. The need, it's growing within me. I fed from a deer and it's done nothing to satiate my thirst. It repelled me. What do I do?'

'You have to abstain. You promised me that you could. We told you the risk. We explained that no-one had ever been able to resist humans. If you can't overcome it, you'll have to come back here until we figure out a way.'

'Okay, I get it, but you know what I want. What do you suggest?'

'Come home. We need to talk.'

The line went silent. A minute later, he heard Steven barely reply. He sounded crushed. 'I'll be there in an hour.'

The line went dead.

CHAPTER 25

JEFF'S STORY

Steven gazed up at the house, a relic of the past. He was the youngest descendant of the Roberts family, Jeff the oldest. In theory the young had much to learn from the old. He needed Jeff's guidance. He got his key out, opened the door and made his way in. A pungent, stale smell lingered. With Judith gone, he doubted anyone had bothered to clean.

'Jeff, are you here?'

The lounge floor was covered in newspapers. Old photographs lay on every work surface. The house was a mess. Worse than that, it looked like Jeff had been wallowing in self pity. He did not blame him.

'Welcome back.' Jeff shuffled into the room, a shadow of his former self. He wore a moth-eaten, striped, dressing gown over his pyjamas. His frame had withered, it was obvious he had not fed, and he looked older, much older.

Steven was consumed with guilty. It was his fault. 'You're not doing so well. I'm sorry I have not called sooner.'

Jeff shrugged his shoulders and made his way to the sofa. 'You've been keeping well? You look okay, a bit paler than usual, but better than me, as you can see.'

Steven could not return the smile. He did not find it funny.

'Hungry right?' Jeff raised his eyebrows.

'Famished.' Steven was torn. He needed help, but then again so did Jeff. 'I can always try to figure it out for myself. You look like you need help to.'

Jeff waved off the suggestion with his hand. 'Nonsense! I know what I need and you know what you need. But, I've thought about our situation a lot and I've come up with a theory. Now, hear me out, see what you think.' He pressed his hands together and rubbed them gently.

Steven wondered if he was cold. Was his resistance breaking down? He focused on what Jeff was saying.

'I think the reason we survived out in the Amazon was because we fed off monkeys. Genetically, they are our closest ancestors.'

That was not was Steven was expecting him to say. 'Monkeys? I never even thought of genetics.'

'I wonder if that might help if you don't want to kill anyone. There is a problem, as you can imagine. There are less monkeys here than people. Not exactly mainstream at university, unless you include those that act like monkeys.'

Steven allowed himself to chuckle. His old friend Adam would have qualified. 'Yes. I know what you mean. There is a Zoo close by; I could get one from there. Is it worth a try?'

'Risky again. All monkeys are accounted for, probably even more than people.' Jeff paused, and looked Steven in the eye. 'Is the girl worth it? Tell me the truth, has she moved on? Should you leave her alone?'

Steven did not want to lie, but he had to. He knew full well she had moved on and got herself a new boyfriend. He should just leave her alone. But, then people don't always do what they should. Without further hesitation, he replied, 'Caitlin is worth it, I'll do anything you suggest.'

'Right well, in that case, you'd better get ready to scale some walls. And Steven, don't get caught.'

'I won't,' he reassured, exuding a confidence he did not have. 'You could come with me?'

'In my current state I don't think I'm up to the job. I'll go out in a minute and get something. Two missing monkeys would also give cause for concern.'

'Can I get you anything? You don't look so good.' He did feel responsible.

'No, I'll be fine. I'm just biding my time. Let me know how you get on.'

'I'll come back.' When he got to the door, he glanced back to see Jeff grasping a picture firmly within his hands. His eyes now closed. He didn't look well, at all.

***

As soon as the door slammed, Jeff made his way over to the entrance window. There was no sign of Steven. He mulled over the situation. He hoped he was right. Steven's future was still so uncertain. Judith always had a way of putting a spanner in the works. Why had she been so certain he could be trusted? Was it the guilt she had lived with in denying Emily what she wanted? He could not help wondering if it was right to keep his promise. Steven showed all the signs of failure. Surely, it was not right to endorse murder.

The dry cough that had been plaguing him for a few days started again and he leaned over as it subsided. His limbs felt achy and sore. It was an unfamiliar sensation to feel old. He was sure he was ageing five years a day. The only way to delay it would be to feed again. The problem was animal blood was not helping. He could have gone with Steven. He just did not want to interfere. Steven had to do this on his own.

The dilemma weighed upon his mind. On the one hand, he wondered whether Judith would want him to kill another human on the grounds of helping Steven. On the other, what was the point of killing someone again to extend his life? Just like she had, he embraced death now, welcomed it. His thoughts were jumbled. They bordered on grey; no decision was ever black or white. For the community, he should recover and take Steven back, just to be sure. It was the premise he had foundered. None of them were meant to live outside. And yet, he had made his wife a promise. It was difficult. Nothing was ever easy, not in the long run.

***

Steven started to run. Hidden within the foliage, he followed the route he had taken the previous year when he went to Marwell Zoo with Caitlin. It had been a good day. Under the cover of night, he moved stealthily, just like a ghost. After hardly any time had passed, he scaled the huge walls of the zoo and jumped over the fence. He made it look effortless. Taking a deep breath he let his senses take over as he tracked his prey. At the enclosure, he surveyed the security. It was going to be tricky.

Eyes peeled, ears focused, he kept out of the line of sight of the surveillance cameras. They made a very slight, clicking sound that no ordinary human would have been able to hear. The change had some advantages. Minutes went by before he found the location for the chimpanzees.

He held the lock in his hand, relieved it did not need a key. As he twisted the dial he listened for the click. Each time the click occurred he changed direction. Finally, the lock gave way. He slipped it off and loosened the catch. Quick as a flash, he grabbed the nearest animal, broke its neck and eased out. As he locked the door he felt sorry for the family left behind. They would miss their companion.

Desperate, he hid in the corner, one of the few blind spots on offer. Without hesitation, he sank his extended fangs into his kill. The taste was different to deer. It was richer, deeper, more filling. Jeff might have been right. This could have been the reason why the Amazon offered them such a fulfilling diet. The burning sensation that had been driving him crazy eased and he made his way out of the area with the dead body. He did not want to leave any evidence behind. He watched and listened. He could not let his guard down now.

Once he was a few miles from the zoo he stopped and checked the dead animal. It looked peaceful – that was the only consolation. A building site came into view so he picked up a shovel that had been left in the corner and took it with him to bury the animal in the dense undergrowth of the nearby forest. He dug a deep hole, laid the animal inside, and covered it up. He added some loose bark and leaves on top as a finishing touch. He had done as much as he could.

On his way back to the house, he tried to put what he had done behind him. His grandfather had been right to question him. He should leave Caitlin alone and go back to the Amazon, to his new life. She had moved on. Steven was too stubborn. He did not want to lose his humanity. He was naïve enough to believe that his determination and will power could overcome his nature.

*

The sight of Jeff on the couch startled Steven. In the few

hours he had been gone, Jeff had got worse. He looked skeletal, practically a corpse. And he was not moving.

'Jeff, are you alright?'

Jeff groaned as his eyes blinked. He barely managed to get them open.

'Jeff, you look terrible, you should be in bed.' Steven picked him up and carried him to the bedroom. Regardless of his strength, he knew Jeff was too light. He was dying.

'Why are you carrying me?' he whispered.

'You are weak,' Steven replied.

What he said next startled Steven. 'I'm sorry. I don't want to live anymore. Not without Judith.'

'I'm sorry too. This is my fault. Okay, look, let's get you comfortable.'

The bedroom was dishevelled to say the least. Steven placed Jeff on the bed and tried to fluff the covers to make him comfortable. Judith had been in the same position not that long ago.

Jeff opened his eyes again and patted the bed. When Steven sat down, Jeff held his hand like a vice. 'I have something to tell you. I promised Judith I would tell you. It's time for the truth.'

'What truth?' Steven had no idea what he was talking about.

Jeff blinked slowly, his eyes sad. 'No-one knows what I'm about to tell you. Well, except Emily, Judith always thought she suspected the truth. That's why Emily was so angry with us. We could have helped her – and we didn't. We just lied to her, told her it was not possible.'

'Slow down, you're not well. Can I get you something first? Water?'

'No, no. Listen. I don't have much time. After you hear this, you can decide whether to let the others know. I have kept the secret for a long time.'

Steven wondered what he could possibly have to say. There was no way he could have prepared himself for what he was about to hear.

'Judith was not infected by the bats, I created her.'

Steven leant back and let go of Jeff's hand. The revelation

whirled in his head. It was not possible. Was it? 'How? And why would you keep something like that a secret?'

'Why do you think?' Jeff started to cough.

'I'll get some water.' Steven needed a few minutes to digest it. He went downstairs and got the glass of water. All the time he wondered if it could possibly be true. It was no surprise it had been kept a secret – it was too big a deal.

Back in the room, he passed Jeff the glass and propped his head up to help him take a sip.

When the glass was safely on the bedside table, Steven repeated the question. 'So, why didn't you tell the others? Didn't you trust them?'

'It was not a question of trust. I didn't want them to see Judith differently. I didn't want them to see us as fictional vampires? It could have got out of hand. That was why I alienated the community and imposed restrictions. I could not let others do what I had done. It was hard for Judith to keep the secret from Emily. When she saw how you suffered she knew there had to be another way. Like I had done all those years earlier, she wanted you to have the choice. That was why she made me promise to stay with you.'

'To help me change Caitlin?' he asked, as the penny dropped.

'Exactly,' he croaked. 'You are so sharp, just like your mother. From the first day I met you and you called us vampires I knew you wouldn't be fooled. I knew you'd discover the truth somehow. And here we are. I don't have much time. You need to listen. Hopefully, it will work again. Just promise me something. Make sure she is willing. Judith was not given the choice – it just happened. You *must* give Caitlin the choice.'

As Jeff continued, Steven listened in awe. He had never considered the possibility of making Caitlin like him. It was impossible, and yet a major result. It had taken a lot of effort for Jeff to tell the tale. Steven noticed him relax after he got the last words out. Now Steven knew everything he needed to know.

Near the end Jeff appeared at ease, he invited death to take

173

him to his beloved wife. Steven watched as his breathing became light and random, his eyes closed. Jeff had saved the last of his energy to fulfil Judith's request. He gave a final gasp, convulsed and became still. It was over. He could rest in peace.

He could not believe what he had just been told – it was a lifeline.

He picked up a blanket and covered the body. There would be plenty of time to deal with the burial. He would make sure his grandfather's wishes were followed and bury him next to Judith. He could not tell the others yet. It would rock the community further. Their father and mentor had died. He had to keep it from them. He needed more time. He gave the blanket a last glance, walked into the corridor and made his way downstairs.   As he did, he considered his next course of action.

Could he really do what Jeff had proposed?

Was it selfish to change the life of the person he loved? It did not feel selfish if she was willing.

That was the crux of the issue.

Would Caitlin ever be willing?

In time, he would be able to win her affections. The thing was time was not something he had a lot of. There had to be a way to get Caitlin back. There had to be a way for her to see him like she used to. She had also fallen in love with him, of that he was sure. And in the recesses of her mind her subconscious would have to find a way to bring it all back.

Steven would have to find a way.

CHAPTER 26

WATERPOLO

Caitlin ran down the stairs and hoisted her bag over her back at the sound of the doorbell, waterpolo beckoned. Without a second thought, she opened the door. With her hand on the handle her eyes jumped out of their sockets as she saw who it was. Daniel smiled and held out an impressive selection of flowers. His jeans and black leather jacket hung perfectly off his frame.

She gawped and focused on the flowers. Orange and yellow freesias drowned within gypsaphelia, wrapped in clear cellophane and a huge pink bow. She looked up at his face. His perfectly groomed, shoulder length chestnut hair surrounded a tanned complexion. It made him look Mediterranean, even though he was born in the outskirts of London and had never ventured further than Scotland. It was the twinkle in his chestnut eyes and the dimples in his cheeks that brought her back to reality.

'Ahhh…,' Caitlin screamed, the bag now discarded on the floor. She flung herself at him and they hugged. She leant her head back and found his lips. The kiss was the hungry sort. Before it got out of hand she pulled back and slapped him lightly on the chest. 'What are you doing here? You nearly gave me a heart attack!'

'I can go back if you like?' he teased, a cheeky grin pasted on his face.

'No, you can't. Come in here, I've missed you.' She grabbed his hand and pulled him in the house. She could not help kissing him again, before a familiar loud cough interrupted them.

Caitlin pulled away and pouted at Gemma who was standing on the staircase with her arms folded, eyes alight, mouth in a half smile.

'Don't mean to interrupt. It's just that the doorbell sounded again. It's a busy night by the looks of it. Shall I get it?'

Caitlin blushed and quickly added, 'no, it's for me.'

Daniel held her hand fast, but she still managed to slip out of his grasp. She had no idea how she was going to concentrate on the match now.

***

Gemma unfolded her arms. 'You must be Daniel then?'

'Yes, nice to meet you.' He did not turn to face her, eyes glued on Caitlin.

The signs were loud and clear, he was totally besotted. Gemma did a head to toe analysis. Nice clothes, cute features, tight butt. Impressive, Caitlin had come good at last.

Caitlin turned back and gave Daniel a pleading, lost puppy, kind of look. 'I have to go for a waterpolo match. Do you want to come and watch?'

Gemma could have laughed aloud. There was no chance he would let up on the opportunity to spot girls in swimsuits, especially when one of them was Caitlin.

No surprise that Daniel replied, 'I'd love to see you play. Do I need to drive?'

Gemma grinned. All men were the same.

'No, there's room for you in the car. Come on, let's go or we'll be late,' Caitlin said, as she reached out for his hand.

Gemma stood in the doorway and watched them dash out, scramble into the car and whizz off. Now you see them, now you don't. The sound of footsteps made her look in the other direction. She could not believe her luck when she saw who was passing by. Regardless of the slippers, she shuffled out in pursuit. 'Simon, is that you?'

He turned to face her. She nearly melted. Daniel was gold, Simon was a diamond.

The sound of his voice was delicious. 'Gemma isn't it? I was just heading into campus.'

'Do you want to join me for that drink now instead?' She knew she was being forward, but it had never hurt before. And she *really* wanted to get to know him better.

Her stomach flipped as he smiled. He was something else. When he made his way towards her, she knew she had caught a big fish – look, line and sinker.

***

Steven could not believe the boyfriend was in Southampton. He kicked a stone in anger as he saw Gemma's head pop out. He could not retract the image of Caitlin holding *his* hand. He had even got all spruced up. Best shirt, jeans, brown leather jacket, gel in his hair. It was a wasted effort. His plan to befriend Caitlin had fallen flat on its face. It had all been for nothing. Gemma brought a different possibility to the forefront. It could be worth hanging around, a drink couldn't hurt.

'So, what are you up to? You look nice.' Gemma's eyes drifted from his head to toe.

Steven wondered if she was the predatory type. 'Like I said, I was heading for campus. I'm the new kid in town so I've got to make an effort.'

Gemma flicked her head to the side and posed. It looked silly when you took into account the dinosaur slippers. 'Oh, right, I forgot. So, what can I get you? Do you want a beer?'

As he stepped across the threshold he breathed deeply. Caitlin had just walked through here, he was sure he could distinguish her scent along with another unwelcome manly one. He focused on the question. 'Sure, a beer would be nice.' He had to be polite. He suspected Gemma wanted to get him drunk; he would not let it happen.

'This way then,' Gemma said, as she made her way to the back.

The house was a narrow mid terraced property so as expected the kitchen was at the back. It had seen better days. The paintwork was peeling and he noticed a range of stains smudged into the living room walls. He did not want to ask, he suspected the worst. 'Nice place you have here.' He hoped he sounded sincere.

'Thanks, it's not the Ritz but it does the job.'

The Ritz it certainly was not. 'Like your slippers by the way, very funky.'

Gemma turned to face him, the hint of blush on her cheeks. 'Fashion statement…'

'It's a good one.'

He was not sure she bought it. Either way, she turned to the fridge and produced two beers. In a well practiced manoeuvre, she flipped off the lids on the table top and handed one over.

'Cheers, to new friends.'

The way her eyes stayed on his left him under no doubt, friendship was an afterthought.

'Cheers, nice one.' The beer was cold. It was the best he could hope for. He had never really been into booze like other students. It was nice, but then water was nice too. He wasn't going to let Gemma know what he really thought just yet.

'So, Simon, I hear from Caitlin that you are a maths genius, true or not?'

'Has she been talking about me then?' As soon as the words left his mouth he wished he could take them back.

'You could say that,' Gemma said, lips pursed. 'So, are you?'

His mind whirled as he considered the implication. 'Sorry, am I what?'

Gemma put the beer on the worktop and used her arms to hoist herself up to sit down. She laughed as she repeated the question. 'Are you a maths genius?'

'Oh. I guess so, I don't know, define genius?' It was his turn to play with words, he was actually enjoying himself.

'Touché. Anyway, she doesn't trust you and she has a boyfriend so don't get your hopes up. I on the other hand am totally available, lucky you.' Gemma batted her eyelids and ran her hand through her hair.

Her frankness caught him off guard. He could have tried to cover up, but he suspected Gemma was one step ahead of him. 'Lucky me, so why did you say that then?'

She slid off the table and made to move towards him. 'What that I was available? That's obvious don't you think?'

He stalled her by talking quickly. 'No, not that, we can get to that *later*. You said Caitlin does not trust me? Why?'

Gemma narrowed her eyes. 'Oh, I don't know. She said

some weird stuff about you knowing her name before she'd told you or something. So, did you know her already?' She took a step closer.

'No, why would I?' He knew he probably came across defensive.

'Why would you indeed?' Gemma hummed, now an arm's length away. 'Anyway, enough about her, I'd like to join your study sessions if that's alright?'

Steven was sure this was a set up. 'Sure, why not?' He moved away from her to the table and picked up the coaster, a picture of a dolphin. It had to be Caitlin's. 'So, are you coming out to campus with me?'

Gemma stopped but her eyes followed. He was sure she was surprised he had walked away. She half smiled. 'Sure.'

He needed to get out of there. He was not sure that staying alone with Gemma was a good plan. He suspected she was Caitlin's best friend. He did not want to hurt someone Caitlin considered a friend. Three times would be heartless.

***

The sound of splashing reverberated off the walls of the pool enclosure. The match was fierce and pretty even. They were losing by one goal to the visitors. Caitlin eyed up the location of the ball and swam quickly to the open space.

'To me,' she called out, waving frantically.

The ball found its way to her outstretched hand as she leapt out of the water. In an effortless manoeuvre, she swam with the ball ahead of her towards the goal. She was quickly flanked by two other girls jostling for the ball. Before they had a chance to steal it back, she grabbed it with one hand and took aim. The ball flew through the air at a perfect angle and fell into the corner of the net as the goalie failed to block it.

The whistle sounded and the girls cheered aloud and retook their starting positions. Caitlin glanced in Daniel's direction at the side of the pool. He winked at her. He looked impressed. The whistle restarted the game and the pace quickened again as both sides sought to take control of the ball. Finally, one of the girls on Caitlin's team threw the ball towards Caitlin. In a quick flip pass, Caitlin passed it to a girl waiting near the goal.

A second later, another goal was scored to the sound of further celebrations.

After they regrouped again the whistle blew to restart the game. The opposing team fought to keep the ball in their possession but were thwarted by the sound of the final whistle. Caitlin's team had won.

'You were amazing,' Daniel gushed, as Caitlin came out of the changing rooms.

A few girls had come out with her. They raised their eyebrows and nudged Caitlin. 'Have a good night then,' one called out laughing.

Caitlin slid her hand into his and they made their way out to the car and got in before anyone else could make any other comments.

Caitlin sat in the back with Daniel. 'Hey, Stephanie thanks a lot.'

'So, are you staying long?' Stephanie asked, from the driver's seat. She was a tall, muscular girl with short hair and boyish features.

'Just for the weekend,' Daniel replied.

Stephanie glanced at the other girl in the driver's seat. 'That's nice. I didn't know your boyfriend was coming down for the weekend Caitlin. You kept that one quiet.'

'He surprised me actually,' Caitlin said, she giggled.

'That's so sweet. I need a man who makes romantic gestures like that. Where can I find one Daniel?'

'Err…,' he replied blankly.

'Don't worry, I don't need an answer,' Stephanie guffawed; she kept her eyes on the road.

Caitlin squeezed his hand gently and he started to trace circles around her wrist. It drove her crazy. Reacting to the slow sensation, she leant her head on his shoulder and closed her eyes.

Finally, they arrived back.

'Thanks again for the lift, Steph; I'll see you next week.'

She gave the car horn a quick toot before joking to the other girl left in the car, 'someone's going to get lucky tonight, I think.' Raucous, they drove off.

'Sorry about them,' Caitlin said. She was sure her cheeks were on fire.

'It's alright.' Daniel shrugged and put his arm over her shoulder.

Once inside, Caitlin turned the lights on and called out for Gemma. After no reply, she turned to Daniel. 'I guess she's gone out.'

'I guess she has.'

Caitlin was sure there were live creatures squirming in her stomach; it was an excruciating yet pleasurable experience. 'Would you like some tea or something to eat?'

'Tea sounds good, and I am actually hungry. I'm easy, anything is good for me.' His eyes delved into hers.

Caitlin marched towards the kitchen and put on the kettle to boil. She was becoming anxious. She was alone with Daniel for the first time. A small, yet poignant fact had started to dawn on her. There was no-one but them around to put the brakes on things developing further.

CHAPTER 27

FEEDING TIME

Caitlin started to open the cupboards for inspiration. She had no idea what she was going to cook. Her food cupboard was pretty bare. All she had was a packet of penne pasta. 'I have pasta.'

'Pasta's good.'

She breathed a sigh of relief and then realised she could not serve pasta on its own. She made her way to the fridge and despaired when she saw the measly supplies. 'We have butter and cheese. Is that okay?'

'Don't stress. I came to see you not to be fed. It's fine.' Daniel eased up next to her and wrapped his arms around her. 'Can I eat you instead?'

'Maybe later,' she stalled. She tried to keep calm. It was difficult, very difficult. They had been inseparable over Christmas. It was too easy to continue where they left off, and they had been so close.

He let his hands drop to her waist, tickled her tummy and gave her a quick peck. 'Harsh woman...let me make the tea then.'

'Fair enough,' she replied, as she twirled around to release herself from his grasp. She took out a packet of pasta from the cupboard. Then she found a pan, scooped two large handfuls of pasta from the packet and put them in before filling the pan with water so that the pasta was just covered. She waited for the water to boil as Daniel got busy making the tea.

'Sugar?' Daniel asked.

'No. Not for me. Thanks.'

'No, I meant do you have any sugar?' He smiled.

'Oh, somewhere, I think, unless Gemma's finished it. She has a sweet tooth,' she laughed. 'It should be in that

Tupperware.'

Daniel found the right one and put two sugars in his tea. He handed her a mug, sugar free. 'There you go. I've made myself useful.'

'Yes, you have.' She could feel his glare burning into her again. She stirred the pasta. It was nowhere near boiling point so she increased the temperature.

She got out the cheese and a grater and started to get it ready. Her hand shook slightly as she worked. She sipped her tea, it had a calming effect.

The sound of overflowing water snapped her out of it. She rushed to the pasta, stirred and lowered the heat.

Daniel had started to read the student bulletin on the table.

She had no idea what to talk to him about. She got the feeling neither of them really wanted to talk. She willed the pasta to cook.

Daniel took his mug to the sink and rinsed it out. 'Are you okay? You are quieter than usual.'

Caitlin wondered whether she should tell him how terrified she actually was. 'I'm fine, it's the chlorine. It always makes me tired.'

'Oh. Okay.' Daniel sat back down again.

Caitlin waited for another question. When none came she was surprised. Gemma would have been onto her. Did he actually believe she was tired?

The pasta looked ready, so she drained it, put a dollop of butter in and swished it round. Then she got two bowls and served Daniel a bigger portion. Then she sprinkled the cheese on top. 'It's not gourmet, but its food.' She handed him a fork and spoon.

'Thanks.' He started to tuck in.

She sat down and followed suit. She was hungry but self conscious. A minute later his bowl was empty. Caitlin still had most of it to go. She hated the fact she could hear her every mouthful. She had forgotten to put some music on, she cursed inwardly.

Daniel stood up. 'Do you mind if I make another cup of tea?'

She swallowed her mouthful quickly and shook her head. 'No, go ahead.'

He put the kettle on again and leant against the counter, arms folded. He watched her again. 'Do you have any music?'

'Yeah, in the lounge, there's a docking station.'

'Can I put something on?' He got up to move.

'Sure.'

In the time he was away Caitlin stuffed her mouth full of pasta and ate as quickly as she could. She hated being watched, especially when she was eating.

The sound of Bruno Mars filtered through, a second later Daniel came back in.

'Are you still hungry? I just remembered I have an emergency packet of biscuits.'

'No, I'm fine. Come here.' He held out his hand.

She put her hand in his and he pulled her towards him and started to sing the lyrics. The fact the topic of marriage was in the song unnerved her, a lot. He leant in to kiss her. Their teeth clashed for a second before his tongue roamed. The kiss was getting very heated. Caitlin pulled back. She did like to kiss him, but she was at odds. She had no idea why.

'I think I need a choccy biscuit. Come on they're in my room.' She held his hand and pulled him along.

He gave her a very sexy smile and followed. It was then she realised what she was doing, but it was too late to back down.

'This is my room,' Caitlin said, as she twirled around. She felt kind of childish, giddy.

'Nice shark posters.' There was a hint of sarcasm in his tone. 'Hope they don't bite.'

'No chance.' She giggled and hated the fact she did. Why was she so twitchy? 'Did you want a biscuit?'

'Not really,' he said, as he eased up to her and wrapped his arms around her. His forehead practically touched hers and he just stared into her eyes. 'Are you okay about me being here? I can sleep on the couch you know. We don't have to do anything you're not happy with.'

Caitlin felt herself relax. 'Can we just snuggle on the bed and watch some telly. I'm shattered and...well, nervous.'

'Caitlin. Why are you nervous? I would never rush you.' He let go and jumped on her bed. 'So, what are we watching?'

Caitlin let out a chuckle. She did not know why she thought he would do anything she wasn't ready for. It was silly really.

Daniel folded his hands behind his head. 'I think I might have a biscuit after all, if you don't mind.'

'Sure,' Caitlin picked up the packet from the shelf and gave it to him. Then she turned to put the telly on. She hoped it would be a comedy night. 'More tea?'

'Do you have any beers?'

'I think so, I'll go check.' At the door, she glanced back and saw Daniel had made himself comfortable, his eyes transfixed on the telly.

A few minutes later, she came back with two beers. She had raided Gemma's supply. She would replace them before she noticed.

'Here you go.'

Daniel grabbed the beer and took a slug. A thank you would've been nice.

'Do you want one?' Daniel asked, as he held out the practically empty packet of biscuits.

'Thanks,' she replied. She nibbled it slowly and edged on to the bed.

'You're not on a diet, right?' Daniel asked, as though he had noticed she was barely eating it.

She put the biscuit down, appetite gone. Did he think she was on one, or should be on one? 'No.'

'Neither am I, don't believe in them. Do enough exercise and you don't have to worry about what you eat.'

Caitlin nodded.

'You don't need to diet at all, you are well fit.' He did not look at her as he said it.

She could not hold back the smile. He thought she was *fit*.

'Come here then.' He held out his arms and looked at her.

She eased up along the bed and snuggled into his arms. It was really comfy.

'You know I have a great party trick.'

Curious, Caitlin turned to face him. 'Really?'

He took the last two biscuits out of the packet and placed them in his mouth.

'Aww, that's gross,' she laughed.

He looked like a hamster as he struggled to chew them. He took a huge gulp of his beer as his face resumed normality. 'I don't suggest you try that.'

'As if,' she scoffed, now in hysterics.

'Did you want to go out at all?' he asked.

'Nah, we can just chill here if you want.' Was Gemma right all along? Was it natural to want to jump his bones?

'That'll be great.'

She felt her cheeks burn. The way he watched her left her in no doubt as to his intent to do more than watch television. She could not lie. She hoped they would do more. The thought scared her to death.

***

Steven walked alongside Gemma. It had been an interesting night. She had drunk a few too many and was slouched against him, arm linked in his.

They made their way up the path leading to the house. 'Right then, well, have a good night,' he said, as he backed off.

Gemma lunged at him and kissed him on the lips, her hands entwined in his hair. She tasted of alcohol and cigarettes, both habits he preferred to avoid. He pulled her off and tried not to look disgusted.

'Best be off now,' he said.

She tried to lean in, but he stopped her. 'You need to go to sleep now. Go to bed.'

Her confused demeanour vanished; it was replaced with a look of obedience. 'Of course, I must go to bed.'

She fumbled with the keys, managed to put the right one in the keyhole and she practically fell through the door. He did not like to use mind control, but in this case it was warranted. The last thing he needed was Caitlin's best friend badmouthing him for rejecting her advances. He made his way to the end of the terrace on the opposite side of the road, leapt up and hid amongst the old chimney stacks. Then he made his way over to the one facing their house.

He had been reduced to stalking. He *needed* to know if Caitlin was with *the boyfriend*. It had been bugging him all night. He clenched his fists. He could not do this. He made his way back to the end of the terrace, leapt down and decided to go for a walk – a long one.

An hour later he returned, unable to keep away. A light was on in one of the bedrooms. A huge oak tree stood majestically opposite the house, but it had no leaves to give him any cover. He retraced his steps and resumed his position amongst the chimney stacks of the opposite Victorian house. From the vantage point he could see Caitlin on her bed, as he suspected she was not alone. They were lying down together – still clothed. That was a relief. The boyfriend was holding her against him as they watched something, probably television. It should have been him with her. A jealous rage overcame him and he fought against the urge to go over and get rid of whoever it was.

This was the reason she was ignoring him – *he* was the reason.

As he mulled over what he should do, his eyes nearly popped out of their sockets as he saw them kissing just as the lights turned off.

A split second later he was on his feet. If anyone looked up now they would see him standing on the roof. He did not care. Taking a leap of faith he lunged towards the roof of her house and flew across the road. He landed in silence. He did not know he could do that. Hunched against the roof tiles, he concentrated hard to hear what he knew he should run away from. The sound of kissing became audible and he groaned. It was leading to more. His expression pained as he heard someone else make love to his woman.

A few minutes later he raised his head in surprise.

She had uttered a name.

His.

CHAPTER 28

CAUGHT OUT

In a dazed state, Caitlin noticed Daniel freeze.

Daniel frowned, rolled off her and stared up at the ceiling. 'Who's Steven?'

'What?' she asked, just as confused.

'Steven, you just said *Steven*,' he repeated, anger starting to seep into his tone.

'I don't know why I said that. It-it just popped out of my mouth. I swear I don't know anyone called that. I don't know why I just said that.' Her thoughts were in disarray.

Daniel barely moved a muscle. 'Can you turn the light on?'

The moment was gone. He was not buying it. She thought she remembered Steven, but there was no way she'd admit her bizarre dreams.

'Sure,' she replied. She reached out whilst holding the covers over herself.

As the light came on, they momentarily squinted and an awkward silence ensued.

'Can I ask you something?' Daniel asked, bitter. 'Have you slept with someone before?'

Caitlin could not believe she was hearing right. 'What do you mean? As in, have I done it before?'

Daniel sat up and folded his arms. 'Yes.'

'No, of course not, you're the first.' Now it was her turn to get angry. She could not believe what he was insinuating.

'The thing is,' he started. He sounded suspicious. 'It did not feel like that was your first time. Trust me I have been with someone who was a virgin and you are not. It sounded like this Steven was the guy who popped your cherry.'

'What are you saying? Are you calling me a liar?' She sat up, appalled. She could feel the constriction on her throat as the tears welled up.

He turned away from her and put his feet on the floor. 'You say you haven't been with anyone when it's pretty obvious you have.'

'How is it obvious?' she retorted, angry now.

Looking at the window, he could not look at her as he said. 'Are you bleeding?'

'I don't know, err…no, I don't think so. What does that have to do with it?'

'You should have been, if it was your first time.' The reply was to the point. He got off the bed; put his pants and trousers back on and started to button his shirt. 'I'm sorry, I shouldn't have come. I'll go back and leave you to think about things. For now though, we're over. I don't like to be deceived.'

This was desperate. She had no idea what had just happened. 'Please, don't go, I don't know who Steven is…,' she said. In mid plea, her expression changed as she saw the face in her mind. The face she loved. A face she knew well. It did not make sense. It was Steven, or was it Simon? It was so confusing. Yet, the face had been a dream, nothing more. She was still a virgin. Nothing made sense.

Daniel grimaced as he studied her confusion.

When the door slammed shut, she threw her face in her hands and crawled in a ball under her covers. The sound of the front door slamming resounded in her head. How had a magical night gone so wrong? She felt like she was going crazy.

***

Steven watched Daniel storm out of the entrance and drive off in his car. A smile inadvertently graced his face. At least he was out of the picture now. He yearned to comfort Caitlin, to wrap his arms around her and tell her that everything was going to be okay. He wanted to explain that she was not insane. He knew he had been right to come back for her, it was not over. If only he could tell her the truth.

Suddenly, the obvious hit and he laughed.

There was nothing to stop him from telling her the truth. Only the truth could get him back into her heart. He knew a way to get her to remember, he had known how to do it for some time now. He just did not realise its potential. It had to be worth a try.

Caitlin's tears ebbed and became a muffled moan. He heard Gemma stumble in to comfort her, but in her inebriated state she was not the most sympathetic. Caitlin told her she was fine and just wanted to be alone. He heard Gemma yelp as she bashed into something a minute later. Shortly after, the light went out.

Steven was tired of sitting on the roof. Indecision clouded his judgment. The black clear sky dotted with twinkling lights above was fascinating; he had studied all of the star systems several times. He had to wait. Soon, she would be fast asleep. He longed to see her peaceful face.

He eased off the roof and climbed towards the window ledge outside her room. He was amazed at the amount of grip his fingertips had against the walls. He made a quick decision and pushed up the sash window. It made a loud cracking sound as it opened. He looked around and climbed in quickly. Then he lowered it again, it made less noise now. He stood frozen by the window and listened. All he could hear was Caitlin's steady breathing.

He tiptoed over to the bed. She was lying on her front partly covered by her duvet. Her hair was swept to her side leaving her neck exposed. It would be so easy for him to take advantage of the situation. He knew what to do now to make her his.

Instead, he knelt down next to her, placed his hands on her head and sent out his thoughts in the manner Eilif had described during a hypnotic lesson. At the time, he had been a reluctant student – the art of hypnosis, memory repression and recall was not a life skill he thought he would need. He was wrong about that. With luck he would do it right.

He concentrated hard on the memories they shared.

The first time they'd met and she'd dropped her bag, their first kiss and the first time they made love. It flooded through him in a wave. He remembered the last night they were together when she had heard the truth about his past, and then he filled her in on his journey to Brazil.

He stopped there. She did not need to know about the rest yet.

The main thing he wanted her to know was that he still loved her and that he did not mean her any harm. Gently, he eased his hand away from her head and took a seat in the corner of the room. When she woke, she would have a lot of questions.

***

The amber eyes, speckled with streaks of gold, entranced her as she leaned in. His firm hold, athletic build and mesmerizing smile turned Caitlin to jelly. She could not hold back a gasp as the kiss became more intense and they started to explore one another. As his hand eased under her top she tensed. Eager to respond, she traced her finger along his back. The way he shivered made her smile. In a wanton trance, they started to peel back the layers of clothing. It was too much – he was too much.

Then the visions started to appear, one after the other, just like a movie. Events in her life that looked so real. Playing pool with Steven; going for a walk with Steven; holding hands with Steven – her memories of Steven. How could she be dreaming something like this, and why?

Her subconscious drifted further into the unknown. All of a sudden the ground swayed and she realised she was sat on a boat surrounded by dense undergrowth. It had the appearance of a desolate and almost prehistoric place. She was sure she had never been there, it just seemed like she was. It was like travelling back in time. She was definitely hallucinating. She could not understand where she was going and then it hit her that she was not going anywhere. It was Steven. He had gone there. She did not know how she knew it was him, she just did.

The scene flicked over again. Steven stood in front of her, soaked to the skin. She leapt against him, so excited to see him again, and could not resist. She had missed him. The feel of his body against hers awakened the raw passion, the lust. She wanted to touch him; she wanted him to touch her. She needed him. She knew him. She was in love with him.

The thought made her rouse, almost in shock, as reality took hold.

She turned in her bed and curled up in a ball. Was she in love with Steven? How was that possible? The dreams always annoyed her, but this one was different. Most of them ended at the good bit, but this time the realisation hit her hard – the good bit had actually happened. It was not a dream. Steven was not a stranger. *This* dream was different. It was real. She just had no idea how it could be real.

Steven's look of despair haunted her. It was weird he had turned up at her door all those months ago. It freaked her out when Steven tried to come in uninvited. Even so, she had never seen anyone so broken. Steven was adamant she knew him; he had even left her a note. He hoped she'd remember him. Did she remember him?

She did not understand what had happened on the previous night. Why would she call out Steven's name whilst making love to Daniel? Daniel was her boyfriend. She loved Daniel. At least she thought she did, until she called out a different name. It was weird, shameful. She had no idea what she would say to Daniel when she next saw him. Was there anything she could say? Was there any explanation she could give that would make everything alright? She doubted it.

With a larger stretch, she spread her arms and legs over the tiny single bed. Her raging mind had woken her up. She did not want to think what the time was. Reluctant, she turned on her back to face the ceiling and slowly opened her eyes. It was still dark. As her eyes adjusted, a strange shadow in the corner on the room caught her eye. Her heartbeat accelerated as she moved her head a fraction and realised she was not alone. Braced to scream, the light turned on.

Confused, she blinked and rubbed her eyes. Then she sprang to a sitting position and gawped, speechless. It was him. Steven was actually in her room. Then again, she could still be in the dream.

'Caitlin,' the familiar voice said.

It was not a dream.

Eyes fixed on the blue and purple covers she replayed the scenes in her mind. She had been in love, besotted in fact, with Steven. That was his real name. Not Simon. It had all gone so wrong. She had been so scared. Those men, they told a story about Steven. She remembered wondering if her life was in danger. The person she thought she knew was a stranger. Steven was not normal. Worse than that, he was going to become a killer. Her eyes widened as she contemplated the thought – had he already become one? She gripped the covers tighter and looked up to face him.

There was no doubt in her mind. He was Simon. Simon was Steven. Steven was Simon.

She had seen things through his eyes. She had felt all of his concerns and emotions. It reminded her of how she'd felt the previous year. Inexplicably sad, as though a part of her had been broken. She remembered now. She remembered when they had made love for the first time. She knew it was all true. Her dreams were true. Steven had been her boyfriend, her first love. She was not a virgin. Daniel had been right to accuse her.

'Don't be scared,' Steven said. His voice was soothing, not threatening.

Indecision overcame her and she fought back the urge to scream. She could not do anything. She could not speak, she was paralysed. She sat without making a noise and stared, still in shock. Only when she saw him blink and move his hand did she believe that he was real and not just a figment of her imagination. He looked back without saying a word. His face was kind, patient – loving. None of it made any sense.

CHAPTER 29

STEVEN OR SIMON?

Caitlin fought the urge to pounce. A part of her wanted to bash his lights out, the other to kiss him. The memory of the dream remained. She suppressed her desire. He was a liar and she intended to find out why. She shook her head and frowned, then blurted out. 'Your name is Steven not Simon. Why did you lie to me?'

'Do you remember me now?' He sounded tentative, worried.

She was taken aback. *He* sounded unsure of himself. 'Yes, I-I remember you,' she answered, as she released the bed sheets. 'I don't understand anything. I-I should call the police. Breaking and entering is against the law.'

He spoke with a trace of humour. 'You should. I am a dangerous criminal that should be apprehended.' She remembered that crooked smile.

'How did you get in?'

Steven smiled. 'The window.'

She leapt out of bed and looked out of the window. 'It's high!'

'I'm very good at climbing walls.'

She became aware of her snoopy pyjamas. She was not expecting company after what had happened. She took cover behind the curtains and studied him. 'Why are you here?'

His scrunched his eyes together. 'Do you remember?'

'I just had the weirdest dream. It *seemed* real. Was it?'

After a few seconds, he replied. 'It was real.' His eyes furrowed, his smile replaced by a frown.

'How?' She could not stand being so close to him anymore. She turned away and sat on the furthest corner of the bed. She needed some space.

She could see him sway as if to get up. Then he stopped and sat still. 'It was all true. That's why I left. They took away my life, my existence. Everyone forgot me, including you.'

She swallowed as the words sunk in. Someone had erased her mind. It all started to make sense. 'But how did I forget everything? How did everyone forget everything?'

'It's just something some of us can do,' he shrugged.

The words rang in her head *some of us*. 'How many of you are there?' What she really wanted to ask was what are you? She still had time for that.

His eyes met hers. They sparkled, amused. 'That's a good question. I don't know. It'll take some explaining.'

'I'll bet,' she sneered. She did not want to be nasty, but she was angry as well as confused. She brushed her face with her hand, her eyes narrowed. 'What are you doing in my maths class? The Steven I knew hated maths. He wanted to be a lawyer.'

He chuckled. 'I never intended to become one of the typical blood-sucking corporate types. I wanted to help people. Remember?'

She was glad he thought she was funny.

'Is it really you?' She leant forward, tempted to get up and reach out to him again.

He matched her and leaned closer, practically off the seat. 'Yes, it's me. I had to find a way to get close to you. I seem to be quite good at math now, don't you think?'

This was definitely not funny.

'Too good for my liking, it was nice to have something I was better at.' She half smiled, she enjoyed their banter. 'Why did you make me remember?'

He stood up and made his way around the bed. 'Can I sit next to you, please?'

'Sure,' she chirped, her voice over the top and way too keen. She should have been saying no. She would be a fool to let him get close. Yet, she was. She couldn't say no.

He sat down, reached out his hand and entwined his fingers in hers. She could not pull back. His touch was unbelievable. With his other hand, he raised her chin, lifted her head up towards his and looked into her eyes. 'Isn't it obvious?'

Before she knew what was happening, he pressed his lips against hers. It was just a light brush, but it was enough to send an electric shock pulsing through her body. She pulled back in surprise. 'Sorry.' She felt like an idiot.

'Don't apologise.'

She wondered if he had felt it too. 'What was that?'

He gave a half smile. The smile that made her knees tremble. She remembered now. It was all flooding back.

'Just us,' he mused. 'There's a lot of tension between us.'

'Is there?' Her voice was barely above a whisper.

'Can I see if it happens again?' he asked, a deep penetrating look in his eyes.

'For experimental purposes only?' There was no way she could refuse.

'Of course.'

He leaned in and took her face in his hands. Then he kissed her again. His tongue caressed hers and she could not stop herself from responding. She gasped aloud as they explored each other. It was just like the dream. It would have been a travesty for something this good to exist only in her imagination.

After about a minute they simultaneously paused for air.

'Caitlin.' He ran his hand through her hair. 'I missed you.'

The words caused a ripple effect that broke down every defence. She took a huge breath as the dam in her throat collapsed. Tears of joy, of heartache, of longing – everything, nothing, they were all rolled into one.

He cupped her face. 'Don't cry on my account.'

The fact he thought that made her cry harder. The sobs continued and she fought to get out the words. After a minute, she calmed down enough to stammer. 'W-Why d-did you tell me the t-truth?'

'I don't know,' he replied, his arms like a vice around her.

In his arms she felt like she'd been enveloped in a ray of sunshine. Even though upset, she could not help the feeling of ecstasy. His warmth was like the heat of a log fire. Something about that felt amiss, but she was too overwhelmed to think why his warmth was unexpected. Emotionally, every heartstring in her body yearned to be with him. Her rational mind was having something to say about that.

She lifted her head, faced him and eased out of his arms. 'Truthfully, I know that I've missed you too. For the past few months, I've been so sad, so lonely. Then I was with,' she paused.

'I know about him, it's okay.'

She felt her cheeks flush and her hands instinctively rose to cover them. He knew about Daniel. She did not want to think how. 'Daniel came along and I thought he was what I needed. I longed for companionship. He said I'd been with someone else.'

'I know.'

'You heard?' Now she was mortified.

'I was around. I have excellent hearing now. Sorry.' The way he shrugged made him look cute. She should be angry with him. She couldn't be.

She carried on. 'Everything Daniel said did not make sense, and then in the dream – the truth. It's surreal,' she paused, troubled. 'I don't like that I hurt Daniel. That was bad. He didn't deserve that.'

'He's not the first to suffer in love.'

The words reflected his pain. Her curiosity overcame sympathy. 'How did you make me see all that stuff in a dream?'

'It's a form of telepathy. I don't really understand it. To be honest I didn't know it would work.'

'It worked.' The vision was still fresh in her mind.

There was no way it was all a dream.

***

Steven reached over and twisted a strand of her red hair in his finger, then let it drop. He wanted to touch her so badly. 'Are you angry with me?'

Caitlin watched his hand and laughed. 'Angry? I can think of a lot of things to be. Anger wouldn't be top of my list. Let's try confused, emotional, bewildered, hormonal…I can give you a whole list. Honestly, I just want the truth. I don't

197

like knowing that for months a huge chunk of my past was kept from me. Do you know, I thought I was going crazy?'

Steven looked away, and eased back gently. 'I'm sorry.'

He could see Caitlin lean towards him in his peripheral vision. 'It's not your fault.'

He stood up and made his way over to the window. Daylight was nearly upon them. It was going to be a long day. 'It is my fault.' He pursed his lips and gripped the window sill.

Caitlin's voice got closer. 'It's not. Look I want to know everything, but we have time right? You don't have to shoot off? I have seen you during the day. I know you're not a *vampire*.'

Caitlin stood next to him and eased her hand into his. The light blue and white colours of daybreak were starting to break over the tops of the terraced houses.

She leant against his shoulder. 'I need to have a shower and get changed. If you're still here when I get back I'll know I wasn't dreaming. I used to sleep walk when I was younger, and right now I'm feeling delusional.'

He gave an amused huff. She always knew how to break him. 'Shall I go and get something ready for breakfast?'

She gave a cheeky smile as she collected some clothes from her drawers. 'So, you still eat then?'

Steven rolled his eyes. 'Yes, I still eat normal food.'

'I'm glad to hear it. I'll be back. By the way, breakfast would be great. I'll warn you though; if Gemma sees you she'll flip. She was quite taken with you – I mean Simon.'

Steven followed her form as she left. He was so aroused when he looked at her, really looked at her. Her petite, slim yet slightly pear shaped figure got him thinking – it was dangerous to think too much sometimes.

Gemma could pose a problem. Strictly speaking, he hadn't done anything the previous evening. They just hung out together, nothing more.

The door creaked when Steven left her room. The smell of dust and damp overpowered. He crept down the stairs and made his way towards the galley style kitchen. A cheap and cheerful pink kettle sat on the worktop. He picked it up and took it to the sink to refill.   A lot of lime scale had accumulated at the bottom so he swirled some water in it first and threw it out before adding fresh water.   Then he pressed the button and waited as he heard the familiar hum.

A small, waist height, fridge sat in the corner of the room. He walked up to it, opened the door and peered in.   The shelves were not marked so he assumed they shared the food. When he was in halls everyone labelled their food, it must be different when you share a house.   He took out the loaf of sliced bread, and margarine.   Toast sounded like a good plan. After he popped two slices in the toaster, he heard footsteps coming down the stairs.   He was sure it was not Caitlin so he braced himself for the confrontation.   He grabbed the local advertising paper for cover, raised it above his head and leant against the counter.

This was going to be fun.

CHAPTER 30

STARTING OVER

Gemma's head thumped. She had no idea what she had done with Simon on the previous night, but the fact he wasn't around meant that for once she had not lured her victim into her bed. Somewhere in the recesses of her mind she recalled that Caitlin had been crying and that Daniel had left. It was a shame, Daniel seemed nice enough. Thing was, she was sure she had just heard Caitlin talking to someone. Perhaps, Daniel had come back after all that. It was typical of Caitlin to have a lover's tiff on the first night. Her thoughts collided in mid thought as she saw a pair of male legs, the trousers looked familiar.

When Simon lowered the paper Gemma stopped in her tracks and stood still, gawping. Had he stayed over after all?

'Good morning,' he said.

She remembered that sultry smile. She could not remember if she had kissed him, but she couldn't have offended him if he was still here. She fought back the urge to holler 'what the hell are you doing here?'

'Can I make you some tea?' he asked. He looked comfortable, as though he lived there.

'Tea? Tea, yes, tea would be good,' she mumbled.

'Milk and sugar?' he asked, in a tone that was way too casual for her liking.

She wished she could remember. Her cheeks flushed as she fumbled a reply, 'err, n-no sugar, just milk, thanks,' she recovered. She scratched her head. 'Sorry, what are you doing here?'

'Tutorial,' Caitlin said, as she breezed through the door.

'Tutorial? On a Saturday morning?' Gemma scrunched up her face. She was not an idiot. Something was going on.

Caitlin took a slice of toast off the plate. 'Is this my tea?'

Simon nodded.

She took a sip and winced. 'I told you he was going to help me.'

Gemma stared from one face to the other, narrowed her eyes, took a seat opposite Simon and folded her arms across her chest. 'Never knew you were that keen to study this *early*. Sorry, erm…Simon. You know you're welcome here and I did have a great time last night.' It didn't matter that she could not remember how it ended.

'Last night?' It was Caitlin's turn to look confused.

'Yes, we went out for a drink when you went out with Daniel.' The look on Caitlin's face called for drastic measures. 'Right, excuse me Simon. I need to have a little chat with Caitlin. We'll be back in just a sec.' Gemma grabbed Caitlin's arm firmly and practically dragged her out of the kitchen as she made her way to the living room at the front of the house. To prevent eavesdropping, she shut the door behind her. 'What's he doing here? I thought Daniel was back when I heard you talking to someone upstairs. But, it wasn't Daniel was it? So, I repeat, why was Simon in your room? And why is he now in our kitchen making breakfast?'

Caitlin grinned. 'Like I said, he came over to help me with my maths.'

'You are full of shit. Last night you were bawling your eyes out over Daniel and today you are happy as ever with Simon. *My* Simon! For someone who has not had a boyfriend until a few weeks ago the tables have turned. But hey, if you don't want to tell your best friend what's going on then fine. I'll butt out and go back to bed,' she said, now fuming.

'Gemma, don't get annoyed. It's over with Daniel. I'm in the middle of figuring something out with Simon. I'll tell you more when I can. I promise,' she pleaded.

Those puppy dog eyes were not going to work today.

'Well, somehow I don't think by *figuring out* you meant maths. Thanks a lot Caitlin. You're a real friend. Fine, I'll leave you both to it. Happy studying!' She could not bear to look at Caitlin any more as she stormed out the door, stomped upstairs and slammed her room door shut.

She could not believe Caitlin. Since when was she the popular one?

***

Caitlin raised her eyebrows at Gemma's performance and made her way back down the hallway. Steven came out of the kitchen carrying the toast and two mugs of tea.

'Shall we sit in there?' he asked, gesturing towards the living room.

'Good idea.'

'I left Gemma's tea in the kitchen. You can take it to her as a peace treaty,' he suggested.

'Might as well,' she groaned, as she let him pass. Even in the hallway, she had to resist the desire to brush up against him.

She found the mug on the table and took it upstairs. She knocked lightly on the door and called out. 'Gemma, can I give you your tea?'

The door eased open slightly after a minute and a pitiful face peeked out. 'Thanks. Sorry if I was a bitch right now. I have no right to preach to you. I guess I'm just very jealous. Anyway,' she added with a slight pause. 'If your studying does not work out tell him to give me a call.'

Caitlin smiled. Gemma was her best friend, but she was not going to let her get her claws into Steven. As she started going down the stairs a few pieces in the puzzle started to fit together. Steven seemed so normal. He was *warm*. If he was a vampire, or whatever that man had said, why was he still so human? Shouldn't he be pale and cold blooded? What about food? It looked like he ate normally. She had a lot to find out.

She found Steven sat on one of the lumpy and smudged sofas. The tea and toast was laid out in front of him on the small, permanently stained, coffee table. Taking a seat opposite him on the non matching sofa chair she picked up the mug and took a sip. It was made just as she liked it. 'I guess you've made me a cup of tea before then.'

'Just a few times,' he said. Then he took hold of his cup and picked up a slice of toast. He took a huge bite and washed it

202

down.

So as not to look ungrateful, she did the same. The sweetness of the sticky strawberry jam amongst the buttery bread reminded her she was starving. She finished it quickly. 'Thank you, I was hungry.'

'My pleasure,' he replied.

'So, do you eat the same stuff?' she asked.

'Yes...'

'But, there is more?' she queried, hesitant.

'There is more,' he added, as he sipped the drink. 'But, we'll talk about it later. Let's go out and get some fresh air.'

'So, you can still go out during daytime?'

'Naturally,' he confirmed. 'You have seen me out and about during the daytime.'

She bit her lip, she felt so stupid for asking. 'Nothing like the stories then?'

'No, definitely *not* like the stories, shall we go?' He deviated from the conversation by picking up the plates to clear up.

She leant in to take her plate, but he beat her to it.

'I'll take them,' he said, the plates perfectly stacked as he marched out of the room.

In the corridor, she took her coat off the banister and put it on. Then she swapped her slippers for her black leather boots. Steven came back out and watched. He was already wearing his shoes and jacket.

She smiled wearily and said, 'ready?'

'Let's go.'

It was like he had always been there. They were acting so normal. As if going for a walk on a Saturday morning was the most natural thing in the world. Then again it was. Just not with a potential murderer, if that's what he was.

***

The sound of the door banging alerted Gemma. They had gone out. She made her way to the bathroom at the front of the house and looked out of the window. They walked side by side just like a couple. They weren't holding hands, but their proximity and way they brushed against each other made it obvious. There was definitely something going on. It was bizarre to see her best friend with two different men in less than twenty four hours. She was damned if she was kept out of the loop for much longer.

***

Considering the time of the year, the air was milder than expected. The previous year it snowed in January. Mid-January, the sun shone on a road sprinkled in frost, the scene peaceful and serene. Caitlin blinked against the bright glare of the sun. It was bizarre to be walking next to Steven, a man she had dreamt of for the last few months for a reason unknown to her until now. She remembered being totally smitten. It just seemed like something from a movie – not memory.

Months had gone by. She was sure she had changed.

Perhaps she was not as gullible as when she first arrived at university. When she met Steven he had made her lose focus, think more of love, not work. Until Steven, she had never felt the urge to be restrained by a relationship. Daniel was a sacrificial lamb. She had to be honest, the reason she thought it might work with Daniel was because he would be miles away most of the time. He gave her space, all the love with no suffocation. Now Steven was back she did not know what to think. She wanted him in her life and yet she didn't. Being in a relationship scared her. Love, marriage – it did strange things. She saw the way her parents talked to each other. She did not want children or to be bound to a man. She wanted to live her life to the full.

Her lips twitched. She could not ignore the facts. She had been so lonely, depressed even. She was not as tough as she wanted to be. There was the wider issue of what exactly Steven had become. The thoughts tangled in her head as she remained silent. She did not know what she was supposed to say. She was not sure he would understand, or see where she was coming from. She did not want to lose him, yet she did not want to lose herself.

She noticed his casual glance in her direction, but she kept her eyes averted. He had succeeded in making her remember him, but if he wanted her back he was going to have to work for it. He had explained a lot by doing whatever it was he had done to bring her memory back, but he still had a way to go.

'Shall we go and get a drink at our usual?' he asked.

Something about that sounded wrong. It was not *their* usual anymore.

'Great.'

She wanted to argue or possibly banter.

She bit her tongue instead.

CHAPTER 31

TIME TO TALK

They walked into the café, ordered and sat down at a corner table. The café was reasonably full with a variety of people taking advantage of a morning drink before work. It was just a normal morning for most people. Sitting opposite Steven, Caitlin looked over her shoulder and noticed a couple deep in conversation, hands practically fused together. They looked in love. Stealing a quick look at Steven, she tensed as her stomach whirled in response. He did look as amazing as she remembered. It was the dark, penetrating amber eyes that had taken her breath away from the first moment they met during fresher's week. Unable to maintain eye contact, she looked down at her drink and took a sip.

'Are you planning to talk to me?' he asked.

She looked up and met his glare. 'I don't really know what to say.'

'Can I ask you the most important thing? Well, for me, anyway?'

She had no idea what was coming. 'Sure.'

He leaned in closer and whispered. 'Are you scared of me?'

She hadn't even thought of that. 'Honestly,' she replied. 'I don't know what to answer. I'm not scared, but I'm not blasé either.'

'So, what do I have to do to reassure you?' he asked, as he took a sip from his steaming cup of coffee.

'Tell me what you are,' she asked, her voice soft, quiet.

He leant back on the chair and tapped his fingers on the table. 'That's difficult. I don't know everything myself. All I know is that I can exert self control and that I am pretty normal, in the scheme of things. I have other needs, but they don't dictate what I do.'

'Right,' she mused. 'So, you don't need, you know, to be *bad.*'

'No, I don't need to be bad,' he assured.

It was a good enough answer, but she was curious about his other needs. 'Why did you come back? Do you want your old life back?'

'I would love my life back, just as it was. It's complicated, not as simple as I thought it would be.' He gave a half smile again.

'You thought it would be simple?'

He laughed. 'No. You're right. I never thought it would be simple, saying that I did actually call *them* simple.'

It was nice to hear him laugh.

'Why?'

He swirled the drink with the spoon again. 'Life with them was different. It was modern, as in they had access to modern things, yet everything they did was communal. And there was no money.'

Caitlin's jaw dropped. 'No money?'

'No, everyone used a barter system.'

'A what?' She had to know how that worked. She could not imagine anything without money working here.

'Well, some cooked, others made clothes, others raised the kids and taught, others dealt with security…' he paused. 'Actually, the jobs are no different to what people do here. There no-one gets paid. They do their job and in exchange take what they need. I know it sounds strange here, but it worked there. The only thing was some, like me, wanted more freedom.'

She nodded and focused on her mug, her head full of conflicting thoughts. 'And this place was in the jungle?'

'The Amazon, in Brazil.'

She found it hard to believe. 'Wow! That's a long way to go from here.'

'It was.' He reached out and started to trace a pattern on her hand.

It tingled.

'So, how did you get away from there? I mean, in the vision

it looked desolate, as in, in the middle of nowhere.

'I was attacked and needed to get better.'

'Attacked by what?' It must have been something scary, like a panther or a leopard.

'A tapir.'

Caitlin blurted out some of her tea. 'A Tapir, what like one of those animals in Dora the Explora?'

Steven gave a slight shake of his head and chuckled. 'They are more vicious than portrayed in a children's cartoon. Anyway, how do you know Dora?'

She wiped her mouth with a serviette. It covered her blush as she attempted to brush him off. 'I have a younger sister remember. Anyway, so what happened then?'

His eyes darkened. 'So, my grandparents brought me back here. I couldn't get better there.'

'Grandparents? Of course, you met your real mum. What was she like?'

'Like any estranged mother would be, I guess.' The frown said it all.

She wondered why he could not get better over there. To think she took another sip, then continued. 'Did you need something you could not get there?'

He looked away. 'Yes.'

'Can you tell me what it was?' If you don't ask, you don't get.

'Not yet. I don't want to freak you out.'

She did not want to ask again. Something told her it was not something she needed to know. 'So how come they let you come back here? You're on your own. Or are we being watched?' Paranoid, she looked around.

'No-one is watching us,' he said. He looked like he suppressed a smile. 'My grandmother died. Up until she passed away no-one seemed to age or die after the change. Now we know it can happen.'

With child like enthusiasm she asked. 'So what's the *change*?'

He finished off his drink. 'Shall we walk and talk?'

'Sure,' Caitlin downed hers and got up.

Once outside, Steven started to talk, lost in his own thoughts. 'The change is when we become different, without human blood we die. It's weird to try to explain something that has no logical explanation. I don't know how much you remember of what my uncle Ian said on that night.'

She pushed her hair away from her face as she considered what he was saying. Did he say uncle? She was sure the men were too young. 'One of those men was your uncle? They scared me. The truth is I was too frightened to take much in. Tell me again.'

Steven looked ahead as he spoke. They were now heading for the Common, a large expanse of trees, a peaceful place. 'Okay. Well, a group of them, my mother included, were attacked by infected bats during the Second World War, whilst they were based in Los Alamos, New Mexico. They think the bats were radioactive. Since then they, and any offspring, have needed blood to survive.'

Caitlin stopped walking. 'Offspring?'

Steven turned back, his expression composed. 'Yep, people like me…although I am the first to be born half human. Offspring have to feed off human blood to enable them to move from adolescence to adulthood.'

She started to move again, she needed to walk and talk. 'You kill the humans you feed from?' she asked, wary. This was going into unfamiliar waters.

He was quiet for a minute or so, the sound of their footsteps just about audible above the sound of traffic. They waited at a set of traffic lights and crossed, then made their way into the common. Large trees welcomed them. Caitlin could hear birds overhead, it was peaceful. It took her thoughts away from the story. It sounded like a story.

Finally, Steven spoke, he sounded reluctant. 'I'm only telling you this because you asked.' He paused, and took hold of her hand. 'Please try to understand and don't freak out okay?'

'Okay.' She did not know what else she was supposed to say.

'Someone has to die to enable one of us to change,' he said, his eyes darkened.

'So, you killed someone?' she spluttered, wide eyed. She was tempted to let go of his hand, she didn't.

His head hung low. 'I'm ashamed to admit that I did. I don't remember doing it. I was feverish at the time, but that's no excuse.'

'So, you *are* bad?'

Two large crows burst through the trees. The way they shrieked made her think of bats – black, deadly, hungry bats.

***

Caitlin's expression had changed from one of curiosity to horror. It looked like some of the *issues* were finally coming home to her. He knew he was being incredibly selfish. He should have left her alone; it was the right thing to do. He just did not want to.

It was uncomfortable to regurgitate Ingrid's words. It hurt him to think of the woman who found him in the first place. 'Well, depends on how you look at it. We all kill to survive, that's the circle of life.' If Ingrid heard him now he was sure she would stick her tongue out at him. He had never been her number one fan in the community.

Caitlin picked up a leaf from the ground and fiddled with it. 'I guess human beings are deadly in their own way. We justify death – a lot.'

'Exactly.'

She cottoned on a lot quicker than he had done. He liked to think she had an ulterior motive for being so understanding. There was a chance she might actually want to be with a monster like him. 'Anyway, when they realised what had happened, they chose to create a new home for themselves in the Amazon.'

'In Brazil, was that was the memory you planted in my head last night?'

He smiled and nodded. He was still amazed it had worked.

'It was actually real? Wow…so what happened after you arrived? What's it like?'

Steven chuckled, her enthusiasm rubbed off easily. She seemed comfortable now. Hopefully thoughts of a macabre nature had been shelved, for a while at least. 'It's like going back in time. In some respects the community is united in a way that you don't see here anymore. And yet everything is controlled. No-one is allowed to leave unless they have permission.'

'Really? You need permission. And they let you go because of the tapir attack,' she giggled.

Steven scowled and then laughed with her. 'It really hurt you know. They are not sweet and innocent.'

'If you say so.' Caitlin carried on laughing.

Steven laughed along with her, infected. 'Come here you.' He eased his arms around her in a warm embrace. Their laughter subsided. 'I love to hear you laugh.' He felt pin prick goose pimples on the back of his neck. He was holding Caitlin again.

He pulled his head back and leant in to kiss her. He was glad she did not pull away. The kiss was slow, tender – it made all his nerve endings go awry. He felt himself react and hoped she would not mind, it had been a long time. Caitlin was so special, the last thing he wanted to do was offend or upset her. He pulled his pelvis back as the kiss came to a natural end. He fought against the urge to do more. They held each other for a while, Caitlin's head on his chest, and her arms around his waist.

He was desperate to know whether he was making any sense at all.

Either way, he relished every second. She was not rejecting him anymore, it was a huge relief.

Caitlin released her arms, pulled back and smiled. It was the smile he had been dying to see every second he had been in the Amazon. He gave her a quick peck. 'So, what else would you like to do? If I know you at all I know you have more questions.' He laughed.

'Do you still need human blood?'

It was just like Caitlin to go for the bullseye.

'Yes…'

Caitlin's eyes widened.

'And…no.'

Her eyes relaxed again.

He held her hand and started to walk again. 'We think the reason they have lived out there without the need for human blood is because of monkeys. Genetically, they fulfil the same need.'

'You kill monkeys?' she gasped, her hand gripped his tighter.

He glanced in her direction. 'In the same way you kill animals for food.'

It was unsettling to have to tell her everything. He was not sure it was bringing her any closer to trusting him.

All he could do was hope.

CHAPTER 32

EXPLANATIONS

The crisp air made Caitlin shiver. She loved the smell of fresh air, there was nothing like it. She gathered he was a new form of human. He could be dangerous. Supposedly, not in a way that was any different to the way humans behaved. In a way she could not berate him for anything she would do herself to survive. She had not been to the Common for a while; it was a good place to talk. It was spacious and near enough empty at this time of day.

They came to an empty bench. She let go of his hand and took a seat. Her head swirled around like mush. It resembles the decomposing leaves on the ground. 'You said they didn't let people leave. Why did they let you go? Why didn't you have to go back once you were better?'

Steven took a seat next to her and leant his elbows on his knees, his hands clasped together. 'My grandparents decided to let me come back. They felt guilty about what had happened to my mother.'

The way he kept a straight face made her suspicious. 'I see, so your mother was forced to return after she had you? Is that why you were raised by your dad? Oh…did she not tell anyone about you? Was that why you didn't know?'

'She kept it from everyone. If Ingrid had not found me, I don't know what would've happened.'

'Ingrid?'

'Ingrid was here on vacation whilst you were away after Georgina's death. She figured out who I was.' He clenched and unclenched his hands.

She was missing something – her brain just had to piece things together. 'So, this Ingrid told everyone about you. And that's why your uncle, Ian right, came to get you?'

'Yes.'

'And why didn't your mum come instead?'

'She is dangerous and erratic. I find it hard to believe she is my mother if I'm honest.' He gave an uneasy chuckle.

Caitlin frowned. His mother was dangerous. The community had to be kept isolated. 'It seems weird to come back to see me if you don't know what you're capable of. Why didn't you just leave me? If you love me, like you say you do, why didn't you stay away?' Her logical brain usually saw things in black or white, this was a definite case of grey.

She was not prepared for his reaction. His eyes seemed to blur and he froze, as though shaken. She had probably been too honest. She could not possibly understand what he had been through, what his life was like. She could not assume anything. Maybe, she would have to allow some room for grey.

Eyes to the ground, he spoke slowly. 'I had to see you again, I just had to. I'm sorry if I was spying on you last night. I promise it was the first time I had ever come around. I would not stalk you. I'm not a psycho…at least I try not to be.' He gave a half smile. 'When I saw your boyfriend leave and I heard you crying, I knew I had to try to tell you the truth. I didn't know it would work. It was lucky it did. At least, I think it was. Maybe you are right. Maybe I should never have come back. If you want me to leave I will. I will never force you to be with me.'

His little angst ridden speech did make her feel sorry for him. She was just not sure she was ready to let him back in just like that. She had to change the subject – fast. 'Did you ever see the message I left you on Facebook?'

'Yes,' he paused. 'I'm sorry. I didn't know what to reply.'

'The truth would have been good.' She knew she was being sarcastic, she could not help it.

The way he stood up suddenly came as a surprise. He practically jogged away. Then he stopped and went perfectly still for a minute before he turned and came back, eyes narrowed, hands clenched.

'That's what I'm doing or trying to do.' He kicked some

leaves away and looked at her again.

It was a deep penetrating stare – it felt like he was probing into her soul.

'I'm sorry, my timing is lousy. You only broke up with your boyfriend last night. I had to tell you why he said what he did. It cut me up. You got deceived. You needed to know the truth.'

'Did you hear me with Daniel?' As much as she was trying to understand, it made her skin crawl.

He bowed his head. 'Sorry.'

'Why would you listen?' Even though he apologised, it was not easy to understand.

'I don't know! It was stupid.' He run his hand through his hair and then dropped both hands to his sides, defeated.

She did not think he was angry with her, more at himself. He took a deep breath, raised his head and added in a soft, almost pleading voice, eyes fixed on hers. 'I needed to know if you loved him.'

'I see.' She could understand that. He wanted to know if he had to move on. 'So, you heard me call out your name?'

'Yes.' There was a definite twitch on his lips, he wanted to smile.

It was her turn to smile instead. 'So, I guess I'm not as *innocent* as I thought I was.'

He sat down again and put his hand on her shoulders gently as he spoke. 'We never did anything wrong. I never…you remember everything now, don't you? Do you remember us?'

His hand radiated heat on her shoulder.

She fought the urge to snuggle into him again. 'Yes.' She could not lie. 'Of course I remember. You've been in my dreams since you left. I just didn't know why.'

'So, you've been dreaming about me?' The cocky smile was back.

Caitlin felt herself blush. There was no way she was going to tell him about *those* dreams. 'Yes, and no – I'm not going to tell you about them.'

'Well, that's just mean,' he said, as he rubbed his thumb against her chin. 'So, am I forgiven for eavesdropping?'

The feel of his hand was making her body react in a familiar way. She was finding it hard to keep her head together and not get distracted by hormones.

She shrugged her shoulder. 'You're forgiven.'

He took his cue, placed his other hand on her face and brought her towards him.

She was desperate to kiss him again, against her better judgement.

The kiss was nothing like the last one. Fireworks exploded, as a series of small lights shot up in different directions just as a huge explosion engulfed the sky. In her head, they developed into smaller yet just as beautiful effects, before a grand finale – everything at once. She lost track of where she was, every sound evaporated. There was no-one else. Just them, as it should be.

The beep of a bicycle horn broke the moment, followed by the holler of a hooded teenager. 'Get a room.'

Somehow, her arms were now firmly round Steven's waist. Simultaneously, they leant back and broke into laughter.

The earth just moved. Caitlin was sure of it. 'Wow.'

'Wow,' Steven repeated. 'Do you see now why I came back?'

'I guess I do.'

She really did.

***

Steven slipped his hand into Caitlin's. 'Come on, let's carry on.'

He needed to walk, to clear his head. She brought out every emotion imaginable. He was so vulnerable with Caitlin.

A few dog walkers roamed in the distance. At a turn in the path a small white Yorkshire terrier stood to attention. A low growl escaped, it was a warning. A man in his twenties came up to his dog and scolded it. The dog stood its ground and barked louder in protest. It looked like it was about to attack. The man attached the lead and apologised profusely whilst dragging the dog away, it had gone mental.

'He knows what you are, doesn't he?' Caitlin asked.

'Animals have instincts that we have chosen to ignore.'

'Why didn't they kill me that night?' she asked.

It caught him off guard. Caitlin was so inquisitive. He couldn't blame her. He just wasn't ready for it. He didn't know how much to tell her. He wanted to open up, to let her in. He just did not want her to run away.

He rubbed his finger against his lips. 'To make sure I did what they said.'

'So, you saved my life already,' she laughed. 'You know, you don't owe me anything. If you want to leave with a clear conscience you can. I appreciate the truth. It's nice to know that I'm not crazy. Sometimes I thought I was hallucinating when things popped up in my mind that did not make sense. I promise not to tell anyone about you. You don't have to risk everything to be with me. I don't think I'm worth it.'

She was doing it again. She was pushing him away. He had never understood that. Caitlin never thought she was good enough for him. She used to tell him enough times. The tables had turned. He was not good enough for her by miles. He gripped her hand tighter. 'I didn't come back because I *owed* you. I'm still in love with you. I always have been. The number of times you used to ask me why I loved you. You never understood. I have no idea why you don't see yourself the way I see you. Surely, you realise *I* am not good enough for you?'

Caitlin fell silent. 'I never thought I was good enough because it's true. Why would you love me? I'm a plain Jane, compared to you. I mean, you're obviously…oh, you know. I'm a redhead, you're like a Greek God…why me?' Her voice was distant, pained.

He gave a throaty chuckle and continued to walk. 'I don't think love is logical. I love your colour hair. I love your fiery nature. I love everything. I don't know that I could ever love anyone like I love you.'

'But *why*?' she repeated, her eyes wide, confused.

He stopped walking and faced her. 'Okay, an easy answer then. No-one swims as gracefully as you do.'

'Oh,' she sighed. That had caught her out.

Steven bridged the gap and kissed her again, he ran his free

217

hand over her back. Perhaps, he needed to remind her of why they were so good together. When she responded he felt vindicated. The passion resurfaced as his heartbeat went into overdrive. Pausing for a moment, he continued to run his fingers through her hair. 'I never want to leave you again.'

Caitlin's eyes darted. She was confused, she had to be.

'I don't want to lose you either. I just don't understand how we can make it work. They said you would be dangerous, not just to me but to others. You said yourself that you don't know what you're capable of. As much as I'd love to be with you, I don't know what will come of it,' she rambled.

'Let me worry about the how. All I need to know is that you still care for me. Do you?'

He hoped not to be disappointed.

CHAPTER 33

FRIENDS

Caitlin did not know what to say, it was not clear cut.

She had never been naïve about love and the sacrifices it demanded. Her parents' constant struggle to make their marriage work taught her that.

Finally, she met his stare and allowed herself to drift into his amber. 'I never thought anyone would sweep me off my feet. I never wanted the knight in his shining armour. Then you came along and changed things. As easily as you came in, you disappeared, vanished. I didn't know why I was so distraught but I felt it all the same. Now at least I know why I've been suffering from a broken heart for all these months. The thought of losing you again is unimaginable. I can't lose you again. I don't want the pain. I just don't know *how* this can work.'

Steven smiled involuntarily as she spoke. He leaned in to bridge the gap, but she held out her hands in front of her. 'But...' she paused.

He cocked his head to the side and gave a cheeky smile.

She narrowed her eyes. 'I need to know what you are. You need to tell me why the dream stopped when you arrived. If we are going to be in a relationship I need to know what I'm letting myself in for.'

'Okay, we'll take it one step at a time. I'll tell you what you want to know.'

She glared now and folded her arms. 'Everything.'

He chuckled. 'One step at a time.'

She unfolded her arms, irritated. What was he doing to her? 'Fine...one step at a time. Do you – Do you think we could continue tomorrow? The truth is my head's spinning. I need some space.'

He sounded hurt when he said, 'if that's what you want.'

She did not want to hurt him but she could not think rationally when her body reacted to his every move. She definitely needed some alone time, some what the hell is going on time, some I must be going crazy now alone time.

***

Caitlin stared at her shark picture, her head on her soft, duck feather pillow, hands over her stomach. The shark was a deadly killing machine yet it was so graceful. Was Steven the same now? She could not think straight with him around. But, with him gone emptiness hit. She was alone and she had asked for it. A knock on the door made her jump. Had he come to see her already?

'Hey.' Gemma.

'Hey.'

'Can we talk?' Gemma asked, more subdued than normal.

Caitlin was all talked out. She did not know what to tell her best friend. She really wanted her opinion; she just could not talk to her about Steven. It was still early, even though it was getting dark outside. They could always grab some chips or something. She needed to get out of the house. 'Sure, let's go out. I need a drink.'

Gemma raised her eyes. 'You're on! I'll grab my purse and be right with you.'

Caitlin grabbed her wallet and made her way down the stairs. She could hear Gemma scrambling above her, in what they referred to as the penthouse suite. It was a better description than the reality – a dingy attic room that smelled of damp.

The sound of laughter downstairs hailed the return their flatmate Sally, who more or less permanently lived with her latest boyfriend. Out of politeness, Caitlin went to the kitchen to say hello.

Sally was cooking over the stove. It smelt like baked beans again. For someone so bright, Sally was a lousy cook. She wondered if she would remember Steven if they met again. Sally had dated Steven's friend, Adam, during the previous year. The latest tall, muscular blonde had his arms wrapped around her waist, his face nuzzled over her shoulder. Was he

220

biting her earlobe?

It seemed rude to interrupt. She did anyway. 'Hey Sally, how're things?'

Sally brushed the latest boyfriend off with a laugh and turned to face her. 'Hey Caitlin. Great thanks. You?'

'Fine, thanks.'

The boyfriend gave Caitlin a quick once over.

'This is Justin. Justin, this is my flatmate Caitlin.'

Justin stepped forward and shook her hand. 'Nice to finally meet one of Sally's friends.'

Caitlin squirmed. 'I'm just heading out with Gemma. If anyone calls round can you tell them I-I went out.'

'Sure.' Sally had a surprised look on her face. It read *why would anyone be coming round for you, it's Saturday*. Caitlin could not blame her – she knew she had a reputation for being a hermit.

She walked out as she heard Sally say, 'the beans!'

Caitlin hoped Justin liked them burnt.

Gemma was in the hallway already. All wrapped up with a thick coat, hat, scarf and gloves. It was only January after all.

'Come on, let's go. There's a band playing later in the union. They've got great reviews.'

Caitlin grabbed her thick red coat and black matching hat, scarf and glove set. Another useful Christmas gift from her grandmother, it was what she always wanted.

'Let me guess, Christmas pressie?'

'You read my mind,' Caitlin grunted.

Gemma rolled her eyes. 'Hey, I got another toiletry set. A lavender one! Trust me you're lucky.'

Caitlin giggled and they headed for the door. It was nice to act normal. She needed to take her mind off things – off Steven.

Gemma made chit chat as they walked to the union. Her course was too hard. Everyone was so keen. She wanted to get good grades, but she was worried she couldn't keep things up. She talked about everything she was thinking – except the obvious thing on her mind. Caitlin was grateful. She did not need a Spanish inquisition at the moment. A queue snaked out of the entrance. It was busy considering it was only six. It had to be a popular band.

'So, where did you go today?'

Caitlin knew Gemma could not hold off for that long. 'To the Common.'

'Nice.' Gemma turned and looked behind them, then looked ahead. 'We might be here for a while.'

'Nah, it always looks worse than it is.'

'As if you've come out that often to know,' Gemma said, more as a joke than a serious retort.

Caitlin still pulled a face and huffed.

Gemma pulled her arm through Caitlin's. 'Joking, I know the waterpolo lot have managed to drag you out at times.'

As if by magic, the queue suddenly moved forward and a minute later they were handing over their student passes and gaining entry to the holy ground, where students let off steam. The union was heaving. It was difficult to know which direction to go in.

'Let's go to the Bar cafeteria. I could murder some pizza and chips'

Caitlin nodded. As they got there she groaned. Obviously, everyone else also had the same idea. There was barely enough space to get in.

Gemma turned and shrugged her shoulders. 'Shall we go in?'

'Go on, we're here now anyway.'

Half an hour later, with a full stomach, they braved the bar. A squash and a squeeze later, they got to the front. Gemma flashed her biggest smile and waved at the barman to get his attention.

'Hey Gemma, fancy seeing you here,' the barman said. He gave her a cheeky wink.

'Dave, be a star and get us a couple of vodka and oranges, please.'

'Coming right up.'

Caitlin could not understand why that never worked for her.

Gemma turned to face Caitlin. 'You said you needed a drink.'

Caitlin nodded. She felt like a puppet on strings, going through the motions.

Gemma handed her the drink after she had paid. 'You can get the next one. Anyway, cheers, to new love, right?'

Caitlin raised her glass to Gemma's. She did not know what to say.

Gemma put her arm around Caitlin's shoulder. 'So where shall we go so you can tell me what's going on?'

'Not here.'

'Okay, let's take a seat down the other end. Not so close to the bar and the band.'

They made their way over and managed to find a seat at the very end. Hardly anyone wanted to be that far away.

Gemma leaned in and whispered. 'So, what happened with Simon?'

'Nothing really.'

'Okay, so why was he there? I know you didn't have a *lesson*. You were really upset about Daniel and then you looked like you were over him. Is it over?'

'Yes, it is over with Daniel. Look, I am seeing Simon, if that's what you want to know but it's complicated.'

'How?'

'Gemma, I wish I could tell you but I barely understand it myself. I have a connection with Simon. And we are just seeing where it leads, that's all.'

'A connection,' Gemma mused, as she rubbed her chin with her hand. 'Sounds ominous.'

Caitlin downed the rest of her drink. She did not want to talk about it. 'Let's dance. Go on.'

'Whatever, we'll dance. Just promise me that you'll tell me what's bothering you if you need a friend. I'm here for you, okay?'

'Okay, thanks Gemma – you're a pal.'

Caitlin grabbed her hand and dragged her on to the dance floor. A lot of students jostled around, hardly any danced at all. It was more of a jump to the beat. Or snog. Or shuffle. Then she saw an unwanted familiar face. Adam. The manslut. After he had used Sally last year, he had moved on to a string of other girlfriends. He always leered at her. She was sure Adam saw women as meat. She grabbed Gemma and pulled her in a different direction. Then she pointed. 'Adam.'

'Good call,' Gemma sighed. 'Shall we go get some shots? Let's get wasted.'

'Let's.'

Caitlin did not usually want to get drunk. Tonight she *needed* to.

*

The smell hit first. The nausea came second. A desire to run was last. It was a pitiful sight. Caitlin bowed over the toilet seat and emptied her entire stomach contents. The acid bile grated her throat. It hurt. A few tears came to her eyes. She could not believe what she had done. She rarely got drunk so when she was stupid enough to do it, it killed. It was agony. She slid off the side of the seat and slumped against the bath, devoid of all energy.

The house was quiet and dark. Gemma had passed out downstairs on the sofa. She may have crawled up to her room by now. She was not sure. Using every last ounce of energy she could muster she got up, swayed and somehow managed to get toothpaste on the brush. She sloshed it around her mouth and gargled. It got the worst of the taste out.

Caitlin collapsed on the floor. On her hands and knees she somehow made it back to her room and hurled herself on the bed. The last thing she remembered was the fluorescent clock, it was very late or very early – she couldn't remember which.

She passed out, still fully clothed.

***

Sunday was like any day for Steven. He was up early and ready to face the next challenge. Caitlin had asked for space, he had given it to her. He was desperate to go to see her, but he had to wait until eleven, the time agreed.

His flat was beginning to resemble a dump site. He hated housework, but it was time to clear up. If Caitlin ever came to visit he wanted it to be decent, or as good as possible. The ulterior motive revealed. He was strong and fast, it helped. The place was beginning to have a decent, lived in, feel to it.

He could actually start to think of it as home.

The option to live in the house was open. Jeff had asked him to take it over. He just couldn't. The residue of death lingered. The house was eerie. He would keep an eye on it. It was the right thing to do. He knew the community members would probably consider him responsible when they found out Jeff was dead. He had contemplated calling Catherine on the mobile number she had given. He just couldn't go through with it. He could not delay forever, but he would stall their return for now. He needed more time and they did know where he was. He had not done anything wrong. It was Jeff's decision.

A shred of doubt lingered.

As far as he was concerned he had *it* under control. He was not a monster – period.

Steven ate rabbit stew a lot, it had grown on him. The blood satisfied to a point and the meat tasted like chicken. He was not sentimental. He had never had a rabbit as a pet. He realised the community had actually taught him many life skills.

The clock read ten o'clock. He could not believe time could go so slowly. He could not drag it out any longer. He could walk slowly, or take a long route. Maybe he'd buy her flowers, be a romantic. Then again, he'd seen Daniel bring her flowers. He wracked his brain for something good, something different. A walk might help.

Outside it was raining again. The weather was so predictable.

He did some window shopping to get ideas. Nothing came. He froze when he saw the toyshop. He could have some fun. As soon as he saw it, he knew it was what he was after. Decision made, he made his purchase and marched towards her house.

Surely, she would not mind if he was early?

CHAPTER 34

Hung Over

The door to the terraced house opened very slowly. Gemma's head poked out, her glazed, red rimmed eyes widened. 'Oh, it's *you*. Come in.'

There was nothing like a warm welcome.

Gemma looked rough, the smell confirmed Steven's suspicion. The alcohol was still evaporating off her tongue.

'Rough night?'

'You could say that.' She glanced at what Steven had in the bag and raised her eyebrows. 'Caitlin's still in bed. I haven't seen her. You're welcome to go up. Just don't tell her I gave you permission. I don't think she'd want you to see her in her current state.'

Something told him Gemma wanted him to see Caitlin. 'Okay then. If you think it's a bad idea, I'll wait here.'

Gemma sulked. 'Just go on up, I bet she'll be happy to see you, especially with that present.' The thought seemed to perk her up as she giggled off down the hall.

He hoped she was planning to drink a very strong coffee.

Steven could not help being confused. Did Caitlin get drunk and sleep in late? They used to be early birds.

At the door, he knocked and waited.

Nothing.

He knocked again. A grunt and thud followed.

He was tempted to open the door, but he resisted. Instead, he waited in the hallway. Patience had never been his strong point. A slow shuffle got louder from the other side of the door. Finally, the door opened.

Caitlin peeked out. Her hair was in tufts above her head, her eyes bloodshot. As she registered it was him, she panicked and shut the door again.

226

Steven knocked on the door gently. 'Caitlin, let me in, it's obvious you've had a rough night. Tell you what. Shall I make you a strong coffee?'

A feeble voice whimpered. 'Yes, please. I just need to freshen up.'

She needed a lot more than that, Caitlin was obviously hungover. He could not believe it. She had never got drunk with him – ever! He had never been a strong drinker and she had *claimed* to not drink either.

It appeared she had changed her mind. So much for principles!

A part of him fumed, another worried. What would make her do that? Steven was no angel, but after seeing his dad on his drunken binges he had vowed never to drink as an adult. It was not worth it. It had been a source of much banter at public school, but he did not care. The girls seemed to like the fact he stayed sober. In fact, being level headed had saved many of his friends of numerous occasions.

He could not take it out on Caitlin. If she wanted to get drunk, it was her choice. He just did not understand why she would, why anyone would for that matter. It was nonsensical.

The kitchen was now empty. Gemma must have skulked off somewhere else. He put down the plastic bag and filled up the kettle. As the hum got louder he looked out of the small window and stared into space. When the switch flicked, he turned and made the coffee. He also made one for himself – he needed one now.

Just as he was taking the spoon out, Gemma came in. 'Nice, I needed another one.'

'Have this one, I'll make another.'

'Thanks,' Gemma said. She smiled, took the cup and slurped. 'Ouch, hot.'

'Freshly made,' Steven said, sarcastic.

Gemma sat down.

He got another mug and repeated the process.

'We had a great time last night. Pity you didn't come.' Another noisy slurp.

He could not figure out if she was baiting him. 'I'm glad

you enjoyed yourselves.' He bit his tongue. He had not been invited and wouldn't have wanted to go on a drunken binge anyway.

'Oh, we did. It was *brilliant*. Caitlin told me all about you guys. Love at first sight, so romantic. Alcohol always loosens the tongue.'

Now he was getting angry. 'What did she say?' He smiled through gritted teeth.

'Caitlin said, and I know she was too drunk by this stage, you knew each other last year. That you'd dated. Then you'd left and broken her heart. And now you're back to make amends, but she doesn't know what's happening. So, tell me Steven. What's happening? Your name is Steven – not Simon. Caitlin told me. Caitlin is my friend and I won't let anyone hurt her. She'd been through a tough time the past year. She doesn't need *complications*.'

'By, complications I guess you mean me?'

Gemma scowled. 'If the shoe fits.'

'Gemma, I'm glad Caitlin has a friend to look out for her. Just let me give you a word of advice. You don't know anything about me and you really don't know Caitlin like I do. So, I appreciate the protective thing you have going – its sweet – but just back off. There is no way I would do anything to hurt Caitlin. I can't say the same for you. You didn't exactly look out for her. It sounds like you got her drunk to get her to open up.' He took a step closer. 'Are you sure you're the kind of friend she needs?' He could not believe he sounded so overprotective. He could not help it.

Gemma stood up, her hands on her hips. Her lower lip wavered as she spoke. 'What the hell do you mean? You don't know what Caitlin was like when I made friends with her. She was lost, *depressed*. Who do you think looked out for her? It wasn't you. I can tell you that in a hurry. Now you come back in and she's lost the first boyfriend she's had in ages. She's lost again. She was happy with Daniel. Who do you think you are?'

'Again, I'll be polite. You need to back off. Daniel was a mistake. I am here for her now. I had to leave, but now I'm back.' Steven put down the mug. If he held it any longer he would crush it.

'So, how come she never mentioned you? How come she didn't know who you were?' Gemma spat, her eyes narrowed. 'A few days ago you were Simon, a new student. Now, you are Steven – an ex boyfriend, the reason for her misery by the sound of it. I'm not stupid. Something is going on. I don't care how suave you think you are. I don't trust you and I don't want you messing with my friend. So yeah, she got drunk. So what? We are students. Liven up. She's in the prime of her life, not looking to settle down. Anyone would think you were her father or something. So what if we got drunk?'

Gemma was shouting now, this was getting out of hand. 'Gemma, calm down, I mean you no harm.' He fixed his eyes on hers and maintained eye contact.

Gemma's hands lowered and hang limply at her sides. She stood still, her eyes glued to his.

Steven got closer, his voice low and controlled. 'You will accept me. You will not ask any more questions. My name is Simon, I love Caitlin. You will trust me.'

When he broke eye contact, Gemma raised her mug to her lips and took a seat. Then she looked up. 'You'd better take the coffee up, or it'll get cold.'

'Thank you Gemma, I'll see you later.'

'Yeah, see you later Simon.'

Job done.

* * *

Caitlin was sure she'd heard raised voices downstairs, even though they were muffled by the sound of her hairdryer. She turned it off and went to investigate. She couldn't hear anyone talking anymore, but she heard the sound of footsteps coming up the stairs. Steven's head appeared.

Caitlin attempted to smile. It was hard, her head was spinning and her mouth was completely dry. 'Everything alright?'

'Of course,' he replied.

She held out her hand for a mug. 'Hmmm, is that coffee?' The first sip was heavenly; she savoured the taste and took a few more slurps. 'I thought I heard shouting.'

'It was nothing. Gemma was upset. It seems you said a few things last night, things that concerned me.' He gave a half smile.

Caitlin wracked her brain. 'Did I? What did I say?'

He walked past her and entered her room. 'Don't worry. It's not a problem anymore.'

The way he said it made a shiver run down her spine.

'What do you mean?' She followed him back into her room. All she wanted to do was crawl back into bed, but she had a feeling something was afoot.

Steven shrugged his shoulders. 'It's all in the past, nothing for us to worry about.'

She bit her inner lip. She had to ask. 'What have you done?' Gemma was not usually the forgiving type. Any man fool enough to cross her had usually experienced her wrath.

'Nothing much.' He put the mug on her bedside table and then moved to the window, pulling aside the curtains. 'This room needs fresh air.'

Caitlin knew it was likely he was not impressed by her current state. She remembered he never understood why people got drunk. 'I don't know what came over me last night, I needed to let go, to de-stress.'

Steven gave her a fleeting glance. 'So, you got drunk?' Then he turned back to the window. 'If I stressed you out then I'm the one that should apologise.' He sounded sincere. He opened the sash window and a gush of fresh air wafted into the room.

Caitlin shivered. 'What did you do to Gemma? Please, tell me.'

He faced her. 'She couldn't know the truth about me. You told her my name was Steven. The name does not matter, the fact I used to be here does. It complicates things if she spreads rumours. So, now she won't anymore. She's none the wiser.'

'Please tell me you did not alter her memory? She's my friend, you wouldn't have. Not without talking to me first.'

'I'm afraid she gave me no choice.'

'I gave you no choice. It was *my* error, not Gemma's.'

Caitlin was outraged. There was no way she could sanction his actions after what had happened to her.

He took a step towards her, bridging the distance between them. 'I didn't do that much, I promise. She hated me. Now she doesn't.'

Caitlin flinched. He didn't think it was wrong. Something about that made her skin crawl. 'You've become just like them. You are willing to lie, to deceive, to have it your way. I'm not sure I understand that. I may have got drunk, but you trick people. It's not right Steven, it's not right.' She took a step back.

Steven's face was shrouded by guilt. 'Do you want me to leave?'

Caitlin studied the floor, torn. 'I think maybe you should.'

'Okay, that's fine,' he chirped.

The fake enthusiasm hurt Caitlin.

'Before I go I got you a present.' He opened the bag he'd been holding and took out a cuddly toy in the shape of a shark. 'I thought you might like this. Even the most dangerous animals can be graceful. They do what it takes to survive.'

Her arms took hold of the soft toy shark.

Steven kissed her forehead and left.

Caitlin did not know what to think anymore. She threw the toy shark on her bed, collapsed on top of it and buried her head in the blue duvet.

***

Steven could not believe she had asked him to leave *again*. He could understand why she would be freaked out. He just hoped she would be more understanding. Then again, he had never accepted things easily either. He could not blame her, but it was too late to take back what he'd done. He could not stop her from talking to her friends. She did not understand the danger – how could she? He needed her so badly and yet, he knew he was acting like an idiot. What made him think he could just swoop back into her life and return everything back to the way it was?

It never could be the same. It wasn't the same.

He had changed. He could do things – abnormal things,

dangerous things.

Why would someone like Caitlin want to be with someone like him? He had been a fool to even think she would take him back. He had never expected it to be easy, he just never thought about *her*. He never thought she would be scared of him. And yet, there it was. She feared him.

It was good really. He would never expect Caitlin to be complacent after what happened. He just did not want to face the facts. He did not belong in her world. Coming back had been a mistake. They had all been right. He was wrong.

CHAPTER 35

MISUNDERSTANDING

Caitlin wiped the tears away from her eyes. She was an emotional wreck. If Steven did not mean anything to her, then why was she upset? Her heart ached. She did not like the fact he had done whatever that was to Gemma, but she knew should not have told Gemma the things she had. They were both in the wrong. Steven was only correcting the mistake she made. She was the fool, she was the idiot.

She nuzzled the toy shark. She was the hypocrite, she considered the Great white to be one of the most magnificent creatures on the planet. So who was she now to rebuff Steven for what he could do. He was only protecting his identity. She could not believe she had asked him to go. He didn't even put up a fight. She jumped off the bed, zipped up her hooded top and raced down the stairs.

She opened the front door and rushed out, frantic she searched the street. In the distance, she saw Steven walking away. He was fast. With no shoes on, she scrambled past the gate and ran in his direction. As she did, she failed to see the recycling bin on the curb, stumbled and fell. More like flew really. Face down on the floor, the tears broke free. She had sprained her ankle. She would not be able to follow.

'Caitlin, are you alright?' Steven. How was he there so quickly? He was so far away. Could he hear her from that distance? She sat up, her lower lip trembling.

'Caitlin, you don't have to be like that. You didn't need a dramatic fall to get my attention.'

She lifted her head and was met with his boyish grin. She scowled. He was teasing her again, just like in the old days. He played the role of the joker very well sometimes. 'You know, I never did get your humour.'

'I know, but a guy has to keep trying. I make you laugh occasionally. Not a few minutes ago, I grant you, but other times.' He sat down beside her.

'You are a very annoying man. Do you know that Steven Thorn? You're like chocolate – addictive, sweet and always tempting even though you are very, very bad for me.'

His finger started to trace the vein on the back of her wrist. 'Addictive, I like that one.'

His finger started to drive her crazy. She pulled her hand away and tried to get up. 'Ouch,' she yelled.

'Come on then, I'll carry you back.' Steven put one arm on her shoulder and the other round the front of her waist. It did help, but his proximity caused a million more fireworks to explode all over her body. He was too close, way too close.

'Thanks.' She hopped along using his full support. After a few more hops she was in agony.

'Okay, this is stupid.' He shook his head.

Before she could stop him, he lifted her up in his arms and carried her inside like a baby. Caitlin had never, ever been so embarrassed.

***

Caitlin had not locked the front door in her haste, it was still slightly ajar. Steven pushed it open and took her into the living room.

Gemma watched them come in with a vacant expression. A second later she came back to life. 'Oh my god, what happened? Caitlin, are you alright?'

Steven put Caitlin down on the sofa.

'I'm fine, I just fell,' Caitlin said. She sounded deflated.

Gemma gazed at Steven in admiration. 'Simon, you are like her knight in shining armour. Caitlin is so lucky to have you.' Then she turned to Caitlin with a serious expression. 'Where does it hurt?'

'My ankle.'

'I'll go get some cold peas or something.'

As Gemma dashed out, Caitlin rolled her eyes towards Steven and huffed, 'mind control?'

Steven sat down next to her and put her feet on his lap. 'You

234

have to admit, it has some advantages. She likes me now.'

He could see she did not want to agree. Hesitant, she added, 'I guess.'

'Anyway, it looks like you're being looked after now. I should leave.' He loved teasing her.

Caitlin's face grimaced. 'NO!'

'I, err, shouldn't leave?' It was fun to play around. He had forgotten what it was like. She was so gullible.

She stared at Steven. In a slow, calculated voice, she added, 'please stay. I was trying to catch up with you just before I fell.'

He melted a little. 'I hoped that was what you were doing. I didn't think that going out for a run without shoes and a hangover was such a good idea.'

She pouted, but a smile lingered on the edge of her lips. Her eyes were vibrant, full of life, just like he remembered. The first time he'd seen that was when he'd beaten her at a game of pool. She'd been angry and impressed. It was always funny to see her upstaged. It was no different at this particular moment. He was convinced she was trying to stay angry at him, but failing miserably. He couldn't help smiling.

'You're doing it again, aren't you?' she accused, definitely sulking.

'Doing what?' He held out his hands and pulled a puzzled expression. He would play along.

'I am not going to tell you. You know what you're doing. We'll leave it at that.' She folded her arms and faced the window.

He massaged her toes. 'Does this mean I'm forgiven?'

She turned slowly and faced him. 'You know if I had any doubt as to whether you had changed at all, you've just dispelled my fears. You have not changed a bit.' She undid her arms and gripped the edge of the sofa seat cushion.

'Is that a good thing?' He was so close to breaking down her defences.

She bit her lip, batted her eyelids and gave him the smile he knew and loved. 'Yes, it is a very good thing.'

Internally, he was shouting for joy – success at last. He

leaned in, he needed to kiss her. Gemma came in and broke the moment.

'Just err, bringing the peas like I said I would. I'll leave them here and err, give you some space I think.' She left the peas and a tea towel on the table and left in a hurry.

Steven got the peas, wrapped them in the tea towel and placed it on her ankle. 'There, now where were we?'

Caitlin smiled and leaned in.

He was home again.

***

Caitlin had to admit that kissing Steven was the best thing she could ever remember doing. Well, maybe not the best thing she'd done with him. A part of her couldn't wait to get further acquainted. If her vivid dreams had been anything to go by she was in for a treat. As his arms wrapped around her every nerve ending in her body yelped. It did not help that it was that time of the month. She always suspected her moods were linked to her cycle. If he was planning to seduce her, he couldn't have chosen a better time.

She pulled back, not quite ready to give in to her needs, and linked her hand in his. She loved his hands. They were much bigger than hers and yet soft, cuddly. She held his hand up to her face and nuzzled against it. They were the best cuddly toy in the world. In response, he leant his head against hers and wrapped his other arm around her for a full cuddle.

Words were overrated. She wanted him back in her life. She did not know what that meant but she did not care. Somehow, they would work it out. Anything was possible.

The next few minutes were intense. Neither of them moved, the sound of their breathing heavy.

He kissed her forehead. 'So, how is the ankle?' His voice sounded croaky. Was it possible he was emotional? She didn't think men did emotions. In any case he had never shown that side of him to her.

'It's fine.'

She noticed his eyes were glazed. She slid her arms under his and leant against his chest. She could hear the steady sound of his heart beat. He was real. He was not a monster or a vampire, a heartless demonic soul. It was a stupid notion. How could he be?

He leant his head on hers again and whispered her name.

'Steven, I'm…'

'It's okay,' he cooed. 'Everything's going to be okay now.'

She wanted to believe him.

'Shall I take you upstairs? You should lie down. I promise I don't have any ulterior motives. I've already seen your room anyway, it's no big deal.'

She knew he meant it. He was a gentleman, always had been. The thing was it was a big deal for her. Thoughts of the bedroom sent her imagination off on a tangent, time alone with him was what she wanted more than anything. So what if something happened? 'Sure, that's a good idea. I-I think you have to carry me.'

'No problem,' he said, as he scooped her up in his arms again. He made it look so easy.

She raised her eyes and asked, 'have you been weight training or something?'

'No, it's just the new me.'

She liked this new, improved Steven. 'Right, another advantage then?'

'Another advantage.'

He set her down on the bed and took a seat on the chair next to the bed. Dialogue was a good idea. She decided to get him talking. 'Do you miss your grandparents? It sounded like you got close to them?'

'Yes and no. They helped me come back, I owe them for that. But, I didn't really get the chance to know them. I miss my parents more.'

She doubted he meant his real mum. 'Your dad and your stepmum?'

'Yeah.'

'Why don't you go and see them? Couldn't you return their memory, like you did mine?'

'They took everything they had away. My dad has no idea he had a son. What would be the point?'

'Erm, you could have said the same about me. I don't regret

knowing the truth.'

He looked pensive. 'I guess, maybe I could go and see them.'

'I'll come with you.' She had always wanted to go on a road trip.

'Really?' His face lit up.

'Of course,' Caitlin smiled. 'We could go next weekend if you like.'

'It's a date.'

She liked the sound of that.

Steven gave a half smile. 'You know, the family house is in the outskirts of Southampton. I can take you there if you like. You can have a glimpse of my ancestral past. Well, on my biological mother's side at any rate.'

'Maybe, when you're ready.' She couldn't imagine he was in a rush to go back there.

'Okay, I'll let you know. Thanks.'

She gave him a cheeky smile. 'You may be able to read me, but I can read you too. Don't forget that.'

'I won't.' His smile said it all. 'Are you hungry?'

'Actually, yes, I am. I think my stomach needs food to recover from my binge last night.' She stopped and thought carefully about her next words. 'I err, don't usually get drunk. You realise that, right?'

'I'm not in a position to judge, am I?' He sat up straight in the chair and shrugged his shoulders.

Her hands felt superfluous on her lap. 'I guess not. I just don't want you to think that it's what I do now. It was just something I needed last night. As you can see I'm not going to repeat that in a hurry.'

'What you do is your choice. I never would. Not just because I never did before, but because now I have no idea what would happen if I did. I might go AWOL. You never know.' He raised his eyebrows in what looked like an attempt to look funny. It just looked silly.

Caitlin could not stop herself from laughing out loud. Once recovered, she asked, 'I can't actually imagine you as scary. What happens? Can you tell me? Are you really *scary*?'

Steven gave a raucous laugh. She did not think it was that funny.

'What?' She wanted to be included in the joke?

'Your face, it's just classic, I have no idea if I'm scary. I don't think so. I know mind control is effective, but it's still early days. I don't know what I'll do.'

It sounded like an honest answer.

Caitlin lay back on the pillow and thought about what she wanted to know. She had no idea where to start. She tried to ignore her throbbing head.

***

Something about the way Caitlin tilted her head back and pursed her lips convinced Steven she was about to embark on her next line of questioning. Yet, he could see her eyes were weary. He decided to make himself useful. 'I'll go make you some food.'

She straightened up and smiled. 'That would be great. I'm famished.'

'I'll get breakfast. Don't want you getting up with your bad ankle and all. Can I get anything?' He knew what students were like from the short time he'd been at university.

'Get whatever, I'll square up with Gemma and Sally later on. A cup of tea would be great,' she gave a cheeky grin.

Steven froze. 'Sally?'

'Yeah Sally, my other flatmate, don't you remember her?'

'I didn't think you got on with Sally, you mean the one that went out with my old mate Adam?'

'Yeah, that's the one. Is it a problem?' Caitlin looked puzzled.

'No, not at all, glad she's still your friend. She just reminded me of a different time, that's all.'

He made his way down and got busy. He hoped he didn't bump into Sally, the last thing he needed was someone else who might remember him.

239

CHAPTER 36

INTRODUCING THE AMAZON

Half an hour later, Steven entered the room with two refilled mugs and a couple of plates laden with sausages, baked beans, fried eggs and a few rounds of buttered toast. He put them down by the bedside table. He had to admit he was impressed with his balancing act. The community had taught him a lot more than he wanted to credit it for. Caitlin's eyes were closed, her mouth slightly open as she breathed deeply.

He leant over and kissed her lips.

The corners of her lips curled up and her eyes fluttered open. 'Sorry, I was just dozing.'

'It's alright sleepy head. Hungry?'

Caitlin stretched and sat up. 'Absolutely.'

'I made you tea this time.'

'Thank you.' She took the cup and practically drained it in the first slug. Her eyes widened.

Steven sipped his coffee and picked up her plate. 'Food is served.'

Caitlin balanced it on her lap. 'Scrummy.' She started to tuck in. After a few hungry mouthfuls, she gazed up. 'So, do you age? Your uncle was not exactly old, he was our age.'

Steven finished his mouthful and gave a half smile, he felt remotely smug. He knew she was going to start with the questions. She didn't miss a thing. He sipped his coffee and replied, 'I will remain this way for a long time.'

'Really, you'll stay looking the same.' She cocked her head to the side. 'That's weird. Guess you won't be able to hang around the same place for long.'

'No, I guess not.' He hadn't really given it too much thought.

After a few minutes, Caitlin put the now empty plate on the

side and drank the last of the tea.

'Another?' he asked.

She leant back on the headboard. 'I'd love another.'

Steven collated the plates and mugs. 'Coming right up.' It would give him a few minutes of respite. He was sure the questions were mulling around in that pretty little head of hers now.

When he returned Caitlin had perked up a bit. Her eyes did not look quite as glazed and she was sat up, a magazine discarded next to her when he arrived.

'The ankle okay?' he asked.

'It's fine.' Her eyes stared into space, lost in thought again. 'So, you said your grandmother died. Shouldn't you all be immortal or something like that?' She gave an uneasy laugh.

He chuckled. 'Well, we all thought so until a few weeks ago. If what I saw from my grandparents is true, in the end the aging process speeds up before you die naturally. It looks like we can choose to die. My grandmother, Judith, decided to let go first, she was back home. I think she didn't want to kill for blood anymore, she told me she had lived long enough.'

'How old was she?' Caitlin fiddled with the duvet cover.

'She was 116 years old.'

Caitlin's jaw dropped. 'Wow.'

'She told me other normal humans have also lived that long, and it is all true – I checked. I don't think she thought she was *that* special.'

Caitlin shook her head. 'It's a lot longer than most people live.

Steven nodded.

'So what happened next?' Caitlin's eyes glimmered. He suspected she found this all rather intriguing.

'Well, my grandfather, Jeff, was devastated, as you can imagine. He didn't want to live without her. So, he gave up on life too.'

Caitlin let out a low whistle. 'They must have been really in love.'

'They were.' Steven gulped for the first time. Talking about them choked him. He took a sip of coffee, composed himself, and continued. 'Anyway, they both abstained from having blood. We have no way of knowing if they would have died anyway, it's an unknown. The only thing I know is that Judith died first and Jeff managed to extend his life by drinking more blood. So, the chances are that there is a link. Then again, different people die at different times. There is no logical reason why someone might not die later from natural causes. We know there is no way to tell how long anyone will live.'

'I guess, but everyone ages in the end, as in there physical appearance changes. Yours doesn't. So, in a way, you really are like a vampire? You needed blood to change and you need blood to stay young.'

'In a crude form, yes, I guess I am. Do I look like one to you?' He cocked his head to the side and snarled, curling his hands.

Caitlin laughed again. 'No, you look silly. Not scary.'

'Well there you go.'

Caitlin sipped her tea. She put it back down. She looked ready for another round of questions. 'So, what happened in the Amazon? The dream stopped when you got there. It looked amazing, by the way.'

'In the middle of nowhere, if you ask me.' He could not help rolling his eyes.

'Tell me about it.' She twirled a strand of hair in her finger.

'You sure you want to know?'

'Yes.' She folded her arms and snuggled under the covers, in the long stay department.

'Right, where do I begin?'

As he started to tell her about the months in the community, he wondered whether she should know everything. Should he tell her about his one night stand with Lucy? Did she need to know *everything*? It might be better to keep quiet about some things for now.

***

Caitlin blinked and tried to stay focused. Her head throbbed, her stomach cramped and she was exhausted. She had asked Steven to tell her about it, now she was not sure she wanted to know. She could not believe he had been through such an experience. To be honest, nothing he said scared her. The opposite, in fact, it intrigued her. What a logical world. What a place. She wanted to see it. She wanted to be a part of that community, away from the constraints of modern life. They sounded so powerful.

Steven stopped talking and laughed. 'Caitlin, your eyes are about to close. Shall I tell you the rest later?'

She pried her eyes open and rubbed them hard. 'It sounds amazing. I can't believe an entire community exists hidden within the confines of the Amazon. And your friends sound nice – Jensen in particular. Don't you miss them?' She fought back against her weakness.

'He's a good friend. I missed you more. Do you mind if I lie next to you? It's been a while. I promise I won't do anything untoward.'

Was she being a complete floozy for wanting him to do something untoward? 'Come here.'

He gave a half smile and sat down on the bed. Since it was only a single bed, she shuffled over to the wall and he squeezed in next to her. At first, neither knew what to do. Caitlin was not going to make the first move. Then Steven slid his hand into hers and started to rub his thumb inside her palm. She turned to face him and before she knew what was happening they were kissing. It was not a hungry kiss. It was soft, gentle, more like yearning.

When they took a breath she leant her head against his chest and he put his arm around her. She closed her eyes, relaxed and floated away to the land of dreams, a place where everything was possible.

When she woke up, she noticed some saliva had dribbled down the side of her lip. She must have been in a deep sleep. Steven was still there, she hugged him tighter. Her mouth had a rancid taste to it – she would never, ever drink again. 'How long have I been out for?'

'A few hours,' he said, and rubbed her arm with his hand.

'Really? Sorry, I'm such a sleepy head. Bad night, I guess,' she gave an awkward chuckle. 'I won't be doing that again in a hurry.'

'We'll see.' His voice betrayed his uncertainty.

'Did I snore?' she gasped, she hated it when he said she had.

'Well, do you want the truth or the polite answer?' He was amused, she could tell.

She did not dare look at him. 'I snored, didn't I?' It was so embarrassing.

'You said it, not me.'

She felt him shrug his shoulders. 'I need the loo, can you help me?'

'Sure.' He got off the bed, and held out his arm.

Her foot hurt more now, she was going to have to take some painkillers. She leant against him, hopped on her good foot and put on a brave face. He practically lifted her off the floor as he helped her out of the room and the pain eased.

Once through the bathroom door, she thanked him and shut it. Then she hopped over to the sink and splashed water on her face. She went to the toilet, relieved she was using it for its standard use again. Then she brushed her teeth. The smell of alcohol and sick still lingered. Finally, she hopped back to the door. He leant against the balustrade. In the dim light of the hallway he looked so mysterious. There was a huge part of her that could not believe he was actually there waiting for her. It was shocking really.

'Ready?' he asked, breaking the image of statuesque perfection.

'Shall we go down and get some lunch?'

'I'm not sure you're up to it. Are you?'

He had a point. 'I'll manage.' She wasn't going to stay in her room all day.

He held out his arm again. With his help, she hobbled down the stairs and made it to the kitchen.

Sally was there with Justin.

'Hey, what happened to you?' Sally asked. Then she turned to look at Steven and flicked her hair. When she did she froze for a moment, but recovered a second later. 'Do I know you?' The way she concentrated on his features was intense.

Justin flinched and did a quick double take. Caitlin couldn't blame him. It did look like Sally was checking Steven out.

244

Caitlin suspected there was more to it.

'This is Simon, my boyfriend. Simon, this is Sally and Justin.'

Steven nodded. Caitlin could tell he was avoiding eye contact.

'Boyfriend? You kept that one quiet,' Sally said, now running her hand through her hair.

Justin came behind Sally and hugged her. 'Shall we go out? Get some lunch. I fancy going out with my girl.'

Sally turned, faced Justin and they started to kiss. It felt like they were at it for hours. It was almost pornographic.

'Let's go then, handsome,' Sally said, as she peeled off Justin, who looked dazed. 'See you around Steven. I'm still sure I've met you before.' The way she laughed was eerie.

But what really irked Caitlin was the fact she stared at Steven when she said handsome. Caitlin could not help the venomous tone as she corrected Sally. 'His name is *Simon*.'

Sally paused, 'what did I say?'

'You said Steven.' Caitlin said.

'Oh, sorry about that Simon, you looked like a Steven to me.' She chuckled as she strolled off.

Sally was such a flirt. Caitlin could not understand how she had managed to share a flat with two of the biggest flirts on campus. It was interesting, she never remembered Sally showing any interest in Steven before. Did she see something different now?

Once they were gone, Caitlin voiced her thoughts. 'Weird? Do you think she remembers you?'

'Maybe,' Steven smiled. 'Anyway, do you have any food?'

'No, I have to go shopping,' she sighed. Two male visitors and she could not impress either of them.

'I have a confession to make.' Steven said, after he helped her sit on a chair.

'Surprise me,' Caitlin said. Was there more?

'Well, whilst you slept I went shopping. I realised your food cupboard was pretty awful. So, you do actually have food.' He gave a cheeky grin.

'Wow...' She really was speechless. It was nice to be

looked after for a change.

'I was going to make pasta with chicken in a pesto sauce, you like?'

'Yes, you know I like. Did you also buy parmesan?' She felt like a giddy school kid.

'I did.' Steven busied himself, pouring water into a pot and putting a proportionate amount of pasta in to boil.

'Wow, you got domesticated. Is it me or did you get housetrained whilst you were away?' There was a real chance she would like this new Steven even more than the old one.

'I had to do a lot of stuff I'd never done before whilst I was away. So, I guess I've got some new life skills.' He glanced back, smiled and then got busy with the chicken. He opened the packet, took the fillets out, placed them on the board and started to cut them up. 'I even got desert.'

She was really, really impressed. 'What did you get?'

'Not telling, later.'

She gave a sly smile and huffed, 'same as always. So…do you turn all the girls' heads, or do you think Sally recognised you?'

'Probably, to both, it was strange.'

'You must have had some attention at the community. You have not told me about that? What about this Ingrid?'

He took out the frying pan, drizzled in some oil and put on the heat. 'I had some attention.'

Watching him cook was hypnotic. 'Annnd? If we're going to be honest with each other, we might as well start here.'

The pasta started to bubble over, so he lowered the heat and gave it a proficient stir before he put it back on the hob. He put the chicken in and it started to sizzle. Her stomach did a flip.

'There were a few girls who wanted to get to know me better.'

'I expected that, and you weren't tempted?' She would have serious competition now. She was gobsmacked. He was too good to be true.

He tossed the chicken around. Satisfied, he opened the jar of pesto and poured it in. The smell overwhelmed.

Then he turned around, his eyes serious, and folded his arms over his chest. 'I only wanted you, you have to know that. It's just well, there was one time. It didn't mean anything. It just happened.'

A part of her was jealous he'd been with someone else, she could not deny it. 'I can't exactly claim innocence, I was with Daniel too.'

'I'm not keeping score.' He turned and stirred.

'Neither am I. I was trying to say that it doesn't matter.' Why had the conversation turned again? She could not help thinking this was what it was going to be like. She was so sensitive.

'It matters to me. I didn't plan to sleep with anyone else. I wanted to be with you. I was just lonely.' His expression said it all.

If her foot didn't hurt so much she would have gone over. She was not bothered – how could she be? He looked so sad, full of regret. Instead, she reached out to him with her hand and motioned him to come over.

He unfolded his arms and walked towards her. As soon as he was close enough she took hold of his hand, pulled him down and kissed him. Mutual understanding reached.

The sound of the pasta boiling over again made him jump up. 'You really shouldn't distract me. I think it's ready anyway.' He got some plates, drained the pasta and shared it out. He placed the chicken on top. A sprinkle of parmesan finished it off.

Caitlin was so hungry, and it wasn't just for the food.

'Your food, señorita,' he smiled.

'Thank you.' She could get used to this. 'Still speaking some Spanish then?'

'A little, it was handy in the community. A huge portion of the population is of Spanish descent.' He pinched the chicken with his fork and took a bite.

'Really?' It was now even *more* interesting.

As they ate, she could not help thinking things had become too normal.

CHAPTER 37

REUNION

Caitlin tried really, really hard to concentrate on the lecture. It was difficult. Next to her sat Steven, her boyfriend. It was a strange notion. He was the first man she had ever fallen in love with, the first man she had opened her heart to, and the first man she had slept with. And yet, until a week ago she had no idea any of it was true. For the past few months she had been living in limbo. Knowing something was missing and not being able to place it. Not until Steven had reinstated her memory. It was lucky she was not going mad after all, although she still had a way to go to convince her brother she was not a bitch. Daniel was his best friend after all. Her brother thought she was heartless.

The week had gone by so quickly. Caitlin had spent every day with Steven. It was tempting to ask him to stay over, but so far they had resisted. The kissing was intense, the relationship was definitely back on track – at least she thought so. Every time she thought of him her stomach churned, the need to be with him grew stronger and stronger. The fact he sat next to her for a proportion of the day made it hard to keep thoughts of him at bay.

'I am beginning to understand why you take maths, this is the most interesting lecture I have *ever* heard,' Steven whispered. He did *not* sound sincere.

'I need to concentrate,' she said. It was exasperating he found it all so easy.

'Don't let me stop you.' He slouched on the seat and put his chin on his chest – snooze position. A slight grin pasted on his face.

Caitlin huffed. She attempted to focus and wrote down the notes, for what it was worth. She had no idea what the lecturer was going on about. Somehow, she doubted Steven would have any problems.

Once the lecture concluded, Caitlin got her stuff together and got ready to leave.

She looked up and saw he was waiting. 'No notes again?'

Steven tapped his head, 'it's all up here now.'

'Lucky you.' She was dead jealous. 'You remember everything, just like that?'

'Just like that.'

'You know people are going to talk. They'll think you're weird you know. Everyone takes notes.'

Steven widened his eyes. 'You know, you've got a point. I'll have to *pretend* to take notes.' He looked cute as he said that. He had not changed at all as far as she was concerned.

'You do that,' she said, restraining her chuckle.

As they made their way out of the lecture room, Caitlin blushed. A lot of girls were giving her the thumbs up. They were obviously impressed and she had to agree, he was a great catch. Somehow she doubted they'd all consider him to be such a great catch if they found out the truth. Caitlin checked her mobile. Gemma had not sent her a text recently – it was not normal.

'Why do you check your phone all the time?' Steven asked.

'Habit, gotta keep in touch. My sister usually sends me messages, but I usually ignore most of them. I didn't know whether to text Gemma. She wasn't around this morning. We are best friends after all.'

'Do you want to catch up with her for lunch? I can always see you later. Give you some girl time.' His smile was genuine.

'You don't mind?'

'Not at all.'

Caitlin sent Gemma a text and waited. After a few minutes she got a reply. 'Gemma's busy again.' She couldn't help being disappointed. She wanted to be with Steven, but she didn't want to lose touch with Gemma. Gemma had been there for her when she needed a friend. Caitlin could not help thinking that she was avoiding her.

'So, pizza and chips it is then?'

'I might be good and opt for the salad. Then add a hot chocolate.' Caitlin gave a cheeky smile.

'What is it with chocolate? If a fat free option with the same taste was ever discovered the inventor would make a fortune,' Steven said, he leant his head to one side.

Caitlin stood up and started to make a move. Steven slipped his hand into hers and they made their way towards the cafeteria. It was packed, as was usual for the time of day. It seemed students rarely went back home for lunch, most opted for a snack with friends or a quick bite. Caitlin waited in the queue and leant against Steven, just as Adam walked past. Adam licked his lips and leered.

Steven's hand tightened its grip. 'Is he always like that with you?'

Caitlin squirmed. Adam used to be his best friend. 'Yes, he is.'

Steven laughed. 'No wonder you always looked so uncomfortable around him. I knew he could be a slime ball, but I didn't realise he was that bad. Funny, he never did that in front of me before. I want to take him out, and that's saying something. He *was* a good friend.'

Caitlin punched his arm. 'Don't, he's not worth it.' Pain seared around her knuckles. 'Ouch, you're arm is like steel.'

'It's just muscle. You're such a weakling.'

Caitlin hummed, not convinced. 'So, what do you have for the rest of the day? I have to go to a Spanish History lecture.'

'I'm going to skip this afternoon and get the flat ready for a visitor.'

'Really, who's coming to see you?'

'You, of course – will you come for supper? I promise to cook something nice.' He looked like a schoolboy, innocent.

'Sure, I'll come.' She gulped at the thought. They'd be alone.

'Great, I'll pick you up at five. Is that alright?'

'Sounds okay, I should be finished by then.' She took a tuna salad and an apple juice and looked ahead. All she could think was 'what on earth am I going to wear?'

***

Steven knocked on the door and waited. Sally opened the door.

'Is Caitlin here?'

Sally gave him a sexy smile. 'Sure, come in. She's just getting ready for the big date. She's very excited.'

'I heard you Sally.' Caitlin's voice echoed from the top of the stairs.

'Sorry, did you hear me tell Steven you were excited about your big date? Silly me, I didn't mean to say it aloud,' she chuckled, as she walked in the direction of the kitchen.

Caitlin came down the stairs slowly. She had changed into a black pair of tight fitting jeans and a loose blue jumper. The blue of the jumper matched the colour of her eyes, now framed in thick mascara. Her reddish brown lipstick completed the look. She looked gorgeous. He could not wait to have her in his apartment, his thoughts ran wild.

He kept his outer thoughts polite. 'You look very nice. Thanks for making an effort. You didn't have to.'

'I wanted to. Got to make a good impression, after all we have only just started dating Simon.' She winked.

'Thanks all the same.' He winked back.

'Sally,' Caitlin called. 'Are you in the kitchen?'

'Yes,' Sally's voice called back.

Caitlin turned to Steven and smiled. 'I'll be right back.'

Steven could hear her perfectly from the corridor. It was typical of Sally to ask if she had *protection*. He held back a laugh. After saying their goodbyes, Caitlin returned to the corridor.

'Shall we?' he asked.

'Let's.'

Truth be told, Steven was apprehensive about taking her to his apartment. It was small, barely furnished and simple. He just wanted her to be with him, in his space for a change. And he was planning to cook again. He knew just what to make to impress her. He made idle chit chat as he drove to deviate his thoughts. He was glad he'd managed to pick up an old Ford Fiesta. A set of wheels that would not draw a lot of attention was always a good plan. 'So, lecture went okay?'

'Spanish is easy. It's fun and much more enjoyable than maths. I know I like maths once I get it, it's just sometimes I don't get it for a while.' She looked sheepish. 'What's it like for you? Are you like a genius now or something?'

'I don't know about that. I just seem to be able to recall facts and information.'

She opened her mouth in awe. 'I would definitely be up for some of that. I'd whizz through my degree then.'

'I'd still rather be studying Law.'

'Why don't you?'

The question was a good one. He could make anything happen, couldn't he? 'Good point, but I'll stick to this for now. I can't sit next to you in Law.'

She nudged him. 'So you are a stalker, the truth is out.'

He laughed aloud, his hands still firmly in control of the car. 'I probably am.'

Steven turned the car to the right and took the first available parking space. He went to get her door, but she was already out. She rarely gave him the chance to be gallant. There was something about chivalry he liked – if only she let him. He held out his arm and she took it. At least he could make little gestures. He entered the pass code and a buzz let them in. 'It's just up a flight of stairs.'

'What number?'

'Ten.'

'Race you,' she shouted, as she lunged for the stairs.

He was too slow to respond. She never ceased to amaze him. So much for the sprained ankle! He made chase, but let her win. When he arrived at the door he pinned her against the wall. They stared at each other, both slightly out of breath. He exaggerated his breathing to not make her self conscious. Simultaneously, they leaned in and kissed. It was a hungry kiss. He took his key out of his pocket, put it in the lock and opened the door, without breaking free from her lips.

The second the door shut, all inhibitions were lost. Food was an afterthought.

***

Caitlin looked up at the ceiling, eyes transfixed. That had been amazing – exactly as she remembered. Better in fact, if that was possible. She focused on her deep breaths and shivered, the chill from her sweat starting to take hold. She turned and wrapped her arms around Steven. He did the same and they hugged. Steven let out a few shivers of his own; she doubted it was from the cold. He had to be just as shocked as she was. That had been one hell of a ride.

She lay there, taking in his scent, enjoying the feel of his body against hers – reminiscing. As she shook again, he let her go and got up. She watched his naked form walk away. It was definitely something to look at. She could not believe watching him aroused her again. A minute later he returned with a duvet and threw it over her. They snuggled under. It was lucky his floor was carpeted. Otherwise, she'd definitely have had to move to the bed.

'Thanks.'

He kissed her again and she responded. They got lost in the moment for a second time, once was not enough. They had always been insatiable in the past, it was lucky Steven was well prepared.

Ten minutes later she lay back and closed her eyes, utterly amazed.

Steven lay just as comatose next to her.

After a few minutes Caitlin sighed. 'Wow.'

Steven voice was low and hazy as he replied, 'Yeah.'

'I can't believe my dreams were real.'

'Dreams?' He leant on his elbow and ran his hand along her hair. 'You dreamt of us?'

'All the time, you're amazing.' Her voice was wispy, far away.

'Correction, you're amazing.'

The sound of her stomach rumble broke the moment.

'Food! Sorry. I promise I did not lure you here to seduce you. I intend to cook you a meal fit for a queen.' He got up and found his boxer shorts, put them on and made his way over to the small kitchenette.

'Did you really *not* plan to seduce me? I intended to seduce you.' Her tone made it clear. It was a matter of fact.

'Caitlin Chance. Are you saying you accepted with a hidden agenda?'

Caitlin laughed, 'not so hidden.'

'Yeees.' He opened the fridge.

She could have offered to help, but she was wasted. Instead, she squirmed over to the iPod docking station on the floor and searched through his tracks. Finding one she liked, she pressed play and cuddled back into the duvet. The sizzle and smell of garlic filled the room. Her stomach protested. She sat up, put her bra and panties back on and then threw her jumper over her head. As she approached, Steven tossed a bowl of prawns into the frying pan, along with the chilli and herbs. It was one of her favourite Spanish dishes – his signature dish – *Gambas pil pil*.

'Yum. Can I help?'

'Nope, just take a seat. Can I get you a glass of wine?'

'I thought you didn't approve of alcohol?' she raised her eyes.

'As part of a meal, it's vital.' He placed the prawns on a plate and put them on the table. Then he put down a bowl with some thick slices of bread, and got the bottle of wine and some glasses. 'Dig in.'

It was rude not to.

Caitlin took a wedge of bread and dipped it in the sauce. She put it in her mouth and hummed. It was delicious.

Steven followed suit, and then took a prawn with his fork. He held it in front of Caitlin, 'ladies first?'

'If you insist.' She was not going to argue over a prawn. Especially, not one as eagerly anticipated as that one. She chewed and took a sip of wine. 'So, where do we go from here?'

Steven smiled. 'Time will tell.'

CHAPTER 38

THE ANCESTRAL HOME

As the sun started to show its face it enveloped the sky in an amazing sunrise. On a clear day like this the effect was magical. The white frost on the ground added to the shiny illusion. Steven turned away from the window and faced Caitlin. Everything was perfect. Caitlin was perfect. The night had been perfect.

They were back as they belonged – together.

Steven knew he had not imagined it. What he had with Caitlin was special, it was worth fighting for. She completed him in a way no other woman could. He was sure of that. He had always been sceptical of true love, but from the moment he met Caitlin no other girl had made him feel the same way. She was the only girl he wanted to be with.

He just had no idea how he was going to explain what he wanted to do. He had been debating the merits of what his grandfather told him, he was not sure if he should even tell her about it. He just did not think he had many options. He did not want to live alongside her and watch her age.

He shook his head. It was too cruel. He had to tell her the truth. He had to give her the choice. The thirst would also raise its weary head. It was pointless to consider staying here forever. Not unless he came up with a very good plan. He had to explain everything to her. He had to be open. He just had to find the right moment.

Lost in his thoughts, he heard Caitlin sigh and return to reality. She opened her eyes and smiled at him.

'Good morning, sleepy head,' he said, as he eased back into bed and hugged her.

'Is it morning already? What's the time?'

'You are obsessed with the time.' He looked at the clock.

'It's seven thirty.'

Caitlin chuckled. 'Someone is stood to attention again. Doesn't he get tired?'

'Eventually.'

Steven doubted he would ever have enough of her, but he kept the thought to himself. Instead, he kissed her deeply. She returned the kiss and he let his actions show her he was definitely not tired.

***

Caitlin stretched on the bed and folded her arms over her face. Her body ached. It longed for more rest and more sleep. She was well and truly knackered, spent – finished. No more. That's what she told herself over and over. Yet, every time he kissed her she reacted. Her body yearned for him like an addict yearns for their addiction after a period of abstinence. She peeked at him from under her arms and mumbled, 'I don't think I can go to lectures today. I'm sure I have an FFF.'

'Nothing wrong with having a fresh face, what was the second F for again?' Steven traced his finger along her leg. 'Not sure we did that one enough.'

She snapped up to a sitting position and lightly slapped his hand. 'No more, behave. Enough.'

Steven pulled a puppy dog face and whimpered.

'Come here.' Caitlin held her arms open as he came in for another cuddle. 'You know even though we're adults, I'm not sure everything we did last night is legal.'

'We haven't even scratched the surface.'

'Ahhhgh,' Caitlin squealed, as she pushed him off. 'I mean it, no more.' She tucked the duvet under her armpits and gave him a determined stare. 'Are we really going to skip lectures? My mum would kill me.'

'What she doesn't know won't hurt her, right?'

Caitlin grabbed a pillow and hurled it at his face. 'You are such a bad influence!'

'So, what do you say? Want to spend the day with me or go to boring lectures? I know it's a tough one, but you have to choose.' He sat down on the chair next to the bed and waited.

Caitlin wanted to spend the day with him. She didn't think if she went to lectures she'd hear a word of what they said anyway. She had nothing to lose. 'You win. Where are we going?'

'Back to bed?' He gave her a cheeky grin.

She sighed. 'Come on now, be serious.'

'Do you want to see my ancestral home? It's desolate, huge and unoccupied. Besides its Friday, we can stay for the weekend.'

Caitlin suspected an ulterior motive, but she agreed. 'Fine, I'll come.' She was curious about his past. Perhaps, his ancestral home would shed some more light on Steven Thorn and who he really was.

*

A couple of hours later they had their belongings in two small rucksacks and were sat in Steven's Fiesta. It felt like an adventure. Caitlin had left a message on the table with a contact number in case of a problem. If anyone asked, she was revising for the exams starting the following week.

Caitlin loved to watch the countryside at this time of year. It was green and luscious, beautiful. Of course, it meant there was a lot of rain, which in England went without saying. She studied the bare, deciduous, oak trees which now revealed an intricate pattern of branches she found fascinating. There was something calming about watching the world go by. They had barely spoken for half an hour, but they held hands intermittently.

'Let's stop and get some food. I don't think there are any supplies in the house,' Steven said, as he indicated into the motorway service station. 'We can get a bite to eat at the café first, what do you say?'

'Sounds good.'

The café was not too busy. They seemed to be mainly truck drivers and a few weary travellers.

'Can I get you anything?' The male attendant asked.

'Yes, please,' she replied, as she leant it to take a look. 'I'll have a hot chocolate, BLT, and a packet of roasted peanuts please.'

'I'll have a latte, a ploughman's, and a packet of bacon

crisps please?'

The man placed the order on a tray. Steven quickly handed over a twenty pound note. 'I'll pay for hers.'

Caitlin blushed. 'Thanks.'

'My pleasure.'

They took a seat by a raised table. Swirling the plastic spoon in the drink, she thought aloud. 'So, how do you pay for everything now?'

'They set me up with some money. They have lots, and I can also get more anytime I want. I have the ability to be *extremely* persuasive. But, I will get a job eventually and earn it properly,' he sighed, raising his eyebrows. Then he casually took a sip of his coffee.

'Is that why I'm here? Did you *persuade* me to come?' she teased.

'I hope not,' he gasped, confused. 'I didn't have to, *did I*?'

'I don't think you hypnotised me – seduced, definitely.' She laughed aloud. 'So, you can make people do what you want?'

'I'm pretty sure I can.'

'So what would you make me do?' Her eyes widened, it was a dare.

'I wouldn't make you do anything, well, apart from maybe fall madly in love with me and run away. Oh, is that what we're doing now?' He pursed his lips, gave a half smile and widened his eyes. He enjoyed teasing.

'Well, it would explain my irrational desire to be with someone *bad*.'

His facial expression changed from cheeky to concerned, as he seemed to consider this seriously. 'Do you think I'm bad?'

'I haven't made my mind up yet.' She pursed her lips and then took a huge bite out of her sandwich.

Following suit, he took his sandwich out of the packaging and ate half of it in one go.

'That's a dangerous bite,' she joked.

He chewed and gave a disgruntled laugh. 'You have not seen the half of it.' He pecked her lips quickly.

Bewitched, she gazed into his eyes. 'Yummy, cheese and ham.'

'I don't remember you being such a joker before?' he mused.

'You know me, I adapt easily.'

'Yes, you do,' he replied. Mouth empty, he leant in for a deeper kiss.

She tried to not respond, but her lips seemed to move of their own accord. When he pulled back she rolled her eyes. 'I'm eating here. Stop kissing me or I'll turn into jelly.'

'Anything you say,' he grinned. 'But, when you finish you're not going to be safe.'

'I'll look forward to it,' she remarked, taking the other half of her sandwich in her hand.

Flirtation was constant. Steven was relentless, besotted. It was great, just unnerving and intense. Either way, she could not stop giggling like a child at every humorous remark.

Twenty minutes later, as Steven took the turn into the desolate countryside, Caitlin's expression turned from joy to surprise. The house they approached was grand and sat on top of a hill. She would have studied it from the distance if she had thought it was a likely destination. 'So, why are we *here*?'

'This is the house my family still owns.'

'It looks like it should have collapsed ages ago. Are you sure it's safe?'

He gave a low chuckle. 'The outside is only like that for appearances' sake. We can't have strangers checking it out.'

Once inside, the house exuded character. Steven turned on the hall light just as the floorboard creaked under his foot.

'This is creepy.'

'Don't worry, I'm here. What could possibly happen?' he said.

It was difficult to take him seriously. Caitlin rolled her eyes. She followed Steven into the lounge and saw him get busy. He started to prepare an open fire. Cosy. It was freezing so any heat was welcome. As it crackled and came to life, he turned back to face her. 'Come, sit by the fire.'

She walked over and sat next to him on a large, fluffy, floor rug.

'Can I ask you something?' Steven said.

Ominous. 'Sure.'

She noticed the colour of his amber eyes matched the fire roaring to life next to them.

'Are you sure you want to be with me?'

Caitlin smiled. 'Silly question, of course I do.'

'The thing is my grandfather told me something the last time I was here. I wanted to tell you about it, in the place he told me. It seems like the right thing to do.'

She waited. He seemed lost in his thoughts as his eyes fixed on the fire. 'So, what did he tell you?'

'I'll tell you soon, first another question.'

'Another question,' she mock gasped. 'Go for it.' She clasped her hands, the suspense was killing her.

'Do you really think I'm bad?'

She leant back on her hands. 'I told you – no.'

It was impossible to think he was bad after everything he had said, she was in awe of him.

Steven took a breath, held her hand and stared into her eyes. 'Do you think you would ever consider becoming like me?'

She leaned forward. 'What do you mean?' She was not expecting that one.

'Don't be frightened, you don't have to. Likewise, if you decide you don't want me in your life, I understand.'

He was not making any sense. 'Is it even possible?'

'Until now, no-one knew it was possible to change a normal human into one of us. But, it turns out that it's been possible from the very beginning. My grandmother was actually changed by my grandfather. She was not infected by the bats.'

'Really?' Her jaw dropped and eyes widened as she took in the information. She focused on the fire. It was hard to believe what he was saying.

Steven voice was subdued. 'I know – what a secret to keep. Apparently, my grandmother wanted *us* to have the choice.'

'Us?'

Steven held her hand. 'Yes, she knew the main reason I wanted to come back was to be with you. She thought that if I was willing to risk everything to see you again, I had to be given the option. Ultimately, she always lived with the guilt of not having given my mother the same choice. If they had told my mother then perhaps she would have led a normal happy life back in the community with my father, and I would have been raised there.'

Caitlin was very curious. Life in the community sounded amazing. Even though there was the *tiny* issue of having to drink blood, she wanted to know more. 'So, what is it? What do you have to do? Will it hurt?'

She could feel the hairs at the back of her neck rising in anticipation.

Steven smiled. 'You actually sound excited. You're weird.'

'And don't you know it,' Caitlin laughed.

'The truth is I don't know how it will affect you. My grandfather only told me *how* it happened.'

Caitlin did not hesitate. 'So, how did it happen? Tell me, I want to know.'

If joining them meant she would become smarter and stronger, *and* stay youthful – she was definitely interested. She ignored the voice at the back of her mind; it warned her to go with caution. She was done with the cautious approach.

CHAPTER 39

REVELATIONS

Steven braced himself to tell Caitlin the story he could scarcely believe. Her enthusiasm worried him, but he decided to tell her all the same. Otherwise the trip home, and his grandparent's death, would have been in vain.

He took a deep breath and began. 'On the night of the attack my grandfather realised everyone, barring my grandmother, had received a series of wounds from the bat bites. They talked about what it could mean but at that point no-one realised what had happened. A few days later my grandfather attacked my grandmother'

'As in he drank her blood?' Caitlin remained wide eyes; she seemed to hang onto his every word.

Steven bowed his head low. 'Yes.'

'It's alright, I'm listening.'

He was surprised she wasn't running for the hills. 'If you're sure.'

'I'm sure. I want to know.' She squeezed his hand, it felt sincere.

'Okay. My grandfather snapped out of his bloodlust with a few minutes to spare and realised she was still alive. You can imagine how disgusted he felt. He checked her pulse, it was weak and she was unconscious. As a trained doctor he knew she needed blood or she would die, so he did what instinct told him to do. He pressed his finger nail into his wrist and let his blood ease into her mouth. To his surprise, she started to drink before she went into a coma. He didn't know what to make of it, but her pulse was strong. He had a feeling she would survive – and she did. In doing so, she became one of them.

A few days later, they killed their first victim together. Then they saw their daughter Catherine and the others do the same.

When Emily and Anna also succumbed to the disease at the age of twenty they were horrified. They felt like monsters. My grandfather said he always felt guilty for what he did to my grandmother. But, he said she always insisted that if he had not done it she would have lost her children years earlier.'

Caitlin's looked up expectantly, awestruck. 'So, blood exchange works. It's *not* just a myth.'

He held out his hand and cupped her face. She was too good for him. 'Supposedly.'

'So you could change me, I could become like you,' she held his gaze.

Steven could not believe she was contemplating it. He leant in and kissed her lightly on the lips. Then he held her in his arms for a minute. He did not know what to say.

Caitlin pulled back. 'What's wrong? Wouldn't you want to? Isn't that why you came back for me? To be with me and to change me, make me one of you.'

He allowed himself to smile, her directness was overwhelming. 'Even if you are willing to try, I'm not sure we should do anything rash. What if I end up killing you?'

She slid her hand into his. Her hands appeared so dainty against his. 'You wouldn't though, would you?'

'I'd like to think not. We don't have to decide anything now.' He knew he had a serious case of cold feet. A change of conversation was a good idea.

She leant her face into his hand and took a deep breath. 'You smell nice.'

'So do you.' He leant in for another kiss.

As they started to kiss he was taken aback when Caitlin ran her tongue along his teeth. She stopped at his canines and pulled back.

'You have very sharp canines. Are they your deadly weapon?'

It was awkward. 'I guess.'

'You also have very big, mesmerising eyes.'

'All the better to see you with, little red.' He rubbed his nose against hers and laughed.

She waved her hands in the air in what looked like an

attempt at mock horror. 'Should I scream and run now?'

'You could try, but somehow I don't think a woodcutter is going to turn up to save you, so I'd stay put if I were you.'

She gave a slight huff and then faced him, all serious. Her eyes were radiant, like the colour of the Mediterranean Sea. As she spoke, she pulled her hair to the side and exposed the left side of her neck. 'So, should I succumb now? Let you take me?'

'What do you mean?' He could not believe she was saying what he thought she was saying.

'Take me. It's the only way we can stay together.' Still serious.

'Are you willing?' He narrowed his eyes, concerned yet intrigued. It would be difficult to pull away if she continued with her antics.

'I'm willing.' She was barely an arms length away.

His rational brain told him to stop. His instinct forced him to lean in and kiss her neck. With every gentle kiss he got closer to her pulsing artery. As he was about to bite, he forced himself back and stopped. 'I'm so sorry. It's not a game. You shouldn't do that.'

Half dazed, she asked, 'do what?'

Steven frowned. Had she been entranced? Had she lost control? Had he done it? 'You don't know what you just did?' he grimaced.

'What? What's wrong? Why do you look so shocked?' It looked like she didn't have a clue.

'I am a monster,' he said. He got up abruptly and paced.

'What just happened?' She genuinely sounded confused.

'I nearly bit you – that's what,' he spat out in disgust.

'I don't remember. It was like I was in a dream and you were coming to save me.'

'I will *not* do that to you unless you are sure.'

'I know, but obviously, you can't help what you do sometimes.' She was arguing the case in a rational way, as always.

Neither spoke, for a few minutes. Steven did not dare to sit closer.

Caitlin broke the silence. 'It's too late for me to leave. What shall we do?'

He looked up and glanced behind her as he spoke. 'I don't know.'

Caitlin broached the distance, knelt in front of him and took his hands in hers. 'Kiss me again, I want to be yours. I'm not in a trance now, I promise.'

Steven refused to make eye contact. 'You don't know what you're saying. I'm probably still influencing you.'

Caitlin grabbed his face in her hands and forced him to look at her. 'Kiss me,' she demanded.

He leant in and kissed her with a fury beyond his control. Lust overtook the need to feed.

Twenty minutes later, they lay naked again. They lay side by side face up, on the shaggy brown carpet.

'That was amazing,' Caitlin whispered, out of breath. 'You know, I'd nearly forgotten why we were so good together.'

'I hadn't,' he said, as he ran his finger over her breast. She flinched under his touch so he stopped and wrapped his arms around her, his body nestled against hers.

'I want you again and forever.'

He was caught off guard. Was she really in love with him? Or was she just under his spell. It was hard to differentiate. 'For the rest of our lives,' he corrected. 'We don't live forever.'

'Make me yours, take me now,' she asked, as she moved to face him.

Steven released her and stood up. He needed to get some distance between them. He threw a blanket over her and went to get his pants and trousers. 'What about your family and friends?'

She sat up and grabbed his arm when he leant down. She pulled him towards her. 'If you could lose them so can I. Do it now before you freak out on me again.'

'Caitlin. NO!' Steven pulled his hand away, grabbed his things and walked away. He did not mean to shout at her, especially not after they had made love. He was just finding it hard to resist. He would not change her unless he knew she was certain.

The problem remained. How would he ever get that reassurance when he was worried she was not in control? Was it even possible?

The sound of crying made him turn back as he reached the door. He could not leave her like that. Caitlin was curled on a ball on the ground, the blanket discarded at the side. He picked up the blanket and covered her. He sat on the sofa. Head in hands, he leant his elbows on his knees. He could not stand to hear her cry.

A long tortuous minute later, he lifted his head and went over to her side. 'Caitlin, don't cry. Listen to me, please.'

Caitlin looked up, her face red, blotchy and wet. Through muffled tears she said. 'I'm listening.'

Steven struggled to find the right words. His hands tangled together. 'I-I, look I don't want you to do the wrong thing, to make the wrong choice. I had no choice – you do. I don't even know if you know what you're saying. I can't tell you whether this life with me will be a good choice. I don't know much about what you'll become. You could hurt people, like I have. I have not told you everything.'

Caitlin stopped crying and stared at him. It hurt to see her like that. With a nod she gave him a sign to carry on.

'I entranced two girls when I bit them. They are both dead now. Are you ready to kill? Do you want to be responsible for death?'

She shook her head and hugged the blanket. 'I want to be with you.'

'I also want to be with you. We just need some time, time to figure this all out.' Steven moved towards her and sat down. 'Please, don't rush this.'

'I know what I want. I will still be human. I will still be me, just like you are. I just don't want to lose you. Not now, not ever.'

Steven held out his hand and grabbed hers. 'I love you Caitlin. You know that don't you?'

'Yes. I love you too. So, stop hurting me. Let me share this with you. You told me to choose and I did. I'm not scared.

We all kill. We'll be careful. Together.' Her eyes were so blue, deep, soul searching. She brushed her hair aside again and exposed her neck. 'Do it now.'

She was breaking him. As much as he wanted to, he could not resist. Not now, not when he was so weak.

Post coital bliss, hunger and bloodlust – a deadly trio.

He could not stop his canines from extending. He could not stop himself from leaning in. He could not stop his natural instinct to drink. Caitlin's blood was the sweetest, most delectable blood, he had ever tasted. Once he started, he knew there was no going back. It was only when she started to go limp that he managed to snap out of his frenzy.

He pulled back, his eyes wide open, and he checked her pulse.

What was he doing? He had not planned to do this now.

Out of options, he laid her down on the floor and bit into his wrist. His placed his wrist to her mouth and let his blood flow into her mouth. He could not believe it when she started to suck, greedy, just like a newborn baby. He saw the colour flood back into her checks and he checked her pulse. It was getting stronger.

When would she stop?

As though drawn into a drunken stupor her mouth stopped sucking and she fell fast asleep. Peaceful, rested. He stroked her hair and then ran his hand down her face. She looked beautiful. He cradled her in his arms, lifted her off the floor and took her to his bed. She would not wake up for a while. If it was anything like what he had gone through, she would have a hell of a hangover when she eventually woke.

He could not believe what had happened.

It was either the most selfish thing he had ever done in his entire life, or the most inspired. When she woke up he would find out. All he could do was hope that he had done everything right. As far as he knew, he had followed his grandfather's instructions perfectly.

CHAPTER 40

CAITLIN

The corridor seemed never-ending – dark, foreboding. A series of large cinema screen size portraits hung on the walls. Caitlin could not make them out. Even though huge they were out of focus. Nothing was sharp, in range. The only thing she knew was she had to keep on walking. She had to reach the light. The bright beam up ahead beckoned her forward. Her feet throbbed and she winced as each step ignited a fresh twinge. It felt like she had been walking for months. Barefoot, in a scanty nightgown, she could not understand what she was doing. It was strange. She was not cold, just restless and uncomfortable. Something was wrong.

She could not understand why she was alone, she didn't like it. Where had everyone gone?

As she got close enough to touch the light a shadow to the right caught her eye. She did not want to look, something told her to fear, but it compelled her. Her eyes veered to the right, to the source, and made out a man. He was tall, dark, and mysterious. If only she could make out the face. The bright light in her face did not help. She shielded her face and peered on, now eager to see who it was. She took a step forward as he turned his face towards the light.

His amber eyes glistened. His square face was strong, handsome and full of character. She liked the look of him. His eyes met hers and he smiled to reveal a set of sharp canines.

Was that normal?

He took a step towards her and she felt herself turn her head in response as he leaned in and aimed for her neck. She could not understand why she was not putting up a fight.

Was she that weak? Was she that helpless?

Her conscience screamed but she remained powerless. His

bite felt like an injection, a form of mild pain. She started to float away, tired

As her eyelids fluttered open Caitlin wondered what the dream meant. She felt exhausted, like she'd swum a mile at full speed, and yet she was wide awake. To her surprise, as she opened her eyes she felt a surge of energy engulf her and tiny tingles all over her body made her alert, on guard. She was lying on a bed. That much she knew. The ceiling looked familiar. She was in the house, Steven's grandparent's house, but where was Steven?

The answer to her question arrived in the form of Steven, as he took a seat next to her. His soothing voice should have comforted her. It didn't.

Caitlin was amazed at the speed with which she moved when she leapt off the bed and flattened her body against the wall. She narrowed her eyes and watched his every move.

Steven stood up and reached out with his hand. 'Caitlin, you don't need to be scared.'

It was an easy thing to say.

'What happened?' She allowed her eyes to survey the room. A clue, she had to find a clue. Her memory was misty, out of focus.

'You changed Caitlin.' His smile looked genuine and she felt a faint flutter in her stomach. She didn't know if she should trust him.

Her confused mind cleared and she remembered her decision. She had asked him to change her, hadn't she? A part of her did not want to dwell on the past, she could not change it. She wanted to look forward. Yet, the decision weighed on her mind. What would she tell her family? Would she have to fake her own death? Was she supposed to just disappear? It was easy for Steven. His existence had been erased. She wondered if it would be wise to do the same for her.

What they had done was impulsive. They had not thought about the implications. Had she made the biggest mistake of her life? She studied his face again.

'Caitlin, talk to me. How are you feeling?' He frowned,

worry lines etched on his forehead.

She wanted him to sweat it out. She did not want to lie.

He took a step closer and she instinctively flinched and cowered in the corner, the love she felt for him had been replaced with fear. She looked around the room and tried to find an escape route. She needed to get away from him.

Steven had done it. It was *his* fault.

***

Steven tried to access the situation. Caitlin was obviously scared and confused. He could relate to that. He knew what it was like. He remembered how much he hated what had happened to him. The realisation of that thought hit him and he gasped. A moment too late, he watched helplessly as Caitlin lunged out of the open window. She flew out in a perfect dive. With no sedative dart he had no option but to follow. He was glad he did not have a dart; he would have struggled to bring her down forcefully.

Hot in pursuit, he chased her out into the open countryside. He could barely keep up; she was camouflaged by trees and shrubs. After a few minutes he found it hard to believe he had not caught up with her. She was fast, too fast. A million thoughts raced through his head. The most pertinent being her intent. Was she on attack mode?

He could not remember wanting to attack anyone. He just wanted to get away. Perhaps, this gave him a clue.

The short cut Caitlin took answered his question.

She was going back to her house. He could not believe how accurate her directions were. Her navigation system was now in tune with his.

After twenty minutes, he stared up at the open window of the terraced house. It was five in the morning. He could risk it. He leapt up on to the ledge just as the window slammed shut. She stared; eyes narrowed, and scowled as she wagged her finger and grinned.

She looked angry. What had he done?

'Caitlin, let me in. We need to talk.'

She put her face against the window and hissed. 'Get away from me. You have done enough.'

270

'What you are going through is normal. Everyone does it. It's instinctive to run.' Steven put his hands against the glass. 'I love you Caitlin, let me in.'

Caitlin cackled and gave a half smile. 'You love me? Love is for foolish people. You made me a monster. I know what we are. Leave me alone.' She shut the curtains in his face.

He stared at the purple drapes and sighed. He was not going to wait. In an effortless manoeuvre he jumped off the window sill and made his way round the back. He suspected the back door would be easy to break into and he was right. The door to the kitchen gave way easily – it was no match for his strength.

He tiptoed up the steps to Caitlin's room and hoped for the best. It had been a joint decision; at least he thought it had. He had to keep positive.

On the landing, he stopped and listened. He did not want to wake up her housemates. Eyes closed, deep in concentration he made out the sounds of deep sleep. The other sound disconcerted him. Caitlin was crying. Her bravado was larger than reality. Mind made up, he put his hand on the door handle and raced in. Before she could react he grabbed her from behind and placed his hand over her mouth.

'Don't scream. We don't want to wake everyone up. If you promise to keep calm, I'll let you go. What'll it be?'

The small nod sufficed.

He took his hand off her mouth. It was wet from the tears on her face. Then he held her tight, the hold becoming an embrace. She shimmied in defiance, but he did not let go. He felt her defences drop and she stopped fighting. He eased his arms off her and she curled up on the floor like a ball. He stroked her back and was relieved when she did not flinch.

The silence lasted for a few minutes.

Caitlin rocked on the floor as Steven stroked her back. Eventually, Steven decided to make her more comfortable. He picked her up like a baby and she nestled into his shoulder. Her fight relinquished. Then he lay her down on her bed. She closed her eyes and started to breathe deeply. She looked so beautiful when she slept. He could not believe how angry she had been and how much she appeared to hate him. He smiled as he recalled that he had been no different after his change.

After ten minutes had passed he had to make a decision. He knew they could not stay there, it was too dangerous. He opened the door and picked her up again, now reassured she was in a comatose state. He made his way down the stairs and left out of the back door. He retraced their steps and made it back to the house half an hour later. His arms throbbed. Once in the house, he lay her down on his bed and spooned next to her, his arm around her waist. He wanted her to wake up next to him. She needed to be reassured he was not going anywhere. They were in this together.

*

A ray of sunshine peeked through the gap in the curtain. It announced the advent of daybreak. The sunlight happened to fall directly on Steven's face so he woke up blinded and moved away from the spot. He turned and looked at Caitlin. If everything had gone to plan they now had a life together, they had a future. He hoped she would wake up in a more forgiving mood. He did not want to leave her, but breakfast might help. It would certainly help him.

Downstairs, the kitchen was a mess. He looked in the fridge and was dismayed to see that all it held was some butter, jam and out of date milk. He poured it into the sink and winced as the smell overpowered. He made his way over to the shopping bags and started to unpack. It dawned on him that he was now responsible for the house. Guilt overwhelmed. If they had not come back to England his grandparents might still be alive. On the other hand, they had both seemed relieved to end their lives back in England. He had brought them back to the place they had once loved and called home. He could not feel sorry for that.

Then again if he had not returned Caitlin would still be normal. There was no point dwelling on that. The deed was done.

Twenty minutes later, an English breakfast consisting of bacon, sausages, baked beans, scrambled eggs and toast were neatly laid out on two large plates. He found a tray and put the plates, cutlery and hot drinks on it. Then he made his way up to the bedroom. He nearly dropped the lot when he saw the bed was empty.

'Caitlin.' He could not hear her, so he put the tray down and looked around. He noticed the draught and saw the open window. Surely, she would not have run away again.

He moved over to look outside and heard her voice, she did not sound angry. 'I'm on the roof. Come up here, the view is amazing. I can smell the breakfast. Bring it up, I'm starved.'

She sounded normal enough.

With a broad smile, he balanced the tray on one hand and made his way up the staircase to get easy access to the roof. On the second floor, he pried open the window which led to a sloping arched roof. He put one foot on the ledge and held on with one hand as he made his way over to where she was sat. Caitlin was wrapped in a blanket enjoying the view of the morning sunrise. The twilight hour had passed. Outstretched in front of them were the green fields of pasture, surrounded by a series of trees and shrubs. Different birds seemed to dart around in an effort to scramble together their own breakfast.

'Here you go,' he said, as he passed her the mug of tea, plate and cutlery. 'Good morning. Glad to see you enjoying the view.'

She flicked her curly hair off her face and gave him a wicked grin. 'I'm enjoying a lot more than the view.'

CHAPTER 41

A NEW DAY

Steven could not believe it, it seemed her breakdown was a thing of the past.

'Thanks for making breakfast.' She sipped the tea and hummed. 'Yummy.' She placed the mug on the guttering and started to tuck in. She looked childish as she dangled her legs over the ledge in a carefree and somewhat dangerous manner.

He took a bite of his own and savoured the taste of bacon and beans. After he swallowed he downed half of his coffee. Wary, he kept an eye on her. So far so good.

As Caitlin scraped the last of her breakfast off the bowl, she licked her lips and put it to the side. She leant back on her hands and shook her hair, the sun made it glisten. 'I have never felt so energised before. It's liberating.'

'You're lucky. You're free, even though...' He allowed himself a chuckle. 'You kind of lost it during the night.'

She clasped her hands to her face and hunched forward on her knees. 'Oh God! Did I really run away from you? I thought it was a dream. How bad?' She peeked at Steven from the corner of her eyes.

He gave a haughty laugh. 'When I changed I also tried to escape. I was sedated with a dart.' The memory made him purse his lips. 'Then I was forced to go back to the community.'

Caitlin laughed at him. 'Ouch. You still have to fill me in on that.'

Steven flexed his arms over his head and placed his hands behind his head. When his hands came back down he reached out for her hand and squeezed. 'By the way, you can get hurt. So, I'd watch it, don't get too confident on the ledge. This house is old after all.'

As if aware of the height for the first time she shuffled back. 'I'll be careful. You know, I was thinking about something.'

'Should I be worried?'

She smiled. 'Maybe…how come you never gave in and let Ingrid seduce you?'

He squirmed in the seat. Was he to be permanently tormented by Ingrid, the girl who changed his life? In a way, he owed her one. It was scary to think about what could have happened if he'd been in England when his change happened. He could have killed Caitlin. The thought was not a good one. 'Ingrid never attracted me. Not that she didn't try, nothing happened, I promise.'

'I believe you.'

Her casual tone put him at ease, until she spoke again.

'You have a way of making women fall at your feet.'

He choked and coughed. 'You didn't exactly fall at my feet.'

'No, I threw all my pamphlets at your feet instead.' She smirked as she twirled a strand of hair in her fingers. 'And I let you change me. I think you seduced me too.'

Her words hit him like an express train. 'I didn't force you to do anything you didn't want to. Did I?'

Caitlin shook her head and bit her lip. 'You had me the first time I laid eyes on you. I'm just confused. I don't regret that you changed me. I just have to get used to the idea and I have to get rid of some green eyed giants.'

'Okay, so how can I help?'

Caitlin ran a hand through her hair and looked up at the wispy white clouds. Then she turned and faced him, serious. 'What happened in the Amazon, with the other girl? You said you had been with someone.'

He didn't understand the reason for the questions; it felt like she was insecure. Either way, he didn't think it was a good idea to withhold an answer. 'The other woman, Lucy, was no girl, and it meant nothing. Anyway, what's this about? You know you're the only one for me.'

He stretched out his hand to reach hers as she moved them under her legs and rocked back and forth.

'I'm just curious and a bit paranoid. Did it mean anything to her?'

He knew he was going to sound defensive now. 'It meant nothing to her, or to me. Look at the bright side. At least you didn't have to hear me making out with anyone else. I heard you with Daniel.'

She gulped and blushed. 'Okay you got me. That did not end well either.'

'So, are we going to sit up here all day?'

'No. The breakfast was great. Thanks.'

She passed him the plate and mug. He stacked it on the tray and passed it through the window. When he turned round he saw Caitlin had stood up. She leant forward and swayed as she allowed the light wind to caress her form.

'What can I do now?' It was an innocent, yet highly loaded question.

'Anything you like,' he replied. He had no idea where the questions would go now.

'Can I jump down? Something tells me I can. So, can I?' she asked, an elfin expression on her face.

'Yes, but I'm not sure the blanket will act like a parachute.'

'Oh.' She passed him the blanket to reveal her attire, an electric blue pair of jeans and tight v-neck blue and white striped sweater. She looked so normal. 'Here I go.' She jumped off the roof, flew up into the air and did a graceful somersault before landing perfectly on the ground below.

Steven gulped. He had not expected her to do that.

He could see her Cheshire cat grin as she waved him down in a challenge. Shaking his head, he waved his hand at her and signalled for her to come back up. At first she stared, put her hands on her hips and pursed her lips dumbfounded. Then he heard her ask. 'Can I jump back up as well as down?'

'Try it,' he said, with a shrug of his shoulders.

She took some steps away from the building and then ran towards it. When she was a couple of body lengths away from the wall she soared up and landed next to him.

'What a rush!' She teetered on the ledge, her face flushed, excited. 'What else can I do?'

'I'm still working it out for myself. Just try and remember that you *can* get hurt. That's how I got my ticket out of the Amazon. I don't know if it'll be different for you, but only human blood can heal us if we're injured. So, don't try and push your luck or you'll end up having to do something you might regret.'

'Okay,' she sighed, her eyes studying the ground below.

To his relief, she looked up, gave him a cheeky smile and scrambled back into the house through the window. As he watched her a feeling of dread came over him. He didn't think he was the best person to fill her in on an identity he barely understood.

The decision to change Caitlin had been rash and unprepared. He had no idea how she was really doing, or how she was handling the decision they'd made. He liked to think *they'd* made it, but a shred of doubt remained. He could not help wondering if he had hypnotised her. Could he be sure she had changed of her own free will? There was nothing he could do about it now.

'We'll have to go and get some supplies if we're going to stay here,' he said, as they got to the lounge. Caitlin had picked a book from the built in stacked bookshelf. Remnants of dust remained on the sleeve.

'Why are we going to stay? We can go back to uni, can't we? You're doing fine. It can't be that hard,' she said, as she flicked through the pages and raised her head for a fraction of a second.

The casual way she replied scared him. He had not prepared her for what she was at all. Of course, he had no way of knowing what she was anyway. When did life decide to get so complicated? He chose his words carefully. 'You want to go back as if nothing happened, to carry on as normal?'

She put the book back in the bookcase and flapped her hands in the air. Carefree again. Too much for his liking. 'Why not? If we need to succumb to any *needs*, we'll find a way.' Again, the way she said it made it sound so normal.

Alarmed, he put his hands on her shoulders and tried to talk calmly. 'Let's sit down. We need to have a little chat. You are freaking me out.'

He sat down and clasped his hands together. He was anxious and getting more worried as each second passed. 'Do you know what you are now?'

'Not really but you're no different so why should I be?'

He gritted his teeth. 'Caitlin.'

She scowled.

He flinched. He held her hand and maintained eye contact. 'There is a very strong possibility that you are going to want to kill people for blood. Do you get that?'

She looked away for a moment then returned the gaze. Something about her was different and it scared the shit out of him.

'Steven, we can't change anything now. We've just got to see how we go. If what you say is true and we don't age then we'll move at the right time. Right now, we're the perfect age for university. Why would I want to leave everything I've worked for? Why would you? I'm sure you wanted your life back just as much as you wanted to see me again.'

Again, she made perfect sense. Flummoxed by her accurate assessment, he grinned. 'I wish you'd been with me when I changed. Your common sense would have been a breath of fresh air.'

She tapped her nose and let go of his hand. 'A woman's perspective.' She sprang off the sofa and paced the room.

He got up and stood in her path. 'You're like a Duracell bunny. Endless energy. Let's go for a run. It might help.'

Her eyes came alight. 'I'm in.'

Before she could run off, he grabbed her hand and pulled her towards him. 'I won't keep you long.' He leant in and kissed her. Caitlin froze, her lips barely moved in response. He eased off and saw her eyes were closed. He stroked her face with his hand. 'All I wanted last year was to have my life back and all everyone told me was that it was impossible. And yet, here you are, with a different way of life in front of you, and you don't even blink. Nothing is impossible for you, is it?'

Caitlin opened her eyes, her cheeks now a pinkish colour. 'I did have a few moments last year when I thought I wouldn't get to grips with maths. I'm not perfect.'

'You are for me.' It was corny but true. She gave a reluctant smile, so he changed the conversation. 'By the way, that reminds me of something. You know any issues you had with maths are now a thing of the past.'

'Really?'

'Are you game to see how advanced you've become?'

'Sure.' Her eyes were really wide, animated.

He enjoyed testing her. 'Okay, what's one million, four thousand and thirty three times twenty four?'

'Twenty four million, ninety six thousand, seven hundred and ninety two,' she blurted out immediately.

She stared at him with huge eyes and shook her head. 'How did I do that?' Then it dawned on her. 'Hang on a minute, now I get why you became very good at maths. She punched his shoulder and frowned. 'What a cheater.'

He rubbed his shoulder. 'Ouch. Anyway, I was not cheating, I just know things quickly now. And actually, so do you. So, if we did go back to uni you would also be cheating, big time.'

'Well, I definitely want to go back now. I'd love to get a first, my parents would be thrilled.'

Backfire.

'So, you want to try to live normally then? Even if we could end up doing something we regret?'

'Definitely. If you think about it logically, some people make bad decisions every day. That doesn't mean they give up on life does it?'

'No, you're right. And you're very wise.'

Caitlin placed her hands on her hips. 'So, are we going for that run now or what?'

'Sure.'

The pictures on the walls of the corridor haunted Steven as they walked past. There were so many memories of a different time, black and white and frayed at the edges. He did not recognise the people in the pictures, but he imagined they were his ancestors. Something about the young man in particular reminded him of his grandfather. He looked important in his

279

suit and bowler hat. He knew so little about them. He wished
he'd asked more questions. It was too late now. He had no
idea what the others would say when they found out what he'd
done.

CHAPTER 42

DOUBTS

Everything felt the same and yet it was different. It was hard for Caitlin to put what she was feeling into distinct thoughts. She was still Caitlin, the same person. Yet, for the first time in her life she didn't have a care in the world. Everything was possible. The world was her oyster, she was filled with a sense of empowerment – *I can change the world* mentality. She understood why Steven was giving her an anxious stare. He had probably always been like that. It's what came with a private education. Everyone she had met at university that had not gone to a state school had it to an extent. Some called it arrogance, she called it confidence. Not outer confidence, a lot of people had that – inner confidence, the one that mattered.

Now, she had it too.

Right now, all she wanted to do was run. She had way too much energy. If she did not let some of it go she was sure she was going to explode. Steven ran alongside her, his face serious.

Caitlin knew she had acted indifferent at the house. She did not dare tell him at the moment, but the truth was she did feel different. She was not overwhelmed anymore, love confused her. She still thought he was attractive, definitely. The thing was she was not in awe of him anymore. Something had changed the way she felt about him. She had no idea what it meant or how she was going to deal with it. It was best to put it to the back of her mind – for now.

Her eyes focused on the trees ahead as she remembered how crazy she had become. She was sure she must have resembled a wild animal. The insanity still bubbled within her like a dormant volcano, a jumble of irrational thoughts lingered.

The bottom line was she had decided to let him change her.

It was not Steven's fault. It had happened in a fit of passion. Honestly, she had no regrets. This way of life made her think of infinite possibilities. Just the academic side alone was mind boggling. The fact she would look the same forever was also a plus. She wondered if she was capable of gaining weight. It was interesting. She didn't think she would gorge herself on chocolate to test the theory, tempting though it was.

'Caitlin, we need to talk. Can you slow down?'

Caitlin wanted to carry on running, but she knew she had to let him in. She slowed to a jog, then a steady walk. 'What's up Steven?' It sounded snappy, she attempted a smile.

Steven walked alongside her and remained quiet for a minute or so. She could have added something but it was easier to let him talk.

'Is something wrong? Are you still angry with me? You seem distant. Not like usual.'

Caitlin knew she could blow her cover in an instant so she held her tongue. She did not want to hurt him. She stopped walking and turned to face him. 'I'm not angry with you.'

Steven gave an uneasy smile. 'That's good.'

Caitlin remembered there had been a time when the smile had made her melt, now it did nothing. She did not think it was a good thing.

'So, what is it?' He held out his hand and took hold of one of hers.

Her hand lay limp in his, the contact made her freeze internally. Just like the kiss earlier. She did not want him. She had no idea what she was going to do. She eased her hands away, put them behind her back and started to walk. She could not handle the proximity. It was difficult. She did not hear him follow for a few seconds. She chose not to look back.

'Caitlin,' he called.

She stopped, looked over her shoulder and gave a nervous smile. Then she started to run again. Now her stomach churned. She could not believe it. How was it possible to be in love with someone one minute and then not the next? She could not understand what had happened. Their plan to be together forever had backfired. If she could not see him as more than a friend there was no future for them. She had no idea where it left her. She could not tell him what she was thinking, she needed time.

***

Steven's jaw dropped as he saw Caitlin run off. He was not stupid. Something was wrong. She was so cold, indifferent even. And he could tell she was keeping something back. He had no idea what he should do. She was a potential killer. He had made her that way. He should have waited. It was stupid, reckless. Lust had driven him to make the wrong choice. If he lost Caitlin it would kill him. He knew the effect of rejection; he had seen it enough times from the other side. It was his turn to be on the receiving end.

He started to run after Caitlin. He stayed behind and watched, intrigued to see where she would go. When they got to the edge of a clearing Caitlin stopped. He came up alongside her and saw what she was looking at. It was the New Forest ponies, at ease, eating grass. There had to be about twenty in total ranging from mottled brown and white to black in colour.

'They are so cute,' Caitlin said. Her childish stance was back as she cupped her hands together in glee.

'They are.' He did not look at her.

'Steven, I'm sorry. I'm not myself okay. Give me some time.' Caitlin sounded worried as she flicked her hair to the side and played with a strand. It was nice to see a familiar habit.

'It's okay. I can't expect too much from you.' He wanted to ask if she still loved him. He wanted to know. He just didn't want to hear the answer.

'I'm thirsty. What should I do?'

'We can go back to the house if you like.'

'No, I mean I'm *thirsty*. You know. Even though the thought of drinking pony blood should appal me right now, it doesn't.'

That kind of thirsty, she *did* have other needs. Steven knew taking down a pony in the middle of the New Forest was not the best way to remain incognito. 'We'll go and find some rabbits. I make a mean rabbit stew.'

Her shoulders slumped. 'A rabbit!'

'No-one keeps an eye on rabbit counts. We need to feed on what we can eat. It's easier. If you get hurt then we'll have to consider an alternative. Until then, we stick to rabbits.'

'Okay then. Bugs bunny is not going to be happy with us.'

He chuckled. The Caitlin he knew. 'I'll have to find a way to make it up to him.'

The rabbit hunt proved successful. They managed to catch four in total. Steven eyed Caitlin as she drained her rabbit of blood.

With a lick of her lips, she glanced at him and shook her head. 'What?'

'Told you rabbit blood was nice.'

'Smarty pants. It is revitalising. Blood leaves me satisfied in a different way to food. It's weird.' She put the rabbits on the floor and leant on her knees, her legs crossed.

'I know. I am still getting used to it myself. I don't have a problem killing rabbits.'

She studied him and bit her lip. 'Will I have to kill people?'

'Not necessarily.' He did not know how much to tell her. She still needed time.

'Why not?' She picked up a twig and started to make patterns on the soil.

'We know monkey blood also has healing powers.'

She threw the twig and clenched her hands into fists. 'So monkeys are better than people. I don't think so. There are a lot of people who'd be better off dead.'

Steven swallowed hard and took a deep breath. This was worse than he thought. 'Caitlin, you can't say that. You can't decide like that. A person is usually tracked or missed. You can't make the call.'

She glared at him, defiant. 'What if they were homeless? No-one cares about them when they walk past them in the street. They're just glad it's not them.'

His anger bubbled to the surface. 'Caitlin! Do you really think that?'

'If it was my life or theirs, then yes.'

Steven gasped, speechless. He had created a monster. 'The only reason I was allowed to come back was because of my firm commitment to preserving life. We are not God. You can not decide who lives and dies. It would make you a killer.'

Caitlin picked up a different twig and started to trace another pattern on the soil as she hummed a tune. She was zoning him out. Not good.

'Caitlin, do you understand what I just said.' It was like he was speaking to a child.

She looked up sharply, gave a hard stare and said, 'crystal.' Then she carried on humming and drawing, lost.

Steven got up and paced. He punched the tree, frustrated.

Caitlin looked up and laughed. 'You don't have to take it out on the tree, you know. It's innocent.' There was a hint of sarcasm in the tone.

Steven's blood pounded as his sense of utter bemusement became exacerbated. He knelt down next to her and put his hand on her wrist. When she looked up, he asked, 'What have I done to you?'

'I'm still Caitlin. I just don't love people as much as you do. I haven't grown up in a bubble where everyone is nice and fluffy. I actually hate quite a lot of people and have often wished some dead. Now I can make it a reality. Call me a killer if you will.'

Steven let go of her hand, his eyes widened in horror.

'Don't look at me like that!' She stood up and put her hands on her hips. 'I don't intend to kill people. All I'm saying is that I would never value a monkey's life over that of a person. Why is that so bad?'

He blinked and pursed his lips. She had a point again. She sounded like everyone else in the community. Was it him that had the problem?

'I understand what you are saying.' His head hung low. His acquiescence came at a price. 'Let's take these back. I don't think we should be out in the open when you're thinking what you are. I'm not saying you don't have a point, just that I don't want you to go to prison for murder just yet.'

She laughed aloud and dropped her hands. Then she leant down picked up the two rabbits and slung them over her shoulder. 'Race you back.' And like that she was gone.

Steven picked up his own pair and made chase. He was totally freaked out. The Caitlin he thought he knew was not the one he did. In truth, they had not known each other for that long. She had never shared her thoughts on people with him. She did mull over things and get annoyed more than he did. But he never thought she would see murder as honourable or an alternative way out. He could not believe some of the things she had said. For a moment there he could have replaced Emily for her and it would have made sense.

Ian was not like that, Jeff was not like that. But the women were. Emily, Ingrid, Catherine, Judith. They all found it hard. Was that why Judith had refused to drink human blood? Was she tired of what she was? Did she want to makes amends? Then again, if she knew what she had become then why would she allow Steven to do the same to Caitlin. Was it her conscience? Did she owe it to Emily? Had he been a fool? Had he failed to consider all of the consequences? He had wanted Caitlin back so badly he had forgotten about the possible outcomes. He had created Caitlin and now it was his responsibility to make sure she did not abuse his gift.

Gift.

He could not believe he was thinking like Ian. Perhaps he had more in common with his uncle than he originally thought.

CHAPTER 43

THE GIRL BECOMES A WOMAN

In the past Caitlin was convinced she failed to meet the mark. She was never the cleverest in the class or the prettiest or the most popular. Just above average, a good achiever. That was now in the past. The future looked rosy. She was fed up of being miss goody two shoes. She wanted to rock and roll. To turn a few heads. She would go back to university and finish her course. She would get a first, the best result possible. She would be popular. She would be the girl everyone wanted to be.

There was only one person stopping her – Steven. Was he supposed to be the love of her life? Or was it just his hybrid nature that had seduced her?

Not any more. The magnets had died.

Was it permanent? She had no idea. At the moment she was not attracted to him. It left her confused, yet excited. Would she be able to seduce others like he had seduced her? She had never been that kind of girl. Could she be? A part of her was curious, very curious indeed.

Back at the house, she dropped the rabbits on the kitchen table and thought of Georgina. Georgina loved rabbits. Her first year flatmate had died because of what she had become. Her shy, quiet friend had not deserved to die. She had been targeted because she was vulnerable. She was someone no-one would miss. In the end, people would nod their heads and think it was sad, but understandable. It was sick. Steven could not justify those actions. Not that he tried to, but she would never kill someone who did not deserve to die.

Steven did, however, have a point. Who was she to choose? Then again, if they had to choose, who would be missed? A student death was so easy to fake, yet she could not be that cruel. She made her way into the living room and picked up the book she found interesting, if educational. She found a comfy place on the sofa and switched off. It was the perfect way to unwind, a good place to escape in. She heard Steven, but she kept her nose down.

A few noises and scuffles later, he came in and stood over her. 'What are you reading anyway?'

She did not look up when she answered. 'Dracula.'

Steven burst into laughter. 'Are you getting tips?'

It was weird. For the first time since the change she thought his voice was a good sound. She liked to hear him laugh. The corners of her mouth rose involuntarily, as her eyes stayed on the pages. 'Funny, so funny. It's actually an excellent read. Now go away and give me some peace.' She focused and tried to ignore him.

Steven waited. When she did not react she heard him give a small sigh before he started to walk out of the room. At the doorway, he stopped. 'I'll go and prepare the rabbits.'

'Sure.' She did not look up.

Even though firmly ensconced on the sofa, she raised her eyes to the clock and was amazed to see that two hours had gone by. She was engrossed in the book. A tasty aroma was starting to make her mouth water.

Lunchtime.

She put the book down and made her way into the kitchen. Steven had set the table and everything. He was so domesticated now. If all the men were the same in the community she would be in for a treat if they went there, it got more interesting by the minute.

'Something smells nice.' She made her way over to the pot and looked in. It was a stew. 'Did you go shopping?'

'Didn't have to.' Steven came up alongside her and gave the stew a stir with a large, silver ladle. 'Most of the veg was in the garden.'

She was momentarily lost for words. He knew how to garden. 'Since when did you learn to become a farmer?'

'The community. They had me digging, cultivating, and hunting. I went back to my roots,' he chuckled. 'Hunter gatherer.'

She felt a faint flutter in her stomach. Perhaps, her feelings for him were just lying low. Dormant.

He gave a shy smile and then held out his left hand. 'Anyway, it's ready. Would you like to take a seat, please?'

He was so polite. He always had been. He was a great catch. She'd be a fool to think otherwise. 'Thank you. I will. Can I do anything to help?'

'No, just sit yourself down and let me serve you. It's the least I can do.'

She took a seat and watched as he got some wide soup bowls and poured two generous potions. He placed one in front of her.

'Would you like some water? We don't have a lot else. There is wine but I don't know…'

'Water is fine.' The way he was fussing was endearing. He was trying so hard. Wine would have been nice but it was best to avoid alcohol for the moment.

The steam wafted up her nose and her stomach growled. It smelled so good, poor little rabbits. She picked up her spoon and helped herself to a potato and some of the rabbit. She could not believe how nice it was. 'Wow, this is amazing. Rabbit tastes like chicken. I never knew that. It's more meaty, but very nice all the same. Thank you for cooking. I'll have to return the favour.'

His eyes met hers. He reached out and cupped her hand with his. 'I'm glad you like it.'

This time she did not move her hand away. Instead she turned it, so that their hands were palm to palm, and eased her fingers through his.

Steven stared into her eyes. It felt like he was reaching out for her soul. 'I love you Caitlin.'

Caitlin could only nod. She was not ready to say it back yet. She let go of his hand and picked up the spoon. 'We'd better eat or it'll go cold.'

He picked up his spoon and stared at his bowl. She might have upset him.

A second later he lifted his head, a sparkle in his eye. 'By the way, I know you're probably not interested, but we can breathe under water.'

He put a mouthful of stew in his mouth and chewed slowly.

She nearly sprayed stew over the table. 'What?!' She would not let that one drop. 'Sorry.' She wiped her mouth with the cloth napkin on the table, glad Steven had put one out. 'What do you mean? We can breathe under water?'

The glint in his eye was back and his lips curled at the corner of his mouth. She could see he was enjoying being one step ahead of her. She felt like touching his face, but she stopped herself as her brain struggled to keep up with a now fluttering heart. Was she developing feelings for him again? She suppressed the thought for a second time.

'Curious?' He swallowed a huge mouthful.

'Of course.' She followed suit and wolfed down a huge helping.

He chuckled.

Caitlin sped up and finished quickly. He followed suit, and before long the bowls were empty. She leant back in her chair, her stomach bulging. Steven picked up her bowl and made his way over to the sink. He turned on the tap, squeezed a dollop of washing up liquid in the basin and filled the sink with water.

'Let me do that.' Caitlin started to get up.

'Nope, I'll do it.'

She folded her arms. He wanted to do everything. This was a treat. Caitlin had never been able to sit still, now it was impossible. She got up, picked up a tea towel and started to dry.

'Well, if you insist.' He passed her the cutlery.

He put the lid on the pot and put it in the fridge.

'It's still hot.' Caitlin said. 'You should wait for it to cool.'

He put it in and got closer to her. Then he wrapped his arms around her and rested his hands on her lower back. 'What would you say to us going away from here?'

'Now?'

'Now.'

'Err...okay I guess.' His proximity was making her nervous. It did feel good to be held.

'So, we have to put everything away now.'

'Right.' She gulped involuntarily.

She stared at him and wondered whether he would kiss her. She thought she did not care for him, she thought she had been hypnotised, she thought...she thought too much. She wrapped her arms around him, bridged the gap and kissed him lightly. Then she rested her head on his chest. It was lucky she was shorter than him. 'Thank you for everything. You are lovely.'

'Lovely, I think I can work on that.' He kissed her head.

She remembered what they used to be like. Even though she had already lost her virginity to him she had a feeling they would have to get to know each other all over again. She looked forward to it and the thought made her cheeks burn. She did not want to do anything right now, the trip beckoned. She wanted to find out about what they could do in water. Convinced, she unclasped her hands, gave a cheeky smile and nodded as she pulled back.

Steven had a cat that got the cream look about him now. 'Go get your stuff. When you're ready, we go. I already got my things ready.'

'How did you know I'd say yes?'

He tapped his nose.

She skipped off. It was exciting.

Once back downstairs she heard Steven in the garage so she made her way over. 'I don't have a swimsuit? Do I need one?' It was not a completely stupid question.

'Not if you don't mind being naked with me.' His eyes narrowed. 'Do you mind?'

Actually, she did. But, she was sure she'd get over it. 'No, it's fine.'

Steven took her bag and put it in the boot. He opened the passenger door of the Bentley and beckoned her in. She was sure it was an expensive car, but she was clueless when it came to it. Either way, with soft tan leather seats she could not complain. She made herself comfortable and looked around. It was just a car.

Steven eased in next to her and put the key in the ignition. 'This car is a classic, but it drives like a dream. I am pretty sure they've done loads of work to it over the years. It even uses normal diesel.'

He picked up little gadget and pressed a button, the garage doors opened up. Electrical – swish. Once the car was out Steven pressed a small button on a remote control device and the garage doors slid shut again.

After thirty minutes of listening to the radio and driving towards Salisbury, Caitlin started to get curious. She had no idea where they were headed. 'So, are you planning to tell me where we are going?'

Steven glanced over and smiled, and then lowered the radio. 'I am taking you to one of the best beaches in England, in my hometown of Ilfracombe. I think we need to get away from everything.'

'But, but, what about university?' she spluttered. It was extreme.

'It can wait. We can get anything else we need when we get there. I-I…just thought we needed to get away.'

The way he hesitated was cute.

'We need to have clear heads if we are going to figure out what we are going to do. And we…' His hands gripped the steering wheel and he paused as though unsure. 'We also need to find out how we feel about each other.'

There. He had said what she had been reluctant to admit. He knew she was having doubts. She couldn't hide it that easily.

'Okay.' She fiddled with her hands again. He knew how to read her. He had been able to do that from the moment they met. He knew. He knew she was having doubts. She had no choice. They would have to talk about it now.

CHAPTER 44

DO YOU STILL LOVE ME?

Steven had let the cat out of the bag. He wanted Caitlin to open up to him. The only way he could see that as possible was if she started being honest. His cards were on the table. Now it was her turn to reveal. In an ideal scenario, she would tell him she still loved him. It was doubtful she would say that yet, she was still acting so strange. He put aside the thought and focused on the road. Given time, she would break the silence. He had said enough.

Ten minutes later Caitlin spoke first. 'Steven, I…I don't know what to say.'

He nodded and kept his gaze on the road.

'The truth is I don't know how I feel about you anymore.'

He heard his involuntary intake. He had been right to suspect a change of heart. He said nothing. From the corner of his eye, he noticed her fidget.

'I am confused. A part of me hated you when I realised what had happened. I know it's stupid since I knew what I was letting myself in for. I don't know,' she stumbled over the words as they burst out. 'It felt like a spell had been broken, like I'd woken up from a dream. A dream in which you were not the handsome prince, you were the devil instead. You won. You had turned me to the *dark side*.' She gave a small uneasy chuckle.

He gave a half smile, and then adopted an ominous tone. 'We are not in Star Wars you know. I am not the Sith Lord out to get you.'

'I know.' The tone of her voice made her sound defeated. He was not helping.

'Anyway, I get what you're saying. I'll give you some time, and we get to know each other again. Then we see. Without the loved up cloud fluff in your eyes you might find something about me you like.' He was trying to sound easygoing. He was not sure it was working. It hurt to think she did not love him like he loved her.

Caitlin turned to face him and he followed suit. She lowered her eyes to the gearbox when she spoke so he faced the road. 'The thing is. If I said I want to go it alone, I don't think I can. Can I? Now that I'm not like everyone else, I don't have the freedom I used to. I want to finish uni and I want to do all the things I wanted to do before.' She hesitated again. 'I don't want to be with you just because I have to; I want to be with you because I want to.'

He gulped. There was nothing he wanted more than to be with her. 'Well, I guess in that case it's my job to make sure you want to be with me then.' He allowed himself another glance in her direction and gave his best *I can be an understanding boyfriend* look.

She smiled back. It looked like a genuine smile, not forced. He could only hope that he could win her back completely. He did not want her to be with him because she had to. 'Anyway, you're going to love what I've got planned. So, stop worrying. We'll figure it out.'

Optimism, priceless.

The sound of Adele filled the car, he increased the volume.

'You like Adele?' Caitlin asked, amused.

Steven shrugged his shoulders. 'This track in particular is very good.'

'Someone like you. I guess you couldn't stay away either.'

Steven licked his lips and held back a cough. His throat had gone dry all of a sudden. He forced the words out. 'No, I couldn't. Either way, it's a great song.'

'Yes, it is.'

The words continued to choke him. He hoped he would not have to look for someone like Caitlin anytime soon. He wanted Caitlin, no-one else. Time. That was all she needed. Things would go back to normal. He had to think it was true. The alternative was not worth consideration.

As the lyrics built up to a crescendo Caitlin pressed the

search button and changed the channel. A dance tune, Steven relaxed. He hoped she didn't want to think about it either. It was a good sign.

'Do you want to stop for a drink?'

Caitlin had read his mind. A service station was just what he needed. 'Sure. Sounds like a plan.'

After they eased into the lay-by, Steven filled up on diesel and then parked on one of the available parking spaces. They made their way into the service station. He resisted the urge to hold her hand. Instead, his hands felt like spare useless appendages, uncomfortably at his sides. The wind had picked up. Dark clouds threatened to congregate. He hated driving in the rain and they still had a few hours drive. He wondered what had possessed him to go back home. It was not exactly round the corner.

A small series of round tables with high bar stools tempted them to sit. At least they'd get a decent coffee here. At the counter, Steven looked at the menu board. He faced Caitlin. 'What'll it be?'

Caitlin stared at the man behind the counter. Her eyes glazed and her tongue ran over her lower lip. He began to think they'd have the coffee to go.

He stood in front of her and blocked the view. 'Caitlin, what'll it be?'

She snapped out of the trance and fixed her eyes on his. 'Hmmm?'

'I'll order for you.'

Shit. This was not good. She wanted a drink. Hot, fresh and of the red variety.

Steven gripped her shoulder to keep her in place and ordered a hot chocolate, a latte macchiato, two croissants and a packet of cookies. Then he added the fuel to the total bill. Caitlin had not moved. Her eyes now fixed on the floor. It looked like she was fighting a battle – of the inner sort. He took the purchases, grabbed her hand and gave a slight nudge to move her along. He led her in the directions of the toilets. 'Will you be okay?'

She looked up and snapped, impatient. 'I'm not a baby.'

Her cheeks were tinged in pink, her eyebrows narrowed, as she flashed a set of canines. The monster on full display.

'Caitlin, you know that's not…'

'I'll be fine!' She let go of his hand and practically ran in.

He rushed to the men's and did the fastest pee he could muster. Outside again, he was relieved to see her come out. Her face and hair wet, remorse all over her face.

Caitlin clasped her hands as she spoke. 'I'm sorry.'

He eased his hand into hers and gave a squeeze. 'Don't be.' It was the least he could do.

She reciprocated and gripped his hand. Her expression was childlike. She was clearly taken aback by her adverse reaction.

As soon as they were strapped in the car again Steven drove off. They could talk on the way. There was no point asking her what was going on since it was likely she did not have a clue either. He had not been prepared for this. He never once imagined the urge to feed would have been so strong for Caitlin. He assumed she would be like him. He assumed too much.

The next half an hour went by in silence. Caitlin leant her head against the window and closed her eyes. She could have dozed off. He was not sure. There were still a few more hours to go before they got to Ilfracombe and if they were not going to talk it gave him some thinking time.

In Ilfracombe they could find a place to hide for a few days. He knew all the good turfs. He really wanted to see his father again but he did not know if that would be possible anymore. He could just turn the car round and go back to Southampton. Then again, what life could they go back to if Caitlin wanted to kill? There was no way they could go back to university and pretend nothing had happened. Not until they knew more. It was so stupid. If he had waited he could have lived a normal life with her, for a few years a least. He clenched the steering wheel in frustration. Nothing had gone the way he had hoped. They would be better off in the community.

The idea lingered.

Should he go back? Should he take her to the Amazon? The community would be able to help. It would let the cat out of the bag in a major way – he had no way of explaining why Caitlin was like them. He would have to tell them the secret, a secret that did not feel his to tell. Was it worth it? He was not in the mood for making another rash decision.

***

Caitlin could have cut the tension in the car with a knife. It was easier to pretend to be asleep than to face up to what had just happened. She had felt her canines extend and a hunger so powerful had taken over. She had nearly lost control in a service station. If Steven had not held her hand she doubted she would have remained calm. She ran her tongue over her deadly weapons. They were dormant again. She should have been horrified, but she wasn't. She was definitely surprised.

It was incredible.

Nothing could have prepared her for what she was becoming. So far she had discovered she could jump up and down great heights. She enjoyed the taste of animal blood. Apparently, they would also be able to swim under water for a period of time. That would be interesting. For the first time she realised her knee had lost its dull twinge. Had her old swimming injury been healed? Would she be able to swim fast without it having any long lasting ill effects? There was so much to be excited about.

At the back of her mind she could not help wondering if Steven saw it differently. He had never come across excited about what he was. She could understand that. She could not understand why she *was* excited. It was weird. It was like a part of her had changed radically. Unfortunately, it was the part that was risk averse. For the first time, ever, she wanted to take risks. She wanted to live life on the edge, do something dangerous. She had no idea what would appease her irrational side.

She stretched and pretended to wake up. 'How long was I out for?'

'A while. We are getting there. I thought we could find accommodation on the Exmoor National Park before we visit my home town. You need to feed again.'

'A park full of animal's no-one will miss. Sounds like a

297

good idea.'

'Exactly.' He glanced in her direction. 'Are you feeling better now?

'By better, do you mean am I not a homicidal killer anymore? Yes, I'm better. Who knows how long it will last. I mean…what was that?'

Steven kept his eyes on the road, his face one of deep concentration. 'I don't know. That's the truth. I have seen someone act like you before.'

'Who was it?' Finally, a breakthrough.

He frowned as he replied, 'my mother.'

That was not what she was expecting to hear. The last she heard his mother was a lunatic. 'Great. That's really good news. So, shall I throw myself onto an oncoming train now or do you have a solution to our problem? If I can't resist human blood what hope do I have?'

The silence was hard to bear. Caitlin shook her head and looked out of the window. Nothing but countryside, cars and gloomy weather. It took several more minutes for Steven to speak.

'The only solution is to take you to the Amazon. The thing is. I don't know what people are going to say. I was not supposed to happen, but you were definitely not supposed to happen. It'll be a shock for them. I don't know how on earth I'll be able to explain it. I might have to call my aunt Catherine and get her advice. She might be able to help.'

'So call her then. Is she nice?'

'She is very nice. Her husband lost all his family during the Second World War. He was Jewish. So they both tend to accept people more readily than others. It could be the only way.' He left the suggestion hanging.

'Right, well, park it is then. Are we nearly there?' A longing burned in the pit of her stomach.

'We are close. Can you hold on?'

The way he said it sounded patronising. She was not a child, even if she acted like one at times. She hoped he'd cut her some slack. The way she was acting was just as frustrating for her as it was for him. 'I can wait.'

CHAPTER 45

NIGHT VISION

In the winter, nightfall comes early. In their current predicament this was an advantage. Steven parked the car on one of the deserted visitor zones and killed the lights. After a few seconds his night vision kicked in.

'Wow…this is so cool. It's like in documentaries. I can see in the dark, yet another perk.' Caitlin sounded so relaxed.

'Just like big cats, we are deadly killing machines with a load of devices at the ready.'

'Yeah,' she laughed. 'I always fancied the idea of becoming a shark. A lion will do instead.'

'Lioness.'

Caitlin held her hands up like claws and growled. 'Even more deadly.'

Steven chuckled and gave a half smile. 'Come on then, let's go. Time to hunt.'

'Hunt? Oh, *hunt*! I'm up for that.' She grabbed the door handle and was out like a flash. 'Tell me we're not hunting rabbits again? Please.'

'No, there's a lot of red deer in the park. We'll go for that. We won't be able to use the body but we'll try to get rid of it.'

'I just hope we don't come up against the Exmoor beast,' Caitlin scoffed.

Steven rolled his eyes. 'The Exmoor beast, as you well know, doesn't exist.'

'What like vampires don't exist?' Caitlin folded her arms and shook her head.

'We are not vampires.'

Caitlin took a deep breath and unfolded her arms. As she spoke she ticked off an imaginary list off using her fingers. 'You're right, we *don't* kill for blood, we *don't* stay young, and we *don't* use hypnotism. Okay, so we *will* die, I guess, and we still eat normal food, and we don't sleep in coffins, and we...okay, fair enough. We're not vampires. Well, at least not how Bram Stoker described them in *Dracula*.'

'We have vampire traits. What we actually are, who knows? I think both of us have a lot to learn. You know, come to think of it we could be the Exmoor beast.'

'What do you mean?'

Steven shook his head. 'Nothing.' It was stupid.

'Go on, spill the beans, what are you thinking?'

Steven thought aloud. 'It's not likely. I don't know, it's just the beast was supposed to kill animals by ripping out their throats. They lost a lot of blood. Considering the fact that our kind only come back every now and again it's plausible that our kind was to blame. They might have been the beast roaming the moors. My mum was around in the early nineties. It's the next large park close to Southampton. I don't know.'

'It could be funny. The Exmoor beast turns out to be a human being with a strange appetite.'

'Possible. Don't think we'll be able to provide a picture of a puma or leopard.'

'No, a picture of a normal human being would not cut the mustard.'

'No.' It was nice to have some banter with Caitlin.

They started to walk into the forested area. Steven wondered what to say. He had learnt from his experience in the Amazon that it was not a good idea to be hasty. 'I don't have a huge amount of experience when it comes to hunting. The only thing I know is that we should hunt together and stay alert. Don't go for the baby, it's likely to be protected. Go for the weak, if they have an injury all the better.'

Caitlin nodded. 'Sure. We do have to find them first.'

'That's the easy part. Watch.' Steven stood still, raised his finger for her to be silent and closed his eyes to focus. The slight, practically silent, sound caught his attention and he knew which way to go. 'This way.'

'What did you do?' She was curious again.

He whispered a reply. 'It's known as human echolocation.'

'What? Like bats?'

'Yes, just like bats.'

'Can I do that?'

'I'll teach you later. Now, let's stay focused. Questions later, okay?'

Her reply was barely audible. 'Okay.'

'Follow my lead.'

Caitlin nodded and their pace slowed as they stalked their prey.

From the cover of some bushes, they watched the red deer drinking by the river. As Steven poised himself to attack he turned to check on Caitlin. He was taken aback when he saw her leap towards one of the deer. In what appeared to be an effortless action, Caitlin landed on the medium sized deer and snapped its head and then sank her teeth into the neck and started to drink. Her stance, aggression and innate ability startled Steven. She was a natural. Not wanting to be overshadowed he listened for another animal. They had all scattered and gone. Caitlin had taken the prize. He made his way over to her and wondered if she would stop. He doubted she could.

'Caitlin, can you share?'

She did not flinch, eyes closed.

'Caitlin, can you hear me? You don't have to drink it all so quickly. See if you can control yourself and stop.'

A shudder from her shoulders, but her eyes remained shut. Steven gave up and took a seat next to her. He could always drink from the animal's leg. He wondered what she would do if he tried. Impatient, he took hold of the animal's leg. His canines extended and he got ready to take his fill. Just as his teeth were about to sink into the flesh, Caitlin's eyes snapped open. She snarled at him and pushed him away with so much force that he landed a few metres away. He could not help finding it amusing and ended up in fits of laughter.

As he laughed, he saw her expression change from fury to anger to frustration to confusion to a smile. She stared at the dead animal then back at Steven and laughed with him. 'You should know better than to try to steal my food. I was never that good a sharing at the best of times, let alone when I'm starving.'

He managed to stop laughing and replied. 'You have one heck of a punch in you. Remind me never to take your food again.'

'I just did.' She wiped her mouth and made her way over to his side. She held out her hand to help him up.

Steven raised his hand, took a firm hold of hers and pushed her down on the floor and then went on top of her and held both of her hands down. 'See if you can get out of this one.'

Caitlin squirmed under him and tried to lift her hands but she couldn't.

'See you're not stronger than me. I can hold my own.'

'Point taken. Maybe I'll have to learn to share.'

'That would be wise.' He stared in her eyes and wondered whether he should kiss her. He wanted to – badly. Did she want him to kiss her? He faltered for a split second.

***

Caitlin liked the fact Steven was on top of her. Even though she resented his superior strength she longed to be dominated. A part of her wanted him to take charge. In her red haze she could still make out the amber irises that had bewitched her from the first moment they met. She wanted him to kiss her. Was he waiting for her?

Simultaneously, they both leaned in, desperate. The kiss was passionate, out of control. They rolled, fumbled and groaned whilst entwined. Caitlin's legs wrapped tight around him. She could feel his need and she certainly knew hers was just as strong.

Impatient, she started to loosen his belt and then slipped her hand in his trousers to touch him. Immediately, Steven trembled in response. His hands went to her trousers and he undid her zip. He struggled with her button and Caitlin had to laugh as they continued to search for each other. When Steven's hand touched her in her most intimate part Caitlin thought she would die. In haste, they discarded trousers. Steven kissed her stomach and touched her again; she arched her back and reached out for his face. She needed to kiss him, hard. As they kissed, they were free to reunite. They moved as one.

Caitlin was convinced she was on fire. The cold, soggy ground did nothing to help. As Steven got into a rhythm she could not suppress her moans as she gripped him tighter towards her. After an incredible climax they lay still, cuddling, out of breath on the floor.

After a minute, Caitlin heard Steven's breathing slow down.

Was he asleep?

She could not sleep. The wet, sticky mud was starting to cool on her legs. It was not pleasant. Why did they have to lose their inhibitions in the forest? A bed would have been so much nicer. Her clothes were also ruined now. She was glad she packed an extra pair of jeans. She knew her sensible side was not strong enough to stop what had happened, but it was having a good old nag now all the same.

'Steven, wake up. We should find somewhere to sleep.' She started to detach herself from his arms.

He pulled her closer and mumbled. 'This is a good place.'

'Steven, stop joking. We can't sleep here.' She sat up and searched for her jeans. She picked up the smudged and soaked pair. 'Ugh, these are disgusting.'

'They're just clothes.' He leaned on his hand and turned to face her, all blurry eyed.

'I'd like somewhere to stay please. We can change in the car and try to look decent for when we find a place.'

Steven sat up and ruffled his hair. 'You are amazing. Have I ever told you that?'

'Thank you, no, not recently. You're pretty good yourself.'

He hummed in agreement as he found his trousers and put them on. 'Shall we go?' he asked, his hand reaching for hers.

'Yes,' Caitlin said, as she found his hand and held it tight. 'I do love you Steven. I *think* I never stopped loving you.'

'That's good to know,' he said, as he leaned in and gave her a gentle kiss on the lips.

She felt her stomach cartwheel in response. Could she want him again? Yes, yes she could. 'I am yours. Let's make it work.'

He gave a beaming smile and wrapped his arms around her as he nestled his face in her hair. 'I love you Caitlin. I promise I will always look out for you. We have nothing to fear. Together, we can do anything.'

She leant against his chest and took in his scent. Everything about him appealed to her now. She felt different. Was it as simple as that? Was sex the answer to her problem? She could not help thinking their relationship meant so much more and yet it was only when they made love that she finally felt a connection so strong it overpowered the ever doubting Thomas in her brain. She did want the relationship to work.

The question at the back of her mind was would they ever live at ease?

***

Emily could not believe she had been lured, like a moth to a light, back to her love. She had finally left the community and all she could do was go in search of Paul, Steven's dad. He had been so easy to find. The internet provided a wealth of knowledge to anyone that asked. He was still an accountant and now ran his own company. He had done well for himself by the look of things.

She hid behind the large trunk of the majestic oak tree at the side of the house and waited. It was becoming a regular routine. Paul always returned at five thirty, without fail. He was nearly forty five years old now, but he still looked good, regardless of his receding hairline. The car headlights engulfed the drive and she took cover. When she heard the car door slam, she peeked out and watched as he put the key in the door lock and made his way in. She would give anything to talk to him. She had memorised the entire layout of the house now and had gone in when the other woman was out. Paul had made a good home for himself. It should have been her home.

She made her way over to the window sill by the kitchen and listened. She could hear Clara – the other woman. She was chattering on as Paul mumbled a few yes and no's in response. He did not love that woman. Emily knew he could not love the other woman. He loved her. In the same way she had only ever loved him. Steven was the proof of their love. The woman was in the way. She would have to think of what she could do to get rid of her. Either way, there was no hurry. The last thing she wanted to do was scare Paul. He would not understand why she still looked the same.

Emily crept back and walked stealthily to the back of the house to wait in the garden. It was lucky for her they did not have any dogs.

CHAPTER 46

EXMOOR NATIONAL PARK

As they drove into the grounds of the country hotel Caitlin eased forward, mouth open. 'We can't stay here. They'll never take us in. We look like tramps.'

'We have some mud on us that's all. Trust me. We'll get a room.' Steven parked the car in the resident zone and gave Caitlin a reassuring smile.

'Are you serious? Can't we go somewhere else? It looks like a really posh hotel.'

Steven found her expression comical. 'You're not scared, are you?'

'No, of course not,' Caitlin said, as she slumped back in the seat. 'I just think, oh I don't know, I've never stayed somewhere like this before.'

'There's always a first. Watch and learn. Come on, let's get the bags and get the best room.'

He could tell Caitlin was all set to protest, but he did not give her the chance. He zipped out of the car, made his way to the passenger seat and opened the door. 'No point sulking.'

'I'm not sulking.' In a fluid motion, Caitlin was out of the car and at his side. 'I'm ready to learn. I should bet something, they'll *never* let us in.'

Steven held her hand and made his way to the entrance. Once through the door, he had to push Caitlin along as she shuffled reluctantly behind. He made his way over to the reception counter and was met by a tight lipped, older gentleman with a bushy moustache.

'May I help you?' The tone made it obvious he did not think he could.

'Yes, thank you kind sir. My fiancée and I had a spot of trouble on the moor with our car and have ended up looking like a pair of ragamuffins. I am embarrassed to arrive at your door in this state. Nevertheless, we will require your best room for the night and the use of your laundry service. I am afraid we are en route to visit the parents in law and, as I am sure you understand, it would not do to turn up in this state.' Steven knew his upper crust accent would not fail him.

'But, of course sir. We do have the one deluxe suite available. We are at your service. Please, if you could give me your name and details I will be happy to take payment. The room is two hundred pounds for the night.' The man raised his eyebrows.

'Wonderful, I can pay in cash.' Steven produced five fifty pound notes. 'Here's an extra fifty for taking care of the laundry for us. Keep the change.'

'Of course, thank you. You are too kind.'

As the man handed over the key Steven glanced at Caitlin and winked. She gave a bemused frown and shook her head. At least she didn't look like she wanted to kill anyone now. It was progress.

After they had entered the lift Caitlin turned on him. 'Where did you get all that money? Did you rob a bank?'

'Well actually, I kind of did. Mind control makes people do the weirdest things.'

'Serious?' Caitlin rubbed her hand through her hair. 'You'll have to show me how to do that. I could easily spend cash.'

'Remember, we don't want to draw attention to ourselves.'

'Oh, but it's okay to take the best room in the hotel and hand over silly money like you just did?'

A challenge, she was good at those. 'He'll have forgotten us by the morning.'

'Serious?'

'Yes, I'm serious. I will try to teach you but I'm not sure I can. I picked up a fair bit in the community.' It was good for something he guessed.

'I need to have a look at this community of yours. It's intriguing.'

'Maybe, we'll see.'

The hotel was immaculate. It had a country feel, on a grand

scale. It did not surprise Steven when they entered the room and found it had a flat screen TV, basket of fruit and a leather sofa. The room was perfect, and very spacious. A large, imposing king-size bed gave him ideas. He did have some catching up to do.

'Can I get you a cup of tea?'

'You know what, thanks but no. I need to shower.'

He remembered the last time they showered together. It was in her halls of residence a long time ago. 'I could join you.'

Caitlin rolled her eyes and smirked. 'Again, thanks, but no. I need some time to think.'

Steven gave a small pout and shrugged his shoulders. 'Fair enough, but don't take too long. I'm desperate for a shower myself.'

'You could always get another room?' she teased.

Steven took a seat on the sofa. 'Cold, Miss Chance, very cold.'

'Ha!' Caitlin slammed the door shut. A second later, she peeked out. 'Just joking, I'll let you in soon, okay?'

Steven raised his hands in defeat. 'Take your time.'

An hour later, Steven had flicked channels so many times he had memorised the order. He was just dozing on the sofa when the door opened. Caitlin had her hair in a turban and wore a fluffy white bathrobe. Her face was flushed. Her pale skin always turned a shade of red in the heat or after exercise. He remembered she always had the same look after a swimming session. He used to like watching her after swim training at university. Her complexion had a shine to it, a glow.

She moved her head to the side as the turban dropped and she rubbed her hair with the towel. Her naturally curly red hair fell loosely around her face. 'Your turn,' she chirped, as she sat at the dressing table and grabbed the hairdryer. As soon as she took it off the wall it started. Automatic, as you would expect in a room of this calibre.

'I might just stay for a moment.'

'No, you won't,' she said, as she pouted and put the hairdryer back as she turned to face him. 'I want to change in peace. And besides you really *do* need a shower.'

'Do I?' He made his way over and put his arms around her.

'Steven! You're going to get me dirty. Look at your hands!'

He started to tickle her; she was irresistible when she sounded annoyed.

As she broke out in laughter, he let her go. 'I knew I could make you laugh, you are so serious. I'm off. I'll be back in a couple of hours, if there's enough hot water that is.' He raised his eyebrows.

'Ha ha. If you take too long I might have to order room service.'

'Room service? Now, that's a great idea. Yeah, order room service, especially if it's full of fat and greasy.'

'In this hotel? Unlikely. I'll do my best. Or, we could go out?'

'You decide.' He closed the door to the bathroom and left her to it.

A second later, the whirring sound of the hairdryer continued.

***

Caitlin stared at her reflection in the mirror as she dried her hair. Did she look different? Did her hair have a shine it did not have before? Were her eyes a brighter shade of blue? Or, did her skin have a glow she could not recall? Had the change done it, or was it the way she had always been? It was so hard to know. She ruffled her hair and removed the clumps of hair that always came off when she washed it. She had so much hair it was never missed.

Satisfied, she placed the hairdryer back and went to find something to wear. She wished she had a better selection. Then again, if Steven had so much money to throw away she doubted he'd mind if she did a bit of shopping. A girl always needed new clothes.

She put on her barely black jeans and purple v-necked jumper, and glanced in the mirror. Purple had always been a good colour for her.

The sound of the door made her turn her head. Steven was already finished. She had not even had time to look at the menu. He had a towel wrapped around his waist. Other than that it was just him. Swimmers build, with broad shoulders and a small waist. His skin was slightly darker than she remembered. His dark, black hair was slicked back and his amber eyes pierced her heart as he smiled at her. She could not believe he was hers. How stupid could she be to even doubt he was the man for her? What an idiot!

'You were quick!' she said, in a casual manner as she picked up the menu and started to look it over. She did not want to stare at him. Strangely, he made her nervous.

'I don't need hours to mull. Besides the shower was okay, but once you've showered under a waterfall normal showers just don't stack up.'

Her jaw dropped. 'A waterfall? You really are holding out on me. This community does not sound so bad after all. Will you take me there?'

'Maybe. One step at a time.'

Steven made his way over to the bag and put on some pants. She turned away to give him some privacy. It felt odd to share so much intimacy. She had seen him change many times in the past, but right now it was new. She studied the menu. When he came up alongside her she tried to act as though it didn't matter. It did. His proximity made her tense. Like static.

'Anything good? Or shall we go out?'

'I think we should…'

Caitlin did not get the chance to finish as Steven leaned in and kissed her. It was deep and longing and she was swept off her feet. Dizzy, he made her dizzy. As she gave in and responded they held each other and just kissed. She had no idea how long it went on for. Eventually, they paused. She realised she had not had a breath, but she was not out of breath. Interesting. She could feel him against her now. She liked the fact he needed her as much as she needed him. But he was a gentleman. He had never acted erratically. Well, until a couple of hours ago. She could not blame him for that one. She could not put the brakes on either.

'I can still get pregnant right?' she asked, as the thought hit her.

'Yes, you can. Oh, yep I'm with you. We can always go to the pharmacy tomorrow and get the morning after pill, if you prefer?'

Sensible, as usual. 'Glad they taught you something at school. That's a good idea. And maybe, we should get some condoms in the meantime, just in case?'

He smiled and continued to get dressed. 'That would be a very good idea, that is, if you don't mind…'

His expression grew serious. He was still worried. She must have really freaked him out earlier. 'I don't mind. I love you. Believe me. I didn't just say it in the heat of the moment. I was just, I don't know, being a woman. I think I doubt a lot more than you do. You never seem to waiver. Is that normal?'

'I guess I'm the loyal type. I promise I will never cheat on you, ever. The only reason I had a one night stand in the community was because I thought I'd never get you back.'

'I know.' She could not believe he still felt guilty about sleeping with that other woman. She could not hold it against him. She had been with Daniel after all. 'Anyway, as I was saying before you swept my off my feet.'

'I swept you off your feet? Excellent!' His face beamed as he moved in closer.

She held out her hand and shook her head. 'Yes, yes, anyway. I think we should eat here.'

'Room service?' Steven gave a cheeky wink.

'No, let's go downstairs and eat together in a normal environment, just like anyone else.'

'A date then?'

'Yes.' She felt the heat rise on her face. Why did he make her feel shy all of a sudden?

Steven gave a slight nod of the head and turned to the door. He opened it and held it as he waited by the side. 'After you?'

CHAPTER 47

DIRTY HANDS

Emily rubbed her hands vigorously in the water. She got more soap and lathered for the second time. She felt so dirty. As she rinsed her hands and got some paper towels she hesitated. She could wash them again. She gave a slight shake of the head. There was no point. Nothing would make her feel clean. The dirty deed was done. The woman was gone. Her path was clear now. He would welcome her back with open arms. She would be his shoulder to cry on, his comfort.

With a cursory glance she looked at the body. It had been so easy to trick her way in. The woman was too trusting. It was lucky Emily had thought to bring the lotion they used to conceal the wound. No-one would be able to tell how the woman had lost so much blood. Either way, she had thrown her down the stairs after she had made her unconscious. With a fractured spine, she would never wake up again.

Emily flicked her hair to the side. It was starting to get long again. She preferred it that way. She never understood why her twin sister Anna always kept it short. Emily always thought long hair suited them better. It was probably Anna's way of being different from Emily. Anna was always so different. Emily browsed through the pictures. Paul had a lot of memories with the woman. A few were missing. Her brother, Ian, took all the pictures of Steven.

It was such a waste.

If she had known Steven would be like her she would have taken him back to the community. She had missed all of the memories for nothing. Then again, she was not sure it would have made any difference. She doubted she could ever have been a good mother.

Slowly, she made her way upstairs. The view was amazing,

the countryside in all its glory. Paul had done well for himself. This was a great house. Shame for the woman it was so deserted. She eased out of the open window and jumped down. Then she walked away and did not look back.

She would return.

First, she would give Paul some time to grieve. He would get quite a shock. If he had taken the car he would have got back sooner. Emily knew he would be another thirty minutes. Paul was a creature of habit. His morning walk for the newspaper provided Emily with the perfect opportunity.

***

Steven could not believe he was back in his home town of Ilfracombe. He never thought he'd see it again, especially not with Caitlin.

'What do you think?' He parked the car in a lay-by with a view of the coastline. 'Want to have a look?' For a change it was not raining and the sun was out.

'Sure,' Caitlin replied.

Once outside they walked to the edge.

'It's amazing. So, this is where you grew up. Not bad. Bet you surf as well then?'

Steven nodded. 'I can ride the waves. We'll have to give it a go.'

'Really?'

'I did tell you we could breathe under water. How else am I going to show you?' He put his arm around her.

'We'll have to get some wetsuits.'

'We don't need them. I think we can handle the cold.' At least he thought they could.

'Yes, but if anyone sees us they'll think we're strange right?'

Always one step ahead of him. 'You're right.'

'You know last night was great.' She leant her head on his shoulder. 'It's like we're in a dream. Do we have to face up to reality?'

He turned to face her. 'Eventually, it's only been a day. Lectures start again Monday. We'll decide what we're going to do tonight.'

'Okay, well in that case. Let's go into town, find a

pharmacy and then maybe we could go and see your dad. That's why we're here right?'

He was amazed she could always see right through him. 'Yes, I would like to see my parents.'

'So, let's go then. Last night was amazing, now we have stuff to do.'

He laughed aloud. Caitlin was a woman on a mission – always.

***

Caitlin found everything so strange. It was too easy. Since they had fed the day before she did not feel so out of control. She did have a slight inclination to attack but it was not strong enough to take over. At the moment all she wanted was to be with Steven. It was just as well she had thought of contraception. The last thing they needed was a baby.

She was looking forward to seeing Steven's father. She wondered what Steven could have looked like when he was older. It was nice to be on his home turf. As the car rounded the bend a series of huge houses came into view. She knew Steven's parents had money but this was in a different league. All of the properties were spread out, a series of mansions with a *lot* of land. She was sure five of her houses could fit on one of the plots.

'So, what's the plan? What are we going to do?'

'We'll pretend we got lost and just ask for directions. I just want to see them again, that's all.'

'What if they're not in?'

'They're always in at the weekend. Then again that was when I was around. I don't know. If they're not in, we'll try again later.'

Caitlin could tell Steven was apprehensive. His finger tapped the steering wheel in a steady beat. All of a sudden it stopped. She looked up to his face and realised he had gone pale. Then she looked ahead and saw some flashing lights.

Not a good sign.

Steven pulled over to the other side of the road and sat still. 'Something's happened,' he murmured.

Caitlin looked across the road and saw a couple of police

cars and an ambulance in the massive driveway. A man stood in the doorway with a serious expression, arms folded. A policeman sccmcd to say something to him. She focused on his lips and rolled down the window. Then his words became clear.

'My stepmother is dead.' Steven held his head in his hands as he leant into the steering wheel. 'Shit. This is bad.'

Caitlin listened in. The man was his dad. 'Shall we go?'

'Not yet. Give me a minute.'

Something made Caitlin look around. She felt like she was being watched. It was weird. She did not say anything. Steven lifted his head, started the car and pulled out.

'Are you sure you don't want me to drive?' It felt right to offer.

'No, I'll be fine.'

As they drove away Caitlin had a final look at the drive. Steven's dad had gone back inside. It was going to be hard to live in a house that size alone. She wondered about the fall. Accidents did happen. The timing just sucked. Steven had not even had the chance to say goodbye, and now he never would.

She reached out with her hand and put it on his. 'Steven, I'm so sorry. I know she meant a lot to you.'

'If only I had been able to see her one last time. Now…it doesn't matter. It was wrong to come back here. We shouldn't have come. I don't know why I wanted to be here. It was…' Steven paused, a serious expression on his face as he performed a sharp u-turn and started to drive back very fast.

'Steven, what's up?'

'A hunch. Trust me.'

Caitlin kept an eye on Steven and an eye on the road. He was driving very fast. As they got to the house he slowed, then parked and got out. Caitlin did not know whether she should follow. Steven glanced at her and beckoned her out.

Steven held out his hand, she took it, and they crossed the road. On the road, next to the house he closed his eyes, as though deep in thought. A second later, his eyes snapped open. 'She's here.'

'Who?' Now she was totally confused.

'My real mother, Emily, did this.'

Caitlin frowned. 'How can you know that?'

'I just do. I know she's been here. Her scent, it's weird. I can smell her. I have to find her alone.'

Caitlin flinched.

'Take the car, find a place to stay and I'll call you in a couple of hours. Please, I don't want her to hurt you. She probably knows I'm here too. Go quickly, before she finds us.'

'Steven I…'

'Go, now. Please.' His expression softened. 'Take this.'

He placed a wad of cash in her hand and then gave her an embrace and kiss. It did little to reassure her; even so she had to do what he asked. Once in the car, she gave him a little wave and drove with no idea of where she was going, on a mission to get far away from there.

***

Steven let his instinct guide him as he walked. She was not near the house, but he was sure she was close by. He walked in the direction Caitlin had gone and picked up the pace. The road went into the forested area they had just passed. He took a turn into the forest away from the main road and continued. He could definitely sense her now. In the same way he had sensed her back in Manaus. After ten minutes, he stopped and looked up. A pair of amber eyes stared back. A moment later she jumped down to face him.

'I knew you were here,' Steven snarled.

Emily laughed and paced up in a carefree manner. 'Aren't you happy to see me? We can let your father in on the secret and we can play happy families again.'

'A family? You are out of your mind. Did you kill my mother?'

She stopped pacing and narrowed her eyes. 'I'm your mother. That woman was nobody.'

'Did you kill her?' he shouted.

'Lower your voice. What does it matter? She was not important.'

Steven lunged at Emily. He could not help it. He pushed

her against the tree and squeezed her throat between his hands as hard as he could.

Emily's face went from a smirk to peace. She closed her eyes as though inviting death. She had no fight in her. Steven could not do it, he had to let go. He struggled to keep it together.

He saw Emily's eyes open slowly as she took a deep breath. 'I knew you would not kill me. You don't have it in you.'

'I'm not heartless,' Steven snapped, now pacing up and down.

As she rubbed her throat, Emily asked, 'who is she?'

'Who?' Steven found it hard to look at her.

'The girl you're with. Her scent is all over you. How did you get a girl? And what are you doing here anyway? Seems both of us are where we shouldn't be.'

Steven got up close. 'Keep away from my dad and keep away from me.'

'And what if I don't? You have not answered my question. Who is the girl?'

Pure hatred and anger surged through Steven. He grabbed Emily by the shoulders and threw her hard against the tree. He heard something snap, it could have been a branch. Emily collapsed on the floor. He picked her up by her throat and held her up with one hand. She choked out a muffled laugh, before she closed her eyes. He threw her on the floor and grimaced in disgust. He did not want to kill her, but if he could make her unconscious it would be a start. There was no way he would let her do anything to his dad and he did not even want to consider the consequences if she found out about Caitlin.

She did not move. Her body was at an odd angle on the floor. He put his finger to her neck to check for a pulse, a weak one remained. Emily was alive, he could not help thinking it was a shame. If she died it would not bother him at all.

He took his phone out his pocket and called up Caitlin. 'Caitlin, drive back. I found Emily. I'll meet you on the road and explain.'

He picked up the unconscious body, hurled it over his

317

shoulder and started to make his way to the road. He had no idea what he was going to do with Emily, but it sounded like a good time to call his Aunt Catherine. Everything was starting to spiral out of control.

CHAPTER 48

NORMALITY

Caitlin glanced nervously at the back seat. Steven's mother scared her and yet Steven looked so much like her. The resemblance was uncanny. She had no idea what they were going to do with her. It appeared swimming was now out of the question.

'I'm sorry about this. I'm sorry about everything. I should have left you alone. I should have protected you not made you one of us. I just…'

Caitlin covered his mouth. 'Don't. It's too late for that. Better that you found her. If she's as dangerous as you say she is, it's good we found her. There is no point in looking at the past now.'

'We have to take her back to the community. You know that, don't you?'

'Yes, I thought you'd say that. It's probably for the best. Life here would not work for us anymore, would it?' She could not believe she was going to walk away from everything.

'No, truth is I don't rate either of our chances. I don't want to become a killer and I don't want to watch you become one either. I mean, not that you would, just look at what she is. We could be like her. I'm so sorry.'

Caitlin watched his head shake, forlorn. 'Stop it! What's done is done. Make the call.'

'Now?'

'Now. Make the call.' She needed to know what they were planning to do, especially since the addition of their extra baggage.

'Okay.'

***

Catherine was taken aback when she was pulled out of her mental agility lesson to take an urgent call. It could only mean one thing. Steven had called. It could be Emily, but she doubted her little sister would ever ask for her help. A minute later, she sat in front of the speaker system. Ian was already there. He did not look happy. She guessed it could only mean one thing. Steven did not want to talk to him.

'Is it Steven?' she asked, out of courtesy. She doubted she was wrong.

Ian gave a curt reply. 'Yes.'

It was a good feeling to be right.

'Steven. How are you?'

'Catherine, glad you could come to the phone. I've been better, but then I guess you knew that.' He sounded nervous.

'Yes. I didn't think you would call just to say hello. How's Dad?'

'I'm sorry to have to tell you this, but your father passed on. He did not want to live without Judith.'

Catherine heard her intake of breath. She felt as though someone had ripped out her heart. Her knees buckled as she managed to sit on the chair next to her. She found it hard to keep her grip on the phone. With considerable effort, she forced the words out. 'Did he suffer?'

'No, not really, it happened quickly. I buried him next to Judith, like I promised.'

'When?' She was barely keeping it together now.

After a slight pause, he replied, 'a while ago.'

She closed her eyes and swallowed. 'You waited to tell me, after you promised to let me know. Why Steven? Why?' A lone tear strayed and ran down her cheek.

Ian snatched the phone away from her. 'What the hell did you do to my father, you son of a bitch? I promised to protect you for them. What happened?'

Catherine could hear Steven's reply. 'Ian, stop blaming me. It was not my fault. He gave up on life, not me. Anyway, I have to talk to you about something important. I have Emily.'

Ian went rigid as he gripped the phone tighter. 'Right, where are you?'

'I'm in Ilfracombe. She was after my dad. All she wanted was him. She killed my mother. I need to know what to do with her, before I kill her myself.'

Ian's tone of voice changed, it became calmer and got to the point. 'Can you restrain her?'

'Probably.'

Catherine could not believe the turn of events. Her younger sister had a lot to account for.

Ian continued. 'Are you alone?'

'No.'

Catherine rubbed her head and then played with a strand of her hair, her eyes fixed on the floor. Not only did Steven have Emily, but he had also got someone else involved. She could not let Ian ruin things. Without hesitation, she wiped her cheeks and snatched the phone away from Ian. 'Steven, I'll come over. I need to say goodbye to Dad. I'll help you with Emily; she is my sister after all.'

'The hell you will…,' Ian trailed.

'Ian, stop!' Catherine gave him the evil eye. 'I will come as fast as I can. Then you have to tell me everything. Can you do that?'

She heard Steven sigh before he replied. 'Yes, I can do that. But, please, come alone.'

Ian started to rant. 'He was my father too. We're all coming over now.'

Catherine held out her hand. 'I'll come alone. I'll call you when I arrive.'

'Okay, thank you, and Catherine?'

'Yes.' She wondered what was on his mind now.

'Sorry, I did not let you know sooner about your Dad.'

'It's okay.'

Apology accepted. What choice did she have?

***

Steven kept his eye on Emily as the phone line went dead. He wondered how long she would be unconscious for. Perhaps he had overdone it. Caitlin leaned against the car, arms wrapped around her. Unsure or maybe a bit scared. He had got her into a real mess and, as far as he could see, there was no way to get her out. He had let her down. He had failed her. He didn't deserve her. All he could hope for was that she'd want to go with him. It was not that easy to forget her reaction after the change. Would she hate him again if she did not like what she saw?

'Penny for your thoughts?' Caitlin said. She sounded at ease.

'It's nothing. Don't worry about it. I guess you heard. My aunt, Catherine, is coming. She will help us.' He could not tell Caitlin what he really thought.

'How are we going to make Emily do what we say?'

'I don't know,' he hesitated. 'We could tie her up but I don't think it will help. I can't do that to her. She did it to me, I won't stoop so low.'

'That's fine and all but how are we going to explain what I am? You're going to have to tell her, you know that right?'

Steven looked up into the trees, in search of inspiration or an answer. It did not come. 'This is just a great big mess. Let's go back to the house. We'll try and keep her there. If all she wanted was my dad then she's done what she came for. She's killed Clara, the only person my dad loved. She won. He will also live out the rest of his days in mourning. I can only hope he might meet someone else in time. Who knows right?'

'He'll be fine. There is nothing you can do.' Caitlin walked up to him and gave him a hug.

He nuzzled into her hair and took a deep breath. It was soothing to be with Caitlin. Together, perhaps, they would find some future worth living for. 'Let's make a move. If she wakes, let me know.'

'I'll drive. Then you can sit next to her. It would be easier if you were there when she woke up.'

'Good idea. You always think of the best solution. Thanks.'

'You don't have to thank me.' Caitlin smiled.

'Yes, I do. I don't deserve you. I love you so much.' He watched her eyes come alight. He was a lucky man if she truly loved him.

Caitlin looked up and met his eyes. 'I love you too.'

The reply was even sweeter. He leaned in and gave her a

loving, tender kiss. All he could do was hope that their love would pull them through what was coming. A part of him wondered if love would be enough.

***

Emily was convinced her spine was damaged. For the first time in years she felt real pain, but she would not let them know. She would not let them know. She would not shout or scream or even move. She would make them think she was asleep. That way she could listen. She would find out about the girl. She had managed to open her eye for a split second as they talked, she was curious. The redhead was pretty; she had a feisty look about her. She could not dare look for longer. She had to play dead. Something told her there was something not quite right? Steven had to have explained what he was by now, or she must have figured out something was out of the ordinary, and yet the girl, Caitlin she thought she'd heard, stayed. Why? She intended to find out.

She would wait until they took her where they wanted to go. She would play along. They were right. Paul was best left alone for now. She could come back for him later. It would be interesting when Catherine arrived. Her sister still owed her one, for lying to her all those years back. Emily did not like liars. She nestled into the back seat and tried to ignore the thrumming on her neck and back. She did not think she could move her legs. Steven had done something to her. Inwardly, she shrugged it off. Human blood would heal her, it always did.

***

Caitlin sat on the driver's seat, adjusted it for her height, and then turned on the ignition. She glanced at Steven in the back, smiled, and then turned on the radio. Music would keep her mind distracted. She concentrated on the road and tried to block out the multitude of thoughts racing through her mind. She could not panic. She had to stay calm. She had to ignore the psycho sat in the back, also known as Steven's mother. She had to prepare herself to meet up with another family member, Steven's aunt Catherine. Would she be as crazy as Emily? She did not sound it on the phone, but nothing ever

323

seemed as it was anymore. She also had to leave everything she had ever worked for behind.

The thought did not hit her as hard as she imagined. Somehow a life of danger and discovery had an appeal that academia could not offer. With her degree she would have probably ended up as an accountant or teacher. A life she might have enjoyed, but nothing to a life in the Amazon. With waterfalls, no money, a shared community. It was bound to be better then an ordinary boring life.

Then again, what if they did not accept her? What if they saw her as an aberration, a freak? How was Steven going to explain who she was, and why she was like them? She did not get the impression Steven had been at ease in the Community. Would it be any different for her? Would the grass be greener, sweeter, elsewhere?

She focused on the track and started to sing along to drown out the thoughts. She had to stay positive. They would work it out. Of one thing she was absolutely sure. There was no way anyone could make her feel the way Steven made her feel. They were soul mates. If they were destined to be, life would show them the way. It usually did. She was sure everything that had happened was just a test. Now their real life could begin. Emily would be dealt with, and they would live happily ever after. The fairytale ending could happen to her.

EPILOGUE

THE COMMUNITY

The sound of footsteps storming down the hall should have alerted Anna. It did, just a few seconds too late. She dreaded to think what could have happened now. In the space of a couple of months, her twin sister, Emily, had gone missing and then her mother had died. She could still not get her head around that. And now her father, Jeff, had opted to stay away. She wished she knew what was going through her father's mind. She could not understand why he was helping Steven. From what she'd heard from Catherine and Ian, Steven did not sound under control; it was madness to let him stay there.

Everything was going wrong.

The community was far from settled. The whole place was in upheaval, questions had arisen that no-one had ever considered. Views that were always on the periphery of the community were now discussed openly. It was not a positive development. These were not good times. She would go as far as to call them dangerous times.

The loud knock on the door brought her back to reality. When it swung open and she saw it was Ian, she groaned. One day she would get locks.

'Anna, we need to talk.' He eyes were puffed, his face haggard.

Regardless, she would not cut him slack; he was always on her case. 'What now?'

'It's not what you think,' he said. His head drooped low. 'Dad's dead.'

She was not expecting that. She swallowed and fought to keep it together. 'When?'

'We don't know. Steven didn't tell us, the bastard.' His eyes widened and he scowled. 'Steven called to tell us he buried Dad with Mum. He has Emily, and it appears he's got someone else involved. Catherine has agreed to go to help him, she agreed to go alone. I don't know what to think anymore.'

Anna frowned. 'Catherine? Since when has Emily ever wanted to talk to Catherine? And who is this other person?' It all felt like a dream, it made no sense.

'You'll have to talk to Catherine. Get some sense into her. She told Steven she would go alone, but if you convince her maybe some of us can follow to help. Steven doesn't need to know we're there. Trust me; I'm just as curious as you are about the third person.'

'Yes, I'll talk to her. Is Dad really dead?' She found it hard to believe.

'Yes. But, we have other problems.'

'More?' What more could possibly go wrong?'

'People are getting restless; you need to calm them down. They'll listen to you. They don't want to do what I say. For the first time...ever...I have lost control.' He slumped on the sofa.

It was always sad when the mighty fell. Anna could not understand why now, after so many years, Ian had finally decided to ask for help. He was such a control freak most of the time. He couldn't handle it when things didn't go his way.

In a firm voice, she replied, 'They don't need me, they need Dad. Now he's gone, what can I do?' Her throat started to constrict.

Ian shook his head, his eyes wild. 'We have to find a way to stop the talk. Can you imagine what would happen if they find out Dad's dead?'

Anna paused and thought about the quandary. Quietly, she added. 'We'll have to arrange for a meeting. Then we can flesh out the issues.'

'A meeting?'

'A meeting with the community, we have to keep people in the loop. The more they don't know, the worse it gets.'

'Yes, of course. First, we should meet up with the originals. Explain what happened. I know that the older ones, in particular, are worried. Hell, I am. I never gave much thought to dying.' He was rambling.

Anna could not remember ever seeing him so insecure. 'Okay, I'll arrange it.'

'Thank you,' he sighed. 'Try and keep Dad's death to yourself for now, we'll talk about it in the meeting.'

Anna nodded. Once he had left, she sat down and closed her eyes.

A mixture of emotions raged through her head. As much as her brother tried to act confident in front of everyone else, he was as mild as a pussy cat behind the scenes. Catherine was no better. She had barely said anything since they'd returned. What could they say? We lost Emily, and Mum died. What they should have said is Dad needs you. She felt like she had let her father down, she should have been there. It was a mistake to leave him alone.

And now Steven was with Emily and someone else, a stranger. Unless, it was the girl he left behind. It was nothing short of a disaster waiting to happen.

Anna never doubted that Emily would find a way out someday; she always suspected that when the opportunity arose Emily would take it. Even so, she had to admit it surprised her. She never expected Emily to abandon Steven again, not when he needed help. Then again, the choices Emily made never failed to amaze her.

Steven also sounded volatile. They had no idea what Steven was capable of, especially since he had a friend along for the ride.

Therein lay the problem.

A lot of people in the community could not understand why Steven was allowed out in the open when they were kept within the confines of the community. If they did not do something soon those that were restless would demand the right to leave. Ultimately, she could not blame them.

In the history of the community there had never been any violence within its walls. Something told her the tide was changing. This was a new era, a new way of thinking. It was dangerous, unknown. It was not something she would be keen to witness, especially if things turned sour.

Her shoulders hunched down and she curled up in a ball, her arms wrapped over her legs. Then she let it all out. Her chest heaved as the tears fell for her mum, dad and estranged sister, Emily. Her twin sister was so different and so reckless.

Anna feared the future.

She had no way of predicting what was to come and what they would discover. She had the feeling life in the community was going to change. Utopia was not meant to last forever.

ABOUT THE AUTHOR

Vanessa Wester is bilingual in English and Spanish, since she was born and raised in Gibraltar. She first moved to England to further her education and obtained a degree in Accounting and Law from the University of Southampton, in England, United Kingdom. Initially, she embarked on a career in Chartered Accountancy. After a couple of years it became obvious she was not cut out to work in an office.

A change in vocation led her to become a Secondary School Teacher of Mathematics, which she loved. For many years, she has been a stay at home mum and gives up a lot of her time towards voluntary organisations. She still teaches maths as a private tutor and has many hobbies which include swimming, walking, reading, singing and acting. She is also a qualified A.S.A. Swimming Teacher and volunteers on weekends at her local swimming club.

Writing is her passion. The day she decided to start writing was the day she found an outlet for her imagination. It is the best way she can think of to express herself and escape from everyday life.

She now lives on the Isle of Wight, another island. It's a small world.

CONNECT ONLINE

Whatever you thought of COMPLICATIONS I would love to know. Please leave a review or connect with me online. Thank you.

Twitter

http://twitter.com/vanessa_wester

Blog

http://theevolutiontrilogy.blogspot.co.uk/
http://vanessawesterwriter.blogspot.co.uk/
http://vanessawester.blogspot.co.uk/
http://festivalofwriting2012.blogspot.co.uk/
http://shortstoriesgroup.blogspot.co.uk/

Community

http://www.goodreads.com/author/show/
6421055.Vanessa_Wester
http://writing-community.writersworkshop.co.uk/members/
profile/4791/Vanessa
http://writing-community.writersworkshop.co.uk/
groups/profile/4874

REFERENCES

History of Manaus, Brazil

http://www.manaus.info/history-of-manaus.html

Bolo de macaxeira or Cassava Cake

http://tudogostoso.uol.com.br/receita/64457-bolo-de-
macaxeira-facil-e-rapido.html
http://www.halfhourmeals.com/recipe/bolo-de-macaxeira--
cassava-cake

AA Route planner

http://www.cutthorne.co.uk/default.htm?welcome.php
http://en.wikipedia.org/wiki/Beast_of_Exmoor

British Empire

http://www.en.wikipedia.org/wiki/Britsh_Empire

15807065R00191

Made in the USA
Charleston, SC
21 November 2012